HORRID MYSTERIES

The Northanger Abbey Horrid Novels

Castle of Wolfenbach (1793)
Eliza Parsons

Clermont (1798)
Regina Maria Roche

The Mysterious Warning (1796)
Eliza Parsons

The Necromancer; or, The Tale of the Black Forest (1794)
"Peter Teuthold"

The Midnight Bell (1798)
Francis Lathom

The Orphan of the Rhine (1798)
Eleanor Sleath

Horrid Mysteries (1796)
Carl Grosse

Horrid Mysteries.

A STORY.

FROM THE GERMAN OF THE MARQUIS OF GROSSE,

BY P. WILL.

—————

WITH A NEW INTRODUCTION BY

ALLEN GROVE

—————

VALANCOURT BOOKS

Horrid Mysteries by Carl Grosse
Originally published in 4 vols., London: William Lane, 1796
First Valancourt Books edition 2016

Introduction © 2016 by Allen Grove
This edition © 2016 by Valancourt Books

Published by Valancourt Books, Richmond, Virginia
Publisher & Editor: JAMES D. JENKINS
http://www.valancourtbooks.com

All Valancourt Books publications are printed on acid free paper that meets all ANSI standards for archival quality paper.

ISBN 978-1-943910-42-7 (trade paperback)
Also available as an electronic book.

Set in Dante MT

CONTENTS

Introduction • vii
Note on the Text • xv

Horrid Mysteries
The Translator's Preface • 1
Volume I • 6
Volume II • 110
Volume III • 202
Volume IV • 319

Introduction: A Defense of Horrid Novels

The novel you hold would most likely be entirely lost to contemporary readers if not for a brief mention in Jane Austen's parody of Gothic fiction, *Northanger Abbey*. Catherine Morland, Austen's unlikely heroine, meets up with her companion Isabella Thorpe who promptly asks about Catherine's progress reading Ann Radcliffe's 1794 gothic novel, *The Mysteries of Udolpho*. When Catherine expresses her delight with the work, Isabella presents her with a future reading list:

> ". . . when you have finished Udolpho, we will read the Italian together; and I have made out a list of ten or twelve more of the same kind for you."
>
> "Have you, indeed! How glad I am!—What are they all?"
>
> "I will read you their names directly; here they are, in my pocket-book. Castle of Wolfenbach, Clermont, Mysterious Warnings, Necromancer of the Black Forest, Midnight Bell, Orphan of the Rhine, and Horrid Mysteries. Those will last us some time."
>
> "Yes, pretty well; but are they all horrid, are you sure they are all horrid?"
>
> "Yes, quite sure; for a particular friend of mine, a Miss Andrews, a sweet girl, one of the sweetest creatures in the world, has read every one of them."

Catherine, and Isabella's sweet friend Miss Andrews, are clearly caught up in the gothic craze that dominated literary tastes and the fiction industry from the 1790s into the early nineteenth century. Hooked on the hugely successful novels of Ann Radcliffe, Matthew Lewis, Regina Maria Roche and other writers of the 1790s, aficionados of the gothic romance were quick to consume any work whose title promised a story of monks, caverns, castles, abbeys, ghosts, forests, witches and all forms of mystery.

Catherine Morland's desire for novels that are "horrid" reveals her hunger for the gothic—haunting romances filled with delightful horrors that keep her immersed in escapist fantasy. Indeed, the presses of the Romantic period had no shortage of titles promising all things horrid: *The Mysterious Hand, or, Subterranean Horrours!* (1811), *Osrick, or, Modern Horrors* (1809), *Bellgrove Castle, or, The Horrid Spectre!* (1803), *The Haunted Palace, or, The Horrors of Ventoliene* (1801), *Valley of Collares, or, The Cavern of Horrors* (1800), *Castle Spectre: or, Family Horrors* (1807), *Cavern of Horrors: or, The Miseries of Miranda* (1802), *Horrible Revenge, or, The Assassin of the Solitary Castle* (1828), *Horrible Revenge, or The Monster of Italy* (1807), *Horrors of Oakendale Abbey* (1797); *Horrors of the Secluded Castle, or, Virtue Triumphant* (1807), and so on. The publication of romance novels grounded in terror and horror was so common that in 1815 a writer using the pseudonym Ircastrensis published *Love and Horror: An Imitation for the Present and a Model for all Future Romances*, a parody of the genre that mocks both the preposterousness and conventionality of contemporary literary tastes.

When Austen puts the word "horrid" in the mouth of her young and naïve heroine, however, the term immediately means more than a novel that evokes horror. Some of the works on Isabella's reading list could also be labeled "horrid" as in rotten—lousy literary productions that aren't worth the reader's effort of slogging through their tortured plots. Readers of Grosse's *Horrid Mysteries* can decide whether or not it fits the former or latter description, or perhaps both. A reviewer for *The Critical Review* clearly did not find much to admire in the work, stating, "More gross and absurd nonsense was surely never put together under the name of adventures."[1] The reviewer also complained that much of *Horrid Mysteries* seems to borrow rather liberally from *Victim of Magical Delusion* by Cajetan Tschink, another German work that Peter Will had translated into English a couple of years before *Horrid Mysteries*.

One of the great mysteries of *Horrid Mysteries* relates to its author, the Marquis of Grosse. Despite his title, Carl Grosse may not have been a marquis at all. He was born in Madgeburg, Germany in 1768. Shortly into his publishing career, he disappeared from record for a couple years, only to reappear as a supposed marquis. He claims to have married an Italian noblewoman who died shortly after the marriage, but his story of royalty has never been confirmed by contemporary scholars.[2] Regardless of his title,

Grosse published numerous romances between 1790 and 1805, and several of his works were translated into English including *The Dagger* (1795) and, of course, *Horrid Mysteries*. Originally published as *Der Genie, oder Memoiren des Marquis von G*, this work was translated into English twice in 1796: once by Joseph Trapp as *The Genius: or, The Mysterious Adventures of Don Carlos de Grandez*, and also in the edition published here, Peter Will's translation, *Horrid Mysteries*.[3]

Peter Will's version was undeniably the more successful of the two English translations of the novel, as evidenced not just by its mention in both *Northanger Abbey* and Thomas Love Peacock's gothic parody *Nightmare Abbey* (1817), but also because it was published by William Lane's highly successful Minerva Press. Lane was an innovator in the publication, marketing, and distribution of fiction. Central to his success was a large network of small circulating libraries housed within other businesses, much like Redbox video distribution today. William Lane was not particularly concerned with the quality or morality of the works he published, and by the early 1800s the press had become closely associated with "bad" writing.[4] Nevertheless, it is undoubtedly the dominance of the Minerva Press in the 1790s publishing scene that leads to Austen's sweet Miss Andrews having such eclectic and dubious taste in reading; likewise, without the Minerva Press, Isabella's would have no list of "horrid" novels to recommend to Catherine.

The plot of *Horrid Mysteries* defies summary, so this introduction is in no danger of providing spoilers. Suffice it to say that the work's central characters get caught up in a secret and manipulative brotherhood that drives them across Europe, and that the work has no shortage of love stories, sexual exploits, supernatural events, and violent murders. Indeed, the novel is so irrational that a character can be murdered more than once. In his important bibliographical work *The First Gothics*, Frederick Frank states that "no novel to survive from the Gothic period is stranger, darker, or more precipitously irrational than Grosse's *Horrid Mysteries*."[5] Michael Sadleir found the book to be the most interesting of all of Austen's horrid novels, noting that it occupies "a different and higher plane of intrinsic interest and importance" than Austen's other "horrid" novels.[6]

The novel is undeniably strange and interesting, but Austen's inclusion of *Horrid Mysteries* is most likely not an endorsement of the work. *Northanger Abbey* constructs a moral hierarchy of Gothic novels. Catherine Morland clearly loves Ann Radcliffe, the best-selling novelist of the 1790s. Radcliffe's *The Mysteries of Udolpho* may have led Catherine to behave quixotically, but the novel itself is quite tame. It hints at, but never actually presents, the type of violence and sexual conduct that could be found in other novels of the period. Radcliffe's heroines keep tight control of their emotions and uphold strict rules of propriety even as they are threatened, kidnapped, and imprisoned by unscrupulous villains. Matthew Lewis's popular novel *The Monk* has no such veneer of respectabil-ity. The novel's problematic representation of the Bible as well as its explicit scenes of sex, rape and violence resulted in Lewis needing to censor the work for the 1798 fourth edition or else face criminal prosecution. In a joke that would have been obvious to eighteenth-century readers, Austen has her insensitive and self-serving charac-ter John Thorpe remark that "Novels are all so full of nonsense and stuff; there has not been a tolerably decent one come out since Tom Jones, except The Monk; I read that t'other day; but as for all the others, they are the stupidest things in creation."

This portrayal of Radcliffe and Lewis can tell us much about the reading list that Isabella provides Catherine. Radcliffe represents appropriate reading, even gaining the approval of Catherine's love interest Henry Tilney who notes that he has "read all Mrs. Rad-cliffe's works, and most of them with great pleasure." *The Monk*, on the other hand, both in Austen's work and in the actual Romantic period literary world, was associated with impropriety and scandal. In short, good characters like *Udolpho*; bad ones like *The Monk*. One represents appropriate reading; the other does not.

But *The Monk* wasn't the only improper book published in the 1790s, and *Horrid Mysteries* certainly competes with or even exceeds Lewis for its representation of seduction, sexual exploits, rape, and violence. Yet this is the novel that Isabella Thorpe recommends to Catherine, and this is the book that sweet Miss Andrews has already read. Isabella's list of "horrid" novels reveals not just how popular gothic novels were in the 1790s, but also how indiscriminating read-ers were. Isabella presents Eleanor Sleath's sentimental *Orphan of the Rhine* and Grosse's scandalous *Horrid Mysteries* in the same breath and as all part of the "same kind" of literature. The reality is that the works have little in common other than falling into the broad category of "gothic" and sharing Lane as a publisher.

"Improper," of course, doesn't mean unpopular. The fleshly, lurid, and violent scenes found in the pages of a gothic novel such as *Horrid Mysteries* may have been condemned by critics and censors, but this forbidden fruit was undeniably part of the appeal to many readers. Consider for a moment my personal copy of the 1798 censored fourth edition of Matthew Lewis's *The Monk*, a treasure I discovered on eBay. Imagine my surprise when I first opened my purchase to find over a hundred pages of handwritten manuscript bound into the printed copy of the book, complete with asterisks marking where these handwritten fragments should be inserted into the printed text. B. Raworth, the original owner of the book, had been so unhappy to have discovered the novel censored that he or she spent days copying out and reinserting all the scenes of grotesque violence, sexual transgression, and religious heresy. The labor involved in reverting this censored text back to a scandalous earlier edition speaks volumes to the type of content the owner desperately wanted to find in the novel.

Whether *Horrid Mysteries* is "horrid" for the terror it evokes, the outlandish plotting, or the immodest content, it is still an important piece of literary history. Certainly many eighteenth-century gothic novels have attracted far more scholarly attention. Well-known and much-imitated works such as those by Horace Walpole, Ann Radcliffe, and Matthew Lewis clearly paved the way for many other novelists in the Romantic period. Then there are works such as Mary Wollstonecraft's *Maria, or, The Wrongs of Woman* (1798) or Charlotte Smith's *Marchmont* (1796) that move beyond the conventions of the genre and use gothic trappings to expose and critique the actual horrors of social injustice. But what about those other 5,000 or so gothic works written between the 1780s and 1820, works even less known than *Horrid Mysteries*, many of which entered and left the Romantic period literary scene almost unnoticed, indeed, many of which have failed to survive the ravages of time? Even these works, horrid as they are, horrid in the worst sense of the word, are worth defending.

As an example, consider *The Castle of Villeroy: A Romance* (1801) by Frances Mary Mills. It's a work that even the most accomplished romanticists have probably not read, and it's not a work I recommend they do read. The story is remarkably unoriginal, the language painfully sentimental. But consider, for a moment, Frances Mary Mills' Dedication, written not to any King or Queen or Princess or Noble Woman or Patron, but to her subscribers:

> In the early and happy part of my life, brought up in affluence and with far brighter prospects than have since awaited me, literary pursuits never occurred to me as a probable resource that could ever be required for my support. But, after having endured the severest calamities—loss of friends—loss of fortune; and, by variety of misfortunes, reduced to experience the bitter feelings of severe hunger, perishing cold, and the want of raiment,—and sinking under accumulating ill health—I must have perished, from absolute want, had not Providence sent me the most unexpected relief; and, while I record these facts, my heart overflows with gratitude to you, who have likewise stood forward the instruments of Providence in saving me from an untimely grave.
>
> Your much obliged, most grateful, and obedient humble Servant
> Frances Mary Mills

Try to picture Frances Mary Mills writing this novel. She is not driven by passion. She does not have a story she feels needs to be told. She simply writes a formulaic and sentimental novel with some conventional gothic scenes. She puts the word "Castle" in the title. And she makes enough money to live. And if I'm allowed to make such a subjective claim, it's a bad novel. I'm not fond of it.

Yet here again is a horrid novel that is worth defending. While the novel itself offers little, its mere existence tells us much. How significant is it that a woman who has been dealt a bad hand, living at a time when women had few options for supporting themselves, can pick up a pen and save herself from starvation through the penning of a gothic tale? It is hard to speak ill of a novel that saved a woman's life.

As another example, consider *The Cavern of Death* (1794), one of the first gothic novels Valancourt Books republished. One must admit that *The Cavern of Death* has a rather evocative title. Readers may be disappointed, however, when they discover that the novel was largely an imitation of Horace Walpole's *The Castle of Otranto* (1764) and Clara Reeve's *The Old English Baron* (1777). And imagine the greater disappointment when readers discover that the cavern is really just a gratuitous addition to the novel, introduced primarily in the final scene just long enough for two men to enter a cave and be mangled into a bloody pulp by a huge falling fragment of rock. It's easy to imagine that the author wrote this work simply to cash in on the popularity of gothic fiction, and it's not out of line to conclude that the title was chosen simply for its ability to seduce readers, like Catherine Morland, who had a craving for all things gothic.

Yet what *The Cavern of Death* may lack in literary quality, it makes up for as an interesting historical artifact. Its gratuitous cavern certainly speaks to the literary tastes of the time, and caverns undeniably had high market value. *The Castle of Otranto* has a central cavern scene. Sophia Lee's *The Recess* (1783-5) begins in a cavern. And then there's *The Romance of the Cavern* (1792), *The Haunted Cavern* (1796), *The Cavern of Strozzi* (1800), *St. Margaret's Cave* (1801), *The Cavern of Horrors* (1802), *The Lady of the Cave* (1802), *The Cave of Cosenza* (1803), and dozens more.

The publication history of *The Cavern of Death* is also interesting. The work made its first appearance not in novel form, but in an incomplete run in a daily newspaper called *The True Briton*. This is not a newspaper that devoted many pages to fiction, and *The Cavern of Death* made its debut amongst reports of the French Revolution, transcripts of criminal trials, letters from George Washington, and accounts of African exploration. These juxtapositions within the newspaper make visible those connections to the larger world that so often hide beneath the surface of even a bad formulaic and imitative novel. Those very features of gothic that make it formulaic— the foreign settings, usurped castles, and imprisoned heroines fall into dialogue with a cultural context defined by political upheaval, gender inequality, and British imperialism.

For *Horrid Mysteries*, these connections are even more profound. Whatever the excesses and improbabilities of the novel, it is very much grounded in the historical reality of the 1790s. For one, it is obviously a reflection of literary tastes, and a product of a rapidly evolving industry of literary production. It also points to the interconnectedness of England with the continent as German texts were quickly translated and made available to English readers. And at the heart of Grosse's outlandish plot is a secret society focused on overthrowing those in power. The main character even finds himself in Paris, swept up in the Reign of Terror. It's a reminder that the violence and chaos we often encounter in the pages of the gothic were also a political reality in the 1790s.

When Austen's Catherine Morland is on a walk with the Tilneys, she breaks an awkward silence by noting that "something very shocking indeed, will soon come out of London." Quixotic Catherine, of course, is talking about the publication of a new gothic novel, one by an unknown "author," a book that will be "horrible" and "dreadful" with "murder and every thing of the kind." Eleanor Tilney hears these words and panics, jumping to the conclusion that actual chaos and violence are planned in the nation's capital. Henry Tilney is quick to mock the young women for their confusion and misunderstanding, but Austen points at a less frivolous reality: the language of gothic fiction is not as detached from reality as one might hope. Indeed, from sexual transgressions to social unrest, the material we find in the pages of a work such as *Horrid Mysteries* was playing out in the streets and houses of revolutionary Europe in the 1790s.

ALLEN GROVE
April 2016

Allen Grove (Ph.D., University of Pennsylvania) is Chair and Professor of English at Alfred University where he teaches courses such as Tales of Terror, Gothic Fiction, Literature and Science, and the Romantic Movement. His research and teaching often explore the interplay between sexuality, science, and genre in gothic fiction. *Horrid Mysteries* is the fourth gothic novel he has introduced for Valancourt Books, and he has also written introductions for Barnes & Noble Books and Race Point Publishing for works including *The Strange Case of Dr. Jekyll and Mr. Hyde*, *Dracula*, *Frankenstein*, and *The Lost World*.

NOTES

1   *The Critical Review; or, Annals of Literature.* Volume 21. (London: A. Hamilton, 1797): 473.
2   Tenille Nowak, *The Gothic Novel and the Invention of the Middle-Class Reader:* Northanger Abbey *as Case Study.* Dissertation. Ann Arbor: UMI, 2009. 291.
3   Montague Summers, *The Gothic Quest: A History of the Gothic Novel.* (New York: Russell & Russell, 1964): 132.
4   E. J. Clery, *The Rise of Supernatural Fiction 1762-1800.* Cambridge: Cambridge University Press, 1995. 138.
5   Frederick Frank, *The First Gothics: A Critical Guide to the English Gothic Novel.* New York: Garland, 1987. 131.
6   Michael Sadleir, *The Northanger Novels: A Footnote to Jane Austen.* Oxford: Oxford University Press, 1927. 10.

NOTE ON THE TEXT

The present edition follows the text of the original four volume edition published by William Lane's Minerva Press in 1796. Spelling and punctuation have been retained from the original, except that a couple of obvious printer's errors, such as the repeated use of "gaol" instead of "goal", and a handful of missing quotation marks, have been corrected. As the book progresses and the story becomes more convoluted, with one character relating to another what a third character said to a fourth, present-day standards would call for double, triple, or quadruple nested quotation marks. However, the original text's use, or misuse, of quotation marks is far from its only incoherency, and we have chosen to retain the punctuation as presented in the original version—the text Jane Austen would have had in mind when mentioning *Horrid Mysteries* in her *Northanger Abbey.*

A final note: oddly, the title page of the original edition gives the title as *Horrid Mysteries,* while the drop-title on the first page of each volume gives the title as *The Horrid Mysteries.* This inconsistency, too, we have preserved.

Horrid Mysteries.

A STORY.

FROM THE GERMAN OF THE MARQUIS OF GROSSE.

BY P. WILL.

IN FOUR VOLUMES.

VOL. III.

LONDON:

PRINTED FOR WILLIAM LANE, AT THE
Minerva-Press,

LEADENHALL-STREET.

M DCC XCVI.

Facsimile of the title page of first edition (1796).

TRANSLATOR's PREFACE.

SECRET Societies have, at all times, and in all civilized countries, either held out private advantages, or pretended to aim at the welfare of whole nations, in order to encrease the number of their members. Amongst the former, the *Rosycrucians*, whose order was instituted in Germany in the latter end of the fifteenth century, and pretended to be in possession of the philosophers' stone, and of many more valuable arcana, were, by far, the most famous; and, among the latter, the association known under the name of the *Secret Tribunal*, acquired the greatest celebrity; if we except the order of the *Freemasons*, which, probably, was the head source whence all other secret associations derived their origin. However, all these associations, avowedly instituted for the improvement of mankind, either in piety, knowledge, or felicity, generally deceived the sanguine expectations of those that suffered themselves to be ensnared by the imposing veil of mysteriousness, which, at bottom, was nothing better than a cloak of their defects, and of the private selfish views of their founders. However good and noble the primary principles of some of these institutions may have been in the beginning, yet they all degenerated, sooner or later, in a most lamentable and glaring manner. The *Secret Tribunal*, for instance, was certainly originally instituted for the noble purpose of putting a stop to the numerous murders and robberies perpetrated by the predatory nobility, whom the German Emperors did not dare to punish for their disobedience to the existing laws on account of their own imbecility; but it soon degenerated into a sanguinary and despotic tribunal, that was deaf to the voice of humanity and justice, and became the terror, instead of being the guardian angel, of Germany.

The secret order of the *Illuminators* in Bavaria, founded by the celebrated Weishaupt, and dispersed about six years since, affords a modern proof of the same assertion. It was founded on masonic principles, and its chief members were freemasons of the strict

observance. The original views of that secret association were to
dispel the dark clouds of superstition and ignorance, which still
obscure the horizon of that and many other Roman Catholic countries, to protect and to assist virtue and merit, to see the places of
public trust occupied by persons of known and tried abilities and rectitude, and to destroy the baneful family influence which distributes
posts of the highest consequence to subjects devoid of all merit, save
what they derive from their noble parentage or the weight of their
purse. The general blissful consequences such an association promised to produce, the alluring prospects of promotion, the veil of
masonic mysteriousness, the hope of attaining higher knowledge,
held out by the secret agents of the society, were powerful allure-
ments, by means of which they prevailed on many well-wishers of
the general good, amongst whom several Princes were, to associate with them, and interested the ambitious and the enthusiast for
their cause. The society soon counted a great number of members,
and rapidly spread all over Germany. The first geniuses of our age,
philosophers and statesmen, were eager to take an active share in
the execution of their, apparently, philanthropic plans; and it cannot
be denied that Bavaria, and some other Roman Catholic countries
in Germany, where priestcraft depressed the energy of the human
mind, and ignorance and superstition swayed with a powerful hand,
experienced many happy effects of the united secret exertions of
the numerous members of that Society. However, it underwent the
same fate all secret confederations, that have a political tendency,
and are unauthorised and unprotected by the government, whose
defects they pretend to ameliorate, are liable to experience. A spirit
of philosophical investigation began, indeed, to pervade the countries that were under its influence, and Bavaria in particular; many
great geniuses were roused from the mental lethargy in which
they had been kept by the priesthood; the hatred against Protes-
tants abated, and gave room to more liberal sentiments: however,
the promising hopes the unknown Superiors of the order had held
out to their disciples soon were visibly shaken. Self-interest, vengeance, ambition, and numberless other baneful passions, began,
by degrees, to guide the influence of the association, which, by
the many injuries it committed against the innocent object of the
hatred of individual members, and by the glaring abuses of its great

power, threatened to become a curse to mankind, instead of pro-moting the happiness of the world, and was, at length, dispersed by the interference of the Bavarian government. One of its supe-riors (Baron de Knigge, who is an honour to the human society) said,* after his secession from the association, of all secret societies in general, and of that of the *Illuminators* in particular, "All these secret associations are useless with regard to their efficacy, because they generally lay too much stress on miserable trifles and absurd ceremonies; speak an emblematical language, that admits of many different interpretations, act after ill-digested plans; are imprudent in the choice of their members, consequently soon degenerate; and although they *could*, in the beginning, have advantages before public Societies, yet, in the sequel, are infected by defects of which the world justly complains. Whoever is animated with a desire of performing something great and useful, finds, in civil and domestic life, many opportunities of doing it, which not *one* improves as he ought to do. It first must be proved that nothing remains to be done in a public manner, or that insurmountable obstacles are thrown into the way of the zealous promoter of the general good, before one has a right to create a secret and peculiar compass of activity that is not sanctioned by Government. Benevolence needs no mys-terious veil; friendship must originate in a free choice; and sociabil-ity does not require being promoted by secret means.

"These secret associations also produce baneful consequences to the world. They are noxious to the public; because all secret trans-actions are justly liable to suspicion; because the executive power can, with justice, demand being informed of the purpose of every activity for which individuals associate; because dangerous plans, and noxious doctrines, may be concealed behind the veil of secresy, as well as noble views and higher knowledge; because not all mem-bers are informed of such dangerous designs, which frequently are hidden by the most beautiful external appearance; because only inferior geniuses suffer themselves to be confined by these moral stays; whereas those that are endowed with superior gifts, either do not long continue in those societies, are spoiled, degenerate, are misguided, or rule over the rest at the expense of their fellow

---

* Veber den Vmgang mit Mensthen. Vol. III, page 135-138.

associates; because *unknown* Superiors frequently direct the whole institution by secret machinations; and it is beneath the dignity of an intelligent man to work after a plan which he cannot overlook, and for whose importance and goodness he has no other security but the authority of people whom he does not know, to whom he engages himself without their entering into reciprocal obligations, without knowing where to apply to if he finds himself disappointed in his expectations. They are dangerous and hurtful to the public, because perverse heads and rogues take advantage of the darkness in which he is enfolded, usurp the supreme power, and abuse the other members for the attainment of their private views; because every mortal has his passions, and of course, brings them along with him into the Society, where they have a more extensive scope to range than under the eyes of the Public, being sheltered by the mask of secresy and concealment; because all these Societies degenerate, by degrees, through the ill-conducted choice of the members that gradually creep in; because they avocate useful citizens from serious civil occupations, misleading them to idleness, or to an *useless* activity; because they become the rendezvous of adventurers and idlers; favour all kinds of political, religious, and philosophical enthusiasm; and, finally, because they are, sooner or later, infected by a monastical *esprit du corps*, cause a great deal of mischief, and afford numberless occasions for cabals, quarrels, persecution, intolerance, and injustice."

This is the confession of a man that was, many years, a warm advocate for Freemasonry, and a superior of the *Illuminators*. The author of the subsequent pages has had but too many opportunities of making a similar experience with Baron de Knigge, and also was a member of the Order of the *Illuminators*, which he left before its dissolution. He has been driven out of his native Country by the secret persecutions of his former brethren, whose intrigues he exposed; and now resides at Algeziras, in Spain, deploring that he has suffered himself to be made a dupe to the ambitious views of a set of men, who promised him the possession of higher knowledge, and a share in the reformation of mankind, while their sole intention was to make him subservient to their private interest; and lamenting that he has sacrificed the best time of his life in hunting after a deluding phantom.

The events related by Marquis Carlos de G****** constitute a great part of his own history, which ought to be a serious warning to all those that listen to the seducing voice of secret, corresponding, and other Societies of a similar nature, that pretend to reform the defects of government, while selfish views are concealed under the imposing outside of philanthropy and patriotism; and the seeds of disaffection to the existing laws and of rebellion, are disseminated under the pretext of applying an healing balsam to the bleeding wounds of the Country.

The subsequent pages are, indeed, no pattern of a *perfect* Romance; however, the defects they evidently have are overbalanced by so many beauties, that the translator flatters himself their appearance in an English garb will, nevertheless, meet with a kind reception. If we consider that the author intended to erect therein a grateful monument to his dearest friends, to give a gentle warning to his numerous enemies, and to exhibit a faithful picture of the formation of his principles and of his character, which has been traduced with the bitterest acrimony; if we consider all this, we cannot but make some allowance for several obvious imperfections the discerning reader may meet with in the course of his reading; for it is much easier to erect a perfect edifice, if we are at liberty to choose our materials at pleasure, than when we design to interweave parts that already exist, and cannot be altered. Finally, the Translator thinks it needful to observe, that if the mysterious events occurring in the subsequent volumes, are not elucidated with that tiresome minuteness which renders many of our modern novels rather tedious than interesting, he flatters himself that the judicious readers will not be displeased at his confidence in their own ingenuity, which sufficiently will be enabled, by the hints the author has dropt to that purpose, to dispel the mystic gloom which he has been prevented to remove by the truth of Voltaire's words:

Le Secret d'en nuyer est le secret de tout dire.

THE

HORRID MYSTERIES.

CHAPTER I.

In the spring of my life, and in the full enjoyment of unimpaired vigour, and of dearly bought experience, do I stop, to look back on the path I went, or, rather, was led. I behold, in all the mazy labyrinths of my career, a visible hand, that, perhaps, is also extended over many of my friends, guides them in the dark, and has wove the thread which they, in careless security, fancy to spin themselves.

The invisible web, which encompassed my fate, is now, perhaps, torn asunder; and, perhaps, not. While I fancy to be free, the fetters which I imagine to have shaken off, are, perhaps, forged stronger, and may soon enthral me again. Be this as it may, I will meet futurity with a cheerful confidence; and I expand my hands peacefully towards you, ye fields of higher knowledge and experience! no matter whether you be strewed with the roses of sweet tranquillity, or the thorns of sorrow. I suffer myself, impelled by stern necessity, and too weak for resistance, to be hurried onward, without anxiety, by a torrent which is limited and directed by a Superior Power.

The history of my eventful life proves how little all human strength, and a well tried and circumspect experience, can prevail over the secret plans of certain unknown persons, who, behind the impenetrable veil of mystic concealment, invisibly watch over a great part of the world. Their plans and proceedings frequently have been closely observed: however, I seem to have been doomed exclusively to penetrate to the centre of their abode. Every action of my life seems to me to have been computed and arranged in their dreadful archives before I was born, they are all directed, in a pre-concerted manner, towards the most horrid crime, to the perpetration of which they wanted to seduce me; and their whole train proves the incontestible truth, that not the application of individual capacities, but only a prudent improvement of reason, can insure an uncontrolled sway over the minds of men.

I must, however, observe, that the course of my history is too rapid, and too complicated, to be plain in the beginning. I shall, therefore, commence with that period which begins to throw some light upon it. All the antecedent occurrences of my life do not only concentre, but are also repeated therein. As for the rest, I am easy about the fate of these sheets, which the world will not see before I am gone to my eternal home; and will take no other revenge on my enemies, than to convince them that I deserved least to be envied in the most envied period of my life.

CHAPTER II.

Count S******, an uncommon handsome and amiable young man, served as volunteer under *Crillon* in the famous siege of *Gibraltar*; and when the latter was forced by *Elliot* to abandon his plan of taking that impregnable fortress, left the service, and took the resolution to travel through *Portugal*, and then to return, by way of *Spain* and *France*, to his German estates in his native country.

He finished his travels in the latter end of summer. I was enraptured to embrace him once more, and found him by far handsomer and more amiable than he had left me, frequently joking with him about the amorous adventures he had probably met with abroad, and, most likely, would meet at home. He returned these jokes; yet I frequently saw, during the sallies of a lively and good-natured wit, something sparkle in his eyes that resembled a tear. Having, however, great reason to imagine a man of his amiable form, character, and rank, could not but have contracted tender connections, I ascribed this to the effect of a sweet recollection which time easily wipes off with a soothing hand, and apprehended not in the most distant manner, that his sorrows sprung from more serious sources.

Having taken the resolution to spend the summer at his estate, he endeavoured to persuade me to keep him company, and I coincided cheerfully with his wishes. The chase, economical concerns, and billiards, occupied the greatest part of the day; and after a frugal supper, we generally seated ourselves in sweet tranquillity by the fire side, our mind being haled by that cheerful philosophy that blesses the soul only after the performance of useful occupations, and sweetens an active life beyond description. Whoever knows what real friendship is, and what congenial souls experience when exchanging harmonious ideas; whoever knows those charming fancies, that are so apt to inebriate our mind by the side of a dear friend, and the glow of innocent hilarity, will easily believe that we were happy in each others company, that we avoided numerous circles, and very rarely had another talker with us besides the garrulous fire in the chimney. We exchanged the adventures of our life and travels when the Count was in a good humour, and frequently were so much absorpt in listening and relating, that neither offered to stir before the dying flame in the chimney and the cold reminded us of Germany and the comfort of a warm bed.

Against the close of April, he looked frequently into the almanack, and laid it down again with the shake of his head. I observed it, but did not enquire the reason of that strange behaviour, leaving the development of this mystery to time and the heart of my friend.

He grew, however, every day, more and more absent and distracted, neglecting the chase, which always had been his favourite diversion; and at supper I frequently missed the jocund hilarity that generally had seasoned our frugal meals: he began to be immersed in thought, and frequently betrayed uneasiness of mind and silent anxiety. I shared his grief, but still refrained from intruding upon his secret. At length, he shut himself up a whole day, and at supper was so melancholy and thoughtful, as not to reply a syllable to my questions. He placed two chairs by the fire side, rang for a servant, and ordered him to fetch more wood. His people being gone to bed, we seated ourselves by the fire: he moved his chair closer towards mine, while I observed these preparations with anxious astonishment, and then inclined his head to me.

I shall relate the tale he now communicated to me with his own words; yet I have just reason to fear it will not be half so interesting as he related it. No man did ever possess that enchanting suavity of speech which rendered his narration so unspeakably beautiful, and made the sweet, melodious stream of his words appear to be only the echo of his feelings: nor did I ever know a mortal that equalled him in the expressive language of his gestures; for every motion of his elegant form, every mien of his went in sweet harmony with his recollection, and his heavenly eye frequently recalled long forgotten tears.

"My dear G******," he now began, "I see my behaviour fills you with anxious surprise; but be easy, my friend. I am going to relate to you the most dreadful scene of my whole life, which, perhaps, will unravel to you the mystery of my deportment. Are you prepared for that tale of horror?"

"You know, my dear S******, that my own fate has made me sufficiently intimate with scenes of that nature: who, therefore, could listen to you with more tranquillity than myself?" However, I gave the lie to that declaration in the very moment I uttered it; a long, chilly tremour flowing down my back.

"Well, Marquis, hearken to the tale I am going to depose into the bosom of my dearest friend! Do you recollect how hastily I passed over my journey from *Lisbon* to *Madrid?* I will fill up that chasm with an adventure which I durst not communicate to you one day sooner, and even now dare relate only partially; an adventure that still is veiled in mystic darkness; so much the more dreadful to me, as I can see no possibility of clearing it up. You know that family affairs obliged me to quit *Madrid* abruptly. I counted every moment. Some disagreeable incidents, but chiefly the impositions of my postillion, forced me to take a roundabout way, and I resolved to ride all the night, in order to make up for that delay. Several robberies and murders having been committed on the road, I was cautioned, previously to my setting out, to be on my guard; yet I relied entirely on the protection of my two servants, who, as well as myself, were well armed. But, when I came to frontiers, and proposed to travel all the night long, my host and hostess exerted themselves in the tenderest manner to dissuade me from my purpose, conjuring me for God's sake to stay till sun rise. They endeavoured to frighten me by the relation of fiery phantoms, of Wills-with-the-wisp, apparitions, and numberless tales of nocturnal adventures and murders. However, the fear of being thought timorous, and the pertinacy which, as you know, is a predominant structure of my character, impelled me to insist on my departure. I persuaded the postillion, comforted my host and his family, and proceeded on my journey.

On that occasion I parted with the ring which you lately missed, giving it to the loveliest little girl I ever have seen, that clung around my knees, and would not suffer me to go. I assure you, my dear G******, the state in which my mind was, at that time, is an evident proof against all sorts of ominous presensions; for I was so cheerful and serene, that I never have felt more strongly what a happiness it is to live, nor ever beheld the objects around me in a gayer attire. Our road led through a forest that commenced at the Spanish frontiers. The night was uncommonly fine; my driver guided his mules mechanically; and my two servants were fast asleep. I was, indeed, awake; however, I dreamed. The silence that swayed around me, the melodious notes of the feathered songsters, the moon, which deceived my eyes with shadowy phantoms, the mystic rustling and whispering in the leaves, and every object around me, procreated dreams in my imagination, in which my friends sweetly danced before my mind. I exchanged with you the most enchanting reveries; collected, as it were, the most mystic sounds of nature, to impart my smiling fancies to you; and only the jostling of my carriage caused now and then a painful chasm in that airy retinue of uncorporeal sensations.

"Being, at length, tired of these unwelcome interruptions, I alighted to walk behind the carriage. Having proceeded about a quarter of a mile, I turned into a bye-path, which appeared to join again with the highway at some distance. Being now freed from all interruptions, my imagination revelled in numberless, extravagant reveries, my steps quickened during that inebriation of my heart, and I compute to have proceeded two miles in that manner, when I stumbled against the root of a tree. My sportive fancies disappeared at once; and I found myself entangled in a ticket, and, soon after, in a mazy labyrinth of underwood, without being able to find the path again; nay, even without the least apparent possibility of retracing it. Supposing, however, that I could not have proceeded a great way, and of course, not be far distant from my carriage, I called several times the name of my driver. I imagined to hear him return an answer, (which probably was nothing but the effect of an echo,) followed the direction of the sound, and relapsed into my former carelessness. Having forced my way, for some time, through bushes and underwood, I was surprised at my having not yet regained the highway. I stopt, and listened. How great was my joy, when I very plainly heard my servant converse with the postillion! I pushed through a thick bush, and imagined to be near my carriage.

"You may easily conceive how great my terror was, when I found myself on the bank of a rivulet, the murmuring of whose waves had deceived me. The painful sensation I felt at this sight was raised to a still higher degree by the idea of being in a strange country, in a dangerous forest, and perhaps at a great distance from honest people. How much did I now repent my heedlessness! I cursed the postillion, myself, and my servants. While I was lamenting my dangerous situation, a little Italian greyhound rushed forth from the adjacent thicket, running along the bank of the rivulet, and crossed a small bridge which I had not observed before; but looking constantly back at me, it fell into the water. The current hurried it rapidly along: I went back, keeping close to the bank, till I could take hold of it. As soon as I set my prisoner at liberty, on the other side of the rivulet, he ran barking before me over a grassy turf, which seemed to be enclosed by a wood. My conductor led me, at last, to a bower, which was embosomed by lofty trees and shrubberies. I entered it without hesitation; but had not advanced many steps, when a soft arm encircled my neck, and pulled me down. A burning mouth touched my cheek, and kissed it fervently. The hand that pressed my face to the lips of the unknown person, glided accidentally upon my shoulder, touching the epaulet of my uniform; upon which the being, in whose arms I was, instantly started up with a loud shriek; but soon sat down again. My situation surpassed all power of description. I was no stranger to dangers, and always had faced them with equanimity: the terrors of war never have terrified me, nor made my heart beat stronger than usual; yet here, where I saw no danger, where I could use my sword, and, to all appearance, was in the company of a female, I began violently to tremble; my knees shook, and, instead of supporting my frightened antagonist, I was supported by her. My heart threatened to burst, and I dropt involuntarily upon my knees. Encircling the stranger with my arm, I perceived that it was a lady. She trembled, but not so violently as I did. My head sank upon one of her hands; my senses were benumbed: I was in a dreadful agony, and imagined the icy hand of death was upon me.

"For God's sake, Sennor, who are you?" a sweet, trembling voice exclaimed at length. I recovered the use of my senses, and rose. My right-hand, which was resting on her shoulder, encircled, by a secret impulse, her taper form, and I pressed her violently to my panting bosom. A vehement passion thrilled all the pulses of my heart, which scarcely had recovered from the highest degree of a momentary terror; my tongue cleaved to the palate, and I stammered, with great difficulty, "A man of honour, Sennora!" Her melodious voice trembled so sweetly, that I fancied to hear the plaintive strains of a nightingale: the darkness of the bower began to be dispelled by the silver rays of the moon, and I beheld the delicate form of a heavenly figure reposing on a seat of green turf. I beheld numberless bewitching charms, yet without being able to discern her features; her heart beat violently under my daring hand, and I was irresistibly impelled to press the sweet enchantress to my enraptured bosom.

"At once, it began to lighten; a sudden brightness illuminated the bower; a dazzling light flirted before my eyes, which, however, were suddenly veiled again with midnight darkness; an icy hand glided down my back, and I was scarcely able to turn my torpid neck: for horrid phantoms, with torches in their hands, stood behind me. I started up; but when I was going to draw my sword, a fifth person rushed upon me from behind, and seized my hands, which were tied together in the twinkling of an eye. I was forcibly dragged into a garden. The rapid transition from the highest summit of ecstasy to the utmost degree of terror, the suddenness of the surprize, and the alarming circumstances attending it, almost petrified me. I was suddenly transported from a world of enchanting reality to the gloomy kingdom of horrid dreams; my senses fled by degrees, my pulse began to beat slower, and, at last, seemed entirely to stop. On recovering my recollection, I was seized with new horrors, seeing two of those phantoms walk by my side. They were covered from head to foot with a white cloth; and I beheld, through a small aperture, such an unnatural, distorted countenance, that I cannot but think that they were masked; though I cannot guess the reason of their having been disguised thus in that place. I never saw such a chalk-white prominent chin, and such a horrid, grinning mouth, which was over-shaded by a crooked red nose. I addressed these monsters trembling, in the Spanish language, but received no answer.

"A little while after, I took the courage to look back after my female companion, whom I heard groan and sob a few paces behind me. She was clad in white; her ash-pale unveiled face was half covered with her auburn tresses, and inclined towards her open bosom, which seemed to expand itself more than usual, in order to receive it entirely. She was led by two guides, that were speaking to her; a chilly tremor, which visibly shook her frame, and a hollow groan, that raised the disordered covering of her bosom, was the only answer she returned. My conductors now dragged me more rapidly along; I heard, only at a distance, low whispers, and could plainly distinguish the name, *Francisca*— But what is the matter with you, Marquis, are you not well?"

"Nothing, dear S******. Pray go on! Your tale is so horrid. The name struck me. Go on, dearest Count!"

The Count gazed a while at me with a doubtful unsatisfied mien, and then resumed:

"The gradually increasing paleness of the moon, and the dawn of the rising day, enabled me to observe that our way led towards a ruinous building, which was half concealed by a cluster of lofty trees, and rose, as if called forth by magic spells, out of grey fog. It reclined against the lower part of a hill, whose barren top beetled over the bushes. It was half decayed, had large apertures, and not one whole window. It seemed to have formerly stood upon the top of the eminence and gradually sunk down into the dreary valley. The doors were half covered with rubbish; and some decayed steps rose out of the black darkness, which evaporated a smell of corruption that straitened my breast. I took leave of the living; a gaping, baseless tomb extended its arms, which seemed to be ready to receive me; stern necessity urged me to bury myself in its darksome womb; I lost sight of the lady, with an excruciating agony, and the icy torpitude of my soul was gradually expelled by a mournful horror. A door was, at length, forced open; my conductors pushed me through the gravelike aperture, which was shut upon me with a dreadful noise. A second door, not far from me, opened at the same instant, and was shut again. Woeful groans re-echoed through the extensive dreary vault. It was Francisca's voice.

"I thought it strange they had not taken my sword from me, which I now recollected. The unknown lady was not far distant,

I hoped she could untie my hands: I was strong, and my keepers were unarmed. Advancing, for that purpose, a few steps nearer to the spot where she was, I found that we were separated by an iron railing, which seemed to extend through the whole vault. I accosted, and begged her to endeavour to thrust one of her hands through the rails; but all the apertures were too narrow. She discovered, at length, a larger opening, through which she could just force her hand. I placed myself sideways to afford her an opportunity of drawing my sword, in order to cut the strings that shackled my hands. The sword sticking, however, too fast, she pulled it so violently that the broken blade wounded her hand.

"In that very moment our keepers appeared at the door. They called to me, and I could not but obey their summons. Francisca was led through the other door: our keepers took us into the middle, and we entered a long passage, which lost itself in the midnight darkness of the back ground.

"I now was at leisure to take a view of my fellow prisoner, assisted by the light of the torches. Alas! my dear G******, not one moment of my life has destroyed a single stroke of that picture, whose exquisite beauty filled me with wonder and astonishment. I never beheld a woman like her. Her heavenly form engrossed my whole attention, and thrilled my soul with rapturous sensations in spite of the dangers that surrounded me. The sight of her would have imparadised me on the brink of the gaping grave. This greatest and most perfect masterpiece of plastic nature seemed to have transported me into a new and better world. I forgot that I was a prisoner, and imagined to breathe in a better atmosphere. Her beauty surpassed all power of description; innocence throned on her heavenly countenance; her coral lips were the residence of numberless graces. No language is adequate to describe the heaven that smiled in her looks. Her face resembled a lily that blushes in the vicinity of an opening rose. She was absorpt in profound thought; a saint-like resignation gleamed in her tearful eye; the convulsive motions of her quivering lips, and her gloomy, downcast brow, bespoke the secret workings of her soul. Her overclouded looks seemed to be directed in fond melancholy towards an object at an unknown distance, and, when returning to me, with a tender glance of pity, appeared to descend from a blessing heaven, to comfort a sinner before their final close.

"I accosted her in French, and she answered me. The passage grew so narrow that only two could walk a-breast. Our leaders were obliged to go before us with their torches; and while they were violently quarrelling about something, she gave me some horrid explanations of that dreadful adventure; but our conversation was soon observed, and we were torn asunder. One of our guides took my sword from my side, and looked at the sword-knot with great attention. I resolved to take advantage of this circumstance for my preservation.

"Having proceeded about an hundred steps, the end of the passage extended itself into a spacious cavern. The light of the torches reflected from the walls in numberless, various colours, as if they were inlaid with chrystal; a soft glimmer spread through the vault; and Francisca, who now joined me, resembled a celestial cherub encircled with heavenly glory. However, this lustre was only a preparation for a still more splendid scene. The cavern contracted itself again into a passage to a second vault, that glared at us with additional radiance. Two large chandeliers depended from the lofty roof into an intense magic mist, which rested awfully upon the objects around. As we proceeded, I observed all the walls around decorated with large mirrors fixed on a ground of black cloth. In our front we beheld an elevation with seats on either side, which seemed to be occupied by a numerous assembly. Two chairs were placed beneath the chandeliers on the brink of a gaping gulph. My first gesture was directed towards that ominous abyss; a cutting blast of wind gushed from between the aperture, and low whispers seemed to ascend from the deep. After a long painful reflection on that alarming object, I directed my eyes at the company that were seated before me. The uppermost place was occupied by an enormous plump figure, the right by four women, and the left by five men. The nearest person towards me was a girl of striking beauty; tho' it appeared to be only the wreck of former charms, which seemed to have been impaired by the most violent assaults of grief and rage. A dying flame gleamed in her breaking eyes, and her bosom was perturbed by a vehement fermentation, that now dyed her features with a crimson colour, and now veiled them with a corpse-like hue. A secret horror seemed to have grasped the whole assembly; every one ceased to breathe when we entered, and the blood in every vein made a long and dreadful pause.

"The young lady knelt, at length, before the monster, whose kindling rage now appeared to give him a thousand arms and a thousand tongues, and the tumultuous passions that agitated his soul broke forth with undescribable fury. The monster accused the girl and myself, charging me with being her lover, and insisted upon our death. Francisca, mean time, was as motionless as a marble statue; life seemed to have taken its flight from her for a while, in order to return, at once, with redoubled warmth. She rose as pale as a corpse, but with marks of firm resolution, and resigned to her impending doom, defending only *me*, and declaring to have seen me the first time an hour ago. Her courage, her more than terrestrial, more than human equanimity, the firmness of her (already unembodied) soul, could have animated a dying man with new life, and kindled in my soul a flame that burst forth in execrations. I pleaded my sword-knot, disclosed my rank, and swore my death would not remain unavenged, and call down their own destruction. My returning boldness, the fire of my eloquence, and alas! (what has destroyed the happiness of my whole life,) my not once mentioning the hapless girl, and pleading only for *myself* and for *my life*, appeared to strike the assembly. But when I had finished my harangue, and the midnight silence returned, I darted a look at my fellow prisoner, and she glanced at me. It was well that I did not die in that moment, for that look would have met me again in another life, and haunted me through the endless realms of eternity. It was a look of angelic greatness, intermixed with a silent, painful contempt of my cowardice. Her tender grief changed into the frigid state of a marble bust; a dying spark seemed, at last, to tremble on its surface, and to demand back all the tender sentiments of which I had cheated her so shamefully. This almost made me frantic; but, instead of rushing into the abyss before me, which opened its gaping jaws to receive me, I raged like a child, struggled to break my galling fetters, and relapsed fainting and weeping upon my chair.

"The stern arbiters of our fate now began to consult with each other in an unknown language. Our accuser frequently interrupted their consultation by horrid howls, and was pacified with the greatest difficulty. A pause of profound silence ensued: the monster, who was ready to faint with inward rage, interrupted, at length, that dreadful interval of stillness, asking me, with a trembling voice, whether I chose to die, or would take a solemn oath never to reveal what Francisca had disclosed to me, and not to mention a syllable of the whole affair during a twelve month? A bible was brought, and I, miserable wretch! swore. I was cautioned not to break my promise, lest I should pay with my life for my perfidy, though I should be concealed in the centre of the earth.

"As soon as I had seated myself, out of breath, and almost bereft of the use of my senses, one of our conductors, who stood behind us, went away. The door was shut with a hideous noise, the lights were extinguished, the assembly disappeared, and the awful silence of a church-yard swayed all around. Francisca only sighed to my left; but soon after was dragged from her chair, and plunged into the abyss before me. I heard her distinctly fall down from step to step, and dreadful screams resounded from the abyss. The hollow groans, extorted by a painful death, were interrupted now and then by woeful lamentations, and the clattering of clanging irons, which clashed against each other. My senses fled on pinions of horror."

These were the last words I heard the Count utter, dropping senseless from my chair. He called for assistance, and I was restored with great difficulty. When I recovered the use of my senses, I found myself upon my bed. My servants stood around me; and the Count sat in speechless stupefaction by my side, leaning his head upon his hand. As soon as I uttered the first sound, he rose, and knelt down before my bed: "What a dreadful mystery!" he exclaimed; and a little while after stared at me, asking, in a kind of agony, "For God's sake! who are you?" It now was *my* turn to collect myself. I took him kindly by the hand; but he tore himself from me, and rushed out of the room. His servants followed him, and I heard him hastily ride through the castle gate.

CHAPTER III.

Morning was just dawning, and I wished to sleep a little, being entirely exhausted. I dismissed the servants, and shut my eyes, but could not sleep. Alas! Francisca! I heard your woeful lamentations, and your groans kept me in a painful stupefaction: a thousand confused ideas arose in my soul, succeeding each other with unspeakable rapidity; but Francisca's hapless fate was uppermost in my imagination. I was suddenly seized with a chilly tremor, and fancied to see her hurled down into her grave. "Yes!" I exclaimed, "Francisca, it is you!" and extended my arms, as if going to save her.

An ice cold hand touched my face, and a secret horror convulsed my nerves. I had ordered the candles to be extinguished; but, nevertheless, perceived a radiant splendor around me. A low rustling announced to me the approach of a superior being. It was *Amanuel.* "What do you want with me?" I exclaimed: "Must you haunt me every where."

"Two years are now elapsed," he replied, kindly, "since you have seen me, but I have never left you for one hour. Remember, Carlos, that I must not appear to you again. You are surrounded every where with invisible spies: I warn you, Carlos!" So saying, he disappeared. The lustre that illuminated my apartment died away, and midnight silence reigned again around me. No sound was heard, and I relapsed breathless upon my pillow.

The Count staid two days away, and no one had seen him since his sudden departure. He returned, on the third day, in visible perplexity. I was just taking a walk in the garden to refresh my exhausted spirits by the exhalation of the budding flowers, and turning round the corner of a bye path, he stood before me, embraced me speechless, and suddenly tore himself from my bosom, leading me to a seat of turf. There he took a sealed paper out of his pocket, and gave it me. Having embraced me again and again, and bedewed my face with tears, he left me abruptly.

I looked trembling at the direction of that mysterious packet. It was directed to me, double-sealed, and tied with a string. The knots being so tight that it was impossible to untwist them, I wanted to take my scissars out of my pocket, but could not find them. Having exhausted my patience by repeated fruitless attempts to open the letter without tearing it, I went to the castle to open it. On the way I met one of my servants, who came to tell me that several neighbouring noblemen were at the castle, and wanted to pay a visit to the Count; but the latter could be found no where, and I was obliged to receive them. We conversed, dined, and sat down to play, whereby I was constantly prevented from reading my letter. The company began, at length, to dance; however, I was drawn into a long conversation, and obliged to stay my impatient desire of knowing the contents of the mysterious paper some time longer. They went, at length, and I hastened impatiently to my closet to gratify my curiosity. I put my hand into my pocket to take the letter out; but how was I terrified when I could find it no where! I searched the whole house and the garden; but all the pains I took to find it were fruitless; and I went to rest, entirely occupied with ideas which painfully combined the whole train of these incidents, and led me to connect a gloomy futurity with past sufferings. However, the vexation of seeing the prospect of future peace again overclouded, the painful notion of being once more reduced into the detestable bondage of spirits that had already repeatedly abused me in the most cruel manner, the adventures of the Count, their probable connection with the incidents of my own life, the familiarity of the place and the persons, Amanuel's words; every, every thing combined to draw a horrid picture before my imagination, which dispelled even the idea of sleep. Being entirely exhausted, and almost stupefied by anxious bodings, I could remain no longer in my bed, and went to the window. The night was beautiful, and a profound, inanimate silence reigned all around; all the pulses of nature seemed to stop. The prospect from my window opened to the seat where I had received the Count's letter. I looked at it, and saw some person sitting on that spot. The moon shone bright and clear; I could not deceive myself. The person was wrapt in a white cloak, and appeared too small for the Count, and much too tall for the gardener. It struck me that this incident, perhaps, would afford me an opportunity of clearing up the unaccountable loss of the letter, and my friend's sudden and mysterious departure.

I slipped my great coat on, opened the garden door softly, took a short way around through the boscage which extended to the turf seat, and went boldly onward. At a small distance from that spot I recollected that I was quite unarmed, which was no small check upon my courage, particularly when I was struck with the idea that every thing bore so much resemblance to the Count's adventure. The moon shone with the same brightness upon a similar ominous scene six months ago; the young leaves floated in a similar manner in the dusky night air, and appeared to tremble with secret horror;

a soft, aromatic gust of air rushed against me, and thrilled me with strange, undescribable sensations: every object around me seemed to be animated with a sense of anxious expectation, and the shades resembled sporting fairies, that appeared to rest on the flowery turf to await the event. Not only my courage was entirely gone, but I also began to tremble. I intended several times to return to the castle; but, at length, took the firm resolution to await the event, and to observe the white figure from a distance.

When I was but a few steps distant from the turf seat, I was struck with astonishment on seeing three white figures, instead of one. The company increased, from time to time, in number, and I had already counted eight persons, when the Count joined them in his usual dress. My hair began to bristle up; I was seized with dreadful apprehensions: my eyes were anxiously directed at the mystic company, to see what would be the consequence of that extraordinary nocturnal meeting. Not the least sound interrupted the awful silence that reigned all around. One of the company unsheathed the Count's sword, and made him take hold of the hilt, without uttering a word. I then clearly saw a tall man touch my friend with a long white finger, upon which he dropt senseless on the ground.

I ejaculated a loud scream; the company disappeared, and I was left alone. Was it, perhaps, a deluding dream? The whole creation around me appeared to be so entirely inanimate that nothing could interrupt my stupefaction. Not a breath of air was stirring; not a leaf trembled; even the moon was not obscured by a single cloud. A distant noise vibrated in my ears; I approached the spot where the Count still was prostrated. He was not stained with blood, but only cold and stiff. Oh! how unspeakably dear was he then to me! I lifted him up, took him in my arms, and spared no pains to recall him to life. All the breath that animated me was concentrated on my lips, to impart itself to him by numberless kisses. His face was dreadfully convulsed. Those beautiful, sweet features, which usually were the seat of juvenile suavity and friendly kindness, were contorted into horrid furrows, and numbered with an icy torpitude; terror had depressed his lips, and a convulsive trepidation moved, now and then, his eyelids and forehead. His right hand had grasped the hilt of his sword so firmly that it was impossible to take it from him.

He began, at length, to move again, opened his gloomy eyes in a ghastly manner, staring at me as if he did not know me, and then closed them again with a loud scream. He seemed to collect himself with great difficulty; but where shall I find words to describe his sudden transition to the most furious passions, and the frightful change which they produced in his face? His corpse-like paleness reddened rapidly; his lips began to quiver; his brows were contracted; and a pair of furious, rolling eyes flashed through the red glow of his countenance. I had recovered my courage, and pressed him tenderly to my bosom, seizing with my left the hand in which he held his sword, and straining him closer to my heart with the right. He attempted to tear himself from me, but his strength failed him, and he relapsed into my arms. His frowning brow now began to brighten up, displaying speaking marks of tender melancholy; the rolling fire of his eyes was drowned in tears, and he groaned aloud.

"Dearest, best Count!" I began, "collect yourself!"

He started back, and tore himself from my embraces. "For God's sake, Carlos, be gone; leave me instantly!—Be on your guard! Don't you see that I am stained with blood?"

"What dreadful phantoms do you behold, Count! Pray, collect yourself: am I not your friend? is not your Carlos with you?"

His head dropt down upon his breast; his lefty hand made a convulsive motion, as if he wanted to drive a fly from his brow: "Rather say, Carlos *was* my friend; for now I hate him mortally." So saying, he started up, but soon dropt down again. "Go, dear Marquis!" he resumed: "do you hear? Make haste to be gone. You are not safe here. Beware of my hand, particularly of my right. Call your servants together; defend yourself!" These last words he pronounced with a singular violence.

"Yes, dear Count, I will call your servants; but not for my sake: it is *you* that wants assistance." I was going to rise, but he pulled me down again. "Hearken, Marquis! I am going to intrust you with a horrid secret! Alas! with a secret that makes me frantic." "Whither could you repose it more safely than in this bosom, which beats entirely for you? Collect yourself, my dear friend, and every thing will be cleared up."

"But will you think it possible? Don't be angry with me, dear Carlos. Alas! I cannot help it: I am urged by stern necessity." With these words, his hair bristled, a dreadful rage convulsed his features, and he grasped my arm vehemently. "Hearken! hearken to what I am going to tell you!" So saying, he drew nearer, and roared into my ear, "I am to assassinate you!"—"Count!"—"Yes, by the omnipotent God!" With these words he rushed upon me like a madman; but I made a sudden turn, and the sword went into the back of the turf seat. We wrestled, and the Count dropt down, unhanding the sword, and pressing me to his heart. "Alas! Carlos, will you believe me?—You that are my only friend! Do you see, I am quite delirious. A spectre haunts me every where. Why will you not die with me?" So saying, he directed his large blue eyes mournfully at me. I was so much benumbed with horror that I lost the power of utterance. "Why don't you answer me? Come, let me pierce your breast; one stroke will unite us for ever. Have pity on me, dear Carlos!" I inclined my face towards him, pressing it to his forehead. "You never have been cruel to me: it will be the last pleasure I shall have on earth. You have desired me to collect myself: do *you* only collect yourself. By the eternal God! (starting up) we both must die this instant."

He searched for his sword, which I had concealed behind the turf seat. "So! Can *you* use *me* thus, Marquis? *Me*, to whom you so frequently have vowed eternal friendship? Why have you taken my sword away? Alas! you have taken every thing from me! Return it me, dear Carlos!" "Count, you ought to thank me for what I have done; your senses are bewildered; you would have repented it too late." "My senses disordered, do you say? God forgive you that lie. No! I am very sensible of what I am doing, where I am, and what I am about. A dreadful mystery tears us asunder. But are you not *Carlos?*" "Yes, your Carlos; your best and most faithful friend." "Well, do you see now that I am not mad?—You are my friend; you have solemnly promised, a thousand times, to die with me; and I know you would die with me now, if it could make me easier. Would you not?" "Willingly, dear Count, if it would make you easier." "Well! then listen to me, Marquis. I have been compelled to swear a dreadful oath; I have been shut up in a dungeon two days; I have been forced to swear!—Alas! I am not delirious:—and, after I had sworn, a white ghost, whom I had already once seen, came, and"—He had, meantime, perceived his sword behind the turf seat, taken it up, and now aimed a stroke at me: however, a Superior Being rushed between us, and the Count dropt to the ground.

CHAPTER IV.

When I came to my recollection, I found myself alone. It was broad day; the sun was risen, and glared me in the face. All the trees around me were enlivened by the feathered songsters, who chirped their matins. The events of the antecedent night hovered only like shades before my fancy, divested of their horrors. My exhausted sensations recovered their usual energy, concentrating into a rapturous stream of serene ideas, and I scarcely missed my friend. I tore myself, slow and reluctant, out of the arms of a voluptuous langour; and my senses were, with difficulty, roused from that sweet lassitude. All the inmates of the castle were still asleep when I returned; I went directly to the Count's apartment; but it was as empty as before. I awakened his servants; no one had seen him. I passed the day in the greatest anxiety; he did not come. Several weeks elapsed, and he had not yet re-appeared. The door of my apartment opened at length, after the lapse of two months, and he entered with a cheerful countenance. The roses of youthful hilarity throned again on his dimpled cheeks; his eyes had recovered their usual lustre; a mild gaiety sported upon his beautiful lips: he looked cheerfully at me, and smiled. "Have I surprised you, dear G******? Well! it is a long time since I have seen you!" He then embraced me with his wonted cordiality, took a chair, and breakfasted with uncommon tranquillity. I beheld all this in a state of petrifaction, and went into the garden to give way to my ideas. The Count joined me in a few minutes; we rambled all over the garden, speaking only on indifferent subjects. He informed me of some improvements he intended to make, and of the sum he meant to apply for that purpose. He seemed not to know that seat of turf where that dreadful scene was acted; not a single vestige of a returning idea of that shocking incident was to be perceived.

The summer passed amid our usual occupations and amusements: my friend was as cheerful as ever; and I joined him with pleasure in his jocundity. We roved merrily from one of our neighbours to the other, frequently had visitors; hunted, danced, played; and arranged our occupations and diversions so well, that the approaching winter did not threaten to make the least change in our plan. When autumn began to dye the leaves with a paler hue, the friendly fire side cemented our mutual intimacy more strongly every day. We spent again our evenings with conversation; a congenial propensity seemed to recal either of us from the bustle of company to the cheerful fire side. We were equally animated with a desire to hear the tale of each others adventures; shewed the same attention to, and the same interest in, our mutual narrations, and were equally ready to gratify our reciprocal curiosity. These hours seemed to be the least important of my life; however, they were the most happy, and I enjoyed them with unallayed tranquillity. The autumn rustling in the trees, the rattling of the windows, and the cracking of the doors, struck us with secret awe, and appeared to bring us into a closer contact.

We returned once, on a serene, frosty autumnal day, from a fatiguing, but pleasant, hunting party. Our supper was soon finished, and we resorted in excellent spirits to the inviting fire side. "Pray, Marquis," the Count said, when we were seated, "don't you think it very strange that I am still ignorant who you are? You have given me only partial accounts of yourself; could you not inrust me with the particulars of your life?"

"I will do it with pleasure, dearest Count; but then we shall want more wood; for I have a long tale to relate."

"I will trouble you only for a part of your adventures to night; but I wish to hear the beginning. Will you do me that kindness?" He ordered the servant to bring more wood, and I began:

"You know, dear S******, that I am born of an old Spanish family, that traces its ancestors back to the first Christians, and has been graced by heroes in the earliest times of the Monarchy. My father was a nobleman of the first rank, and my mother was born of an ancient and wealthy family. Alcantara is the place of my nativity."

"Alcantara!" the Count exclaimed, seized with astonishment: "Alcantara! But go on!" He was for some time lost in profound reflection, from which he recovered only by degrees, and so far as to attend to my tale.

"The amiable qualities of my mother, in particular, had a singular influence on my external improvement, as well as on the mode I adopted to acquire useful knowledge, on my education, and on the combination of all my future hopes with the present time. I was early told that her beauty, which was a particular attribute of the whole family, was the usual inheritance of all its members. Full cheeks, expressive lips, sparkling eyes, and a pair of regular eyebrows, were really my first patrimony. The vivacity of my actions, the first blandishment of my speech, the stability of my disposition, and a little pertinacy, which I knew very well how to apply, assisted me to gain attention, indulgence, and favour.

"My educators, therefore, endeavoured to prolong to me the enjoyment of those happy times. This was, however, the very way of making me lose it the sooner. The solitude which I was suffered to enjoy, served to afford a wrestling place to the extravagancies of my juvenile feelings; it served to imprint my observations more strongly on my mind, to form more voluptuous dreams of them; and my whole spirit seemed gradually to dissolve itself into that uncorporeal mist which bedews with sweet tears all subsequent feelings. Alas! I did not then imagine what sufferings those delicious hours were preparing for me, and how much the marrow of my juvenile strength was consumed by the moments in which my soul floated on cheerful images of the present time into the most distant futurity.

"When I, as a young man, was introduced to society, I was animated with a sensibility and warmth which never fails to make a particular impression on the female sex. I was caressed by the ladies; and they had an hundred defects to correct, and an hundred amiable qualities to unfold; and thus I was seduced under the pretext of being polished.

"I was soon rendered receptive of the caresses of the other sex; but suffering myself to be guided merely by humour and fashion, I generally paid homage only at the shrine of her who was most admired. I improved by degrees in all the arts of gallantry, and very soon had reason to complain more of being constantly teazed by unsought conquests, than of the cruelty of the objects of my adoration. However, the period arrived when I was punished for my amorous frolicks!

"Elmira, Countess of S******, had spent the first fifteen years of her life at the castle of a relation, which was too remote, or too much concealed, to attract the gallantry or the notice of any man. She now came to Alcantara, adorned not only with all the charms of novelty, but also with uncommon natural endowments, which soon raised her above the splendor, and even the jealousy, of her competitors. Her superior beauty, her unaffected wit and jocularity, that charmed at first sight, assisted her to conceal, beneath an ever-smiling form, a glowing heart, a heart that demanded eternal love. Nature seemed to have been in her best humour when forming her, for every expression of her sentiments, and all her motions bore the stamp of the sweetest hilarity, of an indefatigable gaiety, and of innocent blandishment. She admitted my address with that jocund, pleasing openness that redoubles every step, but yet keeps one at a respectful distance.

"One evening I surprised her with her guitar in her hand. She was sitting on a sofa, and the instrument lay on her lap: her head rested on one hand, and the other held the guitar and a pocket-handkerchief. Having entered the apartment unperceived by her, her back being turned towards the door, I heard her heave deep sighs, and saw some pearly tears drop upon the musick book that lay before her. I stepped nearer, but she did not hear me; knelt down before her, seizing her hand, and kissing it; but Elmira seemed to be petrified. She started up, at last, and seeing me by her side, offered to run into her closet: however, I retained her on her seat, yet without speaking a word."

"Alas! Carlos!" she exclaimed, at length, "what have you seen? But if you had heard the sweet affecting air I sung, it would have melted you also to tears: if you wish to hear it, I will play it to you."

"She then searched in her musick book; but I saw that the affecting air could be found no where. She endeavoured to regain her usual cheerfulness, but her efforts were fruitless.

"I now took her once more by the hand, and said; "Dearest Countess, one cannot always find what one wishes to meet with; I am in the same predicament with you. I was melancholy and sad, and expected to find you serene and open, instead of which you are in tears and reserved." "Reserved, Carlos! I never was guilty of reservedness." "Then this is the first time you are, Elmira: I am young in years, but I have ceased long since to be a stripling in love;

and if adoration be not sufficient to deserve your confidence, you will at least unbosom yourself to your friend! You are silent! you weep! Why will you not speak to me? am I not entirely devoted to you? Yes, my sweet friend, every sentiment of mine is your property; all my thoughts and feelings are dedicated to you!"

"Do you then imagine, Carlos," she began at length, rather offended, "that I have secrets to disclose to you! I am, really, not in the least prepared for it."

"Elmira, you misunderstand me."—"To be plain, Carlos, I must tell you that I am in a humour which does not promise to meet your approbation." "Dearest Countess, I did not mean to offend you." "I do not doubt it; you only wanted skill to shape your curiosity properly."

"Indeed, Madonna, I am sensible that I have been too inquisitive. Forgive me, dearest Countess, and let us speak of something else. Who made this guitar?" She stared at me, and began to weep violently: a long, long sigh swelled her beautiful bosom.

"I am troublesome to you, dear Countess: I conjure you once more to excuse my intrusion. Good day to you, Elmira." "Oh! stay, Carlos." "Your tears flow more violently since I am with you." "Don't let me be an object of your anger, if you don't think me deserving of your compassion."

"Having pronounced these words, she left me abruptly. I was extremely angry with her: however, my anger was nothing but the effect of love. That scene affected me so much, that I was obliged to keep my room two days; on the third evening I received the following note:

"We have exchanged our parts, Carlos. I am on the point of becoming the object of *your* pity. You love *all* women; alas! and I only *one* man. To-morrow morning I shall be at the monastery of the Capuchins at St. Jago, and—confess."

"St. Jago is twelve leagues distant from Alcantara. It was necessary that I should set off that very evening; and, in spite of the tempestuous night, and the remonstrances of my servant, I got upon my horse, and rode furiously through the city-gate. Alfonso's prediction was realized; the rain, which, intermixed with thunder and lightning, poured down in torrents, wetted me to the skin; the hurricane threw us off from our horses, and we could not distinguish the road; our poor beasts, who took not the least share in the heat of their riders, sank with every step deeper into the mire; and we knew, at length, neither the situation of the monastery, nor that of the town, arriving at the skirts of a forest, with the greatest danger of our life, and amid the continual fear of being drowned or sinking into the mire. Here a new scene of horror awaited us. The dangers of my journey had still left me so much good humour that I began to sing, to beguile the tediousness of our road. It was a well known popular song, and Alfonso joined me heartily. But conceive our astonishment when the whole forest resounded at once with numberless voices, who sang the same song. I fancied, at first, that it was the effect of an echo, but was chilled with terror when the invisible songsters commenced the second stanza ere we had finished the first. "What is that, Alfonso!" I exclaimed. "Alas! my lord," returned the poor fellow trembling, "I really think they are devils who are going to break our necks."

"I now perceived that we were on a beaten path. Fear had seized my senses, and I gored my horse so violently with my spurs, that he set off in full speed; while my poor servant, who was entangled in the underwood, and roared as if Old Nick and his infernal hosts already had seized him, was incapable of following. I was, in a few moments, so far distant from him, that I could hear his voice no more; and struggling to arrest my horse, he left the road, and got into a close thicket. The sky had cleared up in the meantime; however, my situation was not the better for it. I called my servant repeatedly by his name, but no answer was returned. I alighted, took the horse by the bridle, and went in search of an open spot, where I hoped to discover a road, and, if not, proposed to spend the night. I perceived, now and then, some lights at a distance, which, however, instantly disappeared, when I called out towards the direction where I saw them. One light only remained unalterably in its place; and expecting to find people on that spot, I proceeded towards it half comforted.

"The nearer I came the smaller it appeared: and after I had got, with great difficulty, through marshes and bogs, within a few hundred paces distance from the place where it appeared to be, it concentrated itself, as it were, into a red hot point.

"I discovered, at length, a little hut. The diminutive window in which the light that had guided my steps was placed, was almost totally embost in a thick bush, and entirely covered with leaves; solitary rays only stole through the leafy darkness, and produced an enchanting effect. The sky was entirely cleared up, the tempest had spent its boisterous fury, and a gentle breeze of air only shook the pearly drops from the leaves, which twinkled like little stars through the awful dusk. On stepping nearer to the hut, the sound of different voices, which I had heard at some distance, hushed suddenly. I knocked at the door, but no answer was returned. Pushing violently with my foot against the wooden wall, some person exclaimed within, "Make haste, Maria, and open the door!" The door was opened by a little girl; and I beheld a blazing fire in the middle of the chamber: a female, who had her back turned towards me, was busied in putting some coals under a saucepan; and a little well-made boy was sitting on her left side. As soon as he saw me, he leaned against her bosom, and exclaimed, "Mother! Mother! only look!"

"James, you are very late!" the woman exclaimed, without discontinuing her occupation, or turning round. "Have you brought father with you? Look only, you wicked rogue, I have been obliged to burn, on your account, all the wood which you have gathered with so much trouble: however, I warrant you, James, you will relish your soup." So saying, she took the cover from the saucepan, looking into it with apparent delight.

"Good woman!" I at length began, "it has dreadfully lightened and stormed; and the Spirit of the Wood has passed by." "Poor fellow! I dare say you are wet to the skin. Come to the fire, you wicked rogue!" So saying, she turned around, and seeing me with the horse, who had followed me into the room, the cover, which she had in her hand, dropped down; the saucepan was overturned, and the soup streamed into the fire. She screamed, and endeavoured to save it; but the fright which the sight of a stranger had produced, threw her into such a flutter, that she extinguished the fire by her attempts of saving the supper of poor James; and only the little lamp in the window spread a faint glimmer through the dusk of the hut.

"James will make a fine piece of work, (she now resumed, laughing,) when he finds his delicious soup between the coals." She then got up, and came towards me.

"I beg your pardon, good woman, for having caused that accident. The tempest—I have lost my way."

"Walk in, Sir, (she said, with much good nature;) but the horse must stay out of doors." I went silently back, tied the horse to a tree, and then re-entered her humble abode.

"Well, Sir! I dare say you are pretty wet, and hungry into the bargain. I would light the fire again with all my heart, but I have got no dry wood." I had not seen her face yet: however, her amiable unconcern charmed me. "I have caused your soup to be overturned, (said I,) and shall punish myself for it, by going in search of dry wood." "Pray do, (she replied;) meantime I will rekindle the fire." I went out to fetch wood, but not being able to find one dry piece near the hut, I was obliged to go farther into the forest. Meantime I heard my horse neigh, which he was used to do when he kicked at the approach of a stranger. A loud laugh of several persons ensued, which made me conclude that James was returned, and, with his wife, was diverted by the kicking of my horse.

"I was, at length, so fortunate as to collect a small bundle of dry wood. I returned with hasty strides to the hut, and entered the door; but found the merry scene entirely changed. Neither saucepan nor fire was to be seen; and James, a tall and handsome man, was sitting on the floor, and had taken his wife upon his lap. The lamp, with which she probably had intended to light the fire, stood by her side, and reflected its light upon her beautiful face. She clung with the greatest tenderness round her husband's neck, and her angelic looks were directed at his eyes. James seemed to be enraptured with his happiness, and quite absorpt in his felicity. He lifted his eyes up to his heavenly wife, whose cheeks rested upon his; she imprinted fervent kisses on his majestic brow, and seemed to intend to bury him in her bosom. A look of rapturous enthusiasm glowed on either face, the little boy hung around the neck of the mother, and the most beautiful girl I ever saw caressed her parents by turns. What a *silent*, and yet, what a *speaking* scene! low sighs only were exchanged; and every word was kissed away from the opening lip ere it could form an articulated sound. I never have seen such a feast of tenderness and love; never have I beheld so much genuine matrimonial bliss."

"Oh! God!" James at length began: however, he was interrupted by the boy, who, on seeing me, exclaimed, "The stranger!" James now raised his beautiful burden from the floor, came towards me, and shook me by the hand: "Welcome, dear Sir! welcome to my humble habitation," said he. "You will find very little convenience here; however, it will make us happy to entertain you to the best of our abilities." His charming wife, mean time, was occupied with the fire, and now stepped towards me to bid me welcome, shaking me by the hand with hers, the downy softness of which told me that she was not born to live in that sorry situation. The serenity of her looks gave me, however, just reason to conclude that she was happy in her lowly state. The children too approached me, and began to play with the plume of my hat.

"My excuses scarcely were attended to, and a bench in the back ground of their poor cottage received us. I forgot Elmira and my journey in the society of my amiable hosts and their little cherubs. Another soup was soon got ready, and the same fire served to warm us and to prepare our repast; some fruits, bread, and honey, compleated our meal, and we were soon engaged in serious conversation. James and his lovely wife displayed a polish which was far superior to their situation; and yet their wants appeared to be so few, their happiness so complete, and their virtue so accomplished, that I was frequently put to the blush when I compared myself with that amiable couple.

"I at length took hold of the hand of my hostess: "Excuse my rudeness, (I began,) dearest madam: why do you live in this hut; why did you leave a situation where you would have been honoured, and a world that would adore you?"

"Adore!" she replied smiling: "I assure you, Sennor, that very adoration has driven me into this forest." "Our history is very long, (James interrupted her,) and, alas! very mournful. This sorry cottage was our last asylum: we have sacrificed a part of our life; however, we have saved the rest for our happiness."

CHAPTER V.

Here I was interrupted in the relation of my adventures in a most singular manner. The fire in the chimney began to die away by degrees, and, at length, was entirely extinguished: we were involved

in a cloud of smoke, and the lights threatened to go out. 'The chimney must be on fire!' the Count exclaimed, frightened. He rang for
the servant to look into the chimney; but no fire, not even a single
spark, was discovered. We spent almost the whole night with fruitless examinations all over the house. The Count was tired, and the
room continued to be filled with smoke, notwithstanding our exertions to purify it. We were obliged to leave it in that unaccountable
state, and went to rest.

We were prevented, as it seemed, designedly, for several subsequent nights, to resume our dear conversations. One time we had
visitors, who pleased to stay a whole week; at other times we were
constantly interrupted by the workmen, whom the Count had sent
for in the middle of winter to make some alteration in the castle; or
we had accounts to settle and to revise; and finally, he was obliged
to go to a neighbouring town, on account of a law suit, and to stay
there a considerable time. When stepping into the carriage, he took
me by the hand, and whispered into my ear; 'Pray, think sometimes
of the chimney?' Being, however, entirely occupied with the management of his economical concerns, I could spare very few hours
at night for writing down my adventures, agreeable to the Count's
desire, (for thus I explained his last words,) and I proceeded but
slowly. He had, indeed, meant something else by them; but returning, after an absence of many weeks, he had met with an opportunity of making several discoveries which were combined with my
history, and determined him to take that heroic resolution which
had so great a share in the surprising turn of our subsequent fate.

I shall, therefore, only renew in these sheets, as far as the impressions which I then received, and at the time naturally were much
stronger, shall enable me, the continuation of my history, which
already at that period bears strong marks of those secret attempts
which were intended to prepare me gradually for a horrid purpose.
When I wrote it down for the Count, I had, indeed, only an obscure
idea of the vile machinations which were directed at me, the mystic
veil in which they were involved being dispelled first at a more distant period: however, I was frequently seized, during that occupation, with secret ominous presensions, which I scarcely could drive
back by the idea that every serious reflection upon them would
only render my steps more uncertain and dangerous.

CHAPTER VI.

"Will you give me leave to communicate a part of our history to this gentleman?" said James to his wife. She assented, by a silent inclination of her head; then amused herself with her children, went frequently out of the cottage, and appeared in general, to take some interest in her husband's tale only in the sequel.

"We are born of noble and well known families," James resumed, "but you must give me leave to conceal our names. My juvenile years passed without any remarkable occurrence. Being the youngest son of my father, my little fortune was chiefly confined to the small legacy of an old female relation, which being spent very fast, my family soon got tired of me, and intended to devote me to a monastical life. This, however, did not agree with my inclinations. Having been used to live in a constant bustle, and to lay much stress on my noble birth, I preferred a military career to all other occupations, as it promised to gratify my propensity to splendor, and to afford me, one time, the best and surest opportunity of reaping some benefit from my exalted parentage. Fortune assisted me sooner than I could have expected. A fermentation in New Spain obliged our monarch to send some troops to America, and a regiment that was garrisoned at Madrid was ordered to embark for that purpose. I obtained a company in that regiment by the recommendation of a near relation, and we proceeded to Cadiz, where we were to go on board of a transport. However, the ships of advice, which were to order the preparations for the arrival of the galleons at Carthagena, had been retarded in the harbour by the rogueries of the victuallers, as well as by contrary winds. We could, of course, not hope to set sail before the end of, at least, two months; and that period became the most remarkable of my whole life.

"The town afforded me neither sufficient amusement nor occupation. It being chiefly inhabited by merchants, and only a few grandees, I was entirely confined to the society of the officers of my regiment; and the military being then held very much in contempt, we had not the least hope of being admitted into a good family. My sole diversion consisted, therefore, in walking; and the harbour was almost the only place which I frequented. Afterwards I discovered a more pleasant walk on the south-east side of the town, in the vicinity of the fort St. Sebastian. There I was used to seat myself opposite to the pharos, looking mournfully at the immense ocean, as the only gulph that separated me from the goal of my fond and sanguine hopes; dreamed of wealth and happiness; and was but seldom disturbed in my reveries by the devout pilgrims who visited the neighbouring chapel of St. Sebastian, and more frequently that of the holy Virgin, which is designed for strangers. Excuse my prolixity, Sennor; the sequel of my narrative will convince you that these insignificant circumstances are intimately connected with consequences of importance.

"It happened soon after, that a ship of St. Malo's attempted to export silver without paying the usual duty, and the custom-house officers thought proper to seize it. Two galleons were ordered to execute this resolution, and began to cannonade the vessel. The captain of the French ship was, however, determined to defend himself, and refused to strike; and it being impossible to clear the harbour, on account of contrary wind, he attacked one of the galleons, with an intention to board it, if possible. He could, indeed, not carry his aim; but having rendered the two galleons entirely unfit for farther use, he set fire to the powder-room, and blew his vessel up.

"About twelve persons were saved, and got on shore upon some empty casks and pieces of timber. However, instead of assisting these unfortunate people, the custom-house officers endeavoured to strip them entirely. Being not far distant from the spot where this inhuman scene was acted, I hastened to give them assistance, and interfered with a number of those robbers, who had seized upon a well-dressed young man. I carried him to an adjacent public house, and recommended him to the care of the hostess, but do not know what became of the rest.

"When I went the next morning to see him, I found he had left the house. Being, however, used to meet with ingratitude among men, I was not astonished at it; paid his bill, which was not very moderate, resumed quietly my former occupations, and continued my morning walks. The number of strangers whom the war, which was then on the eve of breaking out, and the sailing of the galleons, had assembled at Cadiz, peopled the environs round my favourite spot so much, that I could amuse myself for whole days by making my observations on those who passed by. A man, who distinguished himself by his form and elegance from the multitude that passed me every day, soon attracted my particular notice. He was wrapt in a large cloak, which covered the greatest part of his face, walked always very fast, finished his devotions in the same hurry, and then hastened back again. However, he never omitted to steal a few seconds from the time he seemed to have dedicated to that pious occupation, to stop at the door of the chapel, and fix his eyes attentively at an inscription which was engraven on the wall; he then inclined his head musing, wrapped his cloak closer round himself, and went away with accelerated steps. His frequent visits to the chapel, his constant attention to that inscription, and the little notice he took of the thronging crowd, arrested, by degrees, the observation of all those that visited that place of devotion. A numerous multitude crowded, at length, from the town to that spot, to stare and gape at the inscription; and the stranger generally found such a crowd of people at the chapel door, that he scarcely could get thro'. He always was received with such a universal whispering, and the words sorcerer and necromancer resounded so loudly, that I apprehended he would come no more.

"He seemed, however, not to pay the least regard to the general notice which his strange behaviour excited, and whenever he could get near the inscription, he stopt, at least, for a few moments, to peruse it. As often as the humming of the people grew too loud, he opened his cloak a little, and his dark eyes examined the whole assembly with scrutinizing looks. An involuntary awe seemed then to seize every intruding gaper; no one attempted to utter a word, nor to look at him, while he was reviewing thus the curious multitude; and the spectators seemed to recover from their awe only after he was gone some time.

"I generally stood in the midst of the multitude, and for some time had endeavoured in vain to decypher the inscription, its half decayed short-hand characters bidding defiance to my exertions, when the stranger arrested my attention more strongly. His gloomy and awful looks were fixed at me twice while he reviewed the assembly, and always struck me with a kind of chilly stupor, from which I recovered only to wonder at my stupefaction. I never have experienced a similar horrid awe.

"We happened, at length, one evening, to meet quite alone at that spot; and on seeing me standing at the door, against which I was carelessly leaning, he viewed me with astonishment; and I directed my eyes involuntarily at the inscription. Having cast his eyes all around, as if he wanted to convince himself that we could not be overheard, he drew nearer, and accosted me with uncommon politeness.

'Sennor, (said he, in a foreign dialect,) your appearance bespeaks a man of honour and courage; may I rely on your discretion?' 'Undoubtedly, Sennor, you may.' 'Will you not give me a denial (he continued) when I beg you to meet me here to night at twelve o'clock?' 'If you will explain to me——'

'You shall know everything (he interrupted me) you at present wish to be informed of: I only wish to converse with you without being interrupted. The moon is bright, and, Sennor, I am an honest man!'—He then opened his cloak, and his large eyes told me the same. 'You may rely upon me, (I replied;) I shall not fail to meet you: I am a stranger to cowardice; and, in case of an attack, I should not fear you!' He bowed, wrapt himself in his cloak, and left me.

"I was at the spot precisely at twelve o'clock. The night was rather windy, and the moon alternately concealed her orb behind the fleeting clouds, and awfully illuminated the objects around. The storm began to shake the windows of the chapel, the weather-cocks made a dismal noise, and the waves of the sea broke with strange accents against the walls. I walked up and down, well armed, and wrapt in a large cloak. Curiosity was at first my chief sensation; and my imagination formed a number of probabilities to remove the painful incertitude which had tormented me several weeks. But when the stranger kept me waiting longer than I had reason to expect, being not arrived at one o'clock, I began to be apprehensive; every cracking of the half-decayed crosses on the graves frightened me, and every rustling of the leaves lifted my hair up. My patience being, at length, exhausted, I was on the point of going home, when he met me on the steps of the chapel, exclaiming, 'I beg your pardon for having kept you waiting so long.' He then took me by the hand, and led me to the chapel door. 'Our time is short, (he resumed,) and

I have to tell you only a few words. Some years back I happened to get acquainted in Germany with a very singular man, who, however, soon after suddenly disappeared at the inn where we lodged in a most unaccountable manner, and without our being able to divine the motive of his clandestine departure. He had left a letter-case behind him, which was brought me. Amongst a number of letters and annotations, which partly were entirely unintelligible, and partly very unimportant, the mystic sense of which I have, however, lately been so fortunate to unfold, I also found the key to an unknown alphabet, to which the characters of yon inscription belong. It has probably been mistaken for an old epitaph, and for that reason fixed into the wall of this chapel: however, according to the key I possess, it contains the following words:

> "Stranger, and thou who art initiated; the friends
> "Are near. A forest and a cavern in the vicinity of
> "Alcantara. The first day of the month."

"I started up at this passage of James's narrative: but he did not suffer himself to be interrupted, continuing with a smile, which he strove to conceal:

"The stranger, having given me this explanation, measured me with piercing looks. 'What do you think of it, Sennor?' he added. 'I don't know what to say, (I replied;) the inscription appears as obscure to me as if it never had been explained. What can we do?'

"He turned round with kindling anger, exclaiming, 'How! can you ask that question? I have been strangely mistaken in your appearance. I advise you to leave me instantly, if you don't choose to feel the edge of my sword.'

'Upon my honour! (I replied,) I am not afraid of it: but don't put yourself into a passion without reason. It is impossible you could be more desirous than myself to know the secret meaning of that inscription, and that exclamation of mine was merely intended to know your sentiments, but not a sign of cool hesitation.'

"This declaration seemed to have reconciled him. 'Very true! (he now exclaimed groaning,) what can we do? We are now in the middle of the month, and, of course, shall be obliged quietly to await the first day of the next. But do you think you will then be able to accompany me?'

"I replied, that I hoped to get leave of absence, if the galleons should not be ready by that time, as I served in a regiment which was going to embark for Mexico."

'Good God! (he exclaimed,) if I had guessed that circumstance, I would not have mentioned a syllable to you; yet I hope you will not betray the secret if you should be detained. I do, indeed, wish you well, without being able to account for it; and offer you my friendship. Do not refuse it; for it may, one time, be of service to you.' 'I accept your kind offer with gratitude.' 'Don't attempt to get leave of absence; it might excite curiosity. I will depart without you; and I swear you shall know every thing on my return, if you are still here; if not, I shall preserve the secret for you.'

"So saying he embraced me, and descended the steps softly, without giving me time to return an answer. I followed him soon after, having first made an attempt of reading the inscription by the light of the moon.

CHAPTER VII.

"In a few days we received orders to prepare for our departure; the galleons were ready, and we embarked. During our whole tedious passage, I was occupied with drawing results from my experience, which afforded me so much pleasure, that I was sorry when we disembarked on the coast of America. The fermentation was soon quelled; and after we had been a twelvemonth in New Spain, I obtained leave to see my family in Europe. Four days were elapsed after my arrival at Cadiz, and I had not yet quitted my apartment, being too much fatigued from my voyage, when I received the following anonymous note:

"You see I am a man of honour. I have been waiting for your return a whole year, and rejoice that you are arrived at length. I have to unfold strange mysteries to you. I shall be with you at nine o'clock."

Here James was interrupted by his children, who shouted, "Father comes! Father comes!" and could add no more, but, "this is the very man, Don Carlos!" I stared at him with astonishment, and was just going to exclaim, "How! you know me?" when the man whom the children had announced stepped into the cottage. His figure was tall, and displayed, in spite of his advanced age, a most regular shape: a sparkling, majestic eye was, however, the only beauty of his face, which he had been able to save from the deluge of passions. His features bore speaking marks that they had successively been the seat of every passion which, after having been nursed up, seemed to have partaken of the general torpitude of his lineaments, which appeared to have been produced by some horrid incident. The wrecks of former violent passions could still be perceived on his countenance; and as one of them reappeared, all the rest seemed to revive along with it: one recollection of former ideas impelled the other, and all the different propensities of an agitated mind flashed alternately over his face. I had sufficient leisure to make these observations; for, after having darted a scrutinizing look at me, he placed himself opposite me by the fire to warm his hands. Without uttering a word, he directed his melancholy looks by turns at the blazing flame, at the children, who were gamboling by his side, at James, his wife, and at me. He seemed to miss something in the cottage, or to be puzzled by some unusual object, and at length took a seat by my side. "You come from Saragossa?" said he to me; and James affirmed it for me. "The night is very boisterous, (he added.) You have been very fortunate to meet with this asylum. This cottage is the only one in the whole forest; and you would have spent the night very uncomfortably, if you had not found it." "The Spirit of the Wood has made a dreadful noise this night," said the young woman, interrupting him.

"The Spirit of the Wood?" he replied, smiling: "Who knows what you have heard, Almeria?"

"I now could refrain my impatience no longer. Having been perturbed and interested to the highest degree by James's tale, I was extremely vexed at this unseasonable interruption. I therefore drew closer towards him, and taking him by the hand, while he viewed me with looks of astonishment, began: "Sennor, don't be surprised at my familiarity: I know you; James has given me an account of you. Give me leave to crave your friendship."

"You don't know the extent of your request, (he replied.) I also know you, Don Carlos: you are of the house of G******. I have seen you lately, and was highly pleased with you. I will do any thing you may reasonably desire. Tell me, what do you wish?"

"Your friend stopped at his return from America, where you interrupted the train of his narrative. You promised to visit him, in order to acquaint him with a secret concerning that strange inscription."

Here he started up, exclaiming angrily, "What! James has done this?" So saying, he stood for some seconds by the fire, staring at the flame: he then turned around, and pulling a watch out of his pocket, said, "Don Carlos, it is six o'clock; I advise you to go to Elmira. She waits for you at the left side of the little chapel. You may return to this place after six weeks; but take care to come without company." While I was almost petrified with astonishment, and could find no words to express my surprise, he disappeared suddenly. "Good God!" I exclaimed, at length, "how wonderful! Am I awake, or is it a dream?" "Do as he has desired you!" James said, rising from his seat. "One word more." "Not a syllable more, dear Carlos: your horse is ready. Make haste to be gone; but I hope you will return?" "Without fail, James."—I embraced him, and perceived a big tear in his eye. My horse stood at the door, he directed me to the road; and when the sun peeped over the tops of the distant mountains, I was in the open plain. Why did James weep? said I to myself. And the beautiful, dear woman, too, wiped her eyes when the old man came. Was it pity, or recollection? And if it was pity, am I perhaps in dangerous hands? Yet it is impossible; that purity and openness of their souls, that innocent bliss from which they scarcely could disengage themselves to welcome me, that sweet domestic harmony of souls, cannot harbour nor conceal a vice. And why did they not rob me if they be robbers? Shall I return richer than I am now?

"I had been hunting in that wood numberless times without ever seeing the cottage, or meeting with any thing suspicious. Strange traditions were, indeed, rumoured about a ruinous castle in the centre of the forest, whither my way never had led me as yet; but I could not learn that ever a particular event had happened in that direction, which could have attracted the notice of the neighborhood to that spot. "But if it be no band of robbers, (I reasoned again,) as all circumstances forbid me to think, what else could be the purpose of that association?" My imagination ranged restless through the whole empire of possibilities; but my reason did not attempt to declare decidedly for one of them.

"While I was thus giving audience to the wild fancies of my heated imagination, my horse started suddenly, and I beheld a person stretched out on the ground close by me. "Don't hurt me, dear spirit!" he exclaimed in a rueful accent. It was Alfonso, who lay prostrated on his face, almost motionless with cold and fear. He trembled violently; and, on my approach, endeavoured to conceal himself behind a bush, contorting his feet anxiously, lest they should betray his asylum.

"For Heaven's sake, Alfonso, what is the matter with you, and where have you left your horse?" I exclaimed, laughing. "Jesus! Maria! is it you, my Lord! Heaven be praised a thousand times, that you are alive. A curse on that forest! How did you get out of that infernal abode of Spirits?" So saying, he crept out of the bush. "But where is your horse?" "Indeed, I do not know, my Lord. Not long after you left me, my poor fellow, in the lurch, it took fright at a Will-o'-the-wisp, threw me down, and ran away. I have been wandering to and fro in the forest all the night long, without being able to find a path. Have the kindness to help me up; for I have sprained my ancle." I assisted the poor fellow to get upon his legs, one of which really appeared to have been hurt, for he could not stand upon it. I made him get upon my horse, and walked by his side. Soon after this incident we perceived an unknown hamlet. We quickened our paces, and it was broad day when we came up with it. We were about four leagues distant from St. Jago. I sent for a surgeon, recommending Alfonso to his care, and arrived at ten o'clock at the cloister.

"I went mechanically to the chapel. Mass was just finished when I approached the door: a numerous multitude streamed out of it; but the crowd soon dispersed: and when I entered the chapel, all around me was deserted and silent. My steps resounded through the vaulted edifice, and a chilling stream of air struck against me within the expanded walls. I perceived a little chapel at my right hand, and a female kneeling before an image of the holy virgin. It was Elmira.

"She prayed audibly, but paused every now and then. Her low sobs told me that she was weeping; her face was covered with a veil, which she frequently removed to dry her tears. Heavens! what a change did I behold on her face whenever she unveiled it for a while! all those enchanting features, which used to be animated with a smiling spirit of cheerfulness, and so easily conquered every heart, appeared to be numbed by a conflict with a tender female anxiety, which seemed to be in expectation of something. Her eyes had quitted the image of the holy virgin, which was standing before her, and wandered with inquietude around the altar, where some more persons prayed, or walked about. I prostrated myself on my knees at the door of the chapel; for I would not have disturbed her on any account. Every moment of which I should have deprived her, would have appeared to me a sacrilege committed against the altar on which my idol stood. Her soul beheld me, at that moment, in a glory before her; and her devotion was raised by the jealousy with which she watched the looks of her guardian-angel. Even at her feet, or regenerated in her arms to a god, I should have missed that part of a bliss which entranced me with unspeakable feelings. Alas! I did then not yet love her with that fervour which willingly sacrifices its own interest to the happiness of its object!

"She began, at length, to stir, and rose up, directing her steps towards the door. I got behind it; and when she was going to step over the threshold, she recollected to have forgot something, and went back to fetch her prayer-book from her seat. Her opening, and looking with visible anxiety in it, prevented her from taking notice of me. A note dropped, at length, out of the book, upon the floor, without her perceiving it. I followed her softly, and having picked it up, exclaimed, Elmira, you have dropt a paper!"

"She turned round, and her knees began to shake: but when I ran to support her, she recovered suddenly from her terror and astonishment, tearing the paper out of my hand, and concealing it in her bosom. She took no notice of my surprise, but viewed me with staring looks, and asked, "Don Carlos! have you read that note?" "No, Elmira!" "I should not have wished you had. It was a letter from my aunt." She added, with more composure, "You are well, I hope, Don Carlos: the weather was dreadful to night; you look a little paler than usual; you have had no accident?"

"(I examined her looks, to learn whether she knew any thing of my nocturnal adventure. Her anxiety to evade my inquiries made me suspect the note. You will see by the sequel, dear Count, how singular the fate of that paper was, and that it unfolded to me, though at a later period, the whole connection of all my adventures. However, Elmira's tranquillity convinced me that nothing but tenderness and anxiety for my peace had prompted her to ask that question.)

"Trifles! dear Countess!" I replied. "Trifles? your looks, and trembling accent, tell me the contrary. But leave me now, Don Carlos, lest we should be observed. Go behind the garden of the cloister: my woman shall meet you in a quarter of an hour, to conduct you to my apartment."

"So saying, she disappeared in the aisles of the chapel. I went out of the back-door, and directed my steps to the garden. Ere long, Elmira's woman joined me, to conduct me to her apartment. I followed her with a beating heart, and in a few moments knelt at Elmira's feet.

"Charming!" she exclaimed: "you are in a great hurry, Don Carlos." Her woman left us, and she resumed, "How imprudent! Will you never act with more circumspection? Rise; I cannot bear to see a man kneeling before me in a cloister."

"But why will you not suffer it? why not allow your confessor to receive the confession of your sins on his knees?"

"You dream, Don Carlos," she replied smiling: "how can you talk of confessors and sins? You don't suppose that I have any thing to confess to *you?*"

"What a misunderstanding, Elmira! yes, I confess that I imagined it. Then you wanted to sport with me! Why did you give me that invitation; and what else can this mysterious visit mean?"

"My good Marquis, don't be so warm. Can you not have a little patience? It is your duty to protect afflicted damsels; and can you not guess what I am going to desire of you?"

"So? Will you be so kind as to tell me how I can be serviceable to you?" With these words I rose coolly, and seated myself carelessly upon the sofa.

"Good Heaven!" she resumed, "what would I give if I could tame this headstrong man! yet I fear I never shall succeed. Well then, Don Carlos, listen to my secret; but first tell me whether your heart is still free?"

"Whether my heart is free?" I repeated, with great emotion: "can Elmira ask that question? Have you never read in my looks that I am entirely devoted to you? Don't be cruel to me. Return me another treasure for that which I have lost."

"No! no! you misconceive me again. I do not desire you to love me; I only wish you would sympathize with me, and pity me a little. I should be so happy if I could interest you for me; for you are an open, noble young man; a man who is too much my friend to refuse me his assistance."

"You may rely upon me. But you speak in riddles; be more explicit, dear Countess, more explicit!"

"Well! let me then tell you the great secret: I am in love, Don Carlos." So saying, she cast down her eyes with a comical modesty, and hid her face in her handkerchief, as if she could not help blushing. "And who is the happy object of your affections?" "A young man." "I do not doubt it, Elmira," I said, with an involuntary laugh: "you are indeed very unfortunate." "He is handsome." "That is still more unfortunate." "Don't rally me, Marquis, for he does not return my love." "This is the worst of all: but do not despair, Elmira; I shall use all my influence on him in your behalf. But you have not yet told me his name. Who is he?" I took hold of her hand, and imprinted a burning kiss upon it. I expected joyfully to hear my own name, and was already prepared to kiss the sweet reluctant confession of her love from her lips; but how was I struck with astonishment when she moved closer towards me, whispering, with an anxious seriousness, "It is Don Antonio, your friend. Oh! Carlos, if you have any power over him, plead in my behalf; but spare my honor."

"I now felt emotions in my breast which were entirely novel to me, and was overpowered by feelings which I never had experienced before. I felt as if I were suddenly roused from a dream, and, on awaking, did behold myself enthralled in irresistible hands. I loved Elmira before she communicated that unexpected secret to me, but my love was only a tranquil tenderness, which, in a constant struggle with caprice and pertinacy, was nourished only by vanity. Thus I had been in love with all women. They always had met me half way, and my heart had found too little resistance, as ever to have required all its feelings for giving vent to its passion. I now did meet not only with a stronger and more resolute resistance, but also an indifference, and a contempt of my address, which I never had experienced before. My heart, which always had been half shut against all tender feelings, and never inflamed with a burning desire by unsought conquest, was unequal to that contempt, and violently agitated by the apprehension of being obliged to give up an expected and anticipated victory.

"I dropt down upon my knees, overcome by the violence of my feelings, and exclaimed, agitated with an unknown pain, "By Heaven, Elmira, this is too much!"

"Having viewed me for some moments with scrutinizing looks, she resumed, "Dear Marquis, stand my friend: I esteem and promise you to have as much affection for you as my situation will allow. What more can you expect?"

"Death! Elmira; have compassion with me: I cannot live and see you in the arms of another person." Here my feelings overpowered me, and I reclined my head senseless on her lap.

"Compose yourself, dear Carlos: you have a noble heart. Should friendship be of less value to you than love? I promise to be your faithfullest, your inseparable friend. I shall not conceal one sentiment of my heart from you; we will teach the world how disinterestedly and strongly two congenial hearts can be united."

"No, I scorn your offer: I despise you: I don't want the miserable refuse which another person will let me have out of pity." Here I rose. "One word more, Elmira: was the note which you dropt to day from Antonio?"

"No, Carlos; I swear it was not. But be a man. Is a present, which I offer voluntarily, of less value to you than an involuntary affection? I feel myself irresistibly *impelled* to love Antonio; and to you I am allied by those soft bonds which owe their existence to the most tender regard. Come, Don Carlos, and be my friend."

"Yes, my doom is fix'd. A life which is bereft of every ray of hope is worse than death. Farewell, and live happy. I am not generous enough to persuade another person to accept a heart, the possession of which promised me an eternity of bliss. Farewell, Elmira!" I kissed her hand, without being able to look at her. Her heart palpitated audibly; her hand trembled violently; I laid it softly on her lap, and went to the door.

"How much have I mistaken you, Don Carlos! Yet, if you are determined to leave me, stay only a few moments longer." I turned round. "Kneel down, Don Carlos!" I lay prostrated at her feet; she

encircled my neck with her hand, and inclined her crimsoning
face to me. Her eyes floated in a liquid fire. "One word more, Don
Carlos! Forgive me! Antonio is no other person but *yourself*." My
senses fled on wings of rapture; I felt nothing but a beating bosom
convulsively prest against my heart; two burning lips in close
contact with mine, and my cheeks were inundated with tears of
unspeakable bliss.

CHAPTER VIII.

"When I recovered from that trance of happiness which the confession of Elmira had thrown me into, I found her large blue eyes
were lovingly rivetted to me; and I fancied to be transported to an
unknown world. "How delightfully do you, sweet enchantress!
atone for the agonizing torments you have inflicted!" I exclaimed.
"Let us be quit, Don Carlos: I have to forgive you as much as you
have to forgive me."

"I have nothing to forgive. Elmira could, perhaps, have offended
me in a former period, but she cannot offend me now. Don't view
me with those looks of jealousy. Do I not now first begin to live? All
is changed; my whole nature is transformed."

"May you never forget, Don Carlos, what you have said in this
happy moment. I have purchased the possession of your heart with
pungent sorrows, but, I hope, not at too great a price."

"Oh! Elmira, my whole existence depends on you. Every sentiment of mine is stamped with your image: you may, therefore,
boldly claim all the feelings of my heart as your property. But
excuse my apprehension! Are you not at liberty to inform me of
the contents of that note, which you so anxiously have concealed
from me?"

"I am; but it would only alarm you, without affording you the
least benefit. Don't urge me any farther." "Your wishes are laws to
me; yet I cannot but confess, I should like to see it." "Just as you
please, Don Carlos; but don't be alarmed: I put more confidence
in my own experience, and in your words, than in that miserable
paper."

"She then gave me the note, which was written with red ink, or with blood, and contained the following words: "Countess Elmira is cautioned against the young Marquis Carlos of G******, for he intends to impose on her." It was signed with three crosses.

"Where have you found that paper?" I exclaimed, frightened. "In my prayer-book." "Do you know the hand writing?" "No; but I can guess who has written the note. Let me intrust you with a secret, Don Carlos. Unknown hands, that direct all affairs, have for some time been dispersed all over Spain. No person knows who they are. They force their way through bolted doors, and to the most retired apartments. You have, probably, heard of the history of Count O****** who carried off a girl against the will of her parents and of those unknown confederates. They were found dead in their bed on the morning after their marriage. Don Pedro D****** quarrelled with his father, and disappeared, after he had murdered his parent by their command. They write only with blood, and sign their letters with three crosses."

"This account struck me with an astonishment which surprised Elmira. "Why are you thus astonished at this intelligence, Don Carlos?" "Tell me first, Elmira, how you have obtained that knowledge." "I have myself experienced their influence, but I dare not mention the particulars; yet you may rely on the truth of what I have told you." [I shall acquaint the reader, in the sequel, with that history which I learnt by accident. It is shocking.]

"I now acquainted her with the adventure I had encountered the preceding night, when it was her turn to be seized with anxious astonishment. "How!" she exclaimed, at length, "Should both incidents be connected with each other? Nothing is more probable. They intended to part us, but did not foresee that our meeting would end in such a manner. They have counted more on my fear than on my love. Give me your hand, Carlos! We will never part: death itself shall not separate us!—Do you hear?"

"Oh! Elmira, never has a vow been offered with more sincerity. Here is my hand. We will live and die together." She embraced me with an enthusiastic, frantic fervour. We were transported beyond ourselves, and I could have sworn, in that solemn moment, to kill her, if she had desired it.

"I will propose something to you, Don Carlos," she now resumed, in a lower accent: "Let us unite these hands for ever. I am provided with a great many valuable jewels, and ready to follow you whithersoever you choose. I shall deem no country too far, no cottage too small. These soft hands shall use themselves to the hardest labour. I shall have no other wish, but to make you happy; no other care, but to clothe you, and to sweeten your life. What do you say to it, dear Carlos?"

"I pressed the heavenly girl convulsively to my bosom. Her looks attested the declaration of her lips. "Alas! I do not deserve you, Elmira," I stammered at length.

"Why should you not deserve me? Love for love. Follow me. I have presaged every thing, and taken proper measures. A priest is waiting for us, and in half an hour we shall be united for ever. Or do you hesitate?" "Elmira!" "Well, then follow me!" So saying, she led me down a secret flight of steps. We went through a long passage; and, at the last, stopt at a door, against which she knocked, exclaiming, "Reverend Father, I am ready for you." The door opened; a priest joined us, and walked silently by our side. We were soon kneeling at the altar; the priest united our hands, and gave us his benediction.

"I cannot omit remarking a circumstance which, during the marriage ceremony, threw me into the greatest consternation. A shrill noise, like the whizzing of a large bat, resounded twice through the church. Elmira grew every time deadly pale; and when it re-echoed a third time, much louder and more piercing than before, she fainted away. Yet she recovered soon, encircling my neck, and said, "Leave me now, Don Carlos. Against evening I expect to see you in my apartment."

"It was already past one o'clock; the sun shone very hot, and I went into the garden. The refreshing coolness of a shadowy walk, and some fruits, which invited my appetite, re-animated me with new life and vigour. The leafy dusk restored me to myself; and the anxiety which had straitened my breast, was dispelled by the expanded prospect before me. The crystal rivulet appeared to me an image of futurity; I only saw the roses which its flowery banks were embroidered with, but did not observe the rugged stones through which it wound itself with difficulty.

"Evening stole, at length, upon me, and I found Elmira on her sofa. Her anxiety had left her, and her cheeks beamed with the fresh enamel of health and young desires. She encircled me with her bridal arms, and drew me down upon the sofa. The hours fled rapidly on pinions of inebriating bliss. We counted every minute, lest it should pass too fleetly, and yet the minutes and hours succeeded each other with unspeakable swiftness. Night surprized us unawares; and when the candles were lighted, we began to think more seriously of our speedy departure. Elmira formed numberless schemes: one urged the other; but not one of them met with our mutual approbation. I sat opposite to her, absorpt in meditating on my happiness, and enraptured with her charms, with the suavity of her youth, with her liveliness, and the fresh roses of her health. She appeared to be more blooming than ever. Her eyes beamed with a heavenly fire, and her mouth opened like a budding, luxuriant rose.

"While I was thus entranced by the contemplation of her charms, I observed that she grew paler, her eyes appeared to be more languid; her mouth less blooming. I stared with astonishment at her; yet ascribed it to the faint light of the candles. However, I saw her soon grow visibly paler; her eyes began to dim, and her upper lip was contorted by a convulsive motion; her whole face grew longer and smaller, and she began to stammer. "For God's sake! Elmira, what is the matter with you?" "Nothing; nothing at all, dear Carlos," she replied with difficulty. But in that very moment her eyes broke, she gnashed her teeth, and inclined herself, with a contorted mouth and staring looks, towards me: the icy face of a corpse touched my lips: her hands violently grasped my arms. I started up, seized with horror, and scarcely could disengage myself from her long fingers. I placed her lengthways on the sofa, and she died under my hands, grinding her teeth. I had not the power to call for assistance, and should have dropt senseless at her feet, if her woman had not come into the room by accident.

"She no sooner saw me lying in despair, and half fainting, by the side of her mistress, and the latter stretched out stiff and lifeless, when she rushed to the place of woe where we lay extended. What a new scene of horror! In such a moment, all distinction of rank and birth ceases. She appeared to have lost a mother, and to have been bereft of her only remaining parent. She threw herself upon the corpse, kissed the livid mouth, and rested her face upon the clay-cold countenance of her mistress. She then pressed the icy hand of the deceased to her lips, and, without uttering a word or a question, her soul seemed to sink under the certainty of Elmira's death; inarticulate sounds only forced themselves through her convulsed lips.

"She recovered the use of her senses at length, and went to fetch assistance. A surgeon came to assist her in her tender endeavours to re-animate the lifeless body of Elmira; but all the application of medical skill served only, as it were, to make it riper for the grave. The air was soon infected with a smell of putrefaction. We were obliged to perform her obsequies the subsequent day.

"Who can form an idea of, and who has experienced, *my* situation? Being hurled down from the summit of the greatest bliss into the most abject state of misery, which bordered on annihilation, it was a happiness for me to have lost the use of my senses so far, that I could not distinguish the sensation of a dream from the heavy pressure of indubitable truth. I stood entirely isolated on one point of the universe; nothing was left near me, nothing that could have reminded me even of the horrors of the time past. The fever of my soul seemed, however, constantly to shake even that sole point; and I was agonized by the apprehensions of an approaching annihilation, without being capable of estimating the value of my existence.

"Alfonso was at that period my greatest benefactor. My danger accelerated his recovery. He never lost sight of me. His warm and truly tender attachment to me, sharpened all his senses to anticipate my wants, and raised the faculties of his soul high enough above the fetters of his prejudices and his rank to gratify them with delicacy. His tender care for me was a continual conflict between the most fervent zeal of being useful to me and the effects of his education, and the latter blinded the former but very rarely; nay, his kindness for me frequently gained additional strength, by his exertions to break the chains of his prejudices.

"The first thing he did for me, was to remove me from all objects which could have reminded me of my loss on the return of my recollection. Submitting patiently to any thing, without being sensible of what he was doing, I was conducted by him to a neighbouring seat of my father's. He informed my parent of my misfortune; and

my whole family came to comfort and to divert me. One amusement succeeded the other; all my favourite occupations were
opposed to the torpor of my soul; and the ladies of my acquaintance forgot their reserve, to convince me, by sweet blandishments,
that I had not lost every thing. Grief was by degrees expelled by
the beautiful retinue of the graces; my senses opened themselves
again, with additional warmth, to long neglected charms; and I
began to miss Elmira less, because I accustomed myself to find her
every where. Uninterrupted amusements diverted one thought
after the other from that object: the images that sported before my
fancy assumed a gayer attire, and their gloom brightened up more
and more every day.

"In order to complete my recovery, I was periodically left alone.
My imagination, which had been occupied by society, suffered, in
those solitary hours, the arguments of cool reason to speak; and I
did, indeed, feel my loss; but soon began to think how I could repair
it.

"Thus the fine season passed; and my disposition was so much
altered at the conclusion of it, that I scarcely knew myself again.
The sweet happy gaiety which formerly had possessed my soul
was vanished; and the seriousness which now occupied my whole
mind scarcely had left the recollection of it. The objects around me
appeared in a more decent attire; the improvement of my understanding began to employ me more than ever; and I owe the greater
accomplishment of my mind entirely to the subsequent period of
my life.

"Yet all these changes of my disposition could not make me
forget the adventure in the forest. I was grown more circumspect,
and even more timid. Not having one friend to whom I could have
unbosomed myself, I wandered from one conclusion to the other,
and nevertheless advanced not a step farther. Don Antonio, the
friend of my juvenile years, had, indeed, sufficient tenderness for
me, but too much levity. I wanted a more experienced and prudent
guide. This want was soon gratified by accident. A young nobleman
of the upper part of Spain, Pedro G******, purchased a seat in my
neighbourhood. Misfortune had visited him earlier than myself,
though still in the prime of his life. He had, according to report,
killed, in the heat of passion, an adored wife and her seducer, whom

he had surprized in the act of adultery; and now suffered for this heedless action in retirement and a cloistered solitude.

"The gardens of his estate bordered close to mine. Both of us being fond of walking, prompted by the situation of our mind, which wanted amusement, I soon had an opportunity of seeing him frequently at a little distance. He was constantly occupied with improving his new residence; and the spirit of building and gardening appeared to have made him frequently forget his misery.

"His form was one of the most interesting I ever beheld. I never have seen so much goodness residing in such a melancholy eye; never such a tranquillity at the miseries of life, blended by such recent impressions of over-powering sorrows. Grief had purified his feelings in a superior degree; and the emanation of his goodness flowed most heavenly and unalloyed upon every thing around him. The whole vicinity soon spoke loudly of his generosity and humanity; and I could not help being involuntarily interested to the highest degree in all his occupations.

"A small rivulet separated our gardens. My side was closely overgrown with shrubberies; and I had ordered a bower to be constructed in a secret corner, where I frequently seated myself on the mossy bench with a book, observing, with sweet tranquillity, the bustle that animated all nature around me, and indulging the variegated reveries of my imagination, while my eyes pursued the fleeting waves of the tinkling rivulet. From that spot I could observe all his occupations through the apertures of the adjacent shrubbery. I soon perceived that he had a sort of tomb erected in the vicinity of the rivulet, where he spent the greatest part of the day as soon as it was finished. He was for hours fixed motionless to his seat, gazing at the urn which was placed at the top of the tomb. He then lifted his eyes up to heaven, raised, as it were, beyond the limits of mortality, as if in search of some object, and declining his looks again to the monument as soon as he seemed to have found it. I watched every motion of his; and the interest I took in them soon became my sole occupation during the day.

"One time he came nearer to the spot where I sat, and started at the sight of me, but saluted me friendly. Sufferers know each other at first sight. Our intercourse was, however, not carried any farther on that day: he disappeared in the shrubbery; but a few days after he stopt long enough to give me an opportunity of addressing him.

"I have so frequently the pleasure, Sennor, (said I,) of seeing you, that I cannot resist the desire of getting more intimately acquainted with you." He bowed politely, and smiled. "You meet me half way, Don Carlos, (he replied;) yet that kindness of yours would not have been required, if I were not so well informed of your history, which made me apprehend that I only should add to the weight of your sufferings by the pressure of my own." "Let us wave that subject for the present, (said I:) futurity and friendship will serve to assuage our mutual sorrows. Let us expect every comfort from these friendly solaces." "I know and esteem you, Don Carlos, (said he.) If *that* will satisfy you, your friendship will indeed make me infinitely happy." With these words he went to a shallow spot of the rivulet, and joined me.

"We continued this intercourse every day. He was extremely civil, but conceived only with difficulty some attachment to me. Our intercourse was gradually prolonged only with regard to time, but decreased in point of enjoyment; yet we became at length inseparable. He was rather weak and irritable, which was very salutary to my pertinacy. The ideas of one served to obliterate those of the other; and friendship began to console me for the disappointment of love.

"Not a single complaint had, as yet, escaped our lips; and we carefully avoided, at the commencement of our intimacy, every thing that could have re-produced the gloomy images of former days. By degrees we began to converse of individual indifferent incidents of our life, and touched only reluctantly upon the more serious and painful part of it.

"One fine morning, when an easy night had expanded our hearts for the influx of pleasure, and lessened the weight of time past, he began to speak of the incidents of his former life as of a dream. He touched only lightly upon the most important of them, mentioning merely as much as was necessary to preserve the connection. His history was affecting, but not extraordinary. He had been married to Donna Francisca L******, who, in the bustle of the great world, became unfaithful to him, and eloped with her seducer. No one could tell what was become of her: the report of her having been killed by her injured Lord was, therefore, erroneous. He still adored her; and would have forgiven her all injuries, if she had returned repenting to his arms.

"I then gave him a faithful account of all the particulars of my history, which struck him with astonishment and pity.

"What is your opinion in point of that mystery?" he asked, at length. "None, but what I have already told you. All that I have been able to conclude from Elmira's information, and from the incidents of my life, prompts me to believe that a great association is dispersed all over Spain, and watches the actions of every individual." "Have you never been able to guess the purport of that secret confederation?" "Never, Sennor!"

"Please only to recollect all the incidents at the cottage: did not one action of its inhabitants betray a vestige of interest? Did you discover no affectation in their miens? Was the unconcern which you mentioned not foreign to the connection of the whole?" "No, certainly not! I surprized them: the woman appeared to have not the least apprehension; and such a tenderness as James and his wife displayed cannot be artificial. The children, too, took a share in it, which they seemed to have been long accustomed to.

"And did the woman really weep, when you left them?" "So it appeared to me: but I am certain that James's countenance changed when I went. It was too visible." "I cannot comprehend it. Yet it appears to me that they have been tools of the old man, under whose command they certainly are. They have probably, at first, been insnared in the same manner in which they intended to allure you."

"But what reasons can you assign for the patience with which they submit to the yoke which is imposed upon them, according to your ideas? What can they fear to lose in that state of extreme poverty and abject slavery, if they flee from their tyrants? Both of them are certainly not born for their melancholy situation; and their resignation and tranquillity is a most palpable proof of their voluntary submission to it."

"This does not at all confound me; but only serves to make me more curious to know the mysteries of the cavern. If both are initiated, and if their happiness flows from that source, what an inestimable treasure for the whole life would it afford, if one could obtain only a few drops of it!"

"I do not think that such an unconfined activity, which remains unalloyed amid all the changes of life, can be derived from principles."

"Principles are not always the only means of rendering man capable to face every storm of life with tranquillity. The consciousness of being united to a society who are allied by the strongest ties, who never suffer a member of their body to sink under the weight of misery, is certainly a great alleviation in every suffering. The more numerous the ports are where we can take shelter in the storms of life, the less are we affected by the dangers and difficulties of our voyage. Every loss points out a new compensation, and every sinister accident is attended with a competent assistance."

"This is very true, Sennor."

"This association, of which we can conceive only an obscure idea, has, besides, another estimable prerogative. Other alliances, whatever view they may have, preclude always from the enjoyment of domestic happiness, if their aim be only in the least important: the ties which unite the father with a faithful wife, and with his whole family, must be dissolved, in order to qualify him for the intimate union which has a more extended purpose in view. The means of gratifying ambition, and of executing lofty plans, can only be met with beyond the depressing limits of a domesticated life; and one conceives a strong and sufficient attachment to the aim only beyond those confines."

"Very true."

"But how different is the nature of that confederation! All appearances point at a deep-layed, powerful, and extensive plan of those men. James, who certainly has a great share in all the views and proceedings of the society, is, notwithstanding this, not in the least alienated from his domestic situation, his wife and his children. He even is no stranger to hospitality, and to the softer sentiments of fellow-feeling."

"But have you forgot, Sennor, the horrid scenes of which Elmira has informed me?"

"We must not judge precipitately of that matter, my friend. We ought to make some allowance as to the extent of their views, and to put a great deal to the account of report, which, if prejudiced, always favours one party, let it take whatever course it may. And,

besides, Don Carlos, you will consider that we are never more apt
to be unjust, than we are too short-sighted to discover the views of
such a society. Who can expect to be capable of unfolding them at
first sight? Let us suppose that they are great and noble, that they
aim at the improvement of all mankind; what is then the life of an
individual, if compared to *that* view? When two men have taken
refuge on one board, which can carry only a single person with
safety on the billowing ocean, either is to be excused if he struggles
to get rid of his rival."

"But, dear Pedro, do you not think it too presumptuous and
unsafe to decide arbitrarily on such an occasion? Who warrants me
that even my best plans, which I either must abandon or prosecute
at the expence of the life of one of my fellow-creatures, are worth
that sacrifice? Who, finally, can be answerable for their success? and
is it not madness to sacrifice an hundred existences to one dream?

"Providence is not so axious as you are. Every thing in nature
presses and urges the other; and a new life originates from every
death. Being entirely taken up by the great plan of promoting the
greater perfection of man, it does not care for the changes which
take place in the creation. Providence knows how to direct every
thing to one great end, and unfolds the last dying point of life for
new plans and designs."

"Very true, Sennor. I should entirely coincide with your opinion,
if we could direct the course of our actions and their final issue with
the same wisdom."

"Shall we never make an attempt, because we do not always succeed? Shall we waste our faculties in a dream of humanity, lest we
should rouse the objects around us from a similar dream? Who
can prove that the *enjoyment* of the moment also is the *purpose* of
the *existence* of that moment? If a whole eternity of times forms a
life beyond the limits of mortality, and if the last point of that life
implies the highest and most perfect enjoyment, if no other end
of our suffering can be found than our gradual qualification for
that supreme bliss; are we then not fools, if we confine ourselves
merely to corporeal wants, and thus place that point longer out of
our reach?"

"I do not entirely comprehend you; but be so good to go on."

"Let us now suppose, that a whole numerous society of men,

who would keep firm to that idea, were to unite, and to prosecute it indefatigably, assisted by a long-tried superiority over the rest of the people; let us farther suppose, that that society should watch the secret process of nature, trace the means Providence employs to educate the human race, and pursue the discoveries which their united exertions should store up; let us finally suppose, that these men should faithfully act as vicegerents of Providence, and strive not to improve, but to accelerate, the actions of the Supreme Ruler of the world; would these men wander from their great mark on account of the lesser troubles of this life?"

"I must confess, this point of view—"

"Is very different from what you have had? However, another point of view is not less obvious. Every life has its natural burden: is it, therefore, not a real blessing for mortals, if they can lay all the weight of future days on the beginning of their career, in order to exempt thereby the evening of their journey from the pressure of sorrow? We have long forgot the tempest of the night, and morn, and the heat of the noontide hours, when the setting sun hales us with a pure and serene light, and finds us in the enjoyment of rest and happiness. The terrors of dangers past, serve then to enhance the value of the blessings we enjoy after a long laborious strife; every object around us wears a gayer attire, and our heart is expanded with raptures which we should be utter strangers to, if former struggles had not purified and exalted our senses."

"I am charmed with that enchanting dream."

"Don't call it a dream, Don Carlos. I reason from *experience*. You do not know that society who have offered to receive you into their hallowed circle. Think of James and his happiness."

"Here we dropped the subject, and our conversation turned on different matters. However, they did not interest me; the ideas which had been imparted to me being sufficient to ingross the reflection of years. I tormented myself to unfold and to arrange them that day; but could not dispel the obscurity in which they were concealed. No other expedient was left me, but to take a firm resolution of prosecuting the vestiges which I already had discovered.

"On meeting with my neighbour the subsequent day, he resumed the thread of his conversation. "Don Carlos, (he said,) should we not make an attempt to ascertain the probabilities we have started yesterday?" This was guessing at the most ardent wish of my heart. I consented cheerfully, and we were just thinking of the proper means, when our consultations were suddenly interrupted by a new incident.

CHAPTER IX.

My friend Pedro had invited me one night to sup with him. He was a little indisposed; and, to avoid the chilling night air, we had retired to a pleasure-house, where we enjoyed the charms of a beautiful night, and the aromatic exhalation of the young orange trees. After supper I began to read to him. He relished the author so much, and I was so pleased at it, that all other ideas and objects lost their influence upon us for some time. He was seated with his back towards the door, his right-hand rested on my shoulder, and his melancholy countenance reclined on my cheek. The book which I was reading had ingrossed my attention to such a degree, that I could not turn my eye from it. A piercing scream suddenly vibrated in my ear. I started up, seized with terror; and Pedro dropped fainting from his chair. I had scarcely time to take hold of and to support him, when I beheld a pale, emaciated face reclining on his hand. It was Francisca. After she had knelt a considerable time, and Pedro, at length, opened his eyes, she rose, and kissed his pallid lips. "Collect yourself, my dear husband, (she exclaimed, with a convulsive firmness;) collect yourself, to grant your forgiveness to a wife who comes to bid you an eternal adieu."

"He had not yet recovered the power of utterance, but stretched out his hand towards her.

"No, my dearest husband, (she resumed, after having kissed his hand,) I thank you. I will not deceive you a second time. A repenting, tormented wife, who escaped her seducer in the very moment which was to ruin her for ever, conjures you to give her your benediction." So saying, she prostrated herself again at his feet.

"No, Francisca, (he replied,) I receive the repenting wife, who returns to me with tender affection, to my bosom. I have forgiven every, every thing, a long time since; and it is certainly my dear Francisca's wish that I should forget it too."

"You are mistaken, Pedro, if you think me capable of abusing your goodness. No, take your heart back again." "Why should I do it, dear Francisca?" "You never can love a criminal; nor shall I ever be capable of making you happy again. No, Pedro, I will not cheat you of every future felicity. Give me your benediction, my dear, injured husband."

"My poor friend was almost distracted. This afflicting coolness of his wife, and these heart-cutting words, pronounced in the easy tone of conversation, excited in his heart a conflict between his tenderness and pride, which I apprehended would prove fatal to his exhausted nature. I thought it my duty to interfere.

"You see, Madonna, (said I,) to what a dreadful state your husband is reduced. If you are come to kill him by your cruelties, your business will soon be done. But, you will give me leave to take care of a life which I have learnt to esteem." I then was going to take her by the hand, and to lead her out of the apartment, but she had grasped his knees so fast that I found it impossible to raise her up.

"Don't let me depart, dear Pedro, without your forgiveness!" she exclaimed. "This man is going to tear me from you. Give me your benediction, and I will part willingly with you."

"The dreadful words, "Give me your blessing, Pedro!" still vibrate in my ears. She rather ejaculated than uttered them with a trembling voice: it was the last dying accent of a person who implores heaven to grant her a gracious reception. Despair had lifted up her hair, which partly covered her face, and partly flowed down her neck, in a frightful disorder. A frigidity, such as I never beheld on a marble statue, kept all her features in infrangible fetters; an unconcern of mien, such as death scarcely can impart, horribly contradicted her words; and she viewed the weeping eyes of her husband with a dreadful indifference. My poor friend sat trembling on his chair, bereft of courage and of every strength; directed his uncertain and inquisitive looks at me, and then at his wife, who kept him fixed to his seat with her hands.

"Will you not give me your benediction, not forgive me, dearest husband?" she resumed. "O! grant me, at least, one prayer."

"I cannot give you my benediction," (he replied trembling:) "to a criminal only, whom one receives, and repudiates again, one gives a benediction as a curse. Come into these loving arms, my dear, my ever adored wife. I was, perhaps, the primary cause of your errors; let me atone for it on your bosom."

"No, Pedro! will you let me suffer the torments of hell in your arms? No, my husband is not so cruel."

"I will not only appease your agony; I will change your despair into love. Do not commit a greater crime in order to retrieve a lesser one. I was unhappy, but never have abandoned all hopes of ceasing one time to be so: will you deprive me also of this consolation; will you rob me of every thing?"

"Be easy, Don Pedro; I must deprive you of it, in order to prepare a peaceful futurity for you. The bosom of your wife has no comfort, no joy to give you. How could uninterrupted eternal torments render you happy? If you should compassionate me, I should rage against your happiness, and reward the raptures of your love with the agony of despair. No! no! give me your benediction, Don Pedro; or, at least, grant me one prayer?"

"And what is it you desire, dear Francisca?"

"She rose, and went out of the door. My astonishment and expectation were raised to such a degree, that I scarcely could make use of the short interval to speak a few words of comfort to my disconsolate friend. She returned, after a few minutes, with a little boy in her arms, who reclined tenderly against her bosom, caressing her with amiable sweetness. He seemed to be two or three years old. Her looks rested painfully on him, and her eyes told me that she was revolving a great design.

"Come, Pedro," she said, kneeling down, "You shall see your father. Look, there he is. Go, and kiss his hand."

"Is this my papa?" the child lisped. "Why does he not speak to me?"

"What does this mean, Francisca?" said my friend, interrupting the child.

"Give me leave to say only a few words more, my husband; then I will go, and bless you." Her bosom worked violently; her livid countenance reddened suddenly, and was, all the time, covered with a high crimson hue. The words she was going to utter, threatened to burst her bosom before she could form them into audible accents. She shivered as if seized with a feverish paroxysm, and we awaited her address with an expectation as awful and agonizing as that which the sinner must feel at the tribunal of his Judge when his eternal doom is to be pronounced.

"You know, Pedro," she continued, "that I carried a fruit of your love under my heart along with me when I left you. It would grieve you to see it in the hands of a reprobate. I will return it to you."

"Alas! Francisca, then you would leave me a living witness of your cruelty?"

"Don't interrupt me, my husband. It is the last will, it is the last sigh of a dying person, what I am now going to confide to you. Do you recollect that day of my bridal bliss, when I sank enraptured into your arms; an immaculate, guiltless virgin?" "Francisca!" "When I imparted to you all the happiness I could bestow, and was grieved that I could not give more, and your quivering lips inspired me with frantic rapture; when every nerve of mine was convulsively benumbed to awake again for new ecstatic sensations of bliss; when my languishing, breathless lips could utter only inarticulate accents; and the voluptuous flame that penetrated my whole frame, scarcely could be extinguished by a stream of delicious tears? Do you recollect that scene of ecstasy? My imagination has cruelly defrauded me of all other joys of former times, to blow up, from that recollection, a burning fire to consume my remembrance slowly upon it. In that hour of unutterable rapture, I received this pledge of your love from you as a security of our mutual happiness, and its everlasting duration: that time is past, our happiness is ruined for ever; I return you your security."

"Merciful God!" my friend exclaimed, "Why did I not die; why must I live to see this scene of unspeakable woe?" Apprehension and suspense had rendered me motionless.

"You have, however, told me, (said Francisca,) that you will have no witness of my cruelty; and I must tell you, in return, that I too will have no witness of my shame. I have hit on an expedient (continued she, musing, and suddenly putting her right hand into her bosom) which will relieve both of us. It is, indeed, an horrid expedient; it will, however, be salutary for you and for myself." With these words she pulled out a dagger, aiming a blow at the boy. My suspicion having, however, been excited by those ominous words, I had watched her motions, and arrested her daring hand. I tore the fatal instrument from her, upon which she exclaimed, "Gracious heaven! I am undone!" and rushed out of the apartment. Neither of us could stop her; and when I ran after her, she was vanished, and every search was fruitless, which made me think she had plunged into the adjacent reservoir.

"On my return, I found my friend occupied with his little boy, A truly great and affecting scene! They seemed to be old acquaintances, and to celebrate the festival of meeting again after a long separation. The boy, who was seated on the lap of his father, did not miss his mother for some time, and only after a long interval began to enquire anxiously about her. I endeavoured to pacify him; and his disconsolate father was inspired by the sight of his child with new hopes and expectations. "Her maternal heart (he said) is attached to the boy; she will certainly return to share this treasure with me."

CHAPTER X.

"It now became the chief object of my care to amuse and divert Don Pedro's thoughts; and I began to unbend *his* mind from its gloom by the same ideas which he, perhaps, involuntarily had excited in *my* soul. The compass of our experience and knowledge soon grew too narrow for us; we separated possibilities and probabilities from the regions of dreams, and produced from these materials one fanciful creation after the other. We turned from hesitation to resolution, from resolution to danger, and at last agreed to encounter them boldly.

"We made every preparation to execute our design with safety. Our death would certainly have been attended with dreadful consequences to our murderers; and what had we to apprehend from them if our life was not at stake? We set out one morning, on horseback, and arrived at the cottage against noon, but it was empty. No vestige of human footsteps could be traced all around. What could that mean? Pedro, who already, on the road, had repented our rash undertaking, made this circumstance a pretext to abandon it entirely; and when I insisted upon the execution of my design, mounted his horse, and left me with visible satisfaction.

"A dreadful wind arose with the setting in of night; the trees were violently shaken, and every new gust threatened to overturn the old, decayed cottage where I had taken shelter against the torrents of rain which poured down from the floodgates of heaven. Having been near an hour in that uncomfortable situation, the intense darkness that involved me seemed to disperse gradually; but the faint glimmer, which now and then trembled through the window, was swallowed up again by black obscurity. My fear made me see every object double; and my imagination was, in these moments of anxiety, dreadfully assailed by the recollection of the adventurous rumours which I had heard related of that forest. My apprehensions were increased by the restlessness of my horse, whom I had tied to a post in the inner part of the cottage; and I may truly say that I never have seen a more dreadful night.

"The awful silence which, for some time, had swayed around the cottage, began by degrees to be enlivened; my listening ear, in which the roaring of the storm, and the cracking of the trees, began to resound again, could plainly distinguish whispers, which seemed to proceed from different people. The whispers grew louder and louder; and I could, at length, plainly distinguish a word. I now began to tremble, instead of rejoicing, at being relieved from my horrid solitude by the society of men. The whispers came, meantime, nearer and nearer; a pale glimmer flashed through the little window; somebody pushed against the unlocked door; it opened, and, to my greatest terror, I saw the old man enter. He had a lighted torch in his hand. As to the rest, he was still the same as when I saw him first; the same awful sternness prevailing in his looks.

"Is it you, Don Carlos?" he exclaimed, as soon as he observed me. "I heard a horse kick and neigh!" "My horse has not neighed." "Perhaps you did not regard it. Are you come to redeem your word?" "Yes; I am come for that purpose," I replied, rising from my seat. "You will not have waited for me; as your occupations—" "I am used to be kept waiting; but don't be uneasy about it; I forgive nothing in the world more readily. Will you follow me now?" I consented. The horse was tied faster: he lighted a second torch, which he had under his arm, and gave it me in my hand. The door was then carefully bolted, and we began to push through the overgrown underwood. But no path being to be met with, every step we proceeded was attended with laborious difficulties. I ran against every protending branch that obstructed our passage, lost my hat, and could not get to an open spot that was before us without leaving part of my tattered garments behind. The old man seemed to be used to that difficult way; he improved every advantage, and followed me without receiving the least hurt. We rested a few minutes on that open spot. I was as tired as if I had walked many miles: the sleepless night, the anxiety of expectation, and the difficulties of our way, had exhausted me entirely: I could scarcely breathe. My conductor looked smiling at me, and shook his head, yet without betraying the least mark of displeasure.

"Let us not tarry long here, Don Carlos," he said; and this was the signal for breaking up. We began to proceed: the great extent of the open spot where we were began to grow narrower by degrees; and we were, at length, confined in a rocky passage, which led through wild shrubberies, almost horizontally, into the deep.

"I could not help being chilled with a secret horror. The way seemed to lead us into a lonely abyss. All objects around us bore evident marks of a chaotic disorder and of violent devastation; yet we beheld every where the wrecks of former grandeur. The destructive hand of nature seemed to have exhausted here all her devastating powers. Enormous rocks, which were already half decayed, opposed a roaring cataract, which concealed its unbridled fury beneath the gloomy darkness of bottomless abysses. Every thing bore the stamp of antiquity. A gray moss mournfully covered the mountains, and the slender shrubs trembled rustling in the flaring light of our torches; the rays of which, reflecting a pallid glimmer upon the darkness of the most distant bushes, along with the trembling shades, alternately raised the mind to the most elevated sentiments, and lulled it again into silent meditation. The change of the light, which sported between the leaves and the deep leafy darkness, every object around appeared to me to be a symbol of my life, in order to conduct me towards a happier futurity. I felt myself, as it were, new created, and dropped the cumbersome covering of time past with enthusiastic boldness.

"Whither do you lead me, Sennor?" I exclaimed, at length, involuntarily.

"Whither a man of boldness and feeling needs not be afraid to go."

"Am I then afraid? Certainly, Sennor, I am a stranger to fear; I only sink under the weight of reflections which never came into my mind; and my soul is suspended between the affliction of a painful experience and the joys of hope. Relieve me only of my suspense."

"Can I do it? Your own feelings ought to tell you what you can expect with certainty. You know James's history. A confederation of *men* awaits you. You wish, perhaps, to take a part in the great views which they prosecute; will you be able to submit to a voluntary yoke?" "Yes, I shall; but what recompense may I expect?" "You will be enabled to throw off an *involuntary* one." "Is that all?"

"Carlos, you ask this question too prematurely. You shall *one* time feel yourself happy. But how can you expect to receive your reward before you have earned it? Purified from your prejudices, united by indissoluble bonds with men of exalted virtue, and of an all-conquering spirit, you will learn to forget the little troubles of life, and be enabled, by the smiling light of truth, cheerfully to bear the burdens of your existence. But, are you unbiassed by opinion? is your mind unfettered by prejudice? do you think you are already deserving of such a union?" "No, Sennor, and this it is that makes me uneasy. Can you say nothing that could dispel my uneasiness?" "Have I not done it already?"

"Can you not point out to me a mean which would enable me to conceal my weaknesses and my defects from the scrutinizing eye of those men whose discerning looks will confound me?" "To give you a mask by which you could deceive us? No, Don Carlos, truth is the soul of our society."

"It is, however, dreadful to appear unprepared before men whom one has learnt to fear. Fear shackles the mind, and suffers the soul to unfold herself but slowly."

"Don't be afraid, Don Carlos; your merits will not be misconceived. They will expect rather too much than too little of you. Why should you then be afraid? If you should feel yourself undervalued, or deceived in your hopes, no one will force ties upon you which require the greatest liberty of will if you shall be useful to the society?"

"But how can freedom of will and ties of that nature be consistent with each other?"

"Nothing can be demonstrated easier than that. The connection of the whole body does not confine the different parts of which it is composed in the motions of which they *can* be capable. The freedom of will, which every member enjoys, suffers no abatement if impelled by its own voluntary choice. The charming garlands which bind a free, but purified, will, are kept together by a union which forms itself voluntarily, animated by a spirit of the highest cultivation. The more you prosecute it, the nicer and the more penetrating your looks grow in the examination of the nature of worlds; the more your perceptibility encreases, and the more sensible you are, that in the inane compass of a retired life the noblest springs of our spirit are lamed, the more powerfully you will be attracted by a point of union in which all the faculties revive as if roused from a lethargy."

"What prospects! what hopes! Sennor!"

"Prospects! hopes!" he then resumed, with a gentle, but sarcastic, smile; what prospects and hopes have been held out to you? Don't speak of it. You are scarcely escaped from a miserable coast, and you presume already to see the shore of the opposite continent! You mistake clouds for the shore, Don Carlos: you see nothing but the covering of rising tempests; a chaos big with terror. The rosy morn opens the gates of day with additional brightness after gloomy and boisterous nights."

"But can I ominate nothing at all? hope nothing?

"How can you form an idea of the enjoyment of a refreshing draught if you never have been dry? how conceive a notion of a height which never has been seen nor measured? Nature conceals in her secret bosom the beautifullest charms of her creation; the enchanting centre of the wonderful web which attracts all her children is concealed in a cave most difficult of access."

"You cannot conceive, dearest Count, how much that dreadful man began to confound my ideas. He excited hopes and feelings in my soul, of which I could conceive no distinct notion: a certain melancholic gloom, an obscuration of all images, deprived me imperceptibly of the consciousness of my ideas; and I found myself, at last, entirely disengaged even from those prospects which had enticed me to visit the mystic forest. His mien spoke, however, more forcibly than his words; he seemed carefully to depress the latter, while the former unfolded itself freely with an awful greatness. His words could not disengage themselves from a certain

mystic meaning, which awed me the more anxiously, the more natural it seemed to be to them. The seriousness of his countenance
was slowly dissolved in that affecting self-contemplation, from
which the soul, when brooding over a great object, unfolds herself
only in single rays. Every thing conspired to imprint the impression
of the circumstances indelibly on my mind; and while I am writing
down this account for your perusal, my dearest Count, those ideas
renew themselves with additional force in my memory.

"We had, mean while, proceeded a great way through the rocky
passage; and the mountains began, at length, to decrease gradually on the left and on the right. A valley opened to our view: the
rising morn filled the apertures between the bushes with a sweet
rosy dawn; and the objects we beheld assumed gradually a more
romantic contour. As our torches began to become more useless
and paler, we found ourselves and the whole valley involved in a
thin vapour, out of which a uniform greenish-red back ground
emerged. The objects around us began to lengthen, and every thing
seemed to have dissolved itself to receive the rising day, and to be
impregnated with its cheering light. Unutterable feelings crowded
upon my senses; a rosy dream had lighted upon my inebriated soul,
and all my ideas were floating in a dubious trance. I had frequently
visited this forest on my hunting excursions, but never descried
that spot, which seemed to be the production of my enraptured
fancy. We entered, at length, a little wood of orange trees. Aromatic odours, and the sweet choristers of the air, who warbled their
matins, seemed to have awaited our arrival to receive us in sweet
unison. A spirit of peaceful tranquillity, and a pleasing life, inclined
the bows of the fragrant trees cheerfully to each other. I fancied to
tread on fairy ground. The shrubberies became again very intricate;
however, the whole romantic scene still exhibited visible vestiges of
a former not quite decayed cultivation. A regular serpentine path
emerged in different places through the luxuriant grass; wrecks
of bowers peeped here and there through the thicket; the regular arrangement of several clusters of trees, wild foreign flowers,
which were dispersed every where, and shrubberies, betrayed the
retracted hand of art. An antiquated fabric displayed itself at length
to our view; a long avenue led towards it. Bending under the pressure of hoary time, its tottering ruins reclined against a hill, which

protended over it in romantic beauty. Most of the windows were decayed; but those that had escaped the voracious tooth of all destroying time, I beheld, to my greatest astonishment, grated with new iron bars. An involuntary horror vibrated through my nerves at that ominous sight. I looked at my conductor, who walked by my side, absorpt in profound meditation. He seemed to have forgot that I was with him; his soul had unfolded herself on his countenance to a great expectation, and seemed to labour under the presension of an anticipated horror. I followed the old man through the gate, and we descended several steps. "Don't fall, Don Carlos," he said, lighting me with his torch. But this *don't fall* almost had thrown me headlong down the steps; I supported myself with difficulty by an iron bar, which was fixed into the wall; and it was high time that we reached the bottom, else I should certainly have dropt down fainting. But I now could support myself no longer. "Give me leave to rest a little," I said to my conductor, and seated myself on the undermost step: "I am quite exhausted."

"The old man turned round with marks of surprise, and viewed me by the light of his torch. (Mine I had flung away at the entrance.) "So soon, Don Carlos?" he exclaimed. "Holy Virgin! how pale you are! Be a man."

"He did every thing in his power to make me easy: however, the apprehension of being doomed to meet still greater horrors, because he otherwise would not have sacrificed the present awful impression, which promised to assist him in the completion of his purpose, rendered my heart inaccessible to every kind of comfort. My not being capable to divine what objects would crowd upon me, my defenceless state, and the visible anxiety of my conductor, gradually obscured my senses. A long passage led us deeper into the fabric; steps which alternately led us up and down narrow ways; spacious caves variegated the scene every minute. We entered at length a regularly vaulted and very spacious apartment. "Stay here, Don Carlos!" my conductor said, extinguishing his torch, and vanished suddenly. Not the least sound, not the most secret motion of air enabled me to find out whither he had turned. Whithersoever I extended my hands, I could find nothing but a dreary vacuity: I was in a spacious grave, the walls of which I could not discover. I stood at first motionless on one spot; but being too much exhausted to remain long in that situation, I resolved to seat myself on the ground, and thus to await patiently the things which were to come.

CHAPTER XI.

After my conductor had left me, one quarter of an hour past after the other without my being relieved from my dreary solitude. My resolution to make myself easy was of short duration; every beating of my pulse, which distanced the time of my arrival, farther encreased my anxiety; and my rising heat turned at length into a violent feverish paroxism, that raised my agony to the highest degree. The space around me began at length to grow visibly lighter, which probably was owing to the rising day, whose rays penetrated through a small aperture in the wall; and I could already discern myself again when a door was opened. Two masked men, with lighted torches, entered, and assisted me to get up. You will be surprised, dear Count, when I tell you that my anxiety was instantly dispelled, and I fancied myself to be amongst brethren. I imagined to meet the expanded arms of an amiable family, who would welcome and make me happy, and whose peaceful society promised me a perfect and unutterable felicity.

"A numerous assembly of men, covered with white masks, offered themselves to my view on our entrance into a hall, which was splendidly illuminated by two large lustres, the light of which was reflected by a number of mirrors. They were seated on low arm chairs, which joined in the centre on an elevated spot, where, as it appeared, the chief of the society was sitting. He had a table before him, on which I beheld some books, a cross, a dagger, a goblet, and some unknown instruments. An empty chair, which seemed to be designed for me, was standing beneath the lustres. A profound solemn silence swayed for a few moments in that awful assembly, till my two conductors had taken their seats, when the chief, who sat opposite me, rose from his elevated seat. He stepped to the table, and uncovered his face. A noble and unspeakably enchanting countenance, where heavenly goodness, mixed with the vestiges of the bitterest experience, was enthroned, struck me with reverential awe. A clear look, which raised itself with peaceful serenity above the confines of this terrestrial life, and a brow, which braved the tempests of sorrow, captivated my soul. The silent plan of a new creation seemed to rest in the former, and the latter was a complete picture of the most perfect humanity. I could have prostrated myself before and adored that great man.

"Thou art come, Carlos, to get acquainted with us?" he now began, in a soft accent. I affirmed it silently. "Unmask, my brethren!" At these words the whole assembly uncovered their faces. What an unspeakably grand scene! A groupe of faces, replete with apostolic humanity. The old man, and my good James, were amongst them. I fancied to have found again a number of old acquaintances. A melancholy seriousness had, however, taken possession of their countenances. Their eyes were mournfully fixed at the face of the old man who had addressed me.

"What is your desire, Don Carlos?" he now resumed. "To get acquainted with this society, reverend father." "And then to become a member of it?" "I have duties incumbent on me as a man; duties which I have been taught to hold sacred: I am ready to become one of you, if you will not violate them." "And what duties are they?" "To love mankind; to be charitable to every one that meets me; to forgive my enemy; to love every one who wishes me well." "Every one, Carlos?" "Every one, my father." "Is this a duty which no circumstances will prompt thee to renounce, against which the arguments of reason, and the persuasion of your heart, never will prevail?" "Neither my reason nor my heart will ever make me renounce it." "Then you are unfit for our society!—Lead him hence, my brethren."

"Do not reject me too rashly, my father, (I replied;) do not condemn me without trial. Tell me what you desire, and what the bond of your brethren requires: I swear to be sincere in return, and to be entirely yours, if I can." "We require nothing of you, Carlos, except the very thing you have declared yourself not to be able to do. If you will become a deserving member of our community, you must dissolve all bonds whereby men bind themselves to men. Our property is only to be found in the world at large. Murder your father, poniard a beloved sister, and we shall receive you with open arms. When human society expels you, when the laws prosecute you, when the state execrates you, then you shall be welcome to us. However, our society rejects the tear of humanity."

"Dreadful!" I exclaimed.

"And why then dreadful? (replied he.) Do we offer no compensation? Whatever you sacrifice for our sake will be compensated a thousand-fold in our society. A single grain you sow bears sevenfold. Or do you account it no gain to call the whole great world your property? Is it a miserable, cheating bargain, to exchange one sister for a thousand brothers? Would you not deem the preservation of millions worth one poor drop of blood from your own breast."

"I understand your words, reverend father, but cannot comprehend their mystic sense."

"Miscreant! remain then for ever a property of your father's dust: may you never be haled by the heart-expanding light of truth; but your breast tortured for ever by the miseries of life!"

"Why do you repel me? I do not reject what you say; only teach me to comprehend it. How can I, being taken by surprise, renounce truths which, as yet, have directed the course of my days, in order to resign myself to principles the consequences of which I cannot divine? Conduct me into the sanctuary of the principles by which your society is guided, and try me whether I am docile enough to be your pupil."

"You came in search of us: it was *you*, Don Carlos, who challenged us to appear to you without disguise. But have you considered what will be the consequence of your having only seen us without becoming a member of our body? The light of knowledge is sometimes so powerful that it will kill the beholder. Are you not sensible that a single word will suffice to remove you for ever from the natural order of things, or at least from the memory of those men to whose welfare you presume to have dedicated your existence?" These last words he pronounced with an agitation which tinged his face with a higher hue. "I am sensible of it, reverend father, (I resumed boldly:) I even have counted upon it. When the smiles of fortune were withdrawn from me, when not a glimmer of hope was left me, I resigned all my claims to a life which ceased to be my property. I look with indifference upon a good which is not entirely in my power, and resign it willingly to him who demands it lawfully from me. But unlawfully?—I have friends, have a father!——

"The whole assembly grew pale at these words, viewing each other with consternation. "How, villain!" my conductor exclaimed, after a pause of universal alarm, "have you betrayed us?"

"I have not betrayed you, because you have not disclosed yourselves to me: I only have exchanged my notions of your society for those of a friend whom chance threw into my way, and who had more favourable ideas of you than myself. Who could have prevented me from uttering suppositions? And was it a crime to solve the obscurity you forced upon me? Have I intruded on your society? Have you not allured me by your influence? When I took leave of those who were around me, in order to follow the secret charm whereby you attracted me, could I resist the apprehension that it might be *possible* I should see them no more? My family will miss me: you know my father. Compare your danger with the value of my death. I have been promised to be at liberty to accept or to decline the union with you: woe unto you if you dare to break this *first* promise!"

"As soon as I had hinted to whom I had confided my secret, the assembly grew calmer; and their tranquillity increased with every minute. They beheld, with an indignant calmness, the emotions of the acutest sorrow and vexation at not having sooner dissolved snares of such a coarse texture. My life was safe; I was sensible of it: however, it grieved me to find menaces where I had been led to expect love. It was only with difficulty I could conceal a disgust which was too natural not to wish for an opportunity of shewing itself.

"Fear nothing, Carlos," the president resumed, at length. "How could we design to force you, as we love you sincerely? In an hour you shall be at liberty; but attend to what I am going to say."

"I am not indocile, my father."

"You know the lamentable state of our country. The grievances of the whole nation cannot but affect you also. All ranks are confounded, or rather, are reduced to *one*, by despotism's galling scourge. The people are miserable slaves. Necessity has formed this society, and oppression has strengthened our mutual ties. Lurking dangers have forced us to be on our guard, and to court retirement and solitude. A century has made us wise. Experience taught us to proceed with moderation. The society chose their members from the ablest geniuses of the nation, who are instructed with all our secrets, are wholly devoted to us, and feel themselves happy."

"Have the views of the association always been entirely general?"

"They have never been otherwise. All countries of importance are ours through the members of our society. Here only is the centre of our united strength." "Do you aim at the dominion of the world?" "To promote the happiness of the world is universal dominion." "And the means?" "You see their symbols on this table. Faith, dagger and poison."—I trembled with horror. "Why does our new brother tremble?" "Did I tremble?—Alas! I was only chilled with a woeful recollection. A horrid, ominous darkness lies before me. I have had a wife, a tender wife! You write with blood! A cross is your sign! Cursed, eternally cursed be your bond! You have robbed me of the greatest treasure!"

"Carlos, you are mad!"—"You are mistaken: my fury is cool, and my intellects are unimpaired. Have you the courage to confess that you have murdered Elmira?" "Carlos, I swear by the eternal God! by the horrors of this mystic cave! by this cross and dagger! we have not *murdered* her." "Then forgive me, reverend father! My despair be on the head of the villain who has perpetrated that atrocious deed." "We shall enable you to find him out." "Do you promise that?" "We do!" "Well! then receive me into your society! I devote myself entirely to you. Tell me, what am I to do?" "Nothing but to renounce every doubt; to confide in our decrees; to obey our orders, and to act your part well. Dagger and poison are the greatest friends of humankind. Thousands of new lives germinate from the urn of *one* man, whose doom is fixed, if the welfare of the human race requires it: his death is unavoidable in that case, though he be a monarch!"———

"You will observe, dear Count, how artfully they endeavoured to prompt me to resign myself entirely to their will. All my passions had been traced out, and excited with unerring art; nothing had been neglected to train me in time to the part which I was designed to act. It was nothing but artful cunning that induced them to touch upon the latter idea, in order to divert me from it with greater ease, because they imagined me to be sufficiently entranced to overlook its real meaning. However, they were mistaken. My imagination had not been able, as yet, to disengage itself so soon from the national ideas I had early imbibed. Thus one word overturned all their fine-spun schemes, obviated their most secret plans at the greatest dis-tance, and entangled them unexpectedly in their own artful snares, which they had spread for me. Yet, although I imagined myself to be cunning enough to conceal the impression it had left on my mind, they perceived very soon what had hurt them most. Both parties wished to deceive each other, and either were deceived; I by them, and they by circumstances which could not be foreseen.——

"Having suppressed my agitation, I exclaimed, with horror, "Shocking! very shocking! The life of a *king*, did you say?" "Yes, the life of a thousand kings. The liberty of man is an unalienable family property. Who steals it is a criminal; who artfully purchases it from the possessor for a false appearance of inane happiness is an impos-tor. Whoever feels himself strong enough to punish crimes, is his natural judge. Our forefathers gave us monarchs; we re-demand our rights, and summon them before a higher tribunal." "But do you judge with more equity than monarchs?" "Our union has more members, and all of them are free: our decrees are never inspired by caprice."

"The monarch owes his existence, as you said, to the voluntary submission of our ancestors: they transferred their inborn rights to him for their benefit and his use: but who has authorised *you* to re-demand these rights? who warrants you the truth of your senti-ments; who the equity of your decrees? Being exasperated against government, you confound your feelings with those of a general oppression; and, scorning to obey any other law than the sug-gestions of your irritated will, you plunge mankind, who are not capable to rule themselves, into the tormenting agony, of being governed by an unknown, foreign, arbitrary power."

"Alas! Carlos, how little do you know us! We retired voluntarily from the lap of fortune, to whom men devote themselves. We resigned the noblest wish of exalted minds, the immortal renown of being useful to a nation who were sensible of our merits, and loudly and publicly courted our friendship; we retired from the splendor which attended us, in order to direct a groaning nation to happiness at a distance; and in solitary seclusion from the plea-sures of the world. A long series of years entirely devoted to that occupation, numberless errors which we retrieved with the greatest difficulty, the unity of our aim, the zeal and the number of our coadjutors, every, every thing has contributed to sharpen our eye; and, without any claim to the pleasures of the world, it sees clear when your looks are overclouded. Believe me, dear Carlos," he continued, taking me by the hand, and looking at me with an eye sparkling with a heavenly fire, "*you* also will, one time, confidently adopt our creed. The hallowed bosom of solitude inspires the soul with elevated, heavenly sentiments; the sublimest plans are generated in the profound darkness of night and obscurity: what an endless bliss to extend one's arms over the whole globe, to be entirely independent, to be no more exposed to the painful sensation of the wants of life, nor to the caprice of circumstances and the blasts of accidents?"

"Being surprised and conquered, I sank into the arms of the venerable speaker. "Approach, my brethren," he resumed, "and receive the oath of eternal love from his lips."

"I was in the twinkling of an eye encircled by every arm; and the horrid vow escaped my lips at the altar, amid the kisses of my new brethren. Being inebriated by a beverage out of the goblet, I dropped down at the foot of the altar, laying my hand upon the cross: my arm was uncovered, a vein opened with the point of a dagger, and the streaming blood circulated in a goblet among all my brethren. The old man embraced me once more. "Go now, my son" said he to me, "go, and receive the reward which you deserve."——

"Give me leave, dear Count, to respire a moment. If I fell, my fall is excusable. My senses were inebriated; and our passions, when dissolved, always melt into a weariness and a wavering of sensations which leave no room for any kind of recollection. The commotion which was excited in my mind by the idea of an atrocious aim of the blackest die, can have been only momentary; and many crimes grow more imperceptible the greater they are.

"I now felt myself not only restored to a new life, full of activity, but all the objects which lighted on my mind were at the same time coloured with the die of that enjoyment, which was, till then, the only one I had learnt to taste. Consider only how I have been educated, and you will excuse me. Although I was early connected with women, I had nevertheless, in their embraces, learnt to love but at a very late period.

CHAPTER XII.

I now was led out of the hall, and the assembly separated. James ascended with me a flight of steps, and shewed me a door, which opened into the garden. Day was not yet far advanced, and the balsamic vapours of the night were still in a conflict with the rising heat of the rosy morn. An ocean of vapours visibly floated in the thin misty clouds from one shrub to the other; a universal life and activity occupied my senses, and I imagined to have been transported to another world. I roved by myself through the garden, sweet bodements lighted upon my soul, and I indulged my imagination to range without restraint through a new world, not caring what now would become of me. What a happy disposition for the charms of love!

The garden had, indeed, a wild appearance; however, it had really gained by the changes which nature had effected in its cultivation. It being sheltered from the parching rays of the sun by its situation, the lemon groves which covered it had been enabled to form a close thicket; little rivulets animated the ever verdant verdure of its soil; "and fruits and fragrant blossoms blushed in social sweetness on the self-same bough:" tottering ruins of former grandeur beetled in different places over the encircling vines, and the creeping evergreen appeared to be the only remaining ligament whereby the half-decayed structures were held together. An ever-serene sky seemed to be suspended over the luxuriancy of this romantic valley, which was cooled by never-dying gentle breezes. A warm breath of fragrant odours floated betwixt the trees, on which the golden load of ripe and ripening fruits, painted with the most beautiful hue of health, beamed through the trembling growth of covering leaves. Every object around wore the gay livery of pleasure, and awakened the desire of enjoyment in every sense. The whole appeared to belong to the peaceful lap of a paradise where even a God could have forgot himself.

"How was it possible I should be able to recal at present to my memory the airy dance of those enchanting images, which were resuscitated, as it were, from all the periods of my whole past life? I floated in a straitening reverie, and nevertheless was unspeakably happy. The whole time past was involved in a roseate cloud, from which the present time unfolded itself gradually like the first rays of the morning sun from the purple clouds of the eastern horizon. I seated myself on the velvet grass in a retired spot, and a low humming in the air, the murmuring of a neighbouring rivulet, the plaintive strains of a solitary nightingale over my head, and the rustling of the leaves, had a more powerful influence on my resolution than the eloquence of a reverend hoary man. How wonderful is my fate, dearest S******! How deceitful, how contradictory is it in the sentiments and feelings to which its singular turns gave rise, and from which always new incidents originated! This heavenly, peaceful disposition, which breathed nothing but the purest innocence, and guiltless tranquillity, procreated a voluptuous inebriation; the effect of which still obscures my whole mind.

"I had not long indulged the sweet dreams of my imagination beneath a fragrant tree, and observed the gentle motions of its boughs, when a distant musick vibrated in my listening ear. The musicians came nearer and nearer, and at length stopped, just when I could discern the different harmonious strains. The sweet accords seemed to be gentle sighs expressed by the soft notes of a flute: the amorous strains of a plaintive voice, which spoke the captive language of voluptuous desires, and the swelling melody of the flute, made my pulses beat with uncommon violence, and changed my blood into a liquid fire. My breast expanded itself in a painful agitation; all my senses were enraptured, and I fancied to be transported to better regions.

"Looking back into the shadowy walk from which the harmonious strains proceeded, I beheld a white female form, of a taper shape, and uncommon beauty. The harmony of her enchanting notes seemed to have imparted itself to all her motions, and lifted the light covering of her bosom visibly higher. Her face was veiled with a thin gauze, and she stopped repeatedly to look timidly back. What a sweetness of features did I behold in her angelic countenance! Her gait was, indeed, rather uncertain and timid: however, the *tout ensemble* of her lovely form was a master-piece of elegance. She drew bashfully nearer towards the spot where I was seated, entranced with unspeakable sensations, and uncovered her heavenly face. Words are inadequate to express what I felt when the unclouded splendor of her unparalleled beauty dazzled my giddy eyes. What a number of beauties had I already beheld in the course of my amorous career! but never have I seen a face like her's. I am of a voluptuous disposition; and I had selected from numerous beauties those charms which flattered that propensity most. An image which I believed could never have its original, had gradually formed itself in my imagination; but here was more than an image of fancy. My enraptured looks beheld female beauty in the highest perfection. Her eyes were animated with a fire which would have kindled the flame of love even in the heart of a stoic: the bright enamel of her face; the blush of morning on her dimpled cheeks; the tremulous motion of a languishing mouth breathed a spirit of wanton desires, which promised more to give than it was capable to receive, and imparted itself to me with irresistible power. Sensations and wishes, which long had lain dormant in my heart, awoke at once, and pervaded every nerve of mine with a soft tremor; a voluptuous fire glided through all my veins; and my arms expanded themselves involuntarily to receive the unknown being. She seated herself silently by my side: the lustre of her beauty unfolded itself more and more to my gazing looks; the roseate colour of her face assumed a higher tinge; her eyes grew more and more languishing, and seemed to invite the wanton sports of love. A growth of silken hair floated in natural ringlets upon her bewitching bosom, and encircled her lily neck. The charms of her incomparable form disengaged themselves gradually from the invidious concealment of her garments; her little foot grew visible; an alabaster knee, whose lilies were intermixed with the blushes of the vernal rose, unfolded itself from the cloud of her vestments, beautifuller, rounder and more perfect, than ever a painter could have delineated, or the most luxuriant imagination conceived. She extended at length her downy arms; I felt myself closely encircled; my eyes were dazzled by the overpowering fire of her looks; a quivering balsamic lip burned on my languishing mouth; my breast heaved against a panting bosom; all my senses were intranced; my blood fermented; my face sank on her knee but she raised me violently up to her bosom; her garments gave way, and—I fell.

"Unhappy me! In the extacy of these embraces, in a furious trance of the highest sensual gratification, which drowns the enchanted being in an ocean without a shore, I was fettered with bonds from which I could not disengage myself for many years; my reason and my firmest principles were totally overturned in the rapture of my senses. It required, afterwards, only the least recollection of those moments of unutterable pleasure to transport me beyond myself, and the noblest resolutions of my, certainly, incorrupted heart could never stand the hope of resting once more on the bosom of that consummate enchantress. Causes and effects had been computed with unparalleled art, and the re-action could, therefore, not miss its aim. With a virgin fulness which enchanted my senses, and with an innocent resignation which charmed, did she combine the art of gratifying me with either. Every seducing art was at her command; she could have thawed the ice of hoary age, and rekindled the flame of youthful fire in the gelid bosom of a Nestor. More than human strength would have been required to withstand the conquering powers which nature and art had imparted to her charms.

"Our mutual trance of sensual gratification was of a pretty long duration, and I recovered first the use of my enraptured senses. She was still extended on the elastic grass in a voluptuous swoon, bereft of the power of recollection. The ecstatic trance in which her senses were drowned dissolved at length; her half dimmed looks seemed to be afraid to meet my languishing eyes; and the blushing spirit of virgin pudency overspread at once the lilies of her languid countenance with a crimson hue. She struggled against my bold blandishments, and, before I was aware of it, had regained a dominion over herself which awed my temerity into profound respect. Her lips began to open the first time; and she said, in a tremulous accent, "Alas! Carlos, what have I done! Will you return my fondness for you with gratitude?" "Angelic girl! how can I ever be grateful enough for the unspeakable bliss you have bestowed on me? My whole existence shall be devoted to you."

"Carlos, your love will be the only return I ever shall claim: but do you really love me, you beautiful rogue?" "I loved you, idol of my soul, when you sat down by my side, adorned with every charm of virgin beauty; when your looks rested with such an unspeakable kindness on me. But now—now—since I have tasted the luxury of your charms, I have ceased to love—I adore you."

"How happy is your Rosalia! how unutterably happy! But who warrants me that you will be faithful to me?" "Your charms, Rosalia, and your kindness to your devoted Carlos." "How many girls have already had charms for you, Carlos! and was one of those whom you loved less kind to you than myself? However, I perceived pretty clearly what would fetter you most, when I saw you the first time. How fervently did I love you at first sight! how boldly did you face the surrounding dangers of death, like a God who fears nothing but the judge in his own heart! How did your Rosalia tremble for you when you refused to become a member of our society! and how ecstatic was my joy when you acceded to it! Dear Carlos, will you ever be faithful to the solemn oath you took voluntarily?" "Undoubtedly?" "Swear to your Rosalia that you will stand firm to your sacred obligations." "I swear by your love; by your blooming charms; by your kindness. I lay my hand upon your bosom as on my most sacred altar, and call down upon my head the most horrid punishment, if ever I break this oath. Will this satisfy you?" "Not quite, Carlos. You have sworn in the solemn assembly of your brethren, and now in the lap of love, to keep faithful to that union, never to quit it, nor ever to waver. Swear to me that you will be active for it with the sacrifice of your faculties and sentiments?"

"Can I presume to engage myself for futurity? Is it not sufficient to be at least a passive member, when reason and sensibility prevent me from taking an active part? Shall I, in the lap of love, renounce the sentiments of humanity, for which you have been animating me just now?"

"That you shall not, Carlos. I only desire you to regard me as a compensation for every thing you shall be obliged to sacrifice. A thousand women will love you, but not *one* so fervently as I do; not one with that anxious desire to be every, every thing to you; not one with my forbearance; not one with the care I have for your happiness; not one with a participation in your enjoyment that will be equal to mine. Dear Carlos, be at least grateful, if you will not love me. Sacrifice to me what you have." "Willingly, dearest Rosalia; but what have I that will satisfy your demands?" "Nothing at present; but, ere long, perhaps, very much. I have an obscure presension of futurity. Are you devoted to none of my sex more ardently than to myself?" "To *none*, dearest Rosalia." "No wife?" "No!" "Did you never love a woman with that ardor which you profess for me?" "Yes, Rosalia, there was a time when I loved with the same, if not a greater ardor. It was Elmira, Countess of ——"

"I know her!" exclaimed Rosalia, with kindling anger. "How! You know her?" She grew visibly pale at these words, and her anxiousness encreased the more she strove to hide her confusion. "Yes, I know her," she resumed, after a short pause; "I have seen her at Madrid." "Elmira never was at Madrid." "Or at Alcantara. Who can recollect every thing?"

"She recovered, at length, her enchanting smile. "Do you not think," she added, when she, probably, recollected that she had interrupted me too prematurely, "that we know your adventures better than yourself? A conquest like Carlos is worth while to engage the whole attention of our society." With these words she encircled my neck with her beautiful arm, pressing me to her bosom, and imprinted a burning kiss on my lips, which had the intended effect. All objections and doubts which her words could have produced were drowned in the rapture which her caresses inspired me with.

"Do you then promise me, Carlos, to sacrifice every thing for me; even your Elmira, if she should be alive?" "Every thing, except Elmira." "And you would abandon me, you traitor, if your Elmira should return from the realms of death?" "No, I should divide my heart between you; I should love either of you with fervent, sincere fondness." "With *sincere* fondness?" she exclaimed, viewing me with astonishment: "No, Carlos can never desire that his Rosalia should be satisfied with half his heart. Choose now between myself and Elmira." So saying, she offered me her hand. "Elmira is dead; I choose you." "I thank you, Carlos! a feast shall crown our love."

"She clapped her hands, and twelve females, clad in white garments, appeared commencing a mystic dance. Their voluptuous attitudes expressed their desires, and excited mine again. The individual enchanting charms of the beautiful dancers composed a whole which inebriated my senses with pleasure. The whitest bosoms and necks, knees and taper legs, which wantonly were displayed by their flying garments; the voluptuous play of their arms

and fingers, the languishing language of their miens, the action and
re-action of their limbs, the visible motions and heaving of their
swelling bosoms; every, every thing my greedy eyes beheld rekindled the half dormant fire in my veins; I pressed Rosalia closer to
my heart, our eyes swam in voluptuous tears, and our pulses beat
with redoubled quickness.

"It is impossible, dearest S******, to give an adequate description
of the pleasures that crowded on my senses, which were alternately
exhausted and animated again with new energy. The sweetest
fruits refreshed my languid tongue; the purest and most delicious
wines invigorated the stopping pulses of my heart. Every object
around seemed to be the effect of fairy art; invisible hands sup-
plied us with the most exquisite dainties; we were left to ourselves,
and yet seemed to be animated by secret voices to spend the day
in fairy revels. The tepid air around us, the most secret bower in
the garden, and the blue enamel of the sky, the joyful rustling and
humming betwixt the leaves, a soft strain of amorous flutes, which
floated through the fragrant air at a distance, invigorated the senses
which that bewitching woman had opened to the raptures of the
most exquisite enjoyment. We roved through the garden arm in
arm, melted, as it were, into one being, and frequently dropped
half fainting on the swelling grass to exchange our souls in burning
kisses.

"Evening came at length on the dusky wings of twilight; the
clear blue of the ether was gradually tinged with a darker hue; and
we beheld already here and there a little star twinkling through
the leaves, which were moved by cooler breezes. The contours of
the objects lost their edges, and gradually dissolved in their own
shade; the dying nocturns of the feathered choiristers grew fainter
and fainter, and the nightingale retired to a more secret and gloomy
spot to sing her plaintive strains in undisturbed solitude. We seated
ourselves on a bench of elastic turf, and Rosalia disengaged herself
at once from my embraces, lifting up her eyes to the starry heaven.
Her looks grew gradually more solemn, and I viewed her with
astonishment. "What is the matter with you, my dearest love?" I
whispered, with endearing caresses, and taking hold of her hand.
She drew it suddenly back, took a poniard out of her bosom, and
lifted it up to heaven. Imagine, dear S******, how great my terror

and astonishment was, when I had reason to fear to be suddenly doomed to destruction in the lap of pleasure.

"Eternal powers!" she exclaimed, with the highest degree of enthusiasm, "to you I am going to devote this victim." (She was no more the fond girl she had been, but quite a different person. I scarcely could think that she was the same Rosalia. She seemed to rush between the Godhead and humanity to sacrifice the latter to the former. Like an inexorable judge, she had raised the dagger to destroy the devoted victim with one blow. What a greatness of look, what a sublime majesty in every feature, did she display!) "Rise, Carlos, and kneel down before me!" I obeyed her stern command. "Hear my imprecation!" "I hear, Rosalia." "Swear as I do." "Here is my hand." "Swear that no other being shall intrude between us; that no living being, not even a thought, shall tear our bond asunder; that we will be united for ever, and keep firm to the society who gave us leave to love each other; that neither of us shall attempt to alienate the other from it." "I swear." "That each of us shall prosecute the faithless party with nameless tortures, and vent the most unrelenting revenge even on the half withered bones of the perfidious wretch; that the burning resentment of the avenger shall not be appeased till every thing that renews the memory of the traitor be extirpated along with every vestige of his love and of his posterity." "I swear."

"And if the reprobate should escape the resentment of the avenger, may then the marrow in his bones dry up, may cankered poison corrode his heart, burning thirst parch his tongue in the midst of water, and an insatiable hunger torment him in the lap of plenty! Even in love's paradise, may infernal agony excruciate his heart and blast his hopes; may he be miserable amid the smiles of pleasure, and become a picture of woe unutterable to humankind. Swear Carlos?" "I swear."

"So do I then consecrate thee to be my faithful husband. May heaven be propitious to our union. Ye invisible powers be witness to our mutual oath!" So saying, she strained me to her heart, and imprinted the bridal kiss on my trembling lips. The voice of my desires was silent in that solemn moment; the stillness of the grave swayed all around us, and even the waving leaves of the trees, ceased to rustle. I pressed my heavenly wife speechless to my bosom, and her large blue eye, animated with a soft fire, repeated the oath her lips had uttered.

"Her hand was still armed with the dagger. She bared my arm, and opened a vein, sucking the blood which flowed from the orifice in large drops; and then wounded her arm in return, bidding me to imbibe the roseate stream, and exclaimed, "thus our souls shall be mixed together!" However, she dropped suddenly fainting into my arms, exhausted by the loss of blood. I started up, seized with terror, bound up her wound with my handkerchief, and with difficulty restored her to the use of her senses. But I was also seized with a sudden fainting fit, having neglected my wound; my eyes grew dim, and my senses fled. Rosalia called out for assistance. Some females appeared, and led me to the castle, where I laid down, and instantly fell asleep.

"James sat by my bed when I awoke the following morning from a balsamic sleep. "You have slept very long, Carlos!" he said: "can you spare me a few minutes for a short conversation?" "Why not, my friend, my preserver?"

"Not so enthusiastic, dear Carlos: Do you hear? Let us now talk in a cool and reasonable manner. You have made me your sincere friend, and it rests entirely with you whether I shall continue to be so or not."

"What can I do, James?"

"First of all, I wish you would listen patiently to me. You was inebriated yesterday: to day you must be sober. Rosalia was, at first, designed only to charm your senses; the girl has, however, conceived a sincere love for you, and this alters the matter."

"Dear James, you speak so candid with me." "Must I not, if I shall be your real friend? I only wish you also would be candid and unreserved. I believe you are in love with Rosalia?" "I adore her." "Will you ever be faithful to her?" "Have I not sworn a solemn oath to be so? I was, indeed, in a state of inebriation when I pronounced that vow; but I call you to witness that I now repeat my oath with the fullest approbation of my understanding."

"I do not doubt your sincerity; she deserves being adored by you. Learn to deserve the heart she has offered you. It was not in our plan that you should anticipate what is only the privilege of a wedded husband. You have tied the bonds of wedlock sooner than you deserved it; you have tasted the sweets of matrimony before you were legally united. Your mutual ties will be more firmly contracted when you first have learnt to be deserving of each other."

"Can I render myself deserving of her by the most implicit submission?" "Yes, this is the only way. I can converse with you only a few minutes longer; and yet have to tell you very much. Let me recommend a few words to your consideration. You will not always comprehend us, Carlos; but let this not tempt you to doubts, and obey without hesitation. After you shall be tried sufficiently, and have given us unexceptionable proofs of your firmness, the veil will be removed from your eyes, which, as yet, cannot bear the strong light of many truths. And besides, we do not know you sufficiently, nor on what trait of your character we can have more or less reliance. Yet, trust in futurity, and you will become an honour to our society.

"Be always obedient. The degree of your obsequiousness will be put to the test; you will be involved in situations in which it will appear to you to promote the interest of our union with your own advantage if you should transgress your orders; but do not suffer yourself to be seduced thereby from your duty; for obedience is the first step that leads to dominion.

"Be always unreserved to us; for it would avail you nothing to be recluse. Being surrounded by an hundred hands, watched by a thousand eyes, you will not be able to conceal the most secret recesses of your heart from us; your eyes will already betray half-born thoughts. Our bond does not condemn bold ideas; we only desire to know them, in order to correct your errors. The opener you are, the more we shall reveal ourselves to you.

"Finally, I must tell you, that I have been sent to make you swear an oath of secresy. We shall intrust you with important papers, by which you will be enabled to get acquainted with the spirit of our society. You must swear to me to preserve them carefully. Who knows the fates of men? There must be places which are out of the sphere of our activity. You may be seduced; but as to this point, you must stand all temptations, and keep faithful to us."

"I promise it."

"Swear by God and your life."

"I swear by God and by my life!"

"Here is the parcel. You will find in it a complete direction how you are to act. Farewel, my dear friend. In a twelvemonth I shall see you again. A *Genius* will attend you every where, and you will be safe if you follow him."

"So saying, he embraced me, and left the apartment with tears of affection. His confidential tone had entirely conquered my poor deluded heart, and my ideas floated in a mixture of noble resolutions and voluptuous fancies. I had just done dressing myself, when a stranger appeared, signifying to me, that he had orders to conduct me out of the castle. I followed him mechanically through several passages of the ruinous fabric, from one vault into the other, and through the garden into the forest. When we came to the cottage, he left me suddenly, and disappeared. My horse was still on the spot where I had left him, and neighed joyfully when he saw me. I took him affectionately round the neck, and his tears seemed to mingle with mine. A great change had, meanwhile, taken place in my mind; I scarcely knew myself again. All my wishes and presensions had been gratified, although but obscurely, yet completely; and now I lost myself again in a labyrinth of new ones, which seemed to be endless. Was it delusion, or a dream? What was to become of me? And, to leave you now, Rosalia, now, a bride after the first bridal night; a wife, after the first embrace; without taking leave, without any other token of remembrance than the picture of your charms, which is deeply engraven in my heart! How unspeakably cruel is the first proof of your friendship, ye dreadful unknown!

During this soliloquy, I had thrown myself down upon the couch where I had rested formerly. My mental and bodily strength was exhausted, and I was half dreaming and half awake. However, the violent kicking of my horse roused me from that state of apathy; I untied him, and went in search of the road to my castle.

"Dear Marquis!" a voice exclaimed, when I approached my garden, "you look very pale. How do you do?" These words were accompanied with a loud laugh, and I perceived Don Pedro at the distance of a few paces.

"Indifferently well, as you see," I answered.

"On coming nearer, he perceived that I was not disposed to listen to his jests, and resumed, in a more serious accent, "So gloomy, Marquis: what has happened to you? If you had come a little later,

I should have gone in search of you with an armed force." "I doubt it very much, Don Pedro." "Perhaps, because I was not inclined to creep with you into the hut. I would lay any thing that you have heard and seen nothing. Is it not true?"

"You are perfectly right, (I replied.) I fell asleep, and had a dream; a long dream, which, as you see, has lasted till now. But, to be serious, Pedro, have you received any intelligence of your lady?"

"This unexpected question disconcerted my poor friend at once; he hung down his head in a mournful manner, dropt big tears, sobbed, and answered not a syllable till we came to his house, when he left me abruptly. I went into my castle, where I was received with universal joy by my servants, who had been under the greatest apprehension on account of my long absence. Different reports about the supposed reason of my absence had, meantime, been rumoured about, and received additional credit, because Don Pedro too had returned but a few hours before me. This latter circumstance, of which he had made not the least mention, did not strike me much at that time: however, his absence was closely connected with my adventures; and you will soon see, dearest Count, what consequences I could have drawn from that circumstance, if I had not been stupefied to such a degree as rendered me entirely unfit for reflection.

"I spent the first weeks with studying the papers I had received from James. They were written in such an obscure stile, that I could only with difficulty gather a few ideas: however, those new notions appeared so sublime to me, that I was quite enraptured with them. What grand pictures did they exhibit, and how great a judgment of composition! I was lost, as it were, in a foreign country, which was shewn to me at a small distance with uncommon charms, and afforded me sufficient opportunities for exerting all my mental faculties to understand the whole, and to enjoy it in unmixed purity. The more I pursued these ideas, the more perceptible did their connection grow; my soul expanded itself, and I soon expected to penetrate to the source of the whole. The remaining part of my time elapsed amid the simple amusements of a rural life. The change of objects amused my mind, and diverted it from the reflection of Rosalia; yet my application to the part which I was to act always recalled to my memory the heavenly charms of her beautiful form.

The latter only was the object of my ideas, because I had experienced too little of the accomplishments of her mind, or was too exhausted to have had a proper sense of her mental excellencies. That smiling, voluptuous image followed me every where, mixing with my amusements, haunting me in my secret bowers, at the tinkling rivulet, and pursuing me to the silent grove, where, on the bloomy spray, the birds with joyous music waked the dawning day. I beheld her every where clad in virgin beauty; and the artless sounds of nature, which formerly had enraptured my soul, had no charms for me, if they did not resemble Rosalia's voice. I cannot conceive, at present, how it was possible that a lively spirit like mine was capable of being sensualized so much.

"Don Pedro appeared again the day after my arrival, and seemed to be very much comforted and tranquil. He was occupied with building, and amused himself with gardening. He was merry and serene, and relapsed but rarely into that melancholy which, in the beginning of our acquaintance, had rendered him so dear to my heart. We generally spent the evenings together, and repeated, in our confidential conversations, the occupations in which we had been engaged during the day. It appeared sometimes to me that his understanding was more penetrating, and his character more studied, than he chose to let me see. His mind frequently developed itself in wonderful greatness and brilliancy. Yet I took those brighter moments for ecstatic transports of an overburthened soul, striving to stun itself by merriment. The deeper I penetrated into the plan of my associated brethren, the plainer I presaged their manner of proceeding and their operations, the more did I suspect every word that was dropt in my presence, and I found in every thing a relation to the notions that occupied my soul. Some time was granted me for rest, and for the study of their system, and two months were already elapsed without any indication from their part. I imagined, at last, that they had forgot me entirely, and prepared to return to *Alcantara*, where my whole family awaited me with anxiety, when an event happened, which at once gave a different turn to my whole future fate.

"I had carefully avoided to mention *Francisca* a second time to *Don Pedro*. He seemed not to have received any farther intelligence of her, and the child appeared to have made him forget the mother.

At once he came in full speed to my house. "I come to tell you news that will surprise you, *Don Carlos*, (he exclaimed on seeing me:) my wife is returned!" "Your wife?—You joke, Pedro!" "Would to God, I did, dear Carlos. But, between ourselves, I now care very little for it. Alas! she is again so melancholy, weeps so much; and when I told her, Don Carlos would rejoice to see her again, her tears flowed more copiously. Can't you guess, dear Carlos, what may be the meaning of it?"

"This unconcern appeared to me very suspicious. His innocent air was not quite natural, and his looks betrayed some anxiety to hear my reply. "So!" I exclaimed, laughing, "I am glad of it. Perhaps she is in love with me!"

"This indifference of mine surprised him as much as his unconcern had struck me. He seemed to be violently agitated, when he saw that he was caught in his own snare, but soon collected himself again.

"What do you mean by that, my dear Marquis? You are very absurd to day, my dear Marquis." "You see, dear *Pedro*, that I am very busy, at present. Pardon my frankness. I shall be glad to see you and Francisca this afternoon. Till then, farewel, dear Pedro." So saying, I offered him my hand. He appeared to be confounded, and left me with downcast looks.

"What does that mean? said I to myself, when he was gone. *Francisca* is returned; and yet the farewel scene between her and Don Pedro was as solemn and so affecting, as if she had intended to see him no more this side of the grave! Did she not swear that she would see him no more? Did she not offer to destroy herself? And, what shall I think of the unconcern with which Don Pedro informs me of her return? He either is a fool or an impostor. And who is to be imposed upon? Carlos! Carlos! If you should suffer yourself to be deceived by a *friend!*

In that moment I stept to the window, and with terror saw the name of *Elmira* written on one of the panes. Gracious heaven! (I exclaimed,) who has done this? In that moment the recollection of times past rushed upon my memory; all those charming scenes when I strained Elmira, that noble, heavenly being, to my heart, were regenerated in my mind. However, the recollection of that blissful moment also re-produced that scene of horror when she closed her eyes for ever in those arms that had expanded themselves to make her happy. A dreadful suspicion rushed like mountains on my heart. She died so suddenly, and in a manner so unnatural! Who spoke so mysteriously of that affair on my reception in the society? And—all-gracious Heaven!—has not *Rosalia* made me swear to love her no more? Of what use was that oath, if she is really dead? And Rosalia betrayed so much anxiety and uneasiness. Should she perhaps be still alive? Should she be only withheld from me?—And for what purpose?—To tie me faster by Rosalia's charms? My agitation almost overpowered me; a torrent of tears gushed from my eyes. How different, Elmira, were your charms from those of Rosalia! How innocent your looks! How chaste was the warmth of your embraces! Never, never shall I forget your noble mind, the sweet harmony and tranquillity of your pure unspotted soul. O! that you never had left me! how happy should I then be!

CHAPTER XIII.

The transition from sentiment to sentiment is a wonderful trait of the human heart. The first part of my soliloquy was entirely occupied by anxious suspicion and lurking jealousy; the second breathed nothing but grief at Elmira's loss, which totally dispelled the former sensations. I was afraid to examine into the probability of Elmira's still being alive; the faint glimmer of hope, that cheered the despondency of my soul, was such a precious treasure to me, that I imagined to owe some gratitude to the confederates for not having precluded me entirely from it. My former fanciful dreams re-occupied my soul, ingrossing my whole consciousness, and I imagined to commence a new life since I renewed the interrupted connection with her. How happy was I! I overlooked from my window, with anxious pleasure, all the bowers and trees with which I had held an intimate communion after the loss of my dear departed wife. I suspended her picture to my neck, kissing it more than an hundred times, and it began to supply to me, by degrees, the original.

"Against evening I saw Don Pedro and his lady coming to my castle. He looked staring at me; talked anxiously to her; and she seemed to take great pains to comprehend the part in which he instructed her. I went down to receive them. Pedro was as friendly, innocent, open, and communicative, as he formerly had been; and his wife did not betray the least perplexity. I received them with common civility, without mentioning a syllable of her return, telling them that I rejoiced at the increase of our society, and we soon commenced an indifferent conversation. Francisca frequently was absorpt in meditation, as if studying the part she was to act; and I surprised her several times in a secret anxiety, which she strove to conceal.

"She was grown much handsomer than when I saw her the first time. A secret grief, that seemed to rankle in her bosom, had spread a languid paleness over her countenance, that wakes sympathetic emotions in every feeling heart, and fascinates the mind; a significant mouth, that spoke the energetic language of internal sufferings, rendered her face an affecting picture of love. I could not help fixing my looks on her interesting countenance.

"Pedro observed the emotions of my heart, which was not usual with him. He made merry at it, and encouraged us to be more communicative to each other. "Have I not a beautiful wife, Don Carlos?" he exclaimed, incircling her taper waist. "Who denies it, Don Pedro?" "A wife that loves the friends of her husband?"

"She stole a glance at me, blushing, and casting her looks down again. This is one part of the character in which he has tutored her! said I to myself, and yet could not help being captivated by the lovely mourner. It is true, Don Pedro acted his part in a masterly manner; and he would have attained his aim, if his wife had been possessed only of one half of his self-consciousness. He involved us in the most innocent, and yet in the most artful, manner, too, in a thousand little situations which gave us an opportunity of growing more intimate with each other. He made me, with consummate art, take notice of the brightest parts of his lady, displaying them in the most advantageous manner, and unfolded all her captivating charms. We grew warmer every moment: however, she blushed more frequently than he probably had instructed her to do. It appeared to me, that she was tutored to perplex me only, without being thrown off her guard; but she watched not carefully enough over her heart, and conceived an inclination to me before she was aware of it. She afforded me less opportunities of making these observations than Don Pedro himself. Without losing sight of me, he gave her numberless little hints not to forget herself; but she gave way to the secret impulse of her heart. At length she acted her part more natural than her husband wished; he rose, and lamented that he could not stay longer with me. When my visitors took leave, Francisca's weeping eyes, and her trembling hand, told me that my suspicion was not unfounded. But how was all this connected? I was implicated in a maze, from which I could not extricate myself. Pedro had some design upon me. This was but too visible. But if it had been connected with that of my associated brethren, it would have been folly to weaken, by the coquetry of his wife, the strong impression Rosalia had made on my heart, which would have been rendered more lasting and efficacious by my sudden separation from that captivating woman. But if he wanted to implicate me in a design of his own (which then was most probable to me) what plan could it have been, if it should compensate him sufficiently for the risk he ran of losing the affection of such an accomplished being? All these reflections produced no other result, than the resolution of being on my guard at all events.

"Several days elapsed before I heard any thing from my neighbours. I was too much occupied to take much notice of it, and omitted purposely to pay them a visit, or to gather any intelligence concerning them from my people. I enjoyed in solitude, and in silent rapture, occupied with the remembrance of my Elmira, all the charms of my residence, indulging my sweet, though melancholy, fancies in the dying breezes of autumn. Every object around me wore the livery of my fancies: I was so happy, so much absorpt in my reveries, as to be afraid of the intrusion of every foreign sensation; I conversed with the tinkling rivulet, and it answered as I wished. Every sufferer loves his grief.

"At the close of the fifth day, I walked slowly down the borders of the rivulet which separated Pedro's estate from mine. I was so much inebriated with pleasing sensations, that I took but little notice of what was doing around me, when suddenly loud sobs vibrated in my ears. They proceeded from Francisca. Her grief was natural, for it was impossible she could have seen me. She sat on the opposite bank of the rivulet, reclining her head on her hand, and mixing her tears with the silver waves of the purling rivulet. Her hair covered part of her pale woe-worn countenance, and her bosom heaved violently under a burden which it seemed endeavouring to throw off. Her attitude was so painful, and the expression of her features so affecting, that involuntary tears started from my eyes.

"At length she started up, and looked wildly around. A rose-bush in full blossom was at her right. She tore the budding flowers off, and scattered the leaves on the ground. At length she seemed to forget that she had intended to tear the fragrant blossoms, collected some of the scattered leaves, kissed them, moistened them with her tears, and kissed them again.

"She is in love! said I within myself: and thou, unhappy wretch, art perhaps, the object of her passion. I stepped nearer towards her, exclaiming, "Francisca! why do you weep?" She raised her head placently, as if the object of her reveries had called to her; her melancholy looks met me; but no sooner did she descry me, than she ejaculated a loud scream, and rushed into the thickest shrubbery.

"Do you see, Carlos, (said I to myself) the hapless woman loves you; and what do you feel for her? nothing but pity! At bottom, I did not know rightly what I felt for the love-sick mourner; but thus much is certain, that I postponed my intended journey on her account. I did, indeed, not love her; my heart being still warmly and faithfully devoted to Elmira; yet Pedro was a villain, and it was worth while to dispossess him of a treasure whose value he could not estimate. This fine ratiocination, whose true source I would not see, prompted me to stay.

"Soon after this incident, Don Pedro visited me. He wanted to appear open and confidential, but I could easily see that something ailed him. I returned his visit the following day, and met Francisca. But she was silent, constantly blushing, reserved, agitated, and pale. "Are you not well, my dear friend?" said I, with a gentle squeeze of my hand, which she returned crimsoning. "She is always sickly," *Don Pedro* replied for her. A torrent of tears gushed from her eyes, and her husband gave her a hint to withdraw.

"I do not know what ails the foolish woman," her husband replied. "You treat her perhaps with too much severity," I answered. "You have not informed me yet of the first reception you gave her; it was, perhaps, not quite such as she could wish; not so warm as

an unhappy, repenting wife may expect. Tell me sincerely, have you
nothing to accuse yourself of, in that respect?" He knit his brow.
"No, indeed not!"—

"Don't restrain her too much. Perhaps she is fond of society;
let us invite the neighbouring nobility. She is perhaps inclined to
amusement and noisy diversions. Let us give concerts, balls, and
masquerades. Take care you don't lose her a second time." This
simplicity opened his lips, and he imagined that he could advance a
few steps farther in his plan without running any risk. "No, Carlos!
You mistake the cause of her grief." "Well, what is it then?" "She
is in love!" "In love? (I laughed aloud.) This is nothing new to me."
"You know it? Well, then, I need not to inform you of it." "No, certainly not; if only the happy object of her flames knows it." "Dear
Marquis, I conjure you to give her no encouragement!" "Do you
dream, Don Pedro? or have you lost your senses?—Of whom do
you speak?" "Of you, Marquis."—"With me she is in love?" "Most
certainly; with you!" "Impossible! That certainly would be something new to me.—But, Pedro, you are a miserable jester!" "No! by
heaven! I am serious!"

"Do you see, that I am right? Your unhappy jealousy renders her
miserable. She sees herself excluded from your affection! Is any
thing farther wanting to make her unhappy.—Fie! be ashamed,
Don Pedro!" "I know very well what I say. But let us drop that subject at present."

"Here our conversation terminated; neither of us being eager to
impose upon the other. I went home soon after. We met several
times, on the subsequent days: but Francisca did not appear, and I
must confess that I was afraid of inquiring after her.

"Pedro was shortly after obliged to make a journey: heaven knows
whither. He seemed to be rather perplexed when he informed me
of it, and took leave with the following words: "If you love me, Don
Carlos, you will remember my request?" He then strained me tenderly to his bosom, and departed. I was not disposed to enter in a
long conversation; it appeared to me as if Francisca's name were
lurking in all my ideas, and as if I did not rejoice at that discovery.
My danger increased. I was but too sensible of it. How distressful
was my situation, if this was a snare for me!

"Yet I resolved firmly not to see her during Don Pedro's absence;

but it was plain that the hapless woman really loved me. She had no share in Don Pedro's art, and her tranquillity and happiness entirely depended on me. Should I render her situation more forlorn than it already was? How easily could she conclude, from my behaviour, that I despised her! That I did not decline her affection from duty, but scorned it. And what bad consequences can one visit produce? I resolved, therefore, to pay her a visit, but to be as civil and reserved as possible. Familiar gambols, and innocent liberties, only threatened to nourish the flame that was concealed in her heart.

"I found her again in a very melancholy situation; her eyes were red and swoln; her pale lips emitted plaintive sighs; yet she endeavoured to conceal the mournful state of her mind, receiving me kindly, and with a blushing placency. I seated myself by her side, beneath a spreading lime-tree, which overshaded a beautiful sumak-shrubbery. The day was one of the finest I had ever seen in autumn. The departing season seemed to bid a smiling farewel to her dying children, and to give her last cheerful benediction to the fading bowers, and the decaying verdure of the autumnal fields. Francisca displayed a mien of composure which I never had observed in her countenance. She was occupied with female work, and now and then stole a glance at me. Her woe-worn, pale countenance, overspread with the charm of an agitated sensibility, rendered it impossible for me to preserve the reserve which I had brought with me.

"Having, for some time, conversed on indifferent subjects, I inquired after her lord. "Will he soon return, Sennora?" said I. "I don't believe he will: for he has ordered me to shut myself up, and to avoid seeing strangers, as much as propriety will permit."—"Probably he has been avocated by family affairs?"—"It may be. He has communicated nothing to me." "You don't seem to be satisfied with his behaviour, Madonna? I am Don Pedro's friend, will you honour me with your confidence?" "Woe unto you, if you are! but I have no secrets to confide to you." "Alas! Francisca, I do not deserve that treatment. No one can love you more cordially and sincerely than myself. But, why these tears, why these involuntary sighs?" You see, my friend, how I kept my resolution. She grew paler and paler, and began to weep more violently; replying, after a mournful pause, "Carlos, if you love me, spare me with your tender goodness; I do not deserve it."

"Who would be more deserving of my tenderness than Francisca? Have confidence in me, my dear friend; let me share your sorrows!" "Carlos, I am a faithless, abandoned woman!" "Has Don Pedro told you so?" "No; Pedro has forgiven me: however, I am agitated by a new conflict with my heart; and this time, alas! Carlos! I shall not conquer." "You are in love?" No answer.

"You are in love, Francisca?"

"She dropt half despairing in my arms, and hid her face in my bosom; seizing my hand with convulsive sighs, and pressing it to her lips and to her heart. Heaven and earth disappeared in that moment from my dizzy eyes; all my resolutions were forgotten; and I beheld nothing more in Don Pedro than a villainous friend and husband, from whose hands one ought to deliver a dear object. I encircled Francisca's waist, and imprinted a burning kiss on her lips. "Carlos?" she groaned, "I can bear it no longer." So saying, she disengaged herself from my embraces, and rose up. "Why do I conceal these sentiments? No, I will be proud of them. Yes, Carlos, I adore you. You are the only being upon earth whose affection can set this poor heart of mine at ease."

"With these words she was going to leave me abruptly; but I was transported beyond myself, and took hold of her arm. "And with that confession you will leave me to myself, Francisca?" "Can I help it, Carlos?" "No, you must not leave me. Unbosom yourself to your friend. Will you unite your fate for ever with mine? Will you flee with your devoted Carlos?" "Yes, I will: but we must not stay in this country, nor in a neighbouring one: they would find you, and tear you from my arms. Do you know some solitary unknown spot beyond the ocean? Forgive me, Carlos: excuse a lovesick woman, that would willingly purchase your happiness at the expense of her own. But take me with you, lest I should be forced to act *against* you!"

"Against me! Then my apprehensions are not unfounded?" "Dark and dreadful things are hid in the human heart. Do not trust your best friend, Carlos. But, I have sworn an horrid oath." She looked around with a fearful countenance.

"We now agreed to elope. The following night was fixed for our flight. I took every precaution to execute our plan with safety, and unpursued. Night set in. A window was the place where I was to meet Francisca. A noise was to be made, as if robbers were break-ing into the house. I intended to conduct her to a place of safety; then to run into the house, under the pretext of tendering my assis-tance, and to pursue her with Pedro's servants in a false direction. A ladder was placed against the house; the window was left open. I entered it masked: but how great was my terror when I found Fran-cisca's bed empty! The whole house was searched. All her waiting women were fast asleep, and she could be found no where.

"I perceived, however, some traces in her room, that convinced me she had been carried off by force. She had, probably, struggled very much; her bed being in the greatest disorder, and a great part of the furniture broken and scattered on the floor, near the bed. It was astonishing that her attendants, who slept in the adjoining chambers, should not have been disturbed by the noise. The ser-vants whom we had awakened, and who were surprised to find that we had got into the bed-room of their lady through the window, protested to have heard nothing but hollow moans, which they had mistaken for the distant howling of a dog. The waiting women were still asleep, and we hastened to awake them, upon which the mystery was unfolded at once. All our endeavours of rousing them were fruitless; and having applied even painful means (to which I thought myself authorised, imagining their lethargy to be ficti-tious) we were obliged to desist from all farther attempts, it being plain that some person in the house, that had an opportunity of mixing somniferous drugs with their drink, was concerned in the affair. Every moment added to my fury and rage. I was almost fran-tic, and threatened Don Pedro's people to massacre every one of them. But they protested unanimously, with evident sincerity, to be entirely ignorant of that mysterious transaction; and it appeared afterwards, that they all had lived too long in Don Pedro's service for being reasonably supposed to have assisted a stranger to carry off their lady. Whom could I now more naturally suspect than Don Pedro himself? I had plain proofs of his low cunning; it was evident that he had a design upon me, whatever it might have been; and had selected his wife to be instrumental in the execution of it. She had returned to his house at the most seasonable period: she was thrown off her guard: it could be foreseen, that, at length, a design would be formed against himself; his wife was, therefore, dangerous to him; he could not remove her without exciting my suspicion, and, of course, carried her off by force.

"This train of arguments appeared to be very clear; though it rendered my situation more intricate and dubious. I was actually on the brink of despair; not so much on account of the loss of Francisca, as of her fate and sufferings. My distress was so much the more galling to me, as I saw myself a second time imposed upon under the mask of friendship. My pride being hurt, the agitation of my mind, originally caused by an unfortunate love, was renewed.

"Several weeks elapsed without any intelligence of either Don Pedro or the confederates having reached me. The country-seat of the former was a real solitude. The servants, that had been left behind, having received neither intelligence nor any instruction from their master, began to quarrel, and part of them ran away: his garden was in the greatest confusion, because every one wanted to be the gardener; and I thought myself bound, as a neighbour, to put a stop to these disorders. Extending thus the compass of my occupations, my reflections on the injury I had received were diverted, my resentment wore off by degrees, and I began to exculpate my former friend with encreasing good-nature, the more I had occasion to interest myself in his external concerns. This mutability of character, which originated less in weakness than in an unbounded goodness of heart, promised before-hand the greatest success to the subsequent wiles with which he deceived my unsuspecting heart.

"The study of the papers James had given me occupied the greatest part of my time. I combined not only my former, but even my innate notions and rooted prejudices with these new enthusiastic doctrines; and the more they became intimate to my open, susceptible soul, the easier I deduced applicable results therefrom, the more did my mind expand itself, and futurity appeared to me in a clearer and rosier dawn. They comprised nothing but ideals, and yet the images pourtrayed therein were so human that my understanding was warmly interested.——

"How sorry am I , dearest Count, that I am forced to withhold from you the noble sensations which the communication of the great and exalted plans these papers contained would produce in your mind, and that I can give you only those few hints my vows do not entirely prohibit me to impart! Though I should be bold enough to imagine myself disengaged from them, yet that Genius that has haunted every step of mine ever since my initiation, still hovers around me. I should wantonly provoke the vengeance of those dreadful *unknown*, whose controul over me may perhaps have decreased; but for their own safety can *terminate* only with my death. Time, perhaps, will unfold more than I am at liberty to do. The influence under which you and I evidently are, must cease sooner or later. Suffice it to tell you, that I gradually have derived from that system, which has intrusted me with the noblest ideas, that tranquil seriousness with which I look forwards into futurity, expecting nothing from it, and taking hold of every thing useful and improving it offers to me. I relapse again with gloomy melancholy into my age, from which I ardently wished to emerge, and submit without either grief or joy to my fate. Dearest Count, let your noble human mind dwell a few moments on this emanation of sensation, the result of the most extraordinary fate; a result which will be able to guide your course when I, as I have reason to apprehend, shall have taken leave of you in some manner or other.

CHAPTER XIV.

Soon after this incident I visited my family at *Alcantara*; but all their rejoicing, all the pains they took to prolong my stay with them, were fruitless. I was entirely dead to those sweet pleasures which the peace of a serene domestic life always affords to uncorrupted minds, that do not groan under the heavy pressure of sorrow. New gratifications had rendered my heart insensible to the former ones; and with the knowledge of the situation of my family, I also had lost all the interest I was wont to take in it.

"It is one of the most lamentable states of mind to be addicted to any good or expectation to such a degree as to be indifferent to all other pleasures. I was misconceived every where. Being from the society of the higher classes, occupied with the ideas of such a noble society, engaged with a constant conflict with myself and my prejudices, I could not but be a stranger to the method of circulating my ideas with ease in the company of that set of people. One stared at me, because he did not comprehend me; another treated me with coldness, because I was used to grow warm on some occasions; and a third shunned me, because I was a disagreeable companion. The natural consequence of it was, that I grew more obstinate and reserved. Taking all those I was connected with for blockheads, I used myself to a tone of condescension that offended. All the offences I gave unknowingly were returned with a vengeance, which prompted me, at length, to leave Alcantara. Having explained to my family the motives that obliged me to leave them, I departed with great satisfaction.

"The vernal season had, mean while, returned; and my heart longing for an undisturbed communication with itself, I threw myself again into the arms of a country life. My grief soon was reconciled again to the world; and the more I secluded myself from men, the more did the gloomy light in which they had appeared to me of late clear up. I soon began to live again for them, yet without being able to love them: while I refined on my enjoyments, I strayed farther and farther from the sweetest and most natural pleasures, and thus appropinquated that point where the whole life is wasted in reasoning, and lost to the community. Finding Don Pedro's house as empty as I had left it, and being unable to discover the least traces of the fate of that couple, I resumed, with additional eagerness, the study of the papers intrusted to me by the confederates, from whom I also had heard nothing since my return from the mystic cavern. The whole system was already become pretty familiar to me; but the more I perused it, the more new ideas did I discover. My mind was occupied all the day long with no other ideas but such as immediately related to the sublime principles contained in those papers, and I even spent whole nights with the most diligent study of that treasure of elevated sentiments.

"In that occupation I was one night engaged. Midnight was already past. Every person in the house was asleep, and I had opened the windows of my bedchamber to inhale the balsamic fragrancy of the young lemon blossoms, and to listen to the plaintive strains of a nightingale that had perched on a large lime-tree before my window, when I suddenly heard a violent knocking against the great gate of the castle. I started up, seized with astonishment, and could not guess the meaning of that unseasonable noise.

"All my servants were asleep. The knocking grew more violent.

The gate was at length opened, as a loud noise re-echoed through the castle, which seemed to be in an uproar. A strange murmuring resounded through the gallery, and the whole edifice was in confusion. Hasty steps were heard on the staircase; the door of my antichamber was opened. Some person approached my bed room, and at length a figure in white entered, rushing into my arms.

"Being half dead with apprehension, and an uncertain fear which I could not shake off, I had shut my eyes, when my nocturnal visitor came towards me. I was so much stunned, that I hardly could open them. The candles did not burn very clear; and the stranger was so much disguised, that I could not discern her features. I imagined her to be Francisca, and was enraptured to strain her again to my bosom. I pressed my lips upon hers, when I first observed it was not Francisca. I pushed her from me, and exclaimed, "Go woman! thou art not Francisca! But who are you?" "How, Carlos? don't you recollect your wife, your Elmira?" Eternal God! it was Elmira. I was astonished at this discovery; it was my sweet, my faithful wife. I knew her by her tender kisses, by the fire of her embraces, by the sweetness and the mildness of her words. Yet she was not the same Elmira that formerly enraptured me; not that heavenly smiling and cheerful being. A death-like paleness covered her torpid features and seemed only reluctantly to give way to the rapture of my sensations. A misty gloom had overcast the large blue eye, staring at me with signs of anxious apprehension; and a painful, but placid, smile asked me solicitously who that Francisca was for whom I had mistaken her with so much warmth. I felt the whole force of that reproving smile, strained her to my bosom to pacify her with blandishments, but found it impossible to utter a word in my excuse.

"Do you still love your Elmira with tenderness?" she at length began. "Yes, my sweet, heavenly wife, I do; but cannot yet collect myself. Are you really risen from the grave, or are you only the ghost of my wife, and returned for some moments to speak comfort to my soul?"

"Let this embrace tell you, my dear husband, what I am. Departed spirits cannot kiss with that fervour. But have you been as faithful to me as I was to you? Be sincere, my dearest husband."

"I was terrified, the joy of meeting again being so short lived, and so suddenly overclouded by anxious jealousy. If that dreadful confederation had taken her from me, she must have been informed of my faithlessness, of my infernal inebriation. This thought, which obtruded itself irresistibly on my mind, bereft me of the power of utterance. At length, I exclaimed, in an agony, "Cursed confederation! thou hast robbed me of every blessing!"

"What does my Carlos say?" Elmira resumed, pressing her pallid face to my cheek. "Be candid to your wife."

"Alas! Elmira, you know my tender heart. You died in my arms, and I was present when you was entombed. How could I imagine that all this was nothing but foul deceit to steal my most valuable treasure from me? I have bemoaned you a long time, and looked for your image in every object which my eyes beheld. You did not desire me not to love a second time."

"No, I did not; I even could not wish that your heart should never give way to a second love. But now, my dearest husband, now you will love me again? Is not Elmira restored to the possession of your heart? She has deserved it by her fidelity, and dearly bought it by her sufferings. Is it not true, my dear Carlos, that you will resign to your faithful Elmira all other women, that you will be wholly mine, and that the restoration of your fond wife gratifies all the wishes of your heart?" "Certainly, my dear, my ever adored wife."

"Though my tender husband should have loved another, yet it was but Elmira whom he fancied to have found in her. If you forgot me for whole days, it was only because you did not ominate the possibility of my return. I forgive you, dear culprit; I forgive you every, every thing. Your heart is capable of rendering thousands happy: but, is it not true, dear Carlos! it can be made happy only by one?"

"The sweet enchantress! I was still suspended between dreaming and waking, while I was enraptured with the probability of having her restored to my heart. I was in the state of a wayward wanderer, who, on the morn succeeding a tempestuous night, is afraid to meet the first rays of the sun, apprehending to mistake it for a flash of lightning. I still suspected that sweet enchanting scene to be only a deluding apparition, and constantly called my senses to an account. It was too romance-like and strange to press the terrestrial form of a departed spirit again to the heart. I had not been surprised when she was torn from me; but could not help wondering to see her restored to me by our enemies. Or had she, perhaps, effected her escape from the den of those tygers? And how was this possible?

No sooner did I begin to place again some confidence in my senses, than I entreated Elmira to unfold that mystery.

"The paleness of her countenance encreased, she looked fearful around, and encircled me with growing anxiety. "Don't let us talk of it now, dear Carlos!" she replied, in a trembling accent: "we are not a moment safe: let us flee, as far as you can, as soon as it is possible! As quickly as you can, if you love your wife. Alas! they will tear me again from your tender bosom!"

"I meditated a few moments. Amongst all my obligations to the confederates I could find none relating to that point: I first wanted a hint to that purpose, and resolved to await it, it being not improbable to me that Elmira had made her escape with their consent; and they could foresee that she would flee with me. Yet, I loved her so ardently, and with such an unspeakable tenderness, that I scarcely would have hesitated to run some risk for her. I, therefore, promised to make every preparation for a speedy flight; I endeavoured to speak comfort and peace to her boding mind; carried her to another bed-chamber, where I begged her to lay down, and to compose herself; and having secured the door and the windows, flung myself upon my couch greatly fatigued.—

"You have seen, dear Count, that my history, as yet, has been an almost uninterrupted train of misfortunes; but the period which I am now beginning opens new scenes of still greater horror, that will shock your feeling heart, and rendered me almost frantic; scenes in which I lost every thing dear to me, the sole object of all my hopes and wishes; in which my feelings were agonized in the highest degree; and which deprived me again, in the most horrid manner, of the only remaining consolation of my former misery. You will behold me the lamentable sport of the most enormous plans, and a victim to black despair.

"Having rested a few moments on my couch, my half open eyes beheld at once a lucidity resembling the saffron glimmer of the dawning morn. I took it, at first, for the blush of the rising sun, and shut my eyes again; but ere long, it grew so dazzling, that it made my eyes smart. I raised myself up, and saw the whole apartment illuminated. I could not discern whence the light came; the whole atmosphere of my chamber being inflamed. Little clouds of light floated in the air, moving to and fro'; and I beheld, with horror, streams of sparkling fire dart through the apartment. All objects around me were clad in variegated light. Low accents, like those produced by a stream of air touching the strings of a harp, vibrated in my ear; a whispering-like rustling of the wind between the young leaves mixed periodically with those mystic sounds. I also heard, at intervals, half suppressed groans, and yet could not see whence they proceeded. I pulled the bell to awaken my servants, but the string broke. I wanted to rush out of the bed, but was held down by an invisible power. I expected that a beneficial swoon would relieve me from those horrors; but my senses being already used to such apparitions, I was denied that melancholy comfort.

While I struggled in vain to disengage myself from the invisible bands that held me down, a thin vapour arose in the apartment, which having attained so much consistency as to overdarken all the objects around, began to form itself into a more distinct shape, and a white being emerged at length from its cloudy womb, darting with sparkling eyes towards my couch.

"Who art thou?" I exclaimed, with an accent of despair. "I am thy Genius, *Amanuel!*" that dreadful being replied, in a hollow, but melodious, strain. "I have been sent to warn thee not to elope with Elmira. Take my advice, for I love thee." "Who has sent you?" "The great confederation has confided thee to my care."

"I had many more questions to ask, and numberless more objections to start; but scarcely had I extended my arm to seize the phantom, when midnight darkness surrounded me at once. The silence of the grave reigned around me, no sound vibrated in my ear, and I beheld the objects around me in their natural form.

"I had not been reclining long on my couch, and was but too certain that I had not yet fallen asleep, and that, of course, that scene could not have been the illusion of a dream. I had been promised a genius, and his apparition was too convincing for me to have mistaken my mystic visitor for an imaginary phantom. He appeared to be a transparent airy being, and amicably inclined to me; my whole belief in the non-existence of spirits was, of course, violently shaken; and I cannot deny that I felt myself happy in my connexion with such a being. On getting up, I found my chamber door fastened on the inside; the windows were strongly barred, as I had left them in the evening; and the whole situation of the chamber rendered a secret communication impossible. Imposition was impracticable, and my reason urged me to believe in *Amanuel's* existence.

"My mind turned, at length, to the purport of his mission, and I repeated his dreadful words with an unspeakable agony. Then I shall resign Elmira to your power? ye incomprehensible *unknown!* She has already suffered too much on my account; and I could be unspeakably, and completely happy with her; I even could, on her bosom, revolve all the notions which you, as requisite for my happiness, excited in my mind. And should I not be happier, and more content, if I never had known you, or were to forget you for ever? I waste the bloom of my years, and the golden age of my life, in mystic presensions and arts, in order to understand and to assist you in directing the happiness of mankind after the lapse of many years. I anticipate, in the prime of life, the gravity and seriousness of hoary age, merely to seek after a felicity which perhaps never will bless me; sacrifice the enjoyment of the present moment to uncertain futurity; sow without knowing whether I ever shall be suffered to reap. How unfortunate, how lamentable is my lot! And do you offer me a compensation equivalent to the sacrifice you demand? How cruel, how incompassionate are you to me!

"I spent the whole night with conflicts of that nature, and was entirely exhausted, when the rosy blush of morn dawned in the east. I went early to Elmira: she also had been debarred from sleep by restless inquietude. We took a walk in the garden, equally restless. A secret visibility depressed the spirit of either; we felt mutually each other's reserve and anxiety, and were afraid to open our lips. I walked mute and gloomy by her side, sighing at every beautiful and secret spot where my fancy formerly had feasted my soul with her image; and when her supplicating eye begged me to disclose my sorrows, I felt myself incapable of realizing those scenes of imaginary pleasure.

"We returned to my apartment without having exchanged a word; but no sooner were we seated, than either hastened to interrogate. We preluded our conversation with fond endearments, and sealed the opening lips with kisses ere they could emit the half-formed words. "Elmira," I began at length, "I am very unfortunate! I cannot flee with you."—"Merciful God! Carlos," she inquired with terror, "why not?" I related the events of the night. She was almost petrified, but insisted upon our flight.

"Rather kill me, my husband, than leave me here. Why would you undo a wife that you have seduced to love you? that was so happy in the lap of her family before she knew you; that from love for you has risked every thing, and patiently suffered unutterable misery. By compassionate, dear Carlos, and kill me!"—

"No, you shall die with me, Elmira. But first let us try whether we can be happy. Tell me, what can I do?"

"Let us fly! This is the only means of insuring happiness. No roses can blossom for us here. Every other part of the globe will afford us more happiness; the farther we fly, the greater will our happiness be."

"But how can I escape those invisible hands that insnare me every where? how can I save my love from their powerful grasp? Put me in a way of doing it. You seem to harbour a secret, let me know it, to save you and your Carlos."

"No; let us save ourselves first: they would murder me in your arms. O! you will learn how cruelly they sport with your good, your noble heart; how enormous and unheard-of is the deceit which is practised upon you; how they endeavour to seduce you, under the mask of friendship, to the most heinous villanies, to the blackest crimes. All the sublime ideas which have been held out to your noble, generous mind, concentrate in one point of the most atrocious wickedness. I have accidentally discovered the whole mystery: I was doomed to die, but I eluded their cunning; and now throw myself in your arms. Have pity on a hapless being!"

"I am astonished! Elmira. Should it be true what I ominated? Should they heedlessly have dropt that hint which I happened to catch in their society?"

"You are certainly not mistaken, Carlos. I know how they abused your heart, and how cruelly they have seduced you. I was forced to witness your faithlessness in Rosalia's arms; I was to be an accomplice in the conspiracy against you. But what rustles yonder, Carlos: did you hear nothing?"—"It is nothing, Elmira. Your imagination deceives you." "Indeed, I heard something, dear Carlos. Take me in your arms; let me die on your bosom."

"There certainly rustled something behind the mirror; however,

I pretended not to have heard it, took her by the hand, prostrated myself before her, and did every thing I could to make her easy. But nothing could dispel her terror. I lavished numberless caresses, intreated her to fear nothing, and even shed tears to prevail upon her to stay at my castle: but I grew weaker every moment; and as soon as she perceived that my firmness gave way, she redoubled her anxious and tender efforts to persuade me to flight; and at length extorted the promise to elope with her to a distant country. In order to protect her at least against open attacks during the short time that was required for the preparation for our departure, I desired two of my most faithful servants to stay with her while I arranged every thing for a speedy flight. Nothing seemed to impede my journey; no obstacle, no hindrance came in my way; every thing was favourable to me. I scorned already the impotence of the Spirit, who, as I imagined, would apply every means of opposing the preparations for my departure. But I was mistaken; the Spirit suffered me to get every thing ready. The night which was fixed for our flight approached very fast. We intended to fly to France, where I hoped to find with Elmira the happiness two congenial souls may expect. I flattered myself to be able to forget in that country the tender objects that made Spain dear to me, and to find a new home. Elmira took a lively share in the hopes that animated me, and we anticipated already so much of our expected happiness, that little would have been left for futurity to add. The mules were already harnessed, the coach was ready, the servants were waiting for my commands, and I went with a loving heart to fetch Elmira. It was already dark; she had two candles burning in her apartment, and sat on the sofa to adjust her travelling dress. She was so cheerful, that we began to joke, and to exchange a thousand little sallies. She had just done dressing, and was on the point to follow me down stairs, when she suddenly started up, overspread with death-like paleness, and said, "Dear Carlos! I hear certainly some noise yonder," pointing at a chandelier that was suspended to the ceiling.

"Yes, I hear the mules kick. Come, let us be gone."

"No, no; I heard something very clearly, just over our head."

"Well, let us quit this inchanted room."

"I took her round the waist, to make her go out of the room, when a pane in the window was shattered to pieces, and fell into the room. The same happened with several more. A loud hissing gushed through the apertures like the whistling of a strong wind. The two candles were extinguished with a loud report. A fire ball flew down to light them again; the doors burst suddenly open, and were shut again. An invisible being ambled through the apartment, and an ice-cold blast of air blew in our face, being succeeded by a burning hot stream, that almost suffocated us. Elmira lay fainting in my arms; however, I had sufficient strength left to carry her to the door. Despair made me furious, and I awaited anxiously Amanuel's arrival to wrestle with him. I could not open the door, and called for help through the window, when it suddenly burst open. I hastened with my precious burden out of the apartment; an uninterrupted hissing and whistling pursued us; the whole apartment was in an uproar, the chandelier fell upon the floor; all the furniture was scattered about with a hideous noise; the whole house seemed to be in a blaze. A tremendous noise arose behind us, pursuing us through all the apartments to the door of the carriage. But I shut my ears and eyes, and held my wife fast in my arms.

"No sooner were we seated in the carriage, than the whole castle seemed to be turned upside down. All the windows were illuminated at once, the doors opened and shut again with a tremendous noise, and large stones were rolled down from the roof of the house. My servants looked at each other pale and seized with terror. They mounted their horses with anxious haste, and even the mules were impatient to leave the inchanted place.

"We soon reached a little wood, and our beasts relaxed from their furious race. At once the carriage stopped, the window was shattered to pieces, and a masked person shot Elmira in my arms.———

"Thus far I had wrote when the Count returned from town, dissatisfied with his affairs, and angry with me, because he had not received a line from me for a long time. I assured him that I had wrote to him several times, and scolded him in my turn. Our letters had been intercepted.

"We re-commenced our former course of life, and were mutually happy in each others society. He did not mention the latter part of his adventures, and I told him that I was writing for him. This made him cheerful; and he frequently repeated, "this will make us understand one another."

"The diversions in which our neighbours involved us, did, however, not allow me to write much; and the subsequent part of my history, to the period when I came to a mutually dangerous explanation with the Count, is the fruit of those hours in which I could steal from his company, the produce of many a night, and of many solitary meditations.

"One day I had been confined to my apartment by a slight indisposition, when the Count returned cheerful from a ball in the neighborhood. "I have got acquainted with a man," he exclaimed, on entering my bed-chamber to wish me a good night, "with a man whom very few resemble, you and myself excepted."—

"The Count was not used to praise too precipitately; my curiosity was therefore excited to a high degree.

"Whence does he come? How does he look?—What did he say?"—I inquired, with impatient eagerness.

"Dear Marquis, what an inquirer you are! He has settled in the neighborhood, and seems to wish being more intimately connected with me. This is the most important point I know of him." "That is certainly sufficient for you; but will you not make me also a little more acquainted with him? How did he look." "His face is rather oval; he has a beautiful pair of black eyes, full lips——"

"Dear S****** this description is very unsatisfactory. Did you not perceive something characteristical, no striking defects? He must certainly have some, and I am very jealous of your partiality, dear Count." "Indeed, I believe he has. A little red scar over his left eye-brow; a little red wart upon his left cheek; and, if I am not mistaken, one of his eyes is black, and the other rather blue. Don't you think, Marquis, that this is a most charming picture? But you don't laugh?—Gracious Heaven! you grow paler and paler!" "Need I not to grow pale? Your description completely suits James's countenance."

END OF THE FIRST VOLUME.

THE

HORRID MYSTERIES.

CHAPTER I.

No one can conceive what sensations agitated me in that moment of horror, when Elmira, my dear, adored wife, lay bleeding in my arms. I saw her angelic soul take its flight amid dreadful convulsions; her heart palpitated fainter and fainter beneath my hand, and, at length, ceased to beat at all. Her lips closed for ever without being able to utter a last farewell. However, I clearly perceived what legacy she wanted to leave me. I still flattered myself that the whole was nothing but a deluding, horrid dream. I had recovered my Elmira in such a romantic manner, and lost her again under such shocking circumstances, that I fancied it was impossible the whole could be any thing more than an illusion of my imagination. I struggled violently to shake off that sensation, but always relapsed again into a state of agonizing incertitude.

"Thus late I was made dreadfully certain that Elmira really was dead. Her blood streamed down my hands; and, on removing her veil, her countenance was entirely disfigured; her features were totally undiscernible; not one trace of her former beauty was left; the loveliest eye was shut by the icy hand of death; not one sigh heaved her bosom; and she rather resembled a marble statue than a corpse. How can I unfold the sensations that thrilled my heart in that moment of agony? I felt no pain, but a burning pressure in my breathless bosom; my tongue began, as it were, to thirst for blood; and her departed spirit appeared to me not to demand tears, but vengeance.

"A mist was, in that moment, removed from my eyes. The whole mystery began to clear up, and all the clouds that had obscured my looks were dispelled. Never had I felt myself so much the sport of those *unknown*, so much their cruelly abused slave. How could they usurp the authority of dictating to my sentiments; and was I to implore, with abject servility, their permission before I could enjoy one happy moment? Life now became indifferent to me. I had vowed to my wife, in the first delicious moments of our connection, not to let her quit the world without me. When she was torn from me the first time, my weakness had absolved me from the performance of that promise. I now was doubly bound to go to my eternal rest; but I vowed to her departed spirit not to die alone.

"This train of ideas was the work of a few moments. A sense of vengeance now was interwoven with my whole existence: the last idea of my bleeding brain, the last drop of blood, streaming from the stiffening heart, would have been animated by that powerful sensation: and in the present hour, in which I am unfolding to you, dearest Count, those dreadful mysteries, I can boldly say, that I have faithfully observed that vow, that I never lost sight of it, that I revolved it in my mind under every pressure of circumstances, and even in the most dangerous situations of my life.

"I mused a moment. My servants leaped from the coach-box: those that had preceded us on horse-back were recalled; the assassin was pursued; my valet fired his pistol at him, and he fell. We hastened to the spot where he lay extended; but he died in the moment of our coming up with him. We tore the mask from his face; I did not know it; however, the mask was dreadfully contorted, like those of your leaders in the garden of which you have given me a description.

"I now removed Elmira's corpse to a corner of the coach, and left it, to examine the body of the assassin. My servants having expected to see me agitated by the most violent eruptions of agony and fury, were amazed at the coolness with which I met them. We had exchanged persons. They burst the coach door open, being impatient to see their beloved mistress once more, to kiss her clay cold hand, and to moisten it with their tears. Happy was he that could catch a few drops of her blood, they were circulated like relics: tears and loud groans were the sole tokens of their affection, and they could not think that it was possible they should have been separated from her so soon. This was the highest triumph of innate goodness and of magnanimity. Elmira had conquered their hearts by her charms; but her immaculate virtue, her gentleness of mind, had insured her conquests.

"I stared with wild looks at that affecting scene; and, after a pause of silent agony, avocated them from their adoration, ordering them to search the murderer. Yet nothing was found upon the villain. The plan of the vengeance I was determined to take was already fixed; and I only wanted the least trace to lead me nearer the mark. Yet all our searches were fruitless; and the progress of time only made me acquainted with the sole way which could lead me to the wished-for scope, and just when I was incapable of pursuing it.

We returned to the castle, and Elmira's corpse was carried to her apartment. Having bolted the door, I undressed her myself, and examined her wounds, to convince myself that she was really dead. Nothing was more certain. Two balls had shattered her breast; a third had lacerated her neck: the blood was congealed, and all her limbs were stiff. I now called her woman, ordering her to undress her entirely, taking her garments with me into my apartment, to examine these more carefully. On turning one of her pockets, a little pocket book dropt on the floor. It was tied with a pink-coloured ribbon, and seemed to be quite new. I tore it open; but it contained nothing, except that note which Elmira had lost at church in my presence, and a packet of papers, that promised to be of the greatest importance to me. Being not at leisure to read them, I put them into a secret drawer of my bureau, which I had made myself, tied the pocket-book again, and replaced it into the pocket from which it had dropt.

"Mean-time repeated attempts had been made to recal Elmira to life; but without effect. The beautifullest form bade defiance to all chirurgical skill. I ordered her to be dressed, and kept above ground three days. I had already once experienced the artifices of the confederation in that respect, and was determined not to neglect the least trifle that could prevent their imposing on me a second time. I made a secret mark on the corpse, and looked every hour at it, lest it should be exchanged. She was so much disfigured, even in her face, by the shot and the powder, that her features bore not the least resemblance to her countenance when alive, and that it consequently would have been easy to substitute another body. Yet a scar, which I never had observed, appeared on her forehead, and it was impossible that mark could be imitated.

"I ordered, for the sake of greater security, several people from my estate, on whose fidelity I could depend, to watch the corpse day and night. After three days, the highest marks of corruption appeared; her coffin was screwed up in my presence, sealed with my family seal, which I always carry about me: no pains were spared to prevent all deception, and I was present when she was intombed in my family vault.

"As soon as I returned from the burial, subdued the agony of an eternal separation, and wiped off a burning reluctant tear, I hastened to my bureau. To take out the papers, to break the seal, and to scatter every thing on the floor, in the hurry of impatience, was the work of one moment. A number of single leaves dropt on the floor. They were not numbered, and it required a long time to arrange them a little. They were, besides, very negligently written, and contained nothing but family accounts. Having run them over, I tied them carefully up, and put them again into my bureau.

"Night stole upon me during these occupations, and I expected to receive a visit from my genius. I ordered lights to be carried to a remote pleasure-house in my garden, to allure him thither, and armed myself with a brace of pistols, with two poniards, and a sword whose goodness I had had several opportunities to try. All preparations were made to give him a warm reception. My fury almost had bereft me of the use of my senses, and yet I waited coolly and patiently for him all the night long; but Amanuel did not appear.

"I waited three nights more for him in my bed-room, leaving the bed empty, and concealing myself in a closet. The fury that rankled in my breast left me not a moment's rest; I watched every motion: the least breeze of air, the least cracking in the wood, made me grasp my poniard. O! I would have given ten years of my life for every moment in which I could have met Amanuel face to face.

"Yet all my diligent care not to miss the propitious moment of bloody revenge was fruitless; and, after having tried every means human prudence could devise to find out a single trace of those unknown friends,* I took the desperate resolution to explore alone

---

* Probably an error for "fiends." [Publisher's note.]

the inmost centre of that horrid web of infernal villainy, to cut the nerves of their motions asunder, and either to find a new existence in their ruin, or to sacrifice my life in the attempt.

"Several weeks elapsed amid the necessary preparations, and the expectation of, perhaps, more distinct elucidations. My resolution was too cool, too fixed, for any difficulties to have shaken. So I thought, at least, at that time. I considered myself as a dying man; I left some dear friends behind me, who had a claim to my consideration, placed my last will into their custody, and, while I prepared myself to bid the world an eternal adieu, my heart became easier, and I imagined to be advanced nearer to the mark of my designs. I committed the management of my estates to Don Antonio, under the pretence of a journey: every thing was in readiness, and I had already concealed a good quantity of poison in the lining of my coat, in order to deprive the confederates, if they should get me in their power alive, of the pleasure of letting me suffer a lingering death; and I only had to fix the hour for my departure, when I was informed that Don Pedro had returned without his lady.

"I was told that he had disgraced himself, in the first hour after his arrival, by the most cruel treatment of one of his servants; that his whole conduct was entirely changed; and every vestige of that benevolence which formerly had gained him the love of all his people, for whose happiness or sorrow he now displayed not the least care, had totally disappeared. I found this report confirmed on the first visit he paid me. He treated me with extreme coldness; however, I returned it with interest. Neither of us was inclined to understand the other; and he sat frequently for whole hours by my side, silent and in a state of apathy, supporting his head with one hand, and moving the other convulsively. I had great reason to be angry with him; but that gloomy, melancholy air, rather gave him an appearance of guiltlessness, and I would not condemn him unheard; yet I durst not trust him in the least; and a personal heat against himself would only have served to betray my plan against the confederation.

"My suspicion was encreased by his changing, unsettled deportment, and the uneasiness he betrayed in our conversations. He grew instantly silent and mute, when I alluded even in the most distant manner to Francisca's probable fate; a shrug of his shoulder, and some significant looks, being the only answer he returned. But he behaved in a different manner when he succeeded to turn our conversation upon the unknown confederates. His whole countenance used then to brighten up; he seemed inly to rejoice at his cunning, wanted to be informed of every thing, dissembled to be interested by every word, and used numberless artful turnings and crooked windings to explore my sentiments and designs. However, I opposed to all his inquiries an unshaken equanimity, a semblance of the most placid resignation to the plans of the confederation, and the oath I had taken to be least communicative and open to my most intimate friends. I frequently contradicted my own opinions; and he was every day more at a loss concerning my real sentiments.

"You are not consistent with yourself, dear Carlos," he said one day; "let us speak more plainly of it. There is nothing in the world so obscure that a friend who is acquainted with the state of our mind could not clear up!"

"Are you really so intimate with the state of my mind? If so, then you will certainly know that I am more consistent with myself than it seems?"

"How do you mean that?" he exclaimed, with evident marks of impatient curiosity.

"I think that there cannot exist a greater self-consistency than to submit quietly to one's fate, to suffer every thing with patience, and even not to murmur. You behold me in that very predicament, Don Pedro. A wife that I adore is restored to me, and I lose her for ever, while I imagine to insure the eternal possession of her. But what can I do? I am easy and chearful nevertheless."

"There you have hit me, Don Carlos; yet you are mistaken, if you think me to be in the same predicament with you. I must confess the confederacy has reason to congratulate itself. Who should have dreamed that the Marquis of G****** would be so content with his slavery!"

"Not slavery, dear Pedro; all is voluntary. Shall I recal to your memory your own words, which you have related to me on an occasion, that has imprinted them deeply on my mind? 'All appearances point at a deep-layed, powerful, and extensive plan of those men: who can expect to unfold the views of that confederacy at *first sight?*' I have been made sensible of this truth, and purchased that sensation with many precious moments; I have boldly exchanged many cheerful prospects of my life for it."

"But Elmira————"

"Her loss was, indeed, a dreadful blow. My soul lost, as in a high fever, all recollection of the time past. But do you see, dear Pedro, I have consoled and cheered myself with your own words? 'Every thing in nature (you told me on that very occasion) presses and urges the other; a new life originates from every death. Providence being entirely taken up by the great plan of promoting the greater perfection of man, does not care for the changes that take place in the creation. It knows how to direct every thing to one great end, and unfolds the last dying point of life for new plans and designs!' And who can have learnt this more palpably than myself?"

"Very true, Don Carlos. But who can presume to comprehend you? You loved Elmira so ardently, all your prospects seemed to be concentrated so much in the possession of her, that one would have sworn the second loss of your idol would distract you, and render life burthensome to you; and now you are so completely a philosopher!"————

"Necessity has made me so; and, dear Pedro, you cannot but confess that this policy, abstracted from experience, of whatever nature it be, is always better than that one mechanically has got by heart, and repeats after rule and measure, like a parrot. Don't you think so, dearest friend?" So saying, I took hold of his hand, shaking it, and looking smiling in his face. This was indeed very imprudent. He was quite confounded, and attempted several times to return that look, but in vain; his eye remained anxiously fixed to the ground. More than half an hour was required to rouse him from a senseless musing, in which he instantly relapsed. I could easily observe that he apprehended I had penetrated deeper into the recesses of his soul than he could wish; however, he was too much occupied with the elucidation of that idea, than to light upon the notion which on my part was necessarily connected with it.

CHAPTER II.

Some days elapsed, and several little incidents led me to observe that the secret agents of the conspiracy began again to render my abode rather unsafe. It appeared to me to be high time to depart. Don Antonio was already arrived at the castle; he was still the same faithful and cordial friend he ever had proved to me; continued to take the warmest interest in my happiness, and to be sincerely concerned for the peace of my mind. The next night was to be the last which perhaps I ever should spend at my castle. Heavens! with what sensations did I see the sky assume a deeper hue; every breeze from my cheerful heavenly gardens was impregnated with secret horrors; and the mild radiance with which the twinkling stars emerged on the dark blue canopy of heaven, straitened my heart in as melancholy a manner, as if the fate of a whole world had depended on my miserable existence. I visited every secret recess of my park once more, took a tender farewell of every bower, and mixed my tears with the tinkling rivulet. Every object seemed to oppose my departure: however, my resolution was too firm to suffer me to yield to my sentiments.

"Very fortunately for myself, and my situation of mind, the whole scene changed against night. A portending tempest overdarkened the horizon; the stars disappeared one after another; the feathered songsters concealed themselves anxiously in the most secret recesses of the park; a sultry, awful stillness swayed over the whole creation; not the least sound interrupted the solemn silence; the pulses of nature seemed to have ceased to palpitate. The solitary chirping of the cricket was the sole sound that by intervals interrupted the universal grave-like stillness, which at length was rendered more awful by the distant rolling of thunder.

"This was a propitious moment for me. Midnight was arrived, and every eye in the castle was closed by the leaden wand of sleep. I fetched the key of the garden-gate, and stole softly down stairs, climbed over a wall into the stable-yard, and began to saddle my fleetest horse. While I was occupied thus, I felt something between my feet. It was *Kusko*, my favourite dog. He had lain in the stable; and having been attracted by the scent, came to caress me; he rejoiced to see his master, bounded against my breast, and howled for joy. Alas! poor Kusko seemed to feel that he should soon be parted from his master. I could not take him with me without betraying myself. An hundred times did I clasp the faithful creature in my arms, and let him lick my tears. I had borne every thing else with coolness, even when I embraced my dear Antonio the last time; but this fare-well scene affected my heart with melancholy sensations. He certainly was sensible of my grief, hanging his head, and whining in low and mournful accents. Alas! he was perhaps the only friend I left behind. However, the affectionate lamentations roused the other dogs in the court-yard, and it was high time for me to be gone. I strained him once more to my bosom, exclaiming, "Good Kusko, thou wilt not forget thy hapless master!" I then locked him up, and shut my ears against his anxious scratching at the door, opening a little back-gate, mounted my horse, and pursued a well known path that led through a chesnut grove.

"The tempest had, mean-time, grown more violent: the night was dark, the lightning flashed in vivid colours, and the thunder rolled in awful majesty. I set spurs to my horse, braving the fury of the hurricane, and the pouring torrents of rain which threatened to drown us; but our strength was soon exhausted; my poor beast began to groan and to puff; I scarcely could resist the violence of the wind any longer, and unfortunately had lost my way. I rode slower, but my horse stumbled every moment over the protending roots of trees, or fell in holes: I found myself every minute entangled in the underwood, or impeded by a branch. If the flashes of lightning had not made me perceive the neighbouring river, I should, with-out doubt, have perished in the Tago; as I certainly should have been prevented by the incessant rolling of thunder from hearing the wild bellowing of the waves. I was, at length, obliged to alight, being unable to proceed farther. I beheld a large cavity in the earth, within a small distance, which promising to afford me some shelter, I resolved to creep into it. My horse, being equally unable to stand the inclemency of the weather any longer, followed me by instinct, and we shared amicably our sorry asylum. He always trembled vio-lently when the lightning flashed through the trees, and pressed closer towards me. No one can conceive what I felt; all nature seemed to be convulsed, and quickly ripening for dissolution.

"The tempest was now over my head; the horizon resembled a billowing ocean of liquid fire, and flaming clouds poured down amid the howling of the hurricane and the cracking of shattered trees. No human ear has ever heard a noise like that which the roaring thunder produced betwixt the neighbouring mountains. Every object around me was violently agitated; and no other choice seemed to be left me, than either to be struck dead by the lightning, or buried beneath the ruins of the shaking cave. The cold of the water benumbed my limbs, and ere long I was unable to hold the bridle.

"What person in my situation would not have repented my mad resolution? However, the commotions and all the horrors of warring nature were nothing, if compared with the torments inflicted by those dreadful *unknown*, who, being acquainted with the most secret recesses of the human heart, knew how to agonize its tenderest fibres, and how to lacerate its most sensible parts. This reflection fired my enthusiasm to the highest degree. Every resistance served only to animate me with redoubled ardour, and a conquered obstacle was my sweetest reward. I looked with rapture at the flaming sky, as if going to collect all the lightnings of heaven to hurl them into that infernal den; I stole the most horrid sounds from nature to appal with them the assassins of my wife; I could have gathered all the torrents of the clouds to deluge those infernal fiends. Thus my fancy was at work even in the most agonizing moments of my life; following only *one* strong current in a great ocean of images, and counting even minutely the drops which fate and chance mix with them.

"The war of the agitated elements ceased at length. When the blush of the dawning morn smiled in the east, not a trace was left of the devastations of the night, except the shattered fragments of some trees turned up by the hurricane, or shivered by the lightning, and the swelling of the water. The air was as pure as if the young creation had just emerged from its maker's hand: the serenity, the sweet smile of appeased nature invited to ardent love; the reconciled creation now appeared in the highest virgin charms, after having been deprived for a short time of its inchanting beauty. The azure mirrour of the smooth waves reflected the verdant verdure of the trees, and only the middle of the river exhibited a curling milky trait. The breath of the rosy morn was embalmed with the sweet invigorating exhalations of millions of little flowers, embroidered with pearly drops; the mystic rustling of the leaves seemed to hale the rising king of day, and showered with every breeze sparkling pearls on the swelling turf. The winged choristers began to chirp their sweet, melodious matins, rejoicing that the horrors of the night were past. All nature was clad in the gayest livery of mirth, and animated with new life. No sooner had I emerged from the wood over a ridge of hills which bounded it, than I was haled by a new charming picture. The heavenly valley of *Placentia*, infolded by the flowery banks of the Tago, smiled at me: on the other side of the river, *Talavera* attracted my delighted looks; and at the left *Oropesa* emerged, surrounded by numberless detached houses and luxuriant villages; a smiling, unspeakably charming landscape, resembling Eden's happy plains.

"The fertility of the exuberant soil was not only cultivated, but also improved and beautified; a phenomenon which one but rarely meets with in *Spain*. A picturesque mixture of vineyards and nodding cornfields leaned in gentle declensions downward to the banks of the Tago; little cottages peeped gaily though the rich clusters of fruit-trees, and the bluish mirrour of the river reflected the blushes of the rising sun through the high grass and luxuriant meadows.

"Nothing interrupted the pleasing exstasy of my enraptured senses. The first village which I arrived at was already in a lively bustle. The inhabitants looked out of their windows, and returned my salutations so cheerful and gay, as if they had already expected me some time. As I approached nearer towards *Talavera*, the road grew more and more populous; whole troops of neatly dressed peasantry joined me by degrees, and, in a short time, composed a large procession, in the middle of which I proceeded on horseback, ridiculed by the merry swains for my woe-worn countenance. At first they were rather reserved, not knowing how to address me properly; but as soon as I had accosted them, a general joy pervaded the whole cavalcade. They informed me, amid the laughter of merriment, that an excellent fair was held at *Oropesa*, and that they intended to celebrate it in cheerfulness and jocundity, because they loved to do honour to that festive occasion. We grew at length so sociable, that they began to dispute whose guest I should be at the next alehouse.

"We stopped at several places on the road, and met every where with prosperity, innocence, and hospitality. That happy valley seemed to be entirely cut off from the rest of the country, and to be possessed of innate treasures. The innocent hilarity of its inhabitants, the neat and simple elegance, and the playsome gaiety of the tawney girls, their lively loquacity, their little caresses and endearments, made my heart heavier with every step. "How happy, (I exclaimed repeatedly,) how happy should I be if I could live amongst you!"

"Pray, dear Sir, do settle in our village," a young, robust peasant, who walked hand in hand with his cheerful consort, replied: "follow my example, and choose a wife amongst our girls; no one will refuse your hand." "But you don't consider, my friend, that I should not be able to work as hard as you: who would assist me?"—

"We all, dear Sir, if you will stay with us. We have not been long acquainted with you, yet I am sure you are a good man, and we love you already. We compose but one family, and would gladly receive you too in its lap. Is it not so, my dear friends?"—The whole troop replied, with the most amiable good-nature and openness, "Certainly!"

"And thou, little enchantress yonder," he continued, "that looks so slily at us, would you hesitate to take this gentleman for a husband?"

Her countenance was overspread with the virgin crimson of modesty. "Don't be a child, Clara," he resumed: "come, give me your hand. She is my wife's sister, dear Sir: you see she is a pretty little rogue; and, notwithstanding her levity and humoursome pranks, a very good-natured, honest and endearing girl. What! you cast your looks down? Have I perhaps said too much in your praise?" Clara, casting a most bewitching leer at him, said to me; "Don't believe him, Sir: I am good for nothing. Yet—if you will run the risk with me—I don't dislike you."

"Sweet creature!" I replied, "how sorry am I not to be able to accept of that happiness at present! I have a father and a mother, a proud family, and, alas! am of noble birth."

"So am I, Sir," said the peasant; "and it is a question which of our families is the most noble. Have you ever heard of Count O******?" he whispered in my ear.

"Gracious Heaven! are you Count O******, who eloped with a young lady, and afterwards ————"

"How! Sir, you know my history?—Pray, who are you?" I whispered my name in his ear. He looked at me with astonishment, checked his pace, and viewed me with scrutinizing looks from head to foot. Having gazed at me a while, he turned to his company, and said, "Children, I recollect just now to have left something at the last public house; proceed on your way, I shall soon be with you again." His companions asked him what it was, and every one begged to be suffered to fetch it: however, he whispered in my ear, "Don Carlos, you are an honest man; but I must see you no more;" and left us abruptly.

"Every one was astonished to see the peasant turn back; the whole society was vexed at it; yet I was surprised to see that they were more and more reconciled to his sudden departure, the longer he staid away; and while they agreed that he would not return, the former cheerfulness began again to enliven the whole troop. "He has sometimes strange whims," one of the company said; "it is a pity that such a good man is so melancholy." No one could conceive what was the reason of his gloominess, as he had fertile fields, a house, a good wife, and children.

"Yet his consort, who could not conceal her noble extraction, and her genteel education, was far from being pleased with the arguments of her companions. Being, probably, conscious that her husband did not indulge such singular humours without reason, she was extremely terrified by his sudden departure. She gazed at me with melancholy looks, as if apprehending that I should disturb her present happiness. Clara too took a very lively share in that incident. I was utterly confounded, and did not know how to behave in that dilemma.

"Perceiving that the lady seemed to be inclined to speak in private with me, I separated imperceptibly from the company to give her an opportunity of doing it. She guessed the motive of my loitering behind, and stopping under some pretext, approached me. It is impossible to describe the affecting perplexity in which she was.

She seemed to cast, with weeping, mournful eyes, a look into futurity, on which her whole present happiness suddenly threatened to be wrecked. Before she could disclose her mind to me, I endeavoured to display, in my looks and air, that sympathising interest which my heart really took in her deplorable fate, and let her read in my eyes all the consolation that could afford her comfort in her affliction.

"Alas! dear Sir!" she began, with a deep sigh, "we are very unfortunate."

"Indeed, charming Countess," I replied, astonished at that preamble, "I am sensibly interested in your misfortunes."

"I see, Sennor, my consort has been so imprudent as to disclose our rank to you; yet I am not uneasy about it; as I do not doubt for a moment that you are a man of honour. But why did he leave us so abruptly?—Why does he not return?—I know him; he was violently affected."

"You need, indeed, not to suspect me of want of generosity, and may count on my sincere friendship for you. I consider the knowledge of your rank as a secret which I ought to hold sacred. I shall bury it in my heart, Sennora."

"I am satisfied with your promise."

"As for the sudden departure of your lord, I am in a greater incertitude than you can be. I only can faintly guess at the reason of it. You know, probably, the rumour that was circulated about your marriage. Count O****** married against the will of a confederacy of certain unknown persons."

"I am astonished, Sennor!"——

"Don't be astonished, Madonna—I also am connected with those Unknown."

"Merciful God! woe unto us!"

"What are you afraid of, my lady? did you not hear that I said, I also am connected with them. That relation was perhaps far more painful to me than yours. I have been more dreadfully abused than you. I even am deprived of those means of saving myself from misery that were left to you. Do you comprehend me now?

"Perfectly."—

"I received very plain hints concerning that point; they acquainted me with *your* history, perhaps with exaggerated circumstances; which, however, is perhaps dreadful enough without these additions. Who has a greater right of being interested in it than myself, whom it so nearly concerns?"

"I said just now, Sennor, woe unto us that we have met you. I now recall my words, and say, how fortunate are we!"

"I soon perceived that I had hurt myself very much. She grew visibly more reserved, and I could not prevail upon her to unfold to me the mystery of her history. If, on the contrary, I had availed myself of the dubious moment of her terror, I might probably have learned her story; whereas she now appeared to have suddenly forgot every part of her fate that could have interested me. She evaded, with an admirable dexterity, every captious and tempting question I put to her, and turned my own arms upon me. Her eyes only spoke, perhaps, more than they ought to have done.

"In this state of mind we arrived at length at *Oropesa*. The fair was large, and crowded with people. All the neighbouring villages seemed to have depopulated themselves to render it splendid. A merry, variegated mixture of characters and dresses afforded me sufficient room for observation. This motly crowd amused me for some time; the bustle of the multitude hurried me from one diversion to the other: now I stood before a booth of jugglers, in the midst of wondering gapers, and now involuntarily was entangled in a bachantic dance. An inexhaustible diversity of new objects, the clamour and the noise of the joyous populace, quarrels and blows, scolding and bursts of laughter; all this composed a medly that would have amused a novice in such scenes a considerable time.

"Having diverted myself for some hours, I stopt at a ring which a number of peasants had formed round a dancing dog, when suddenly some person tapt me on the shoulder, exclaiming, "How do you do, Marquis?" Turning round, I beheld a stranger, whose face I could not recollect ever to have seen. "You are certainly mistaken in the person, my friend," said I, startled at that unwelcome address. "I beg your pardon, my Lord," resumed the stranger; "I know you too well; you are Don Carlos, Marquis of G******. All eyes seemed, in that moment, fixed on me. I was almost petrified, and a chilly tremor seized me, when I fancied to have seen that face, and the countenance of the two companions of the stranger who mean time had joined him, at the mystic castle in the forest. I rushed almost senseless through the gaping multitude, mounted my horse, and galloped away at a furious rate.

"Hapless Carlos," groaned I within myself, "there is not one spot on earth where thou canst find an asylum; no place where thou art not surrounded by the myrmidons of those fiend-like *Unknown*. Their snares are spread every where. Alas! what will be thy fate, if they get thee in their power. What new torments will they invent to punish thy disobedience! What new wiles will they devise to entrap thee in thy own perfidy, and to delude thee by thy own madness! Thou wilt catch a phantom of thy own fancy, when thinking to be near the butt of thy pursuit, and the laboursome structure of thy presumptuous wit will miserably sink down into its own pit.

"And what will it avail to have recourse to force? Two weak arms, of an unnerved body, against a thousand vigorous men; one poniard against a thousand swords; and one solitary brain against the artful shiftings and turning of a numerous set of cunning deceivers? It is true, thou art provided with poison, and couldst shorten thy torments; but what remedy hast thou against their pity, against their silent contempt, if they should catch thee in thy own snares, and generously release thee again to convince thee of thy pitiful impotence? This would be more tormenting than the agonies of a lingering death! It certainly would be wiser to contrive means of escaping their powerful grasp, than to wander from place to place in search of them, guided by nothing but an obscure presension."

CHAPTER III.

Amid a melancholy and irresolute soliloquy I reached a forest at the borders of the valley of *Placentia*. Being used to meet in every dark wood with a scene of strange adventures and incidents, I prepared myself with tranquillity for the worst. My imagination was at such a romantic and turbulent stretch, that it always anticipated dreadful events with anxious rapture. Every vestige of ancient times filled it with ominous images; I mistook every cavity in the ground for an entrance of a horrid cavern; and every uncommon mark cut in the trunk of a tree was suspected by my harrowed fancy of some mystic meaning. I met a traveller in the gloom of the forest. He was

a man of common appearance, and his address was equally insignificant. Merely the want of society seemed to prompt him to accost
me; and a secret impulse to court the assistance of men against
design and chance, that haunted me every where, made me willing to receive his addresses with kindness. The cause of our keeping company was also the theme of our conversation. The forest,
danger, apprehensions, adventures, and conjectures, were the chief
subjects of our discourse.

Our conversation turned, at length, on the proprietor of the tract
of country to which the forest belonged, and a spirit of communicativeness seemed to have seized him on a sudden: he introduced, in a
simple, natural manner, a number of strange events, and seemed to
become more inexhaustible the longer he enlarged on those topics.
The proprietor was a widow; her husband had suddenly disappeared; and she seemed to be ignorant of what was become of him;
having, at least, spared neither time nor pains to find him out. All
her searches having at length proved abortive, she had retired from
the world, to spend the rest of her days in solitude. It appeared, by
the narrative of the stranger, that she was an enthusiast; yet the
extravagancies of her imagination were so amiable and gentle, that
Heaven seemed to have sent them to make her forget the sorrows
of her afflicted heart, and to reconcile her to her lamentable fate.

"Evening had set in; no inn was to be found within several
leagues, and the lady received every traveller with kindness and
hospitality. The stranger assured me that her hospitable disposition
extended to all ranks, and I had just reason to hope that I should
remain unknown beneath her roof. Her voluntary seclusion from
the world, her melancholy, which seemed to guide almost all her
actions, the mysteriousness of her history, and particularly the
sudden and unaccountable disappearance of her lord, had pre-
occupied me in her favour. In the painful incertitude in which I was,
the society of every human being would have been agreeable to
me, how much more the meeting with a being that, expelled from
the world by events similar to mine, perhaps by the same fiends that
had ruined me, had already executed the resolution to which my
state of mind, and the dangers of my situation, were just going to
impel me!

"We now came to a bye road, which led to the village where

my companion resided, and that, as he informed me, was several leagues distant. My horse was almost knocked up; I myself was tired, and impelled by curiosity; which determined me to proceed to the castle. My fellow traveller assured me I could not miss it: twilight was yet faintly struggling with the setting sun; why should I, therefore, hesitate to direct my course to the hospitable abode of the unknown recluse?

"I had not long separated from my companion, when I beheld the turrets of a large building emerging from the misty vapours that began to rise. I had expected only a simple, unadorned edifice, and was struck with an agreeable astonishment, to see a majestic fabric hailing my gazing looks through the dusk of eve. It seemed not to be a residence of tranquillity and rusticated retirement, but the abode of a man of the world, who seemed to revigorate his relaxed senses by the change of the luxuries of a rural life.

"The avenue to this elegant fabric led through a garden, which embroidered it with a variegated verdure. It seemed not to be laid out after a regular plan, the most perfect art being concealed behind the charming veil of simplicity; yet an internal sense impelled me to admire the elegant taste which had guided the forming hand of nature. The soft, pellucid verdure of the vine, blended with purple clusters, blushing through the leaves, mixed itself so artfully with the darker green of the luxuriant turf; the variegated leaves of the trees exhibited such a pleasing contrast; the colours of the objects were so strikingly, and in such an enchanting manner combined or separated, that it was impossible to overlook the spirit of elegance and taste that had regulated the whole, and prevailed in every part of the *tout ensemble*. I was animated with a secret pleasure at the internal sense that told me I should not be able to withhold my regard and admiration from the amiable disposer of that fairy scene.

"As the avenue approached nearer to the castle, the alleys grew straiter, the clusters of trees more regular; the enchanting wildness of the walks, where the relaxed senses were left entirely to the invigorating hand of artless nature, now dissolved imperceptibly in more artificial regularity, and terminated, at length, in a beautiful flower garden. The statues, that only wanted breath to be completely alive, seemed to refresh themselves in the cool dusk of twilight, and in a fragrant atmosphere of sweet scenting lemon and orange blossoms. Some temples, and a number of pavillions, that with a sumptuous splendor enraptured the eye through the darkening dusk, offered themselves to my looks on approaching the castle, which was situated in the centre of that fairy spot. Every object I beheld displayed the wealth of the possessor, and her elegant taste. A benevolent fay seemed to have exhausted here all her supernatural power, to prove that a paradise could be produced on earth.

"In the back ground the whole of this sweet flower garden was terminated by the castle, an edifice which was noble in its structure, without parading with groteske ornaments. An extensive turf was in the front; two alleys, in a half circular form, led to the portal; and a marble staircase wound itself up to the entrance of the edifice.

"This paradise was, however, lifeless, and appeared to be uninhabited. The birds retired gradually to their roosts; a solitary finch chirped in the shrubbery, a little snake rustled in the leaf; the evening breeze whispered in the odorous foliage; but no other motion, no sound, no human footsteps vibrated in my ear. I alighted; my horse pranced in the court-yard, and hailed the stable by his neighing; no person seemed to take notice of it. I ascended the steps, opened the door; no sound met me in the anti-chamber; and only the echo of my footsteps was heard in the empty apartment. I mounted boldly an alabaster staircase; passed several lofty rooms, and observed every where marks of splendor and luxury, but no trace of an inhabitant. At length a door opened; a servant, in mourning, came out of it, but kept his eyes fixed to the floor. I accosted him; yet he took no notice of me; and before my astonishment suffered me to come up with him, he disappeared.

"By Heaven, Carlos!" I exclaimed at length, "thou hast met with many singular events, but never with one similar to the adventure of this night." So saying, I opened the door which the servant came out of, and entered a dark apartment, lighted only by two torches, which were standing near a silver crucifix. A lady, in black, knelt before it; looked at me, on my entering the apartment, and gave me a signal not to disturb her. I stood near half an hour at the door, agitated with strange sensations. To be so unexpectedly received in such an unaccountable manner; to be treated with so much indifference, blended with cordiality; to behold the enchanting effusion of the noblest sentiments, without knowing how far they might be relied upon; all this would have confounded a man of greater equanimity than myself. With what eyes was I to behold the woman that lay prostrated before me in such a heavenly ecstasy, occupied with the idea of God, of her heaven, or of her lover, betraying so much sorrow and tenderness, soaring above this world, and yet animated with benevolence, without affecting not to perceive what was doing near her, and showing so much goodness to the disturber of her devotion? In what light was I to view myself? More intimately related to her soul than she could ominate in that moment, or insnared again in a new imposition, in a pre-concerted delusion? Ratiocinations and presensions alternately succeeded one another in my soul; I did not know what to think of that singular event.

"The ornaments of the apartment were not splendid, but simple and neat: ash-grey hangings, embroidered with garlands of roses, and two pictures, were the only embellishments of the room. It was no exhibition room of grief and mourning, but only harmonizing with the disposition of its owner. The table with the crucifix, before which she lay prostrated, stood near the sofa; and a harp was standing in a corner. In short, every thing was in the taste of a family apartment in which one loves to be at home.

"At length she rose, wiping a tear from her eye, and stepping towards me with a candle in her hand. The effervescence of her devotion was still visible in the crimson hue of her sweet countenance; but the traces of great sorrows, and of many years of affliction, glittered in her large blue eye. A dewy languor of her looks pointed treacherously at the place where she had deposited her wishes and her hopes, and whence she just had returned. She had prayed at the throne of her Father for strength to perform every duty of sisterly piety and of benevolent charity. All this my harrowed mind read in her eye and in her speaking looks. I was surprised to find her so young and so charming. My senses spoke at first sight louder in her praise than they ought to have done. How could that angelic being have been an impostor! My self-consciousness being assailed by such repeated and sensible blows, began gradually to lose its energy: I could scarcely think it possible that all this should have been pre-concerted. So many men, so much labour, such exquisite charms, so much understanding and skill should have been combined so studiously, and, frequently, reluctantly compressed; for what purpose? for the miserable end of fettering and fixing the whole existence of a being that already, for a long time, had been tired of that existence; it was impossible means and end could here be proportionated to each other with that wisdom and exactness one could expect of such a confederation as my unknown tormentors already had proved to be.

The meeting of these incidents was, indeed, wonderful enough; and I frequently found the confederation most unaccountably implicated in those very objects where I had the least reason to suspect their agency: there was even a long period of my life when I could not proceed a single step without meeting with some vestiges of their omni-presence, as I justly may call it; yet at the same time I was not far distant from them: the humor of chance, too, contributed, perhaps, now and then, to combine the incidents in such a striking manner, and they found it less difficult to ensnare me than at present when I was farther distant, and rendered more circumspect by many a sad experience.

"Who are you, Sennor? and how can I serve you?" the lady asked me with a winning grace.

"A strayed traveller, Sennora, who flatters himself you will not deny him an asylum for this night," I replied. "I shall not apologize for my intrusion," I added, "as this would be doubting the veracity of the general report of your hospitality and humanity." She seemed to find my reply rather inconsistent with my appearance, and viewed me with scrutinizing looks.

"Sennor," she returned, at length, "I beg your pardon: you do me much honour: but may I crave your name?" I made use of the name of a friend of mine, whose family, relations, and situation, I was completely acquainted with; adding, that if she knew my name, she also would not be ignorant how little my slender fortune corresponded with my rank, and pretended to have been impelled to travel by a desire of seeing the world. During this elucidation I had kept a strict watch over her features, but not one mien seemed to betray or to conceal any thing from me. She recollected my name, my family, and situation, with artless civility, protesting that she would detain me some days at her castle, ordered her servant to shew me to some beautiful apartments, and begged me to return as soon as possible to supper. Her address and replies were delivered in such a simple tone of conversation, that I had no probable reason to suspect a preconcerted plan.

"It was, at length, time to go to supper: the changing of my dress, the contemplating of the beautiful situation of the castle, and the examination of my elegant apartments, retained me so long, that she was obliged to send the servant twice for me. I was astonished to find a young man in her company: he was one of the handsomest and most interesting figures I ever have seen: the energic vigour swelling his sinews, the consciousness of innate nobility, throning on his graceful countenance, and the traces of secret sorrow, which were legibly written in his looks, made him appear a melancholy Apollo. I took him for her brother, and treated him accordingly; but soon perceived, by the interchange of eloquent glances, that a more tender relation united them. They concealed their mutual sentiments so little, and so entirely disregarded my presence, that they soon obliterated the dissatisfaction their behaviour at first had excited in my soul. I considered them, in a short time, as destinated for each other; viewing him with reverence and envy, as the instrument of Heaven to reconcile the heart of that excellent woman with the world and her fate, and seconded with pleasure with mutual effusion and interchange of their tenderness.

"He spoke but very little, but what he said was excellent. His words seemed to emanate from the profundity of a noble heart, and bespoke a fertile imagination and a high-soaring understanding. Notwithstanding my being constantly on the watch to catch something on which I could have grounded the suspicions which haunted me every where, yet he always eluded my snares with so much dexterity and artlessness, that I could discover nothing that could have justified my apprehensions. I either was not subtle and dexterous enough to over-reach such a genius, or he was innocent. At last I found that it would be most prudent in me to display my little accomplishments in the most advantageous manner, and to try whether I should be more successful in that method of attack.

"We had, mean-time, finished our supper amid indifferent conversations. I was extremely fatigued, and retired in good time to my apartment. Soon after, I heard the young man pass my door, and retire to an adjacent apartment, accompanied by a servant. Gen-

eral silence began gradually to prevail in the castle; the gates were
shut, and a profound, awful stillness reigned all around. I could not
sleep in spite of my weariness, the night being extremely hot, and
my blood in an unnatural fermentation. I also imagined to hear the
sound of a musical instrument; and getting up, opened the window
with all possible precaution to listen whence the melodious strains
proceeded.

I was not mistaken, distinguishing the sweet notes of a lute,
accompanied with a harmonious voice. The general silence that
prevailed in the environs of the castle, soon enabled me to discern
the words of a popular song and the voice of my hostess. The tune
may, indeed, have been printed literally in the book as she sang it;
however, no person, that did not feel the meaning of the poet in the
strongest manner, could have sung it like her. The notes seemed to
emerge from the deepest recesses of an afflicted heart, and were so
plaintive and affecting, that their powerful charm glided irrestist-
ibly through every nerve of mine, and touched the inmost fibres of
my senses.

"My heart sympathized, in that moment, feelingly with hers.
Elmira, my sainted Elmira, stole upon my fancy, arrayed with all
the beauties of her lovely form, and with the charms of heavenly
glory, recalling the events past to my memory. Every plaintive
sound that touched my ravished ears seemed to appertain to her;
I imagined to be transported a better world, and there to hear the
sainted darling of my heart vent her grief at our untimely separation. Alas! how oft had she sung that tune to me! All my ideas were
drowned in the great, over-powering ocean of the wonderful events
of my life past, and I had no sense for the time present. The view
from my window commanded a great part of the garden. A long,
over-grown path led, by several windings, to some edifices which I
beheld through the gloom of night. The plaintive strains seemed to
proceed from one of those buildings, which emitted a faint gleam
of light. My whole attention was now directed to that spot; and, ere
long, I beheld a white figure, resembling my hostess in her form and
gait, carrying a lamp in one hand. The air blowing rather strong,
she screened the light with her hand, which prevented me from discerning her face. On coming nearer to the castle, she turned into a
side path, and chancing to cast a look at my window, saw me lean-

ing out of it; the lamp dropped on the ground, she screamed aloud, and concealed herself in the next shrubbery.

"I did not know what to think of that strange incident. Was it surprise or terror that frightened her so strangely from my aspect? Did she, perhaps, imagine to have been taken unawares in a sentiment or an expression which she had reason to conceal from me? Nothing is more uncertain and deceitful than the grimaces of women. How frequently had I already been mistaken in my judgment of their actions; nay, I had just reason to aver that I had not once hit the truth, and acted accordingly. Though I was the sport of women from my early youth, and had constantly been allured and repelled by them, yet that treacherous sex had not exhausted its wiles to mislead me anew. I was become mistrustful; but this only afforded them additional means of misguiding me.

"Was that unaccountable incident (said I to myself) perhaps a new design upon thee? Was the scene I had witnessed premeditated to mislead thee again to some sinister step, or only to excite thy curiosity? Sympathy is, with good, or only enthusiastic minds, the son of curiosity; love is the sister of sympathy. They are more akin in thy soul than in that of a thousand other persons; the secret motives of thy plans, the combination and the instruments of thy actions, either are known, or they endeavour, at least, slily to sift them. Thus I reasoned within myself; but it served only to increase my perplexity.

"I spent the night in an unspeakable agitation. I awoke again from a comfortable slumber of sly observations; my ideas began gradually to interchange their nature; what seemed to be trifling and insignificant, now appeared to me to conceal some danger; but noisy incidents did not alarm me. Appearance, which already naturally is deceitful enough, was now nursed up to a state of the completest delusion. All the circumstances were so visibly connected, and every thing contributed involuntarily to cement that connection, which rendered it so much the more dangerous.

"However, who can unfold the wonderful mazes of the heart! All these ideas were active in my mind only while the resemblance with Elmira struck me, and my soul was occupied to find out a probability of her having appeared to me here; for my agitated imagination surmounted every obstacle, and was capable of effecting any kind of delusion.

"Yet as soon as these dreams, that were intimately connected with my whole existence, disappeared, or their connection with the most distant probability began to grow more invisible and dubious, the light in which my hostess appeared to me assumed gradually more cheerfulness. The interest she could have had in alluring me by her charms, her visible attachment to some object of her grief, rendered it very improbable that she could have any design upon me; and if any thing in the world could gain upon her affection, and claim her attention, it was certainly the handsome young man whom I had seen with her, and whose excellent qualities far out-shone my poor accomplishments. Her eyes confirmed this conjec-ture in a most striking manner. What a great distinction did they make between him and myself! and why should I not believe their language?

CHAPTER IV.

"In the morning a servant called me to breakfast. The lady was alone, and informed me that the other gentleman had gone on a journey. She met me with a pale and languid countenance, but with-out any sign of perplexity. She enquired so tenderly after the state of my health, that I was thrown into an anxious confusion. We soon were engaged in deep conversation. She seemed to be desirous only to unfold her ideas and experiences of certain philosophical princi-ples, and thereby betrayed me into an explanation of my opinions. All her notions were the offsprings of overstrained enthusiasm.

"It was visible that she had totally, and already, for a long time, retired from this sublunary world, to be happy in another, which she decorated with her romantic dreams. I behaved, as much as pos-sible, merely in a passive manner, being sensible that it was not yet proper to submit my ideas to her investigation.

"In this mutual relation several days elapsed, and the young man was not returned from his journey. She seemed to be surprised, but not much vexed at it. Two souls, that communicate with each other for some time, and can converse without being interrupted, are more intimately allied every minute, if only the harmony of their dispositions renders them more congenial. Ennuy and civility kept

us, in the beginning, tolerably together, but we soon grew inseparable, our communication being cemented by more tender ties.

"I intended every day to leave that enchanting house: however,
the charms that retained me grew every day more attractive. The
hours were connected by a certain unaccountable tie of desire and
satisfaction; our conversations grew more interesting the more
we disclosed the secret recesses of our hearts to each other, and
interchanged our ideas and sentiments. Roving the garden from
morn till night, we left our senses no time for enjoyment: we flut-
tered from pleasure to pleasure, and soared, on rosy wings of fancy,
beyond the limits of reality, without having a clear perception of
our imaginary transport.

"The garden terminated in a little lake, on whose flowery banks
a grassy knoll formed our favourite spot. Here we sat for whole
hours, indulging our imagination in its airy flights. The undulation of the curling waves; the serene sky, reflecting from the silver
lake; the amorous gambols of the playsome swallows, sporting on
its surface; the peaceful tranquillity that reigned all around, gave
wings to our fancy, and procreated sweet sensations in our hearts.
We wandered beyond the limits of mortality, and our imagination
transported us to the golden age of a futurity beyond the grave. We
visited the kingdom of spirits, peopled it with the offsprings of our
roseate dreams, and roved through the boundless realms of eternity on pinions of smiling hope.

"Thus we spent eight days by ourselves. The moon soon saw us
walk arm in arm though the mazes of the garden; and at length,
infolded in rapturous embraces, attracted to one another by the
secret ecstasy of our ideas. It was no sensual love that united us so
tenderly, but an internal sense of the congenial harmony of our
souls. "What a boundless realm of sweet ideas does fancy com-
prise," she exclaimed, one time, when we just were returned from
one of the boldest flights into the realm of spirits, "so sweet, and yet
so melancholy."

"How happy am I, Sennora, to know only the sweets of it! Being
almost deadened for the bustle of human forms and circumstances,
I have settled in those bodyless realms as a cheerful and peaceable
citizen. My new country is subject to me, and receives my laws; it is
a soft and pliant mould in my forming hand, and is rendered happy

by me. I am the great omnipotent spirit in this creation of mine; and spreading my bliss-abounding hand over its realms, every thing ripens to maturity, affords me the purest enjoyment, and contributes to the happiness of the whole. "A beautiful fiction, my friend! But is your creative fancy never disappointed? is the creator never displeased with his creatures; never wearied by his work?"

"I cannot but confess, Sennor, that disappointment, dissatisfaction, and fatigue, now and then steals upon him; but not in such a degree as to destroy the enjoyment of the blissful hour. Even weariness is sweet in a certain point; and one is yet happy, though the strength decreases, when one has done every thing duty and necessity require."

"But, Carlos," said she, taking hold of my hand, "if a realm of spirits like that which our imagination has created should really exist?"

"So much the better, Sennora."

"No, Carlos, you mistake me. I am serious, my friend. If you were more intimately acquainted with the events of my life, you would be convinced that I have a melancholy, dearly-bought right to speak that language."

"How wildly you talk, Sennora! If you speak that language with me, I must answer you as your friend. I respect the offsprings of your imagination; they are emanations of an accomplished mind; your dreams are dearly-bought creations of an amiable heart. I follow you with pleasure to the realms of friendship, love, and peace. I also hold a communion with a life beyond the grave dear and sacred, because the events of my former days have rendered me unsusceptible of earthly bliss. But, dearest friend, do not mingle the least shadow of reality with those charming children of glowing fancy, nothing that might destroy the happiness which every journey to that enchanting country affords."

"How happy you are, Sennor, that your senses have not convinced you of the truth of my assertion! Other people are less fortunate. And pray, dear friend, what can reason object against the existence of such an intermediate realm, whose spiritual inhabitants can communicate with men?"

"I can, indeed, not absolutely deny it; yet it affords strong arguments against a belief in the existence of such a realm of spirits, whose citizens communicate with the human race. Why should they be endowed with that capacity? To render *us* or *themselves* happier? *Us?* Can any mortal maintain ever to have had a clear perception of their existence or influence on earth-born men?"

"You are too rash, Don Carlos."

"Why, Sennora, too rash? Neither you nor I can speak of it from experience. To improve their own happiness thereby? How could that be possible? Through the recollection of their former life? How few of them would be able to derive happiness from that source! To continue the improvement of their capacities, interrupted by death? Would this world afford them more proper opportunities for doing it than yon blissful realms beyond the grave? To watch over the happiness of mankind? Is the omnipotent all-wise Ruler of the World not powerful enough to promote our happiness without the interposition of such a miraculous agency, that would overturn all the wise rules of nature?"

"You may say whatever you choose, dear Carlos; you will never be able to prove that it is *impossible* such an agency of intermediate beings can exist. I could oppose an argument to your reasoning that would confound you at once."

"And what argument could that be, Sennora?"

"Reality."

"Reality!"

"And my own experience."

"Your experience? You astonish me."

"Yes, yes, my experience. Are you my friend? my real sincere friend?"

"How can you doubt it, dearest woman?"

"I don't, indeed, Carlos; but I am so anxious, so anxious. I don't know what it is that lays so heavy upon my mind. I am afraid I shall suffer, shall painfully suffer, for my communicativeness; but let the world be dissolved, and the sun be extinguished, if I but purchase a friend for all eternity." Here she paused, and having looked anxiously around, resumed: "Look at me, Carlos, and behold the paleness of my cheeks, the melancholy wreck of an extinguishing fire in my eyes, and the visible decay of my constitution. Sleepless and tormenting nights prey upon my health. My strength declines gradually, and I behold myself at the brink of the yawning grave. A Spirit does not permit me to enjoy a moment's rest."

"A Spirit! a Spirit! did you say, Sennora?"

"The departed Spirit of my Lord."

"Eternal God! this is *Amanuel!*"

"What sound did I hear? Have you said any thing, Don Carlos?"

"I only said, What a strange illusion of fancy!"

"No: that was not the sound I heard: it was some name."

"The wind rustles in the leaf, Sennora. Pray go on."

"I have been frightened so much, Sennor. The most secret, mystic sound of nature terrifies me violently. I tremble at the least rustling near me. Every thing torments me: I can enjoy no pleasure unmixed and pure. Let me give you a brief account of my history. You know my family. Five years since, I was married to a man whom my heart had chosen. He was the most amiable, the best of men, and an enthusiast like myself. Being captivated with a country life, and retirement from the bustle of the world, he persuaded me to live with him on his estate. Want of regular occupations, and of cheering amusements, the total seclusion of this castle from the world, and our own susceptibility, infected us already in the first years of our union with a kind of pensive melancholy, which heightened the charms of our imaginary dreams. In a fatal hour of ecstatic enthusiasm, we vowed mutually to extend our reciprocal love beyond the confines of the grave, and to continue our communication after death. I lost him soon after we had exchanged that vow, and now he visits me regularly every night."

"I am astonished, Sennora, at your wonderful tale. But was no person present when you interchanged that vow?"

"Who could have been present? We were quite solitary: no person visited us; and my Lord kept only that young man whom you saw with me on the first night after your arrival to take care of the management of our domestic affairs, and of the preservation of the estate. Besides him, we suffered no person to be admitted to our conversation, and he was at the time absent on some business."

"Wonderful!—Every night, did you say?"

"Every night: he omits but very seldom to appear."

"And what does he say to you on these visits?"

"He has never uttered a word; but only seats himself at the bottom of my bed."

"Have you never attempted to touch him?"

"Never!"

"Have you tried every means to discover whether you are not imposed upon?"

"Every thing, Sennor. My bed-chamber is bolted on the inside, and it has no secret door."

"This renders it certainly more incomprehensible than I imagined. I am a man of courage, Sennora, and of no small bodily strength; you have confided your secret to me; give me leave to examine it!"

"No, Carlos; I have too much affection for you as to suffer you to endanger your life so much."

"I fear nothing for *my* life, Sennora, but much for yours. I have courage, and a more than common bodily strength. I shall arm myself against any attempt against my life; only let us proceed with caution."

"No, you must desist from your design. You are dear to my heart, are the only friend I have in this world. It would render me unspeakably miserable, if you should thus wantonly rob me of the only good that has some value for me. The few moments of my life are counted; let me linger them away, at least with some shadow of peace, and do not shorten them."

"Thus we fought for some time the conflict of love and friendship, and only after much persuasion I could prevail on her to suffer me to engage in the adventure. Having mutually agreed to preserve the profoundest secrecy, and that she should admit me to her bed-chamber before midnight, I prepared myself in a manner which promised to insure me success. A good cuirass, which I generally used to wear, a well-tried poniard, a strong agile body, courage, and presence of mind, which I acquired through a variety of surprising adventures, were no despicable armour for such a hazardous attempt. I was confident not to lose my firmness entirely, however terrified the apparition should be. I awaited the setting in of night with impatience. The wished-for time arrived at length. We endeavoured, indeed, to exhibit a semblance of tranquillity at supper; but who can conceal emotions like those that prevailed in our soul? We exerted every sense for wit and gaiety to suppress those for fear and anxious expectation, or, at least, to conceal our emotions in an unaffected manner, and succeeded in our attempts tolerably well.

"We separated at the usual time, laughing and joking. I bolted my door carefully, extinguished the candle, and laid myself down. Having laughed pretty loud in my bed for some time, I drew the curtain, and began to snore. The night was not dark; however, the wind was fortunately so high, and the dark clouds were driven with such an impetuosity through the air, that I could not be observed in my apartment.

"The castle clock struck half an hour after eleven, when I crept softly out of my bed, this being the time the Countess had fixed. I armed, and wrapt myself in a counterpane, unbolted my door as silently as possible, and began my pilgrimage.

"On the long corridor, which I was obliged to pass on my way to the chamber of my hostess, I almost was betrayed by a large dog, that was sleeping in the middle of the way. It was so dark that I did not observe him 'till I trod upon him; and I could not prevent him, by all my caresses, from barking violently. But as the tempest fortunately shook the windows of the castle in a violent manner, and the dogs in the court-yard also began to be very noisy, I flattered myself to have escaped observation.

My hostess opened her chamber door as soon as I had made the signal we had agreed upon. She was in great agitation when I entered her chamber, and almost swooned in my arms; and although I exerted all my eloquence to make her easy, yet she continued to be in a dreadful state of fear and anxiety. She exhibited the most singular conflict between dread and curiosity, between womanhood and enthusiasm, shame and expectation. She seemed not to fear so much *for* as *of* me; and I succeeded only after numberless attempts of availing myself of her passions to inspire her with some hope.

"I cannot deny that her situation was dangerous enough. If she had fore-known it in its whole extent, I should probably not have persuaded her to such an attempt. The tempestuous night, which usually makes two congenial souls more familiar; her situation, which precluded her from all assistance; the disorder and negligence of her dress, and the agitation caused by her fear, would have endangered the virtue of two firmer characters. I cannot but confess that, on my part, scarcely one half of these incitements would have been wanted to stir up my senses if they had not been occupied too much with my own danger. Every thing that had wounded my heart in the former periods of my life, or awakened any dormant passion or sensation within me, appeared to me to point at that moment. Much of my own history could be elucidated here, and all my resolutions would receive an impulse to a different direction for the future. Although the history of the lady was not immediately connected with a part of my own, yet its development served to make it useful to me in the sequel.

"The momentous hour of midnight drew nearer and nearer. We made some preparations, chilled with mutual horror. She concealed herself in a corner of the apartment, and I occupied her place in the bed, wrapt in my counterpane, and listening with the greatest attention to every motion around me. The least vibration of the air, nay, I almost might say, the respiration of a fly, alarmed my imagination. Nothing appeared to me so trifling or insignificant as not to be capable of begetting some horrid apparition. The barking of the dogs, and even the crowing of the cocks, was suspicious to me.

"At length it struck twelve o'clock. A gentle, almost imperceptible, rustling vibrated in the air. The rain beat a little stronger against the windows; the wood work of the bed and of the whole apartment began to crack; the objects grew more visible and distinct, and the moon-light clearer; every thing around me trembled in an undulating glimmer. At once the curtains were drawn; and the whole bed having been moved a little from its place, a human form, encircled with a milk white light, seated itself at the bottom of my couch. The first terror stunned me so much in the beginning, that I could discern nothing but the outlines of the phantom, and I distinguished only gradually the face of a man already advanced in years, disfigured with blood, and fixing a staring look at me. He moved his hand slightly, as if going to speak; yet without uttering a syllable. Having looked at him a few seconds, I started suddenly up.

"The apparition staggered back at that sudden motion, which inspired me with additional courage; and when I had entirely disengaged myself from my disguise, he rose terrified from his seat to retire. I even imagined to hear him utter a sound which was not unknown to me, and could not appertain to a spirit. This determined me to attack him. I darted upon him, and in that moment was completely convinced that he was no airy phantom. He wounded me in the arm with a poniard, and only my cuirass protected me against a second stab, which otherwise would have put an end to my life. I seized him so powerfully that he could not stir, opposing to a more than human strength, which perhaps was heightened by fury and despair, firmness and agility, parrying his repeated, violent thrusts with my arm, or rendering them harmless by my cuirass. We wrestled without uttering a word, or making a great noise, like two furious lions, and came suddenly to the ground. Being almost exhausted, I was obliged to save my life by the last dreadful expedient: I unsheathed my dagger, and terminated our conflict by two violent thrusts. He died without uttering a word, heaving a long and heavy groan. His stiffning arms grasped me powerfully in the last agony of death, and enfolded me so furiously that I could not disengage myself.

"The lady came to my assistance, lighting a candle in the antichamber. We divested the corpse of its disguise, and were seized with dreadful astonishment when we beheld his face. It was the young handsome man whom I had seen the first evening after my arrival.

"My first look was now directed at my hostess. Numberless passions, which I had not expected to behold at one time, changed on her countenance; astonishment, curiosity, grief, and at last, indignation, convulsed her features. The latter prevailed over the rest. I now expected that she would thank me for having hazarded my life in her service; but I was disappointed. Having contemplated the corpse for some time in dumb horror, she put the candle on the floor, dropt on one knee, applying her handkerchief to the bleeding wound, and kissing the pallid lips of the youth. I gazed at the strange scene, seized with astonishment. Her convulsive features convinced me that her agony was of such a violent nature as to deprive her of the use of her speech.

"Having remained for some time in that posture, she rose at length, and staring at me with that gloomy, melancholy frigidity which distinguished the commencement of our acquaintance, exclaimed, "again a *murderer!*" So saying, she left the room abruptly, turning round once more to look at me. I was almost petrified with astonishment, and had not strength enough to follow her.

"I returned to my apartment without being able to conclude how all this would end. Was it love for the dead young man that repelled her from me in that decisive moment which she had anticipated with effusions of the most grateful enthusiasm? Was it horror at the bloody termination of the conflict? Was it the consequence of terror; or what was it? I never spent a night in more painful perplexity, and awaited with impatience the dawn of the day; yet it afforded me no more light.

"I went to the apartment of the lady at the usual hour of breakfast. It was locked. A waiting woman of my hostess came to tell me that I could not see her. My breakfast was carried into the garden, where I spent the whole forenoon. I went again to her door, at noon; but was a second time denied admittance. I found my dinner in my own apartment, and the following sealed letter upon a plate:

"You have again perplexed me in my opinion of your sex. Don't inquire for the *reason* of this assertion. You have undesignedly robbed me of the greatest felicity that could have alleviated my distress. I can see you no more. Don't deny me the favour of delivering me of the sight of you, which has become to me the source of unspeakable misery. Forgive a poor, disconsolate woman, that deserves your compassion, and forget me."

"I was seized with deep indignation at reading the note, and wrote the following reply on the other side of the paper:

"You know the motives that have prompted me to risk my life to restore peace to your heart. You know the love with which my soul met your's; but you also must know the ambition that guides my actions. If chance does not throw me again in your way, you will have seen me the last time in that bloody moment. I wish you may forget an unhappy man, whom you cruelly wrong."

"Having wrote this letter, I rose, and left the apartment. After I had waited a painful quarter of an hour in the anti-chamber, one of the waiting women appeared. I gave her some pieces of gold, and the letter, desiring her to deliver it to her lady, ordered my horse to be saddled, and rode away with the coldest tranquillity, without once looking back at the castle, and returned the same road I came.

CHAPTER V.

"I should find it difficult to give you, dearest Count, an idea of the sentiments of that moment; for, to be sincere, I thought nothing at all. I was in a state as if I had been suddenly roused from a dream, and could not recollect myself. The world appeared to me as if new created, as an extensive space, and I myself only a solitary point in it.

"Being arrived at the spot where I had parted with my travelling companion, I turned mechanically into the road which he had taken when he left me. I was sheltered by lofty and thick trees against the scorching rays of the sun. The depending branches breathed a profound peace, which gradually communicated itself to my soul. I rejoiced in that moment with inward rapture at having escaped the danger which had threatened me; my whole life appeared to me like a dream, and it soon began to give me pleasure. I let it pass the review before my imagination in the rosy hue it had assumed; and was totally absorpt in meditations on events past.

The path grew wider and wider, and at length extended itself into a spacious turfy plain, on which I beheld, at some distance, several tents, in the front of which a number of ladies and gentlemen appeared on horseback. I soon observed that they were preparing for a chase. The number of splendidly arrayed hunters and beautiful huntresses encreased every moment; the hounds swept the plain in large packs; the winding of horns, mixed with the yell of dogs, and the neighing of horses, filled the air. The chase drew near, and I turned from the high road to let it pass, and to admire the dress of the beautiful huntresses at leisure. The whole train exhibited a splendid scene; jewels, gold and silver, and most admirable embroidery, variegating with the most exquisite taste and elegance.

"The troop past the spot where I stood in slow solemnity, and no one deigned to look at me, my appearance and dress being too humble to attract their attention, when suddenly one of the hindmost horsemen, who attended some ladies, came up to me, staring at me, and exclaiming with a roaring laughter, "Upon my life and honour! this is the Marquis of G******—How are you, Don Carlos? How the devil came you here in that splendid attire?"

"I saw myself discovered to my utter confusion. The young Duke of S******, one of the most intimate friends of my earlier years, stood before me; the whole chase was thrown into confusion; and in a few moments I was surrounded by a number of gay ladies and gentlemen, who did not know what to think of the adventure. At length I made the best of this unexpected incident, laughing aloud, and embracing the Duke. He introduced me to the company, adding, that I was an adventurer who ought not to be suffered to proceed; and I consented at last, after much persuasion, to stay some days at his castle. I was provided with a hunter, and desired to attend Donna Augusta, one of the most beautiful ladies in the whole company. The chase began, and after we had shot some game, we returned to the castle amid loud peals of merriment.

"It is impossible to find a more charming society than my companions composed, and to behold a more pleasing mixture of forms and geniuses than that which they exhibited. There was no form that did not strike the eye; no character which did not contrast with some other. The richness and variety of the beautiful group did not invalidate the internal value of the whole picture, which rather had more intrinsic worth than it promised at first sight. Wit and humour animated the whole company; one pleasing sensation urged the other; and the most perfect elegance was united with natural simplicity. Every one seemed to study only how to contribute the largest share to the diversion of the whole.

"Don Edwardo, Count of V******, was the paragon of the whole society. It is my duty to avail myself of this opportunity to erect, in the heart of my friend, a little monument to that excellent young man. I have felt, with the warmest rapture, what a happiness is to be his friend: I have pursued my thorny and painful course with more success and courage while he guided and comforted me, and the recollection of his conversation frequently steals upon my mind amid tears of affection. Count V****** was descended from an ancient Greek family, that had settled in Italy. Having left his native country at an early age, and being gifted by nature and education, with all those endowments that render man susceptible

of every object, he soon became naturalized to a country where
the foreigner in general is easily discerned from the native. His long
and almost continual travels had enabled him to gather and combine in himself the peculiar accomplishments of different nations;
he spoke several modern languages with facility, and in great perfection, and had no superficial knowledge of the sciences and arts.
Being a complete man of letters, a perfect observer and courtier,
he could conceal and exhibit as much of his accomplishments as he
chose.

"His amiable wit, his great judgment, and the tenderest pliability
of his thoughts and notions, convinced me, at first sight, that he
was born only for society. His form, indeed, was not perfectly handsome; his hands and legs could have been better shaped; however,
his deportment was easy and engaging, and his countenance was
the most winning I ever beheld. His large blue eyes spoke to the
heart: he was master of all his movements, and thoroughly skilled
in the great art of accommodating himself to every situation, and
imitating what is peculiar and natural to every rank. In the elegant
circles of the great world, he was the most consummate courtier: in
the middle classes, an agreeable and well bred citizen; and amongst
country people, an inquisitive and artless swain; but in each situation equally amiable.

"But how shall I be able to give you an adequate account of his
heart, which was adorned with every sentiment that ennobles man?
The Count was in every respect fit for his age, but his heart was
too good and too feeling for the present time. Immersed in the pro-
fundities of former ages, he lived only for the remotest futurity:
without presuming to confound a world in which he found so many
objects that could attract him, he was animated with an enthusiastic desire to form it for the enjoyment of a heaven. Nothing in this
world could give him grief or pleasure, except the sorrows or the
happiness of his friends. He loved, and his whole soul was occupied with the objects of his affection: however, his fancies generally strayed beyond the limits of this world, and he only was happy
when he could transplant his sentiments into the most distant ages,
amid roses, and beneath the ever-smiling sky of a peaceful, pastoral
life.

"He had been frequently deceived by men; his friends had repeat-

edly betrayed him; his kindred had renounced, and his mistress
jilted him: he had experienced all the bitterness of life which an
open heart must expect in an artful world. He had no where met
with a congenial soul, that knew to estimate and to repay his worth.
His mind now unfolded itself only in the narrow circle of his most
intimate friends.

"Donna Augusta F****** was the object of his affection, and
could not but be happy. Her susceptibility for manly greatness, and
her fond attachment to her Edwardo, could not but render his love
the greatest blessing to her. I must confess I never beheld a greater
harmony of souls than that which united these two happy lovers.

"Augusta's form was uncommonly charming. It is possible to be
handsomer than her, but not to be more enchanting. The ever juvenile suavity of her looks, the easy play of her mien, the winning
smile that graced her rosy lips, the beautiful symmetry of her features, and the freshness of her tint, will scarcely be found united in
such perfect harmony in any other female form. A taper shape put
the finishing stroke to the whole charming picture.

"Her cheerful humour, and even her whims, imparted an uninterrupted flow of jocundity to the whole company. She spread
laughter and merriment around, by the inexhaustible sallies of her
lively wit, without hurting the feelings of any one, or trespassing
the limits of virgin modesty, and was assiduous to make every one
happy, without neglecting her Edwardo.

"The society was besides graced by some other members, who
contributed in a different manner to complete the happiness of the
whole. Our host, the Duke of S******, was a character of the first
rank with respect to general amusement. I had known him already
many years as a very amiable man, who knew how to attach me
to his person by his fondness for me; and although his subsequent
connection with the court and the great world, and the flatteries he
received, had changed some beautiful features of his character, yet
he had not ceased to love his fellow-creatures with sincere ardour,
and to deserve their reciprocal affection. He was the most subtle
courtier among the whole society, a kind of chameleon, without
possessing any colour of his own, changing all forms with uncommon ease, and gifted with a most pliant tongue, a high degree of
judgment, and a fertile imagination; a flattering mirror for every

one that had a mind to make use of it. His refined epicurism, which always confined itself within the bounds the tone of the company in which he was and circumstances did prescribe, contributed a great deal to the pleasure of the whole society. He was the most refined voluptuary I ever knew, sporting with pleasure, which assumed a thousand different shapes under his forming hands. He made all circumstances subservient to his joviality, was proof against all attacks of sorrow, indifferent to all the incidents of life, and unruffled by passions, except that of enjoyment. Even sadness served him to procreate mirth, and he transformed, as it were, every tear into a rose-bud.

"This disposition made him the favourite of the ladies. Without being gifted with a great stock of natural wit, he had acquired an artificial one through study and reading, and was endowed with the great art of adorning and displaying a limited number of ideas in a manner which made every one believe that he possessed an immense store. Dancing, music, the play and the chase, in short, every thing that contributes to smooth the stream of life, seemed to be his favourite amusement, and he knew the imposing surface of all sciences. The make of his body agreed perfectly with the disposition of his mind and heart, it being neither athletic nor manly handsome, but rather luxuriant and pliant. His shape displayed the greatest symmetry, without approaching to effeminacy; his mien and muscles were in constant motion without being antic; numberless passions changed continually on his pretty countenance, without precipitation; the most beautiful, smallest, and whitest hands, a little foot, and a handsome calf, which he knew how to display to advantage, composed an enchanting *Alcibiades*.

"His brother, Don Pablo S******, on the contrary, acted the philosopher. Count V****** seemed to have divided himself in two parts to produce this couple. The Duke had received his charms, and Don Pablo his seriousness: either of them only had it improved in his own way, and exaggerated. Don Pablo was dryness itself, endowed with a kind of humour which excited general laughter, without his changing a feature. His imagination was poor; but he possessed a great store of substantial knowledge, which he had gathered from all the philosophers of ancient times. His mind and body were robust and gigantic; and his disposition would, undoubtedly, have been tiresome to the company, if one of the ladies had not found the means of taming that lion, which impelled him to miss no party of pleasure, and to exert every faculty to shew himself in the most advantageous light.

"Donna Elvira, the Dutchess of S******, deserved the first rank amongst the ladies, after Augusta: she was the wildest, most contradictory being on earth; half a man, and yet provided with a good number of female whims, and of a pretty firm character, which, however, was a strange mixture of bad and of charming caprices. She possessed the most excellent heart, breathing nothing but philanthropy, but was sometimes severe, merely to conceal her humanity. The latter, having been imposed upon and abused several times, she imagined an affectation of severity would be the easiest way of avoiding a repetition of a similar ingratitude. Yet she had frequently reason to repent her whimsical behavior, and then had much to do to repair the mischievous effects of her affected severity. She wept and laughed frequently without the least cause; only because she had a whim to do so. Sometimes she found sadness very droll, and at other times drollery very sad; admired in one minute what she abhorred in the next. She possessed so much wit and eloquence, as to be capable of convincing one half of the company, and of persuading the other, that all were in the wrong, except herself; and of proving, a few minutes after, that it had been absurd to applaud her. It was a misfortune to be in love with her, which was the sad lot not only of her brother-in-law, but also of several other young gentlemen of the company. All of them were obliged to pay for her whims with a total slavery, which afforded us ample scope for merriment, as they were a sort of philosophers. No one could keep her a little in order, except Count V******, who flattered her humour without the least derogation from that manly dignity which always is sure to gain the female heart.

"Elizabeth B******, a young English Lady, whom the Duke had brought with him from his travels when she was a little girl, and who now was a charming beauty, was one of the principal ornaments of our society. Her form was, without doubt, the finest in the whole circle. The education which the Duke and his Lady had given her, and which was intended to train her up to the voluptuous disposition of the Spanish clime, had produced just the contrary effect; a coolness without measure, notwithstanding her fiery imagination, indifference blended with lively ideas, and an unbounded propensity to study and the improvement of the mind, amid the amusements and the luxuries of the warmest clime. She had improved every opportunity of forming her mind, and produced the most astonishing effects by little means. Although she confined herself chiefly to this serious sort of amusement, yet she had not renounced the pleasures of the fine arts, played on several instruments in a masterly manner, and was versed in almost all sciences which serve to sweeten life.

"The Duke had the misfortune to be deeply enamoured with his foster-daughter. She returned his passion with the coldest indifference, as far as her gratitude would admit, and had a very salutary influence on his character. He grew more serious, and paid a greater attention to the choice of his pleasures, renouncing many of his favourite amusements, because they displeased his Elizabeth. He found a new way to pleasure by indulging the most delicate secret love.

"Our circle was graced by several more very interesting characters. Yet I will not tire you, dearest Count, with a minute description of them, as it would contribute nothing to render the course of my narrative more distinct and clear. The whole society composed a charming picture, and not one member of it was superfluous. Every one was happy in being at liberty to pursue the principal idea of his mind, and of his disposition.

"I was, in a short time, completely initiated in that spirit of sociableness, or rather infected by it. We seemed to live in a fairy land; amusements of the most exquisite kind followed each other in rapid succession, and always had some charm of novelty that pleased the senses and the heart.

"A new interest soon attached me with more tender ties to the society. I became gradually the rival of the Duke in his affection for the beautiful Elizabeth. I wanted to conceal it from myself; however, my inclination had already diverted the whole company before I was aware of the situation of my heart, being the last that discovered that secret. Being no longer fit to join in the witty sallies and gambols of my companions, an internal instinct urged me to have recourse to philosophy. Growing more intimate with the fair enchantress that represented it in human shape, and being deemed worthy to receive a kind reception, I soon paid for my boldness with the loss of my liberty. You see, dearest Count, what an unsettled being I still was, without the least firmness, without a fixed system, and yet burning with an ardent desire of attaining it.

"Elizabeth B****** seemed not to dislike me. Notwithstanding her apparent reserve, she possessed a certain self-consciousness, which was not reluctant to communicate its greatness and beauty; yet she was destitute of a companion that could or would properly understand her. In that moment I offered myself unto her. The love of the Duke probably was only transitory, and certainly without any fixed aim; but me she could expect to enthral for ever. I will not presume to maintain that she felt for me what generally is called love; yet I may make bold to say, that it was a certain nameless sensation which frequently represents the former in a most illusive manner. Yet the little enchantress was so coy as to conceal her inclination for me with consummate art; or, at least, was so niggardly in conferring her favours on me, that I was frequently more impatient to know her real design than to be treated with more indulgence. I discovered, however, at length, at a great feast, which the Duke gave, that she entertained more tender sentiments for me than she chose to let me know.

CHAPTER VI.

"Great preparations had been making for the Duke's feast for some weeks. It was to be a theatrical amusement for the night; and he had fitted up a convenient spot in his garden for that purpose. The theatre was only composed of hedges: the decorations consisted of a charming mixture of lemon and orange trees; and the whole, being illuminated with variegated lamps, seemed to be the work of enchantment. Two little brooks were carried to an uncommon height, to fall down again thro' silver tubes into an alabaster bason, to refrigerate the hot summer-nights: the trees concealed a number of nightingales in cages, which being animated by the soft notes of flutes, mingled their melodious strains with the tinkling of the descending waters. An harmonious unity pervaded the whole, which augmented the effects of the *tout ensemble* to an astonishing degree.

"The piece, which was to be the introduction to the feast, was a farce composed by the Duke. It had little intrinsic merit, but produced a most enchanting effect on the eye. The splendor of the dresses and decorations, the excellency of the orchestra, and the unspeakable sweetness of some voices, but particularly the skill of the players, rendered the whole piece excellent in its kind.

"The plot was extremely simple. A young nobleman falls in love with the daughter of his gardener, courts her favour, and not being able to prevail upon her to crown his wishes at an easy price, promises to marry her. The girl being, however, pre-engaged to a young peasant, marries her lover at last, notwithstanding the numberless arts employed by her father and mother, who are flattered by the high rank of the young nobleman, and in defiance to the menaces and solicitations of her family not to reject the splendid fortune offered to her.

"The parts were distributed in the following manner. Elizabeth B****** was the handsome gardener's daughter: I acted the young nobleman, which was natural; but it was still more so that the Duke played the part of the young peasant. No one could start the least reasonable objection against this arrangement before the conclusion of the play: however, the Duke felt the bad consequences of it as soon as the curtain was drawn; for the peasant was most unfavourably received by his inamorata, and the nobleman was in a fair way of gaining the heart of the fair damsel. Nay, she even forgot herself several times so much as to confound the two rivals, and to dish up for one what was prepared for the other. Yet the whole piece went off tolerably well, without any material interruption; and she was, at length, going to bestow her hand, which she had reluctantly drawn back more than ten times, upon the happy swain, when the play suddenly terminated with a catastrophe widely different from that which the author's book contained. A large cat, who wanted to have her share of the luxuries of the feast, had probably been on the watch for some time to seize a propitious opportunity of running away with one of the nightingales; and, in that critical moment, ventured a leap from one tree to another; but missing her aim, dropt in the midst of the enraptured family, who were bestowing the blessings on the happy couple. It is impossible to give an adequate description of the terror which this unexpected accident excited. A general scream and confusion ensued. Elizabeth, being ignorant of the real cause of the sudden alarm, withdrew her hand from her swain, left father and mother, and ran anxiously to the discarded nobleman for protection. The cause of the alarm had, meantime, decamped; the society began again to resume their respective stations and attitudes; the screams of the frightened ladies changed into loud laughter, and the disordered features gradually arranged themselves in proper order: but Elizabeth seemed to be transformed into a statue, staring speechless at the spot where the alarm arose, and encircling me to support herself. She was all in a tremble. When the rest of the company had recovered from their panic terror, and perceived the chief person in my arms, they approached us, and we were obliged to lead her to a seat, where she recovered slowly, and displayed the greatest confusion. "This incident," said the Duke, at the close of the feast, "has taught me two rules; first of all, never to court again a peasant's daughter; and, secondly, to avoid, in future, to celebrate my nuptials in the open air."

"The Duke was inexhaustible in amusements of this kind. I only shall give you a brief account of the two last feasts of that sort at which I was present. The first was called the *Feast of Neptune*; but more properly aught to have been denominated the *Feast of the Fauns*. The whole was nothing but a great masquerade, to which all the neighbouring nobility were invited, who crowded, with the first dawn of day, to the place of rendezvous in their different masks. The centre of the garden was occupied by a small island, where an artificial grotto had been erected, and a sumptuous dinner provided by the Duke's order. The latter was dressed as *Neptune*, and swam in a golden shell upon the lake, provided with all his attributes, surrounded by a number of sea-gods, and drawn by blowing Tritons. He then made a long speech, prepared for that occasion, in which he invited all his subjects, even the nymphs, dryads, and hamadryads, included, who probably did not know how they came to that honour, to be merry, and to enjoy the pleasures of the day. The gods and goddesses that were assembled on shore, and impatiently had expected that invitation, did not want much persuasion, but instantly made every preparation to be carried over to the paradise in shells, which were provided for that purpose. Thus far the company was pre-informed of every thing; but what follows was an impromptu of several members. When the fair ladies just were going to embark in the shells, a great troop of Fauns suddenly rushed out of the neighbouring thicket, every one seizing a nymph, and retreating with his fair prize to their ambush. A general cry of surprise was raised, and soon made room to universal laughter. However, the gods on shore being not inclined to part at so easy a rate with their better halves, put themselves in motion to fetch them back by force. The Fauns having entrenched themselves so well that it was not adviseable to attack them, they returned to get assistance. The Triton and Nereides quitted their element, and advanced in a threatening posture towards the enemy, who received them with a roaring laughter, and a shower of pine-fruit. Neptune himself quitted his car to restore order, but in vain. The gods were obliged to capitulate, and to resign the nymphs one half of the evening to the Fauns. The feast concluded with a supper, excellent music, and a dance.

"The last festival was *the Vigil of Venus*, for which purpose the Duke had built a beautiful temple of marble in his myrtle grove. That piece of architecture seemed to have been borrowed of the finest period of the Greek art, uniting uncommon splendor with the most exquisite taste in a very small compass. The alabaster statue of Venus stood in the middle on an altar, half alive, but speechless. The temple was adorned the antecedent night with garlands of myrtle and roses, in a simple but noble stile. Two golden censors were waiting for the frankincense. Twelve of the most beautiful girls were selected from the adjacent villages, and dressed as priestesses by order of the Duke. They had been taught the proper hymns, and an excellent band of musicians was assembled.

"When evening was setting in, a solemn procession proceeded from the entrance of the park. The priestesses of Venus were in the front, clad in white silk, and burning torches in their hands; they were followed by twelve beautiful nymphs; then Venus succeeded on a gilt car, accompanied by the *graces*, and contrary to custom, drawn by four milk white horses. The company concluded the train, being joined in couples as accident or inclination had paired them.

"The girl that represented Venus seemed to have been expressly formed for that purpose; a soft, extremely luxuriant and inviting beauty, animated by the spirit of her disguise, and her new rank. The Duke led his Elizabeth, Count V****** his Augusta; the Duchess walked by Don Pablo's side; and I was, to the greatest diversion of the whole company, coupled to a gouty lady from the neighborhood, a woman that, in spite of every deformity of old age, was puffed up with the presumptuous belief to do honour to the feast. The rest of our company were followed by six young couples, whom the Duke intended to portion and to marry on that occasion. Every one carried a torch.

"We arrived at length at the myrtle grove, amid the loud acclamations of the gaping multitude. A sweet symphony of flutes received us, and we joined in a chorus in the hymn which was sung by the virgins. Two sylvans gave, at the entrance of the grove, two garlands of myrtles to every lover; one for himself, and one for his companion. It had been agreed that every one should kiss his lady when crowning her with the garland; and none had protested more violently against that ceremony than my antiquated companion, though none submitted with a better grace to it than herself.

"We beheld the splendor of the temple and its illumination already at a distance. The dark verdure of the surrounding myrtles served to set off the variegated light with which it was emblazoned; the excellent music, the silent solemnity of the procession, and the truly Greek simplicity of the melodious strains, the neat dresses, and even the exhalation of the myrtles, reflected upon the whole a semblance of reality. I imagined to be transported to the isle of Cyprus; and, when the temple raised its milk white marble colonnades, decorated with garlands of myrtles and roses, through the reddish blaze of the torches, and displayed its simple elegance more and more distinctly; when I ascended its steps, I fancied for some moments to live in that golden age, when man could enjoy all the beauty of art, when every passion contributed to embellish it, and every one knew how to avail himself of its variegated graces. The illumination was so artificially concealed, that we perceived nothing but its effects. The censors emitted two columns of an aromatic exhalation; and the twelve priestesses knelt around the altar opposite to the statue of the goddess. The latter disappeared suddenly, as if removed by enchantment, when the Deity whom it represented alighted from her chariot. She was conducted to the altar, and seated herself upon a throne, which emerged from the pavement. We formed a circle behind the priestesses; the vigils were begun, accompanied by solemn music.

"At length, the priestesses began their solemn rites, the music grew softer and softer, and gradually died away in languishing strains, imitating the palpitation which pervades the anxious heart at the approach of a solemn vow of love; and the six couples drew nearer to the altar to receive the benediction of the goddess. They seemed to be highly sensible of what they received; their happiness was legibly written in their speaking looks, gazing with delight at the objects of their love; and a reverential awe seemed to pervade them when the priestesses encircled their temples with the chaplets they received from the hand of the goddess. All this was accompanied with a suitable address, and with mystic ceremonies.

"We all now stept forth to be crowned, and prostrated ourselves, raising our eyes up to the goddess; but, gracious heaven! what did my eyes behold! One of the graces seemed to be *Elmira*. I imagined to be deluded by a dream, and rubbed my eyes, but still beheld the same countenance, the same striking resemblance of features, the same beautiful energy of *Elmira's* looks. Now she glanced at me; but her looks pervaded almost instantly the whole spacious building, as if in search of some dear object. She found it, at length. Gracious heaven! how placidly she smiles! her eye speaks the audible language of internal delight; her bosom palpitates more violently, lifting the Greek garment; she is near her heaven, has found her lover. No, it is not Elmira. My Elmira cannot have forgot me *thus*; my senses fail me; a chilly tremor pervades my nerves, and stops the pulses of my heart. All the objects around me seemed to be over-darkened by a thick mist. I suffered myself mechanically to be crowned with my companion, and, with a kind of senseless apathy, submitted to the eruption of her excited sensuality, scarcely attending to her voluptuous sighs and the pressure of her hand: I only had eyes for my nymph, and for her resemblance with my sainted wife. Her looks met me, at length; but she did not blush, and only smiled. Her eyes now wandered indifferently from my person to rest longer on the other groups. Ere long they began again to sparkle with a secret desire: I envied the happy object of her silent fondness, following her looks, and, alas! they rested on Count V******, assuming an additional lustre, and sparkling with uncommon rapture, while that happy man, absorpt in the contemplation of his Augusta's charms, did not even observe it.

"The whole company rose at length, and having received the blessing of the goddess, crowded towards the garden, which, being illuminated with coloured lamps, displayed what one chose to exhibit, and hid what another wished to conceal. Cool grottos, elastic seats of swelling turf, concealed in the most secret recesses of the mazy shrubbery, the beautiful night, and the aromatic exhalations of the myrtles, and of numberless sweet scented flowers, invited with a powerful charm the enraptured senses to enjoy the pleasures of love.

"Fortunately I lost my antiquated companion in the crowd; fled into the darkest labyrinths of the garden to escape her, and went in search of a retired spot to collect my confused thoughts, and to commune in solitude with the ideas that perturbated my mind. However, I met in every secret path a couple that was animated with a similar desire for solitude; or, while I was going to seat myself down in a retired place, interrupted another that already had found what I was seeking after. The Duke met me out of breath, and agitated with all the furies of disappointment. He had lost his Elizabeth, on whose account he had given the feast, whose senses he had intended to surprise, and whom he had expected to animate with sweet sentiments propitious to his love. He was in despair, and stopping every nymph, examining every secret recess, and disturbing the raptures of each happy couple, was whipped through the grove, according to the laws of the feast. I left him to his foolish fury, and directed my course to a favourite spot in the neighbourhood of a cascade, which so frequently had invited me to sweet meditations, where I already had so often arranged my confused ideas, and cheered my hopes, lulled into tranquillity by the harmonious murmurs of the descending waters. I found it occupied by three persons, who were engaged in friendly conversation, and laughing, as I supposed, at the Duke, who had overlooked them in the heat of pursuit. As I came nearer, I descried the Count of V******, Augusta, and Elizabeth, and seated myself by their side, silent and speechless. They asked me what ailed me; and apprehended I was not well. I was going to reply, but a torrent of tears gushing from my eyes, I began to sob violently, and dropt to the ground. Elizabeth felt so much concern at my lamentable situation, that she forgot the reserve natural to her sex, and encircled me with her arms. However, I was insensible of these tokens of her affection, and the Count restored me to my recollection with great difficulty. He then endeavoured to discover the cause of my affliction, taking Elizabeth's hand, and putting it into mine. She not only suffered it, but even attempted to cheer me up by the most tender caresses; yet I did not return the emanations of her affection, turning my eyes from her tender looks, and casting them melancholy to the ground.

"I fear," the Count exclaimed, at length, with tenderness, "I fear our friend is very ill. The night is damp, ladies; your dress is light; you too expose yourselves to the bad effects of the chilling air. Let us return to the castle."

"Having seen the ladies to their apartments, he took me affectionately by the hand, led me back into the garden, and being seated on a bench, began in soothing accents: "Here we are beyond the reach of observation, Carlos: you know I am your friend; I insist upon sharing your grief." How could I have resisted his affectionate caresses, and his generous warmth? I informed him of the most material part of my history, and acquainted that dear friend with the cause of my affliction and grief.

"He listened attentively to my tale, comforted me tenderly; and when I had finished, said, "The lady whom you have seen, is not Elmira; I know her. Your plan of going in search of the *unknown*, and of taking vengeance on them, is extravagant, and bordering on madness. Endeavour to find out an asylum where you can remain unknown, and there attempt to recover the peace of your mind. This is the advice of a friend who sincerely loves you; but leave this place as soon as possible. You see you have gained Elizabeth's heart; don't excite wishes in her bosom which you never *can* gratify."

"He then conducted me back to my apartment, and stayed the whole night conversing with me on my situation, and giving me counsels which I afterwards recollected but too late. He entreated me not to return to my native town before I should have made farther discoveries, and promised to take all possible pains to serve me, for which reason he wished me to remain in the neighbourhood, proposing Madrid for my future place of residence. His penetrating and experienced eye discovered, with an uninterrupted equanimity, connections which I had entirely overlooked; and his great and noble heart took such a lively share in my fate, that it would have proved dangerous to himself, if he had been possessed of less experience and prudence. If Heaven had blessed me for a longer space of time with the happiness of his society, and if an unforeseen change of circumstances had not removed him from the situation in which it was possible for him to make some discovery in my behalf, we should probably have been enabled by our union to come at the bottom of the matter, and, in time, have prevented an evil which, by its consequences, gave reason to presage the most baneful effects.

"Being completely convinced by his sage advice, he promised me to speak to the Duke, in order to render my sudden departure as little suspicious and surprising as possible. A palpable pretext for my journey was invented, and I took leave of the company on the subsequent day. You may think with what emotions I bade a last adieu to the amiable Elizabeth. The lovely girl had gained on my affections by a partiality for me, which, in the latter days of my residence at the castle, threw off all reserve. She would not let me depart before I had given her a solemn promise not to forget her entirely, and, if possible, to see her once more under happier circumstances. I quitted that charming society with a heavy heart, accompanied only by the Count, who went a few miles with me.

CHAPTER VII.

My journey to Madrid contains nothing worth notice, at least nothing that related to my situation. The safety and the peace with which I continued my journey, made me once more believe that it was possible I could escape my tormentors; I already began to dream of future serenity of mind, and to form airy plans of happiness. I travelled incognito, and my cheering imagination reflected a mild light upon all objects; I enjoyed my independent situation with internal delight. I can truly say, that that period was one of the most cheerful of my life. The consciousness of having left some friends,

who took a share in my concerns, and even my tender affections
for the Count, gave a purity to my disposition, of which I thought
it never could be capable. Thus light and darkness succeeded each
other alternately in my fate.

"When I came to Madrid, I took a house, and furnished it as if I
intended to remain there a long time. I had agreed with the Count
that he should furnish me with the requisite money, and began to
choose a circle of acquaintances and friends in which I could hope
to spend those months which I considered as a probationary time
tolerably happy. Connections with people of middle rank, music,
the play-house, and reading, diverted me almost a whole year in the
most agreeable and satisfactory manner, when an accident, which I
drew upon me by my own folly and imprudence, deprived me again
of that happiness.

"In the companies which I visited, it was not always possible to
avoid playing at cards; but as my income was uncertain, and easily
could be stopt by my persecutors, I carefully avoided all experienced players and noted gamblers. Yet my ill stars would have it,
that my secret tormentors should find out the way by which I was
provided with money; for I received neither money nor letters from
the Count in the course of six months, notwithstanding my writing frequently to him. My regularity had, 'till then, preserved me
from want, and promised to do so for some time to come, when,
one fatal evening, I was so much inebriated with joy and wine, that
I staked more money than I was used to do, and was so unfortunate
to see my cash gradually dwindle away under the hands of cunning
thieves. I saved only as much as would serve to maintain me a few
weeks longer. I waited several weeks for letters from the Count; and
being, at length, reduced, by despair and shame, to the last extremity, I resolved to quit Madrid, and to return to Alcantara. I sold my
furniture to pay my debts, and was obliged to travel on foot for want
of money. Thus I was again reduced to my former unfortunate situation by my own imprudence, notwithstanding the sage counsels
and exhortations of my friend, and in spite of my firm resolutions.
I gave myself voluntarily up to my secret enemies, from whom I
seemed to have delivered myself for some time, with so much
trouble and through such great sacrifices; and while I was furiously
enraged at my not being able to escape one misfortune, I ran heed-

lessly into the very mouth of a still greater one. What ought to have bent down my spirit, only animated me with additional courage; what, at some other period, would undoubtedly have exhausted my firmness, raised it now to a higher degree. While I was poor, a helpless beggar, and exposed to every danger and distress, I cheered myself with hopes of which my wearied soul would not have been susceptible amid all the encouragements of a smiling life.

"Negligence, and a want of knowledge of those little advantages which are so useful to a traveller, soon lessened my little wealth rapidly; and I was scarcely a few days journey distant from the capital, when I had but very little money left. Yet my courage did not forsake me: the remainder of my cash was just sufficient to purchase a miserable lute at the next town: I have some talent for music, and knew then a number of popular songs by heart, which I had learned in better days for my amusement. My misfortunes and my enthusiasm animated the miserable instrument: I addressed myself chiefly to the female sex, and being gifted with a tolerably good form, I obtained every where bread and a favourable reception: for, studying the temper of those whom I had to deal with, I only played such tunes as were agreeable to their situation and disposition of mind. Thus I finished one half of my journey, pretty well satisfied with my situation, animated with bodily strength, blessed with serenity of mind and with a cheerful countenance.

"On a sultry afternoon, when the heat of the sun, hunger, and fatigue, had exhausted me entirely, I was just going to quit the high road, and to rest my weary limbs in the refreshing shade of a distant wood, where I expected to find some fruit, when I descried a little cottage, at the foot of a hill, not far off from the highway, in the centre of a small garden, and a neat grove of fruit trees. A bell, which was suspended near that humble mansion, told me that it was the residence of a hermit. The whole bore such an inviting aspect of neatness and elegance, that I was pre-occupied in favour of its possessor. The God of plenty seemed to have blessed that little Paradise. Blossoms and fruits were most beautifully blended with each other. Every little spot nourished some plant, and every plant was covered by a cooling shade. A tinkling rill crept from the neighbouring mountains towards that enchanting asylum of solitary piety, and seemed to creep slower through the luxuriant verdure of the garden, and to leave it with regret. I have never beheld a more charming picture of peace and cheerfulness than that residence of sequestered pleasure. Its beauties unfolded themselves more distinctly and charmingly the nearer I approached. A small grove embosomed the whole: every corner was adorned with a blossoming bower; and the murmuring rill was received in the centre by a bason, to protect the flowers and plants against the heat of the noontide sun, and to refresh them with its cooling exhalations. A refrigerating coolness pervaded that terrestrial paradise, and the whole exhibited a picture of rest after a toilsome labour.

"I rang the bell at the little gate. The hermit stepped out of his humble mansion, looking for his guest; and when he saw me, went to open the garden gate. While he performed that hospitable task, I looked at his countenance. What an interesting aspect did my eyes behold! The grief of many years, and the felicity which he seemed to have found at last, had produced features which penetrated into the deepest recesses of my heart. His looks bade defiance to the imposing deception of external appearance. Silent seriousness rested in his mien: his countenance displayed the vestiges of a dear-bought conquest over every warring passion of former years: his reverend brow was furrowed by early misfortunes: a faint gloom of melancholy sat upon the pensive eye: the tone of his voice was full and charming, but awful even to the innocent; and his whole form exhibited a most interesting picture of virtue, purified from every dreg in the furnace of adversity; of humanity, that seemed to embrace every fellow-creature; unassuming nobility, paternal goodness, and of silent internal contentment.

"I had forgot the words I intended to address to that reverend being when I approached him, and stood before him seized with speechless awe. All the images of venerable suavity and humanity, which I had borrowed from the mystic cavern, and still carried in my mind, blushed at the sight of that reverend countenance. Here I saw happiness united with peace: I approached her humble abode with blissful dreams, and now trembled to be so near its venerable inmate. I had taken the first resolution to preserve equanimity in every scene of life, to meet every hope and fear with tranquillity: I had already made a toilsome beginning and nevertheless had remained constant to that resolution; but here, at the sight of that picture of terminated years of sorrow, the former weakness, so natural and so dear to the human heart, awoke again, and I again began to tremble for my happiness.

"He was, besides, no hermit of the common sort. He had, indeed, secluded himself from the sight of men; but he did not abscond himself in inaccessible caverns, nor in the most secret recesses of impenetrable forests. His peaceful cottage was situated on an open spot; a happy, encouraging example; it admitted every one, and was a comfortable asylum for the weary wanderer. He had retired from a smaller circle of his brethren only to be enabled to serve in peace a greater one. My grateful heart, so irresistibly attached to the hoary sage at first sight, dissolved with reverential awe into sentiments of virtue and humanity, which I had become a stranger to. "Step in, poor stranger," he said, on perceiving my weariness and astonishment: "walk in; rest yourself in the shade of my trees; refresh yourself at my spring, and eat of my fruits." "Forgive, reverend father, (I said, while I approached him:) I am astonished and confounded: forgive me that I cannot return your kind reception as I ought to do. Yet I hope my silent thanks will satisfy you."

"He squeezed my hand without replying a word; shut his garden-gate, and went to open his cottage; fetched an easy chair, and having covered it with a mat, placed it for me beneath a spreading walnut tree, which over-shadowed his humble mansion. He then fetched water from the spring, and having placed it before me with a little basket of figs, peaches, and grapes, seated himself upon a wooden bench against which my chair was reclined, and said, "Eat, dear friend, and refresh yourself: you seem to want it."

"How happy are you, reverend father, (I resumed, taking him tenderly by the hand, and looking in his smiling countenance,) to live in the bosom of this terrestrial paradise, where you represent the image of the all-bountiful Father of nature amongst men whose warmest gratitude you deserve, and, without doubt, are rewarded with."

"Happy! Yes, I am happy, at present, my young friend. I rejoice at you and my brethren whom I can comfort."

"He then appeared to be absorpt in a transient reverie; but I soon roused him with these words: "I am quite exhausted, good father: will you give me leave to stay at your cottage to-night?"

"With pleasure, my son; to-night, to-morrow, as long as you choose. It is, in general, not my custom: however, your countenance inspires me with confidence, and I will readily make an exception from my rule."

"Do not think that I shall waste my time in idleness while with you; you are already bent down by the burden of hoary age; the vigour of your body is fled: your garden requires labour; these arms are sinewy, and I understand a little of gardening."

"Well, my son, I give you leave to stay with me as long as you choose: I shall be a tender father to you while you are with me. You seem not to be born for the situation whose badge you wear. You will assist me, and I shall not let you depart without salutary advice and relief." So saying, he inclosed my hand tenderly in his. I rose, and kissed it with filial affection. Burning tears, which I could not retain, bedewed that reverend hand; and I dropt at his feet, in the fullness of my heart, encircling his knees. His heavenly eyes too swam in tears, and his bosom heaved higher. I beheld his noble countenance brightning up with a heaven of amiable sentiments which had lain dormant, and now pervaded all his features with speaking vivacity and redoubled energy. He strained me to his bosom, calling me his hapless son, and promised to convey comfort to my mind from his parental heart and experience. I felt my whole existence changed at once, in that sacred moment of purest reverence, for a being of a higher order; and my spirit was straitened by novel, unknown sensations and new prospects.

"He raised me, at length, and made me sit down on the bench. "Refresh yourself now, my son; we shall be sufficiently at leisure to unbosom ourselves to each other: you may relate your history to me to-morrow, or at any other future period, and ask my advice, if you choose. I now shall leave you, to work in my garden: you may follow, and assist me, if you are not too much fatigued." He dropt my hand, and left me.

"No sooner was I in private, than I was visited by pleasing fancies. I had longed for a peaceful asylum as the highest object of my ardent wishes, and here I had found it, at last, in the arms of a tender father and a loving friend. I was already so happy in the moment, so content, that I forgot the stern frowns of futurity; being chained to presence by its smiling aspect, I abandoned myself so entirely to the first charm of new hope, as if they were already realized. The recollection of time past vanished suddenly; I could not recal to my memory even the most trifling incident of former times: my life being at once cheered up by the unexpected dawn of roseate joy, appeared to promise an uninterrupted train of pleasing enjoyment. The last moment of terminated sufferings is always a sufficient atonement, and even a sweet reward, for misery past; and being rendered more sensible and susceptible by pain, we gradually ripen in the mutable changes of life, for the most rapturous bliss.

"A short, tranquil slumber having invigorated my whole frame, I rose, taking up a spade, which the hermit had left for me at the entrance of his cottage, and went the way he had pointed out to me. I found him at work in the midst of a beautiful spot of ground, covered with a gay tapestry of variegated flowers, leaning on his working tool, and looking at the children of his diligence, absorpt in secret joy. Hearing me approach, he smiled kindly at me, asking if I had any knowledge of the cultivation of vines; and, upon my answering in the affirmative, directed me to look after a little vine-yard bordering on the south-end of his garden. We worked till the sinking sun had hid his radiant orb behind the western mountains; he smiled frequently at my diligence, applauding my assiduous dexterity; and I was happy beyond the power of description. "Can the noisy bustle of the world," he exclaimed repeatedly during our work, "afford that sweet and tranquil pleasure one enjoys in the society of the plants our diligence has reared and softened, and in the unclouded conversation with that modest, gentle part of the creation? Animated by their example, and their passiveness, com-forted by the mysteries of their nature, with higher prospects, and refreshed by their fragrant exhalations, I have frequently, in their society, forgot men, and even learnt to cherish them. I have exam-ined their structure, and am become the confident of the rose that refreshes me with its spicy odour, of the fruit that nourishes me, and of the grove that spreads its cooling shade around my cot-tage. I have found friends amongst them; their life serves me as an example and a rule; and I am grown a stranger to sorrow. How fre-quently has their silent growth recalled to my mind the sweet dor-mant images of my juvenile years; how often have they animated me to keep firm on the road of unsullied virtue and wisdom! Even a dream exalts the mind, if it occupies it sufficiently, and renders it happy in the midst of its occupations."

"Thus he entertained me with cheerful and instructing lessons of wisdom till evening was setting in; and I saw the sun decline with unusual contentment and inward rapture. All the objects around smiled, and seemed to share my happiness. We took our working implements, and returned to the cottage; seating ourselves upon an elevation of elastic turf before the door of that humble asylum of contentment and tranquillity. "You have worked well," said my venerable host, "and deserve a proportionate reward." He then fetched some fruits, a loaf of white bread, and a bottle of wine. We ate with a keen appetite, and seasoned our meal with cheerful talk, transported into the golden age of yore, till the last ray of the sun had died away, and a sparkling host of twinkling stars covered the azure firmament in silent majesty. A simple couch was our bed, and I never had enjoyed such a sweet and profound sleep, nor had I ever risen so early and so cheerful.

CHAPTER VIII.

Several days elapsed equally serene with the first, and divided between labour, rest, and happiness. Whatever the hermit spoke, contained sage precepts, rules of virtue, and directions of happiness. His actions were of the same nature. I always went to rest happier than I had risen, and always rose more content than I had laid down. The hoary hermit preserved a constant silence with regard to my history, putting not one question to me concerning my fate; and I was too much occupied with my felicity, to reflect on misfortunes past, and introduce that painful subject.

"One evening I was sitting later than usual upon the turfy seat before our door, contemplating the charms of my new residence, and the solemn beauties of the serene night. The hermit was already gone to rest, and I left to myself. I was entirely absorpt in profound meditations on my peaceful situation, and yet open to all the charms that surrounded me. I inhaled the refreshing exhalation of the trees, and the balsamic odour of the spicy flowers, diffusing their rich perfumes through the nocturnal air on wings of cooling breezes. I was lost in the capacious space of time: eternity represented itself before my flowery imagination, with its numerous train of never-fading blessings, as a just rewarder of well-spent years. The mystic strains of night unfolded themselves gradually from the general silence of the creation like harmonies from a better world; the undulation of the night-air, the rustling of the leaves, the chirping of a cricket, and the dying tinkling of the rill, vibrated in my listening ears like whispers of an invisible train of spirits sporting on the wings of fragrant breezes. The creative dusk, composed of the misty vapours of the night, and of the silver light of the rising moon, ethereal images, and the trembling rays of the Queen of night, which stole timidly through the half transparent leaves, painted them with the pale dappling mist of the realm of spirits. The murmuring rill represented itself as a gleaming streak, which lost itself in the nocturnal stillness of the valley. Solitary bushes, whose tops nodded on its banks, formed dancing phantoms on its smooth surface. My elated soul, conscious of her innate power, soared through the vapours of the night and the mystic dusk, which enfolded all objects around the curling clouds and the milky way. The stars disappeared without returning again: I lost myself in the populous realms of my busy fancy; penetrating to the world where Elmira resided, where she awaited me, hoarding up joys unspeakable for her Carlos. I enjoyed her conversation, and dreamed myself encircled with heavenly glory in her arms; my bridled passions were silenced, I had improved in virtue, and felt myself deserving of her never-fading love. What a moment of bliss! what a numerous train of years was concentred in it! No joys surpass those of a glowing imagination, and of enthusiasm, if they are occupied with a dear object.

"I now had reposed my presensions and my wishes in her lap, and returned with additional contentment to myself. I recollected my lute, and went on tip-toe into the cottage to fetch it. Having found it, I returned to my former place, and began to unburden myself in melodious strains of the rest of those overflowing sensations which painfully straitened my bosom. All the feelings of my soul imparted themselves to the artless strains I drew from the melodious chords. All nature seemed to listen to my nocturns. The recollection of the bliss I had enjoyed in Elmira's arms, now made my fingers run quicker over the sonorous chords. However, the cheerful strains soon died away in swelling plaintive notes, when my imagination began to cool, and the painful remembrancer in my heart reminded me that she was no more. At once the joyous hope of a future re-union with the darling of my heart lighted upon my mournful soul, while triumphal strains resounded through the air, and sweet tranquillity was restored to my agitated bosom. I fancied to see Elmira's spirit throning on a silver cloud, and listening to my raptures. I had never felt with so much energy how dear that heavenly woman was to my heart, how indissolubly she was united with my whole existence, than now, when I saw her again, when I enjoyed her purer and without senses, contemplating myself in her heavenly mind as in a mirror. I felt, to my astonishment, and with unspeakable rapture, that she was no more the same Elmira I knew formerly; she now appeared to my fancy as a sainted angel, disencumbered of all terrestrial qualities and defects; a pure unspotted beauty, glowing with fervent love for me, notwithstanding her raptures, which sprung from the consciousness of her exalted virtues.

"While I was yet absorpt in these ecstatic reveries, I heard a noise close by me. The cottage door opened, and my benevolent host joined me. "A new talent," he said, smiling, "which I am rejoiced to discover in you: you sing and play in no inferior stile. You have waked me from my sleep in a most agreeable manner. But what means that tear in your eye, my poor friend? Come, let us beguile the rest of the night with confidential talk." So saying, he seated himself by my side. I was not able to reply; but took his pale trembling hand, pressing it tenderly to my bosom, and looking with heart-felt gratitude in his smiling eye.

"Either the recollection of former times," he continued, "lays heavy upon your mind, or futurity fills you with anxious bodings. But it will be wiser to enjoy the present moment. What need you to care for joys or sufferings which are nothing else but a dream? and what will it boot you to guess at futurity, since the charm of the present moment directs our inclinations, and every thing that does not resemble it appears terrible to us?"

"No, my father, I do not grieve at the present time, nor am I anxious about futurity. You have provided for either with equal kindness. You surprised me only in a conversation with beloved, sainted friends; and my tears were tears of joy, produced by our re-union.

"Beloved, sainted friends, did you say? Your looks, my son, speak of great and early sorrows. I am most affectionately concerned for you, and take a parent's share in your sufferings. You know me already sufficiently to be convinced that we are related in that point. You shall learn my history at some future time. Tell me now a part of the incidents of your life, if you have no objection to it, and want any advice or comfort." How could I have resisted the confidential request of a father, how could I have withstood his tenderness and his concern? Being already sufficiently prompted to it by the disposition of my mind, which just was returning from the land of peace and fraternal comfort, my heart readily consented to gratify the wishes of the good old man, and unburthened itself of a heavy load of grief and melancholy by sharing it with a friend. I related to him, in that night, my history to the present period, and nearly in the same manner in which I have communicated it to you, dear Count.

"The hermit listened patiently to my tale, and without any apparent surprise; scarcely *one* mien bespoke his concern or compassion. He seemed to be absorpt in a dream, in which his feelings took a moderate share, without being once stopt or interrupted in their gentle course: they only seemed to be sensibly interested in the conclusion, which had brought me to his cottage. As soon as I came to that point, he folded me in his arms, without uttering a single sound. I reclined my face against his heart, which audibly beat more violently than usual. I was exhausted, and half fainting: incoherent accents, mingled with sobs, stammered my gratitude. The enthusiasm of filial love, which had been weakened and interrupted by early misfortunes and sorrows, awoke again with redoubled force. While I searched for my lute to express my grateful sensations, I found a language deserving of him and of myself.

"You have lost every thing, Carlos," he resumed; "parents, wife, and happiness. I am as sensible of your loss as yourself; but hearken; one treasure has not yet been taken from you; you have still a friend left, and I will convince you that I deserve that sacred name. You are, therefore, not isolated nor forsaken, as you dream. Renounce, for a short time, do you hear? only for a short time, your lofty wishes, and you will be enabled again to hope to find happiness and peace."

"Oh! I have already found them in your society, in your parental

goodness, in assisting you, and in returning your love. Look! here is
the goal of all my wishes. I am in want of nothing further."

"And my happiness too will encrease, if you continue to be my
friend, dear Carlos, and to stay with me. My hair is already bleached
by age; my hands tremble; and being bent down by the load of
years, I stagger already towards the grave: you shall be my heir; not
the heir of this little estate, but of my experience and principles.
Wait only a few years longer, and then mix again with the world,
to practise them; and if you find them useful, and have improved
all your faculties amid the busy crowd of incidents and perplexing
situations, as you *can* and *ought* to do, then return to this solitude to
enjoy them."

"Mix with the world, did you say? with men who have deceived
and repelled me so frequently?"

"Have you not also left *friends* behind you who love you? Don't be
unjust to them, dear Carlos."

"No friend whom I have not found again in this peaceful solitude;
no pleasure which you could not give me too; none of the purest
and most beneficent enjoyments, which I could not find in this
paradise, without painful trouble and disappointment."

"I will believe, dear Carlos, that this could suffice your heart for
years, yea for the rest of your life. You certainly would find around
this cottage plenty of work to occupy you, and sufficient gratifications to keep you always awake and to charm you: but you say you
would be able to procure them without painful trouble: I only ask
you, has the refreshing shade and the cooling spring ever given you
so much delight after an idle walk as when you enjoyed it after a
long fatiguing journey?"

"But, my father, have I not gathered a sufficient stock of experience, have I not lived long enough? Has my heart not been nursed
up amid grief and woe, and the vexations of disappointed hopes?
Is my mind not sufficiently formed, has it not means enough to
render these cooling shades constantly charming without fatigue,
and always equally desirable?"

"No, Carlos, you are mistaken. Stay with me till I am gone to my
eternal home, and you will be sensible of it. Grief is no good pupil
of wisdom: and believe me, not here, but amongst men, you will
find peace. Peace of mind does not consist in the oblivion of our-

selves. To rush senseless out of the bustle of the world, is no step nearer to perfection; and flying the society of men, without knowing them from experience, does not sweeten solitude. But when you have enjoyed the world some time longer, and more frequently seen your hopes and dreams frustrated; when you have attained a proper knowledge of things, and of their intrinsic value, and thus obtained a right to reflect on, and to judge of them; when you have seen the sufferings of others, and frequently felt how trifling yours are if compared with theirs; when you, inspired and supported by the expectation of a peaceful end, have contemplated every thing with the firm look of true liberty, and nothing in the world gives you any more pleasure or grief; then, dear Carlos, then wisdom and solitude will cheerfully receive you in their bosom. You must not go in search of them as an exile from your house, nor filled with rancour against your neighbours; no, you must go voluntarily, and quit the society with a cheerful farewel.

"If you reflect now on the time past, you behold nothing but an empty space, nothing but ungratified and lost dreams of your imagination. You have experienced a sufficient share of adversity, and lived long enough; but you have been surprised by the too rapid course of your fate, and one half of your experience is irretrievably lost for you. I pity you; yet it would be better for your future happiness, if the greater part of it were still before you.

"You live in this moment entirely upon the sweet expectations of futurity, without being aware of it. Hope is always the first dawn that lights upon our heart when it opens again for the reception of social happiness. If some accident, against which you cannot guard yourself, should drive you one time out of this cottage, and this solitude, your happiness would be irrecoverably lost. You would not have strength enough to seek it elsewhere."

"But, my father, what business have I with human society? How shall I converse with men? Being used to the company of your honesty and love, I should suffer myself to be deceived again."

"That you shall, Carlos. You shall launch again into the billowing ocean of the world, to learn the real value of things by repeated trials. Then you never will miss in your solitude what your imagination at present sees only at a distance; and while you shall be able to enjoy the present moment, because you are grown indifferent to futurity, you will, at the same time, have it in your power to console yourself with distant prospects, when the unavoidable trifling sorrows of the moment are hovering over you. The philosophy of life is nothing but an accurate occular knowledge of the vicissitude of all things."

"And is this all that I am to acquire by connecting myself again with men, to be content at the close of my life?"

"This will, indeed, be sufficient to make you content, but not to raise you to the highest degree of that happiness of which you are susceptible. This requires a great deal more, makes it requisite that all the powerful passions of your mind should have been active on the great stage of the world, and finished their ever-changing play. You must have acquired the power of stopping them in their rapid course, and of directing them to that point where they can be useful. You courted the favours of love, follow now the banners of laudable ambition."

"Is fame a good that will contribute to brighten the close of my life?"

"Fame in itself is certainly no good; but the desire of attaining it is the criterion of an exalted mind. Your faculties will gradually improve while you make the general love and regard of your cotemporaries the aim of your pursuits; your happiness will by degrees become less subjected to be tainted by those trifling incidents which mix so much bitterness with the life of the greater part of mankind. You will, indeed, not be happy while your career hurries you without rest from deeds to deeds; yet while you court the gratitude of nations, and roses blossom for you at the limits of time, you will wean yourself from your inferior passions. You will then one time awake from your dream: your present disposition, which was too early and too firmly interwoven with your feelings, warrants the truth of this prediction: and if you survive that period, the rest of your life will amply reward you for the misery and struggles of former days."

"I grant it, my father; but will my soul not be wearied too much by the repeated blows of adverse fate, as to be able to have a due sense of that reward? will she save her pure and beautiful susceptibility from the tempests of misfortune and disappointment?"

"Undoubtedly! provided you never lose sight of your aim, and

beguile your gloomy hours with cheering prospects of future happiness. Take it as a golden rule of happiness, to enjoy the present
moment, when your feelings are awake; and to console yourself
with the prospect of future times, when you perform the duties of
your station."

"But has a pastoral life, has that sweet uniform growing of the
faculties in the lap of nature, no charms, has it no gratifications to
bestow? Is it no happiness to lead a life in which every thing charms
and pleases, in which labour and pleasure aid each other in an eternal rotation, upon which no year of satiety and regret can intrude,
and every hour is bestrewed with flowers by the graces? You smile,
my father; but you will forgive me my enthusiasm. How could it be
otherwise in this delightful paradise, where I inhale the odour of
fragrant blossoms, where the evening breeze whispers gently in the
leaves, where the flower raises its dewy head, nodding sparkling in
the silver light of the moon: where peaceful tranquillity lights upon
my soul in the hallowed dusk of night; where I feel only what I am;
where time past smiles at me only as a cheerful dream, and futurity
amuses me in various pleasing shapes? How sweet is it to enjoy, in
this silent grove, the peace which is our work, to eat of the fruits we
have grown for our use, to live in the shade we have planted ourselves! And, when our senses grow weary, when the modest gloom
of the grove, when the mirror of the peaceful pond, when the fields
and the night cease to charm, the spirit still continues to live amid
an eternal change of new and unknown apparitions and pleasing
phantoms, our looks, which learn to extend themselves from individual parts to the whole, return with gathered treasures, and with
additional contentment, supplying the mind with an inexhaustible
store of materials for never-fading luxuries."

"I have suffered you to go on, Carlos, without interrupting you.
Nature and the few peaceful days you have enjoyed have inspired
you with a poetical fire. I rejoice at it, but fear that it will not be
of long duration. The enjoyment of the country, and of peace of
mind, is yet too novel to you. Your images will soon be exhausted.
And believe me, Carlos, even if accident and your noble soul should
render this retired life constantly new to you, yet you would regret
this happiness at the close of your days; for your spirit rather would
lose itself in the contemplation of your days past than be pleased

with them. A tranquil course of time renders the moments cheerful, but wearies the hours; and if it continues to flow in the same easy tide, without exerting its powers, without being roused by obstacles to an additional exertion, it becomes an image of tedious inanity. If, on the contrary, you have devoted the greater part of your life to a higher purpose; if you have sacrificed peace and enjoyment to the passion of extending the compass of your activity; if you see the dream of your wearied hours, fame and adoration, gradually rise, in the realms of futurity, to reality; how different are then your sensations! Your glowing soul does then with rapture reflect on the minutes elapsed without enjoyment; the time past ravishes your mind with a train of noble, laudable deeds; every particle of time is marked with the consciousness of internal applause; joy and grief, pain and recreation, compose a pleasing picture; and you behold, at the end of your career, your name respected by posterity, and adorned with the glory of immortal renown. If, at that period, the pastoral life of rural retirement still has some charms for you, then you may make the silent groves your residence, and bury yourself in the solitary gloom of secluded grottos. The recollection of your deeds will then surprise you in your solitude; you will reflect with fond delight on a well-spent life; your achievements will be your companions; and the consciousness of your virtues will make you forget the corruption of the age you live in. Your memory will always supply you with pleasing images; the source of your pleasure will be inexhaustible; and you will never want means of beguiling the tediousness of solitude."

"What you have said may be true, my father: my understanding comprehends you, but my heart is yet a stranger to the happiness you have set before me. However, you have more experience than I, and I ought therefore to be silent."

"You cannot but know, dear Carlos, and your own feelings will tell you, that joy avoids us when we seek for it; that it comes uncalled; that it oftentimes surprises us in the most rapturous shape, amid our labours and disappointments; but pays no regard to our solicitations, and resists all violent efforts of seizing it by dint of force."

"I have frequently experienced it."

"Stay here, and pant after happiness: anatomize the essence of things, and see what they afford you; nothing but tediousness and disgust. On the other side, apply your faculties to useful labour; search for knowledge: do not first sift the objects how far a more intimate acquaintance with them can afford you pleasure, but throw yourself without hesitation amongst them. If you do not find enjoyment during your labour, you may be sure to obtain it at the completion of your work, collected in one cup. And wherewith would you now fill up the time of solitude; by what ties combine the hours when circumstances interrupt your enjoyment? Your experiences are far from being science. Endeavour to improve in any branch of human knowledge, and you will become sensible that you are destitute of every thing that can sweeten the hours of solitude. Knowledge only preserves the innate energy of the mind, chases discontent and weariness from our solitary retirement, and accompanies us in every occupation, always charming and cheering, and offering us in every sorrow a certain, never-failing asylum."

"I feel, my dear father, that you are right. All the experiences I have picked up are nothing but the children of accident and necessity; study has not yet shaped them into a harmonious whole. But will it be worth while to undergo sufferings in order to acquire knowledge? are we not here near the source of the most beautiful and sublime wisdom?"

"Very true; but if you will find it, you must first have learnt to examine; you must prepare yourself by a long exertion of your faculties before you can value it properly, and acquire a nice and unerring sense of discerning the wisdom of the creator in the smallest object of nature, and cherish beauty wherever you find it. The misfortune you are so anxious to avoid is, besides, no real evil. Only take care not to deserve it; act with circumspection, and undertake nothing without having a sufficient ground for it. Even grief can afford joy to the enlightened: the conversation with dear departed friends produces tears of pleasure; and the reflection of times past thrills the human heart with a sweet, luxurious melancholy. Those sufferings that improve the mind by exerting its faculties, are certain gain for mankind. When we stand at the mark, absorpt in nature, with our pains and disappointed hopes, and some object in it seems to take a share in our grief, the bitterness of heart dissolves itself in a secret sweet melancholy, which exalts every pleasure, and discerns and catches, sometimes even at the brink of the abyss of time, every moment of contentment which, otherwise would, perhaps, have been lost to us. In short, peaceful retirement is salutary and pleasing only when it has unfolded itself from the scenes of the most energic exertion of our faculties, when we first have mingled with the world, and contributed our share to the general happiness: it is a blessing only to the weary wanderer, who has struggled with the difficulties of a long journey, and can sit down in the solitary shade furnished with a good store of useful observations gathered on his pilgrimage. No one can enjoy solitude better than a man who is bent down with the burthen of age, and has made a wise use of his life. He can look back with pleasure on a long train of gratifications, and converse in his retirement with the useful actions of his former days: his contented, satiated imagination represents all the past scenes of his existence in a mild and pleasing light; the adversities of former days are buried in oblivion; he recollects only the happier hours; the world is his friend; and the peaceful consciousness of his deeds encircles his temples with the garland of immortality."

CHAPTER IX.

The hoary hermit frequently discoursed with me in the hours of night, after the fatigues of our labour, while cooling breezes whispered in the leaves, and the silver rays of the moon gaily skipped on the surface of the rivulet. The philosophy of futurity stole upon my mind, while I imagined to empty the cup of present happiness: the observation of the moment gradually delineated to me rules for similar events; I learned to husband my hours, and to apply them properly; accident ceased to frown at me, because I learned to improve it for my benefit; and I soon began to consider the world as a game for a trifle, in which it is indifferent, when one rises, whether one has lost or gained; and in which one rejoices at one's skill and dexterity, and repents only the faults one has committed.

"The cultivation of the garden afforded us sufficient amusement during the day; every thing prospered under our hands; we were delighted at the growth of our plants, and derived a wholesome subsistence from their fruits. The evenings were sacred to rest and wisdom. A bower of odorous woodbine received us then in its refreshing coolness. The mystic whispers of the evening breeze did, indeed, mix something enthusiastic and melancholy with our ideas; however, this served only to mellow the feelings of my heart. The mind of the venerable hermit unfolded itself gradually with less restraint and more serenity. As soon as he perceived that I was desirous to share his ideas, he began to be more communicative. Though he never entered into a minute detail of his history, yet I learnt the greatest part of it from a thousand little strokes of its secret effects, events great in their cause, developement and consequence. I perceived plainly, by his conversations, how an exalted mind educates itself, how rapidly it runs through all the accords of joy and grief; how it derives benefit from either, and improves moments for hours and years. A great variety of events had urged him from sentiment to sentiment; and yet he had maintained himself, after a certain period, which he applied to a resolute reflection, in an equilibrium of unconcern and joy. His just and virtuous consciousness floated peacefully on the current of time towards a happy or unhappy eternity; either of which he awaited with a firm equanimity. He carried his paradise in his heart, created within himself a consoling and cheerful companion, and needed no other society. This was the man who called me his son, and educated me for this life, and for eternity, in spite of all misfortunes, and even of happy incidents, which prevailed upon my weak heart more than all the tempests of adversity; for I generally lost in one rapturous moment of joy what all the storms of life could not take from me. However, this philosophy of my sage instructor did not find access to my heart till after a certain period, and only after he had gained all my little passions in its behalf; for the former required exertion and activity, and the latter panted after a luxurious and gratifying rest. I was at that period already too much disgusted with life, as to wish to extend it through labour; and being too much flattered by a new and unexpected peace, I was rather inclined to shorten it by a uniform and imperceptibly passing joy. Neither weariness nor disgust, which the hermit had prognosticated to me, was to be apprehended for some time after such a general exhaustion; the rosy days of my life returned once more adorned with greater charms by experience, by a long train of disappointed hopes, and involuntarily bridled passions.

"We were now and then interrupted in our daily labours by pilgrims, who refreshed and rested themselves in our cottage. They were all welcome to the little comforts we could bestow, and our happiness increased in the same measure in which we could be useful to our weary visitors. Our humble abode frequently resembled a cottage of the golden age. Our frugal meals were composed of fruits grown in our garden, of excellent bread, which every day was brought to us from the neighbouring village, and of cyder and wine of our own making. Two goats furnished our table with milk and cheese; and some bee-hives with fragrant honey. Every thing appeared to be twice our property, because we saw it grow under our hands; and even our joy was two-fold when we could share the produce of our toil with the needy. We entered into confidential talk with our pilgrims; our hospitality and kindness unlocked their lips, and they generally left us a part of their history. It is surprising how much the conversation with such different characters improved me; how I deduced from those relations, assisted by the hermit, rules which proved salutary to me all the rest of my life; and how I grew more satisfied with my fate, when I saw other sufferers not entirely comfortless under a heavier and more pressing load of sorrows. The hoary hermit was, besides, the oracle of all the surrounding neighbourhood. His humanity and great experience were generally known. He lent his assistance wherever he could, and commonly was successful in his advice. Two days in the week were devoted to that business; at other times he did not like to be disturbed. Our neighbours knew it, and behaved accordingly. Our little cottage was the temple where the wishes of numberless suppliants were deposited, and many found relief. They rejoiced to shew their gratitude, loading him with presents of fruits and meat; yet he accepted nothing for himself, but distributed the gifts he received among the poor who assembled before his door. This situation might well have filled up the rest of my life.

"My happiness was, however, too great to be of long duration. The hermit's health began to decline some months after my arrival at his solitude. His soul, being too pure for his body, gradually began to disengage itself from the ties which united it to its terrestrial part; his strength was exhausted, he left off working, and prepared himself seriously to leave this world. Dear Count, that melancholy event gave me the greatest and most pungent sorrow I ever experienced. It was a most afflicting sight to see that beautiful spirit gradually extinguish, that great and noble heart grow cold, and those heavenly features of the most expressive countenance stiffen by degrees. How frequently did I encircle his knees with my trembling arms when he sat on the turf-seat to enjoy the cooling breezes of the night, taking the most lively interest in my happiness, paying the greatest attention to every thing that could improve and instruct me, and contemplating, with inward rapture, the beauties of nature, though he was already on the brink of eternity. He slowly took leave of this world, which omitted nothing to make his parting as painful and affecting as possible. Autumn never was more beautiful; never did I behold his hermitage adorned with so many charms, nor embellished by nature's forming hand in a more delightful manner. Nature exhausted itself to appear in its gayest attire before he parted for ever from its numberless beauties.

I never shall forget those nights in which I so plainly saw his peaceful mind gradually ripen for a better world. The theme of his discourses was more sublime than usual; he soared with me beyond the milky way, dwelling with more than common warmth on the amiable attributes of the great Creator of the universe, and on the prospects of unspeakable bliss he has opened to our view. The harmony he descried throughout the boundless realms of nature, the paternal care of Providence for the happiness of man, and the preservation and nourishment of the brute creation, which struck his mind, on the verge of mortality, with additional force, the numberless wise means the great Author of our existence employs to educate his children, and to qualify them gradually for the enjoyment of greater bliss, made his eyes beam with joy and hope. His disembodied mind roved with inward rapture through the boundless realms of eternity, anticipating the happiness of a more intimate connection with that nameless Being whose ways are often hid in midnight darkness, but are ever wise and ever good.

"He grieved only that he should leave *me* behind. He wished much that it might have been in his power to form my mind completely for my own happiness, and that of my fellow-creatures. He foresaw that I should never attain the mark entirely without an experienced guide: however, his love, and the impressions his death left on my heart, saved me many a painful experience, rendering me unfit for it by the disposition of my mind; and you, my dearest friend, will soon see me act with a firmness, which, at first sight, will appear to you totally heterogeneous to my unsettled character.

"How frequently did I, at that melancholy, heart-rending period, lay prostrate at his feet, bedewing them with my tears! how frequently did I recline my heaving breast against his bosom, uttering convulsive sobs! Every evening made me apprehend it would be the last I should be able to converse with him: when he went to rest, I kissed his trembling hand so fervently, as if bidding him an eternal adieu; and as soon as I awoke, made it my first business to steal on tip-toe to his couch, to examine whether his lips were still warm, and to see whether his bosom continued to heave; and when I found my apprehensions contradicted, I repaired with rapturous joy to the garden, enjoying the beauties of nature with additional delight: every object that met my sparkling eyes, seemed to be new born, and to exist only to give me pleasure. However, the melancholy parting hour drew visibly nearer; and one day, when he had fatigued himself more than usual with his little occupations, he threw himself against night half fainting on the turf-seat, folding his hands across his breast, and gazing with a staring look at the setting sun. A saint-like glory throned already on his countenance; and I could not help being pervaded with a chilling awe, when I beheld the fervent emanation of his devotion, and the silent serene joy that sparkled in his looks, a harbinger of his approaching happiness.

"To day I shall see you for the last time, dear Carlos," he began at last. "I part reluctantly with that beautiful spot the residence of joys and pleasures; with that peaceful cottage, the silent witness of my happiness. Yet Providence has ordained it so, and I submit to the will of the best of Fathers. If I could have been useful to this world any longer, my God and heavenly friend, thou wouldst not yet have called me hence. Father of man, a faithful obedient child returns to thy bosom." So saying, he extended his hands in silent rapture to Heaven; his drooping head hung on his heaving bosom, and he began to reel. I started up, and received him in my arms.

"Are you here, my son?" he whispered: "I thank thee, God, that I can die in the arms of a beloved child. Don't forget me, dear Carlos, and follow me."

"With these words his eyes closed, as if overpowered by a sweet sleep; his pallid lips opened once more, uttering a whisper, which I could not understand; his breast heaved once again with a deep sigh, and the faint pressure of his stiffning hand, with which he took an eternal farewel, died gradually away in mine. The best of men, the tenderest, most affectionate father, the friend of human kind, was no more; he had conquered the last foe. In vain did I press my mouth upon his clay-cold lips, almost petrified with agonizing sorrow; in vain expend all the breath of my heaving bosom to warm them again; the pulses of his heart ceased to beat, and his inanimate body sank motionless into my arms. I could not yet believe that I had lost him for ever, endeavouring to persuade myself that he only was asleep, and carried him to his couch. Yet I was scarcely returned into the garden, when I grew sensible of that melancholy truth, and felt the whole extent of my loss.

"All the objects around me assumed a grave-like appearance. The stillness of the approaching night never had been so awfully silent, the solitude never so solitary. Not one bird sang a doleful dirge, or my stupefaction prevented my hearing them; not a single cricket chirped; even the rivulet ceased to tinkle: I was isolated, left alone in the extensive creation, without friend, without father, and without a protector, being deprived of them at the moment I began to be most sensible of the value of the treasure I possessed.

"I will not tire you, dearest Count, with a picture of the just grief which perturbated my desponding mind, when I recovered the use of my senses, ascertaining the solitary situation in which I was left, and feeling myself at once deprived of every thing I had formerly been in want of to my greatest misfortune. "Is Heaven just?" I exclaimed, in the height of my agony. "Is Heaven just, in repaying me for *years* of woe with happy *hours?*" However, as soon as my mind grew calmer, I implored the Allwise to pardon my murmurs. I, ungrateful wretch, had forgot what an unspeakably great gratification he granted me in lieu of those trifling sufferings, and that he had made even the latter subservient to lead to greater future bliss.

"The most afflicting scene was yet to come. As soon as the death of the venerable hermit was known in the neighbourhood, numerous crowds of people thronged to our cottage; husbands and wives, whom he had made happy; parents and their families, whom he had

assisted with his sage counsels; hundreds of poor, whom he had
fed and relieved, came to sacrifice at the shrine of gratitude. It is
impossible to give an adequate description of that scene of general
woe. You cannot conceive, dearest Count, how deeply it affected
my sensibility, to see them surround his corpse, bedewing his clay-
cold hands with burning tears, contending with each other who
should be the first, and imploring Heaven to reward his virtues.
I did as much as lay in my power to assuage their grief, promised
not to leave them, and to become a faithful representative of their
and of my father and benefactor. Yet they paid little regard to what
I said, being too much occupied with the loss they had sustained;
and while these poor people dwelt only on the pain of the present
moment, they made me secretly indifferent to their future fate.

"The throng of visitors increased when I announced the day on
which the dear corpse was to be interred: hoary men, bent down
by the burden of years, women and children, in short, people of
every age, flocked together; all the inhabitants of the neighbourhood seemed to have assembled. Every one wanted to assist in dig-
ging his grave; and those that were not provided with the proper
tools, made use of their hands. He was at length interred beneath
a spreading chesnut-tree, on a spot which he had pointed out a few
days before his death; and as soon as the grave was filled with earth,
the whole multitude dropt on their knees, sending fervent prayers
to Heaven. They afterwards desired me to divide his garments
amongst them; every one contended for a rag, and carried it home
as a relic. His tomb was for several days crowded with visitors. The
night was the only time when I was left to myself; and I devoted
it entirely to the conversation with my sainted friend, repeating in
silent ecstasy his valuable principles and rules. I believed to hear his
spirit when the nocturnal breezes shook the leaves of the chesnut-
tree, and was every where haunted by a mystic sensation of his
presence, which followed me to all my labours and amusements. I
fancied constantly to hear his voice, whispering applause or blame
in my listening ears; was in a solitude without being alone.

"I returned, however, to the realms of reality before a month was
elapsed. The remembrance of his virtues remained always equally
strong and active in my soul, but I began to be less frequently
reminded of him. The nature of man and humanity resemble each

other every where. The enthusiasm of the neighbouring peasant decreased gradually, and the number of visitors grew less and less every day. I was soon left to myself, without company, and without the support the hoary hermit had received. A trunk, which stood in a secret corner of the cottage, and contained, besides a sum of money he had hoarded up, or saved from the wrecks of his fortune, all the papers relating to his history, and some loose reflections, occupied and diverted me for some time. Yet this source of amusement too was soon exhausted, and I entirely left to the reflection of my own history.

"My solitary situation, which began to grow irksome to me, and the promise I had made to my sainted friend, prompted me soon to mix again with the world, to gather new experience, and new means of restoring peace of my mind. I prepared myself for my departure, resolving to return one time to the cottage, which I always considered as my last asylum. I prevailed upon an honest peasant, from a neighbouring hamlet, to live with his family at the hermitage, and to promise to keep it in proper repair. Having paid a last farewel visit to the grave of my benefactor, I took my papers and my lute, and descended the hill with cheerfulness, which, however, was blended now and then with anxious apprehension.

CHAPTER X.

I was now going to launch again into the wide ocean of the world, presaging many interesting events, yet without having a clear prospect before me. Although the sum I found in the hermitage would have been sufficient to carry me through a part of Europe, yet I preferred my former manner of travelling as a minstrel and lute-player, having used myself to mix with the lower classes, where I found many little joys and means of pleasure, which the higher ranks would not have afforded me.

"Having wandered over a great extent of country, I chose, one evening, an old ruinous public-house for my night's lodging. The external appearance of the house was, indeed, sorry enough; but when I entered it, I was hailed with the laughter of merriment and jocundity. All its inmates seemed to be happy; the young men and girls were dancing, and the old ones playing at cards. Some lutenists and flute-players united their efforts, in a corner of the room, to animate the dance and the merry songsters. The scene of joviality was extremely welcome to me; I sat down, and joined the musicians.

"I scarcely had begun to touch the strings of my instrument, when something pulled me by my cloak, and turning round, I beheld a large, ugly, scabby dog at my elbow. He bounded joyfully against me, and I found it difficult to repel his caresses. He began at length to raise his voice in a most doleful accent, and I knew him at once to be my faithful Kusko, the play-fellow of my juvenile years, and the companion of my gambols and youthful sports. But, alas! how much was he altered! All his former beauty was gone; he had only one eye left: his ears were cropped; his hair was fallen off; and his present master a shabby beggar, who held him by a string. I was deeply affected by his misfortunes, the traces of which were legibly imprinted on his miserable carcass, and exasperated at the ingratitude of those who had expelled him from my house after many years of faithful service. The tears started from my eyes; I embraced him as a long-lost friend, and found it impossible to separate myself again from the dear companion of my youthful years.

"On inquiring after his present master, I learned not only his but also a great part of my own history. One of my grooms had sold him to the beggar for a trifle. "The young Marquis of G******," the beggar said, "is gone abroad, and no one knows what is become of him. He has committed the management of his estate to his friend Antonio, who lives in a constant round of pleasures, without considering that he may be called to an account sooner or later. A strange lady, and a little boy, live with him, and nobody knows whence they came. She leads, however, a very retired life, and walks frequently weeping in the garden, where I have seen her several times."

"He also informed me of many little circumstances which concerned my domestic affairs, and gave me plainly to understand, that the source of his intelligence was not very pure. Yet I could not but believe that the chief and most striking parts of his information were true. "A strange lady with a little boy! Who can that be?" My imagination reviewed in vain all possibilities; I could not trace out the least probability.

"And Don Antonio abandons himself carelessly to all sorts of pleasure, forgetting a friend who loves him so tenderly, and for whom he also seemed to entertain the sincerest affection?" I tormented myself in vain to find out a connection between those little excesses of joy and the unaccountable presence of the melancholy lady. I believed, however, that if she was no relation of his, her presence at the castle must be owing to some new event connected with my history, and had just reason to apprehend that the cause of it would endanger again my peace of mind. I am naturally disposed soon to forget past misfortunes; however, my cruel imagination torments me in return with all the terrors of future adversities, which I apprehend not to be able to avoid entirely. It exhausts itself already at a distance, as it were, and, fortunately for me, leaves little difficulty for the moment behind.

"Could any thing be more natural, under these circumstances, than the idea of examining every thing myself under the concealment of my disguise? As soon as this thought came into my mind, I ceased to ruminate on the intelligence I had received from the beggar, and, while I anticipated the execution of this resolution, I was as satisfied as if I had already obtained the wished-for elucidation. The plan in itself was not difficult to be executed. A long beard, which I had suffered to grow from negligence, a sun-burnt countenance, and a tattered coat, afforded me the greatest reason to hope to be taken for a beggar or a vagrant knave. I bought my faithful Kusko for a trifling sum of the beggar, took my lute under my arm, and having provided myself with a knotty club, began my pilgrimage with the first dawn of day.

"Don Antonio's residence was not far distant from the public house where I had spent the night. The beggar had informed me of this circumstance; and I soon convinced myself of it, on meeting with different objects which I knew. I recollected to have hunted sometimes so far in the vicinity of my castle. Allowing me but a short time to prepare myself for the part I was going to act, I began seriously to fear for my firmness. I recollected but too plainly that it had been frequently shaken on similar occasions; my heart was attached to the objects of my happier days with too much warmth,

and a too visible inquietude than that I could expect to conceal the
emotions of my mind. However, my attempt terminated otherwise
than I had expected.

"I beheld the turrets of my castle already against noon, and a few
small hours later arrived at the wall which enclosed my park. I was
surprised to find myself accidentally on the same way I had taken
in that dreadful night in which I left the castle. I was very much pre-
occupied against Antonio; however, every step that brought me
nearer to the castle, reconciled me more and more with him. I discovered a number of alterations in the garden; but they were so
judiciously made, that I could not but be pleased: and I perceived
plainly how much my friend had studied to gratify my taste at the
expence of his own, which was widely different from mine. Order
and cultivation prevailed every where in such a degree, that my
former affection for him soon returned. He had erected some neat
buildings on spots where I had wished to see them without having
had time to execute my plan, and even had adopted some ideas
which I recollected to have dropt in the course of conversation.

"I thought it would be best to untie Kusko from the cord by
which I led that faithful companion, lest he should betray me.
He had for some time displayed a strong desire to get loose, and
instantly made the best use of his liberty, running with the greatest
haste to the castle-gate, without caring any farther for me. Finding a little garden-gate open, I stole cautiously to a covered walk
which led to a wing of the castle: but a great noise, and loud peals
of laughter, which I heard at a small distance, prevented me from
proceeding farther, and I concealed myself in an adjacent arbour.
This retired spot was formerly the silent witness of many hours of
bliss and sorrow, and perhaps had witnessed, during my absence,
scenes of the greatest importance to me: but, alas! could tell no
tales. All the leaves and flowers around me seemed to welcome me
as a friend who was thought to be lost for ever; the trees were old
acquaintances, and their tops nodded friendly to me. I heard the
same gambols in the high grass around me, the same humming in
the air, and the same murmuring of the rivulet, to which I was used
to listen with so much rapture. Numberless different sensations
crowded upon my heart: and my fancy recalled all the pleasing pictures of youthful vigour and pleasure, which thrilled my soul with

delight, but at the same time gave me pain. Yet the consciousness of being again at my own estate, and of being able to say, This bower is mine; that shade, which infolds me so friendly; that odour of sweet scenting flowers; that rustling and murmuring around me, is mine, expelled all other ideas.

"I was soon interrupted in my reflections. A little boy went close by my hiding place, running after a large dog; an excellent child, full of energy, and of a beautiful form! Openness throned on his black eyes, and the smile of good-nature sat on his rosy cheeks. I could have given half the world for that sweet, heavenly cherub. Soon after I heard more steps approach, and soft whispers vibrated in my ears. I beheld a lady, through the leaves, leaning upon a man, and walking slowly by his side, with down-cast looks. When they came nearer, I discerned the person of Francisca; of my sweet, dear Francisca, and my friend Antonio. She was extremely melancholy, and seemed to labour under a secret grief. She had wept, and, if I was not mistaken, seemed to hope, and, at the same time to fear, something; and Antonio appeared to comfort her. She was paler and more languid than ever I had seen her. Her eye was doubtfully fixed to the ground; and all the lustre of her innate, innocent cheerfulness, was over-clouded by a passion or a grief, which she seemed to have confessed to herself in that moment with deep blushes. My affected heart felt itself reluctantly insnared in her engaging charms, my senses were suddenly over-clouded; and I forgot to avail myself of that propitious moment, as I had intended.

"While I hesitated a few seconds to make myself known, and to rush into her arms, the propitious, most favourable moment was vanished: they had passed the arbour where I was concealed, and I was again left to myself. What an absurd inconsistency of my character! I was come to watch them secretly; and in the first moment of seeing them I burned with a desire to embrace her. The propitious moment escapes without being improved. I was angry with myself for my childish behaviour, and almost shed tears of anguish.

"The best thing I now could do was to return to the castle, and to await them there, for I had no farther wish to watch them, the state of my mind being entirely changed. The grief of my Francisca, which was the more afflicting to me as I was ignorant of its cause, though I imagined to guess at it, had softened my mind to pity. These circumstances were no longer dark to me, though I could not perceive the least connection between them. The recollection of that sweet period, in which Francisca had unbosomed herself to me, and in which I was made sensible of the congeniality of her soul with mine, made me suspect the source of her melancholy, and the distress of my own situation vanished entirely in that moment.

"I directed my steps towards the castle, and heard, already, at a distance, a most doleful howling. I distinguished the voice of my Kusko, whom the servants seemed to beat. This cruel reception of the faithful animal gave me great reason to suspect that I should not be treated much better. He perceived me, at length, from the court-yard, bounded into the garden, and ran howling towards me, as if imploring my protection. Some servants pursued him with sticks and several dogs. Their faces were entirely new to me, and I could not recollect one of them. As soon as they saw me, they exclaimed with one voice, "What business has that beggar there in the garden? Let us cudgel him out of it;" and began their attack by throwing stones at me. This was certainly one of the greatest difficulties which ever befel me. How could I expect to escape their dogs and their cudgels?

"I could have killed every one of them if I had had a sword. They drew nearer, brandishing their cudgels; and the dogs began already to show their teeth and to snarl. Yet they seemed to have still some pity in their bosom, hesitating awhile to set the ferocious beasts at me. My old faithful Kusko looked anxiously up to me, and, notwithstanding the blows he had received, seemed ready to defend his poor master.

"Villains!" I exclaimed at length, in a fit of despair, "Don't you know your master? I am the Marquis of G******." "The fellow is mad," they replied, raising a roaring laughter. One of them was so daring as to offer to spit in my face. I collected myself as much as possible, and exclaimed, with a pathetic grandezza, "Call Don Antonio, and you will hear who I am." This was, perhaps, the most ridiculous step I could have taken in my aukward situation, and produced the effect I could naturally have expected. "As true as I am alive," one of them exclaimed, "the fellow is a drunken Hidalgo." Another replied with a violent blow on my shoulder, adding, "Don

Antonio greets you, and sends you this!" A general horse laugh drowned the words of his companions.

"I now grew frantic with rage, levelling such a violent blow at one of them, that he dropt roaring to the ground. I gave him a furious kick into the bargain, and rushed upon the rest, laying so effectually about me with my stick, that I dispersed them instantly. My boiling rage gave me more than human strength. However, what could I do against three stout fellows, whose fury bordered on madness, when they beheld the temerity of a beggar, and their companion weltering in his blood, which cried for vengeance? In vain did I drive them back twice; in vain did my faithful Kusko exert all his strength to keep off the attack of the dogs; and in vain did I roar with all my might, in hopes of drawing Don Antonio to the field of combat. No one came to assist me; my poor lute was beaten to atoms. Kusko already gave way to the two dogs; my stick was split; my small cloaths, cloak, and doublet, were torn; and I was obliged to take to my heels. I fled on wings of despair, gained with difficulty a little back gate, pursued by the dogs, jumped over a deep ditch, and saved myself at length, amid a shower of stones, in the neighbouring grove. There I flung myself upon the ground with sore limbs, a bleeding face, and lacerated hands, weeping and gnashing my teeth. I was entirely exhausted, and almost senseless. "A fine welcome, Carlos!" I exclaimed, at length, in broken accents; "to be cudgelled by thy own servants! How much is every thing altered! Formerly they would have licked your feet; and now you are a miserable beggar, that dares not enter his own house." This soliloquy, which would have reduced me to despair, was seasonably interrupted by Kusko. That faithful partner in my misery seemed to have more comfort than myself; he had already forgot his blows, and licked my bleeding hands. He caressed me so affectionately, his looks bespoke so much tender pity, that he succeeded at length in consoling me. I was animated with new courage, and began to consider what step I should take, the result of which was a resolution to proceed to Alcantara. I shook off the dust of my feet, looked with indignation back at a place which formerly had charmed me so much, and had not the least doubt that my faithful friend had infected the servants with his example; proceeding with bitterness and thirst for revenge in my heart towards my native town.

"I was so much exhausted by the blows I had received, and the tempest of passions which raged in my mind, that I wanted two days to accomplish that little journey. I beheld at length the steeples of Alcantara, on the morning of the third day; and was thrilled with pleasing sensations by the sweet recollection of my juvenile years, blended with inward anguish by the reflection on the sufferings I had experienced since. The cruel treatment at my own estate deprived me of every hope of being better received any where. Alas! how weak and inconsequential is the human heart! It always assumes the shape of the present moment, painting futurity either gloomy or smiling, guided merely by external circumstances!

CHAPTER XI.

I now went to my paternal house; knocked at the gate, and it was instantly opened. The first object I met was Alfonso, my faithful servant, who, after my secret departure from my castle, had repaired to Alcantara to await my return there. He stared at me with speaking marks of amazement and doubtful looks. Yet he soon recollected me, exclaiming, with astonishment, "Eternal God! In what a pitiful state do I see you again, my Lord! What misfortune has happened to you?" He then grasped my hand, kissing it with looks of pity. His good-natured, honest countenance expressed at once astonishment and rapture, blended with a certain anxiety of mind, which struck me, because I could not account for it.

"He conducted me instantly to the apartment I had formerly inhabited, where he informed me, with that open frankness which is the attribute only of great and noble minds, that my father had died during my absence, and my mother only was alive; that, to his knowledge, she was the sole heiress of my father; that she had been almost distracted by my sudden disappearance, and that no one but Count V******, who was at present an inmate of our house, had been able to succeed in comforting her. The latter intelligence contributed very much to console me for the afflicting news he had communicated to me: I hastened to throw myself into the arms of that excellent parent; who received me with the most flattering maternal tenderness, and on whose bosom I rested from all my misery, and forgot all the apprehensions which had perturbated my boding mind. Count V******, who, at the first intelligence of my arrival, hastened to embrace me, surprised me in her arms, and pressed me with unaffected sincerity to his noble, generous heart. He assured me, the interruption of our correspondence had not been owing to neglect or any fault on his side, that he had written several letters to me, and sent bills of exchange to a considerable amount. His investigations, with regard to the secret confederation, had been equally indefatigable, but fruitless. He had learnt several instances of their incredible influence and activity, which he communicated to me. He also informed me, that Francisca was returned to the castle of her lord, and that Don Pedro had disappeared; adding, he had seen her several times at my castle, without having been able to gain her confidence, which he had been anxious to obtain on my account: she seemed, however, to live on too intimate a footing with Antonio, than that he should not know a little more of her history. He assured me, at the same time, that Don Antonio had increased my fortune considerably, advising me to inform him and Francisca of my arrival. I did it, and soon had the pleasure of pressing them to my heart.

"Finally, Count V****** informed me of his present situation. His family had separated him from his Augusta through some artifices. He had lost her irrecoverably; and although his noble heart cherished the world and humankind too much as to be entirely overcome by his grief, yet his peace of mind was gradually undermined by secret anguish. Being conscious that he deserved to have at least a little share in the joys of this life, he saw himself entirely deprived of it; and while he was only occupied to avoid being urged by his misfortune to do some rash deed, he saw, to his greatest grief, the opportunities for great actions vanish under his hands. And yet he always retained so much equanimity, as to be capable of administering comfort to his friends; and those that were not intimately acquainted with him could not but think that he was happy. Soon after my return to Alcantara, he took leave of me to recover his peace of mind in another clime, or perhaps in a different part of the world, and I exerted myself in vain to divert him from the execution of his plan. His short stay with me was like the apparition of an angel which quickly passes away. May heaven bless that worthy friend! His noble soul was not fit for this world.

"The arrival of Don Antonio and Francisca produced a scene peculiar in its kind. I hastened down to receive them when they got out of the carriage. They rushed with rapture into my arms; strained me alternately to their heart; put numberless anxious questions to me about my health, and evinced the liveliest sorrow at the paleness and the scars of my face. I was seized with a transport of joy, and felt Heaven's bliss in their tender embraces.

"My old servants had, mean time, assembled around me to express their joy at my return by thousand caresses. One of them took my hand gently from Francisca's shoulder to cover it with his kisses; a second took hold of my coat; a third wanted to say something to me without being able to find words; and a fourth shouted for joy: they all jumped and danced around me. The affection of these good people moved my heart sensibly; I shook every one by the hand, and told them how glad I was to see them again. On turning round, I beheld some more figures in the back ground, leaning against the carriage, and holding their hats in their hands. They seemed not to know whether they should weep or laugh; exhibiting striking pictures of perplexity, and of a secret anxiety to see the event. I recollected their faces instantly, and clearly saw that they also knew me again. They bowed mechanically when I looked at them, made some motions with their hats, and uttered some unintelligible sounds. I nodded friendly to them, and thanked them with a motion of my hand. Kusko was, however, of a different opinion; for as soon as he saw his old enemies; he put himself into a posture of attack, shewing his teeth, and snarling at them. He could never forget the injury he had suffered from them, snarling whenever one of them came in his way, and pursuing them occasionally.

"You may easily conceive, dear friend, that I availed myself of the first opportunity to enquire after the particulars of Francisca's mysterious fate: however, Don Antonio knew no more than myself: and Francisca was uncommonly reserved. She displayed the most heartfelt affection for me, but kept the secret locked up in her bosom; and soon after I observed that her former passion for me was on the decline, that Antonio had found means to gain upon her affection, and was the idol of her soul. It is astonishing how suddenly the inclinations of that charming woman altered their course, and, never-theless, were always firmly and completely devoted to the object which attracted them.

"Don Antonio informed me that several secret attempts had been made to gain him over to that dreadful confederation. How-ever, he had conceived such a rooted disinclination to that society, that I doubt whether they ever succeeded to gain him entirely for their cause. His soul was artless, great and open. He hated every thing that was adventurous, romantic, mysterious, and intricate. Even Francisca had lost a great deal in his opinion by her behaviour and her mysterious looks. He had conceived an aversion from her, which she could not overcome for a considerable time. Being never afraid to act openly, and ready to give every moment an account of his actions, he required that no action of his friends should shun his eyes, and detested nothing more than the crooked proceedings of certain people, who imagined to ensure thereby his affections more firmly. He was the dearest of all my friends, Count V****** excepted.

"Being pleased with my new residence, and having renewed sev-eral old connections, I had taken it into my head to stay some time at Alcantara, and to enjoy the peace which seemed to be within my reach. However, I got, on that occasion, acquainted with an evil which afflicted me so much the more painfully, as I never had suf-fered by it before. It was nothing less than the evil of gossiping, and soon obliged me to quit my native town again.

"Some antiquated dowagers, soon after my arrival at Alcan-tara, took the pains of racking their brains to find out where I had been all the time. The strange manner in which I returned to my native town was quickly circulated through the whole place. I never could conceive how one can talk of subjects in which we have not the least interest; having been always too much occupied with the nearer concerns of my heart, and of my mind, either surrounded by congenial friends or by myself, I never had taken the least notice of other people or their opinion; but now I was connected with a set of beings whose understanding was scarcely sufficient to direct their own affairs; I was obliged to communicate with people who already were infected with the rage of gossiping, and a new friend was ready every moment to inform me of the strange rumours which were circulating about me. I was as if dropt from the clouds; without being able to guess what all these people wanted of me, I was obliged to listen to their tales: and while I began to be attentive to their officious communications, I actually was vexed at the unsolicited concern the town took in my affairs. Don Antonio, being more used to it than myself, ridiculed me constantly about my vexation. The reports and suspicions about my person, which were circulated in all companies, encreased every day; and, having offended some of the chiefs of the town by my unconcern, and made them my mortal enemies by the contempt I treated them with, it being, at the same time, inconsistent with the private interest of some sneaking priests to see me well received in certain houses, which they found means to resent, I took suddenly leave of all my acquaintances, and quitted Alcantara. Count V****** had advised me several times to reside for some months at a university, and to apply myself to the study of some sciences, which could be useful to, and qualify me for, an active life, which he had pointed out to me as the best means of recovering my peace of mind. I resolved to put his advice into practice, and chose Toledo.

"I perceived, however, plainly, on that occasion, that I and my happiness were not qualified for a certain kind of civil existence. One cannot make that observation in a circle of select friends, and if occupied with other ideas. In such a situation one is always an happy hermit, and never can accommodate oneself to the frivolous nonsense one is obliged to take up with in the connection with men of the world.

"I arrived at Toledo attended only by one servant; for I had formed the plan of living here retired, and of devoting my time entirely to my studies. This would certainly have been the most prudent way I could have taken; however, my open and too obliging character frustrated my wise resolution, and played me some tricks which produced very disagreeable consequences towards the end of my stay at Toledo. I had not resided two months at that seat of learning, when the kindness of Count V****** displayed itself to me in a very conspicuous manner, receiving, thro' his intercession, unexpectedly, a very acceptable offer of a place at the court of Madrid, which was connected with business abroad, where I could make a good use of my knowledge and the practical good sense I was gifted with. I accepted it with pleasure, under the condition to have half a year more to myself.

"During the first time of my residence at Toledo, I sought and found new opportunities of violating the resolution I had taken to live as retired as possible, and to dedicate my leisure hours to the improvement of my knowledge. But, alas! the amusements which I indulged myself with encreased the more I got acquainted with the world in which I lived: I was, indeed, still unknown enough; however, my singularities soon made me an object of general notice; and the intrusions of the curious, who were desirous to obtain a more satisfactory knowledge of that eccentric fellow who denied himself every pleasure, and whose language and manners betrayed a higher rank than that which I had thought proper to assume, exposed me frequently to the importunity of the greater number. Amongst the new acquaintances which I thus was obliged to form, I found some that were worth while being cultivated; and seeing no other means of leading a quiet life, than to accommodate myself to the humours of the generality, I connected myself, by degrees, with a circle of friends: Mr. de B******, a Frenchman, whom family affairs had brought to Toledo; Don Pablos F******, Don Bernhard H******, and Count S******i.

"Mr. de B****** was the most accomplished amongst them, possessing a great deal of learning, much knowledge of the world, a practical penetration, polished manners, and a most captivating eloquence. Our conversation never stopt a moment when he was with us; and I still recollect with pleasure the little tales which he related in our confidential circle with a most luxuriant humour. His imagination had been extremely well fitted for it by a journey which he had made to the Orient; however, he had conceived such a strong predilection for every thing uncommon and romantic, that he infected with it every one that was frequently in his society. He beheld so many events of former times, so many occurrences of life in the same point of view in which Count V****** was used to see them, that he easily gained my friendship and confidence. He possessed as much gallantry as I did, but displayed a most striking and general dislike to the female sex. In this point he differed very much from Count V******, who entertained different notions of the dignity of the sex, whom he always treated with respect and indulgence, which, no doubt, originated in the consciousness of his own superiority. It is very probable that the amorous adventures Mr. de B****** frequently went in search of, and carried on at the risk of his life, while in the Orient, were the chief cause of that aversion. He never contradicted, never entered seriously into a contest, except when the conversation happened to turn on the ladies, and some one took the trouble to defend them against his sarcasms. Whenever he happened to be in an ill humour at our evening meetings, and began to philosophize, we were sure to rouse him from his phlegmatic disposition through some anecdote in honour of the female sex; he then grew generally very violent, and sometimes exasperated at the whole company; yet always related, at last, some charming stories, which he had collected, or invented, to prove that the ladies are a sort of cats whom we must stroke without ever losing sight of their claws. This acrimony was evidently serious, and indubitably owing to some secret cause of importance. But what rendered this singularity more striking was his keeping a mistress whose shape and character was that of a dragoon. Yet no one ever exercised a more arbitrary sway over a woman than Mr. de B****** maintained over his charmer. He called her his night-lamp, because he insisted that she displayed the greatest lustre in the dark; though I am pretty sure he never did examine that quality during our connection. We frequently spent the evenings in her company, to be amused by her antic tricks, her manner of expressing her ideas, her mimicry, and her droll behaviour. Her lover was always the first who quitted her society.

"Don Bernhard H****** was his natural antagonist; for while Mr. de B****** insisted that all women were good for nothing, his mistress excepted, whom he always respected in some manner, Don Bernhard maintained the contrary, declaring that the whole sex was good, his mistress excepted; and what was most ridiculous, either endeavoured to prove his assertion by his own experience. Don Bernhard was the most singular man I ever knew, his character being the strangest medley of two diametrically opposite tempers. He could be choleric and rash in the highest degree, and on the other side indolent and easy beyond belief. I believe, however, that the former temper was natural with him, and the latter acquired through philosophy, and gradually became habitual to him, although I could not perceive their transition.

"His soul was swayed by a seriousness which had transmoulded his whole being. I have not once seen him laugh; and whatever he contributed to our, frequently, excessive joviality, was accompanied only with half a smile; and this seeming unconcern was not the effect of a violent exertion, or an internal convulsion, but originated in the natural disposition of his soul. I also must observe, that, amongst the many trials he had undergone, only those prevailed in his mind which must have contributed to produce the coldness; for, previous to the greatest misfortunes a mortal can experience, he had enjoyed an uninterrupted train of pleasures and luxuries, had tasted misery and happiness, and nothing could now disturb the equanimity of his mind. Nature seemed to have exhausted herself in the formation of that dreadful man, and had nothing left that could affect or retard him only for a moment in his career. Like a God did he behold the agonies of suffering humanity, without shedding a tear; without love, without concern, without sustaining an increase of his internal happiness, or his secret consciousness, did he behold the flow of joy and pleasure he had spread around himself. No prayers, no remonstrances, could move him; no offence could provoke his anger: with a steady eye, without one weak moment, without being ever thrown off his guard, without caring for his fame, or the talk of the multitude, or even for the opinions of his friends, did he pursue a fixed and dear-bought plan of a rigid virtue, which, as he was wont to say, would lead him, at least, with equanimity through an unfortunate life.

"Considering this, it is certainly highly remarkable that he was far from being a zealous preacher of virtue; for he patiently suffered and beheld vices and follies, even those of his friends; however, he generally repaired them silently. He never defended an opinion, or attacked the principles, of others; never spoke of other people; yet without despising them. He had read very little, and a book which could tempt his curiosity must be of a very singular tenour. He had borrowed his principles neither of a philosopher nor of a moralist, but derived them with stoic coolness from the great book of nature and experience, from his communication with mankind, and from his own fate; for which reason they never deserted him when happening to fall in with those objects from which he had abstracted them. His practical virtue did not flow from his heart, but rather was the effect of habitude. Actions which other people call sacrifices, he performed without the least struggle or hesitation; his actions and wishes were the voluntary produce of his nature.

"He seemed to have rendered himself entirely independent on all his senses; for, although his sensibility was refined to the highest degree, yet that soul which perceived was entirely different from that whereby his resolutions and actions were ruled. He was careful of his body merely to preserve his health; for he maintained that a prudent care of it was the chief means of being virtuous. No one could be more sober than him; he never drank wine or heating liquors; he made only one meal in a day; and chiefly lived upon bread, butter, and dried fruits. This rigorous diet seemed to encrease his blooming health every day, and kept him in the possession of the full use of his faculties, instead of weakening his constitution, as it is commonly thought.

"Count S******i was of a different character, not less remarkable, and the Adonis of our circle. His form was uncommonly elegant and handsome, graced with female meekness, and stamped with a deep impression of angelic goodness. He was so amiable, and so heavenly gentle, that I doated upon him. His pure imagination, the gentle disposition of his mind, a memory which seemed to exist only for the scenes of mild virtue, were charmingly blended with a soft affecting melancholy, and a meek enthusiasm.

"He had sacrificed at the shrine of love only once in his life, and was unfortunate in his attachment. The hearts of all women were open to him; he was the idol of all girls; only the object of his passion was cruel to him, and rendered him miserable for the rest of his life, notwithstanding his excellent qualifications for happiness. His disappointment had, however, not secluded him from his brethren, nor rendered him indifferent to their welfare; he rather loved mankind, from that period, with additional ardour, and with a more active interest in the happiness of his fellow-creatures. No man living has ever done more good in the compass of his activity; and when it was out of his power to afford effectual assistance, the affecting emanation of his silent virtues were sure to administer at least consolation.

"He was entirely formed for this unfortunate age. His beautiful accomplished form was made for the sensuality of his time, and his heart, open to every species of sorrow, for its misery. He was fondly cherished by all those who knew him, and almost adored. His gentleness, his pure smiling innocence, his artless goodness and modesty ingratiated themselves with every feeling heart; one felt affection and love for him already before one was properly acquainted with his worth. He was passionately fond of the fine arts, and practised several of them in perfection. He resembled Apollo attended by the Graces.

"Don Pablos F****** was an amiable, sweet fellow, but at bottom rather insignificant. His mind was jovial, constantly serene, cheerful and happy. He possessed more humour than wit; yet it was irresistible when it began to display itself in its full force. He was, indeed, not exactly fitted for the characters of the rest of our society, but nevertheless had rendered himself so necessary to us, that we found our little suppers always very irksome when he was not present. We rested ourselves, as it were, in his genius, and gained many ideas and little pleasures by the gentle flow which he contrived to give our discourse. He was perfectly versed in the art of conducting a conversation; never interrupted the speaker, but suffered every one to talk as much and as long as he chose, connecting only the thread of our discourse where he perceived a chasm. He generally did it by starting some easy and pretty observation, which he had been sufficiently at leisure to make, but always fell into the course of our conversation, as if by accident; or by interweaving some little, droll anecdote, which, as it were, dropt from the clouds, by his neat simplicity, and, sometimes, by a more than common lustre of wit; and we never separated at night without being charmed by his remarks and his little stories, though he had spoken least, and was more frequently interrupted, than any one of us.

"Our amusements received an additional charm by a mistress whom he kept, a neat, little, humorous girl, exactly like himself. It is impossible two people could agree better than that charming couple did. Their souls seemed to be united into one. If he happened to be serious, which, by the bye, was not frequently the case, she began to weep for rarity's sake, laughed whenever he desired it; and he did the same at whatever she chose: they frequently happened to laugh at each other. Their hatred against Mr. de B******'s

mistress was mutual, and you may easily conceive what ridiculous
scenes this produced.

"It is impossible to give an adequate description of the little
charming bacchanals which we frequently celebrated at night;
for every one had generally fatigued himself so much during the
day, that he came to our jovial suppers with the best disposition to
divert his mind as much as possible. B****** and Don Pablos took
great pains during the day to collect little anecdotes and town stories, which were related at night, and generally occasioned one or
the other of us to treat the company with a similar occurrence of
his life. Don Bernhard seasoned all this with his extensive knowledge of men, and with remarks which were extremely moral,
without having the least appearance of it; and Count S******i
with his tender enthusiastic philanthropy, which sweetened all the
bitterness of wit and humour. We always were sure to be entertained by a smart contest between the two ladies. The mistress of
Count S******i exerted all her wit and humour to parry the attacks
of Mr. de B******'s masculine inamorata, and occasionally to put
in a thrust: we took gradually a general part in their bickerings,
which lasted till the table was cleared, when B****** made them
conclude a truce. We then formed a semi-circle before the cheerful
fire-side, and spent the rest of the evening with that pleasure which
only uninterrupted harmony, unoffending wit, and sound humour,
can afford. Our peculiarities could here unfold themselves without
restraint, and our mutual remarks added an additional polish to our
character.

"Thus we spent our evenings; but give me leave to say also a few
words of the application of our days. If the former served to elucidate the progress of my adventures, the latter contributed to give
them a peculiar direction. My connection with the *secret confederation* was almost entirely dissolved; I had not been formally expelled;
but as they had acted against our mutual agreement, I thought
myself at liberty to cancel all obligations which I had taken upon
myself, and they could clearly perceive what they had to expect
from me. I have, besides, never given a promise, not to speak of
their union, and always shall respect the oath which they made me
swear never to divulge the papers which they intrusted to me. Nothing could, therefore, prevent me to drop now and then as much of

my adventures as was sufficient to excite and attract the curiosity of congenial souls.

"B****** was the first that pressed me to explain those hints; and one night paid me a visit at a late hour to meet me alone: having more than ten times broken off the thread of the discourse, contrary to his custom, and taken it up again most miserably, tossed himself as many times to and fro on the sofa, and several times vexed me with curious, scrutinizing looks, began, at length, with a deep sigh, "Hearken, Carlos! I can brook your damned reserve no longer. You have some secret on your mind, and it grieves me that you keep it to yourself. What is the meaning of your mysterious words, and of your obscure hints? Can't you let me into the secret? You don't know how you torment me by your sullen silence."

"I could not help laughing at his impatience; but at length consented to give him a brief account of my adventures. He smiled repeatedly, even when the sad recollection of sufferings past made the tears start from my eyes, and when I had finished, exclaimed laughing, "Upon my honour, Carlos! you can tell excellent stories. But I protest it won't go down with me."

"He had taken hold of my hand, examining my countenance with scrutinizing looks, to see what effect his fine speech would produce on my features. I flung his hand violently on the sofa, and went to the window, exclaiming, in an angry accent, "Don't say a word more on that subject, Mr. de B****** if you value my friendship." Indignation had choked my voice so much that I was scarcely able to utter these words. He stared at me, seized with astonishment; then cast his looks on the floor, and mused a few moments.

"That would be a horrid tale, Carlos," he resumed, "if you did not mean to make game at me."

"You will do well to go home," I replied: "you see it begins already to dawn, and I am fatigued."

"Are you?" he replied, in a tragi-comic accent: "Well, I wish you a good night, and will endeavour to digest properly what you have communicated to me." He now stretched out his hand, adding, "I hope, Carlos, we are friends?"

"I hope you will be convinced that I am your friend, when you have more seriously pondered on the confidence I have shewn you."

CHAPTER XII.

The mind of Mr. de B****** seemed to be uncommonly agitated the day following our late conversation: however, he mentioned not a word about that affair, hanging his head, and meditating, without appearing to be sensible of it. On the third day he resumed the subject. After the tale of horror I had disclosed to him had sufficiently fermented in his mind, he seemed at once to have come to a resolution; and the manner in which he explained himself was entirely different from what my knowledge of his character had led me to expect. He had, at first, excited my indignation by his unbelief; but now his enthusiastic soul had blown up the spark, which I had thrown into his mind by my relation, into a blazing flame, and he gave now the most implicit credit to the tale which he, at first, had taken for fiction. He was impatient to sift the whole matter to the very bottom, and importuned me, with numberless questions, about one particular point, about the purpose of the confederates, which was to myself a secret hidden in the profoundest obscurity. It was, therefore, not in my power to satisfy his impatient curiosity: however, we found, at length, a probable cause of that mysterious association. A secret fermentation had pervaded the kingdom already for some time. The affairs of the state, and of private persons, were guided by unknown hands; but no one, even those not excepted who had suffered by their powerful grasp, had been able to discover the secret agents to whom they belonged. Neither of us was favourable to revolutions: we were sensible that a monarchical government is always the best for the general welfare; and burning with an ardent love for real liberty, we were firmly persuaded that we always should be capable to extricate ourselves, by prudent conduct, from the pressure of despotism, without a rebellion against divine and human laws; and without sacrificing one of those advantages which the regularity attending the commands of *one* head, must impart to the connection of the whole community.

"These ideas, which we gathered from our experience and our observations, gradually engendered a regular plan. The uninterrupted combination of ideas to which B****** was urged by the novelty of the subject, and its affinity with the natural propensity of his character, and I, by the lively interest he took in it, enlarging it, we formed the wild plan to make a *counter-confederation*, and to try what our weak and individual exertions could do. We were so fortunate as to prevail on Don Bernhard to unite himself with us, and began our labours with the most sanguine hopes of success, and with vigorous ardour. Our intimate connection with Count S******i and Don Pablos did not allow us to exclude them entirely: we therefore assigned to them a subordinate part, which rendered it impossible the mildness of their souls should spoil our plan.

"Thus we began to execute our design, which, for some time, had consisted only in theory; and every member of our small society contributed a sufficient sum of money to defray the unavoidable expences. We drew every one, that promised to be useful to us, in some manner or other into our interest; and connected ourselves in a more distant or intimate manner, as circumstances required it, with all the men of genius we knew. Yet these preparatory measures did not hinder us from proceeding with all possible circumspection, to conceal our ideas, as much as it could be done, behind the veil of commonness, and to keep a careful guard even upon our miens during our little suppers. We omitted nothing to secure ourselves, and exerted all our faculties to make rapid progresses, when, at once, our plan was thrown into the utmost confusion by invisible hands.

"The six months of my furlough being elapsed, I had the greatest difficulties to encounter when I petitioned for half a year more. After I had taken incredible pains to carry my aim, I was, at length, indulged with three months more, receiving, at the same time, the strictest order to prepare, at the expiration of that term, for my departure for Paris, the place of my destination.

"The money we had collected for defraying the expences of our plan diminished visibly, although I kept the chest in which it was locked up in my bed-room, and concealed it beneath the bedding. If we added a sum one day, we were sure to find it decreased to half the next, and in the same proportion every subsequent day. We carried the chest from one member to the other, and every where took the same precaution, without being able to prevent the gradual decrease of our treasury. It is inconceivable what an astonishing effect this trifling circumstance had on our union. The weaker part of the members were thereby disheartened, because we were incapable of unfathoming even such trifles; and it damped our spirits, as it convinced us that our secret was known. We also were rather terrified to see those whose artifices we intended to discover and to destroy, so dreadfully near us before we had made the least discovery of their plans. Our affairs were interrupted by that unaccountable incident, because we had now the greatest difficulties to encounter before we could collect the necessary sums; the propitious moment was frequently past, and our ardour had evaporated before we could make up the money requisite for our purposes.

"Our papers had the same fate, the most important passages being carefully cut out, so that we plainly could see that our secret enemies must have read them at leisure. The letters we sent away, either were intercepted, or the directions altered in such a manner, that our correspondents received orders which they could not execute, the letters being forwarded to the wrong persons. All our labours were lost, and our exertions rendered ridiculous into the bargain, which reduced our union again to its former nothing.

"The confederates were, however, not satisfied with having rendered our plan abortive, but at the same time convinced us that they could separate and unite us at pleasure, when and wherever they chose. The family affairs of Mr. de B******, which could not have been more unfavourable than they were, promised at once such a propitious termination, that he thought proper to return to France to recover his fortune. The cold, dry, and stoic Don Bernhard was, at a ball, heated to such a degree, by some drug or other mixed with his drink, that he began to quarrel, and killed his antagonist, which obliged him to save himself by flight. Count S******i fell in love with a beautiful Italian, who had just arrived, and soon made him entirely her slave. Don Pablos was, at length, caught in the same snare; and I was drawn in by a girl who absolutely would marry me, intricated me in numberless difficulties, and finally obliged me to quit Toledo. Our little suppers were, previously to that catastrophe, entirely interrupted in the short space of eight or nine days, and all my friends taken from my side, or literally alienated from me. Previous to that period, an incident happened which I cannot omit inserting here, and, in every respect, was so dreadful, that I cannot reflect upon it without being thrilled with an involuntary horror. I had planned the whole association, was the boldest and firmest member, and even had formed the design to have recourse to the assistance of the police to find out the lurking place of the confederates, for which reason they owed me a more sensible chastisement than the rest, which actually was inflicted upon me. I had hired a small country-house before the town, where we used to have little feasts, to dance and to sup some times; returning very rarely before midnight. Being entirely occupied with our plan, we loved to talk of it on our return to town, and to discuss the measures we had taken and the discoveries we had happened to make, in the day. We left, therefore, only one of the society with the ladies, and rode together in the same carriage. One evening we had been uncommonly merry, and I had drunk more than usual. Midnight was already past, and we hastened to break up. Every thing was ready, but I could not find my hat. The night being rather damp, I would not go without it. I saw it, at length, after a long search, on the top of a set of drawers; and while I got upon a chair to take it down, the rest went into the yard. Having extinguished the lights of the chandeliers, I hastened down stairs to join my friends, and found my carriage at the gate. I stept in, the door was shut, and the carriage drove away.

"My spirits being in an excellent flow of hilarity, I jested, and talked without interruption, but received no answer from my friends, whom I had seen step into the same carriage. Their obstinate taciturnity struck me at length; but thinking they were in a sporting humour, I did not much care for it. However, my eyes were suddenly opened in a dreadful manner. I observed, to my greatest terror, that my companions were dressed in black, and masked. I boded with horror in what society I was; the words died on my lips; my hair bristled; a chilly tremor pervaded my whole frame; my teeth began to chatter, and my knees to tremble violently. Yet the death-like silence continued uninterruptedly.

"My dreadful companions began at length to stir. One of them, who sat close by me, broke the top of something, and a flame burst forth, lighting the wax taper he held in his hand. The faces of my fellow-travellers were unmasked at once; and, merciful God! I beheld James, and two more of the confederates of the cave. I was ready to swoon; but three glittering poniards directed at my heart kept me alive.

"Do you know us?" James exclaimed, in a dreadful accent, extinguishing the light. The former church-yard silence resumed again its ominous sway, and strange sensations thrilled my soul with terror and dismay. James pulled the string; my companions got out of the carriage, and ordered the coachman to go on, disappearing like a midnight phantom.

"When I came home, only the two ladies and their companion were returned; and my three friends, in whose company I had, at first, imagined to be, were not yet arrived. I sent my carriage back, and afterwards was informed that they had taken a walk in the garden, and waited for me. I was very ill, and half fainting. No sooner was I carried to bed, than I lost the use of my senses entirely; and my friends were struck with horror when I afterwards related my adventure. All of them were thrown into the utmost confusion, except Don Bernhard, who said, with his usual equanimity, "The miserable wretches! I certainly should have lost my life, if I had been in your place."

"Soon after this incident, the above-mentioned changes took place. Numberless teasing disagreements with some families with whom I was more intimately connected, inspired me with such a deciding disgust against Toledo, that I awaited my dispatches, and the order for my departure, with the greatest impatience. They arrived at length; and I never drove through a city-gate with a more cheerful heart than that of Toledo.

"Paris is a place where one never is in want of pleasures. My station did, indeed, not allow me to be idle; yet I was no stranger to an active life, was endowed with a sufficient share of dexterity, and could easily accommodate myself to every department, if nothing else was required but exertion and attention; and when I had laid down my pen, and divested myself of my official dress, had sufficient time left to take a share in the gaieties of Paris.

"I was extremely fond of masquerades, because I enjoyed no where a greater liberty; nor could I any where indulge, more innocently and safely, my propensity to little adventures and amorous sports, and was sure never to miss an opportunity of amusing myself in that manner.

"My occupations left me, besides, sufficiently at leisure to collect a numerous circle of acquaintances around me. Yet I had only a few friends, amongst whom the young Duke of F******n occupied the first place. He was a noble enthusiast; of an open, untainted heart, which had not yet been deceived; conscious of his elevated dignity, and adorned with all the generosity of a noble extraction; good-natured, and yet sufficiently prudent; of elegant manners, and yet candid and undisguising; winning and faithful to his friends. He was spoiled for a courtier; not because he wanted the external qualifications, but only because he was too indolent for those little attentions which are necessarily requisite for a court-life. Yet he was always ready to make sacrifices to love and friendship, which surpass the power of corruption of common men. We were inseparable; went to the same hotels; played with a joint-stock, and visited the same companies. Is it possible a more intimate connection could subsist between two men of the world? Yet we went still farther, communicating to one another subjects that belong only to the forum of the most intimate friendship. My heart had the fault not to be reserved enough, whereby it was exposed to every illusion and imposition, and circumspection was never on the register of my virtues.

"The whole society which formerly was connected at Toledo gradually met again at the gay capital of France. One after the other arrived, and every one protested to have been drawn to Paris by some important motive. We began again to meet frequently, and to talk again of our former association; and what was worse, initiated the young Duke in our mysteries. The great distance from the supposed seat of the confederation, and the tranquillity we had enjoyed for a long time, lulled us into a deeper security than sound reason could approve.

"One evening we sat at a masquerade, before a cheerful chimney in a bye-room, fatigued by the bustle and the sports of merriment; and I related at large the apparition of Amanuel at my flight with Elmira. It grew late; the fire died gradually away, and the torches began already to emit a fainter light. We were by ourselves, and only a few masks, who went from one apartment into the other, passed us now and then. We took little notice of it, being too much taken up with my adventures. A general gloom prevailed in our little circle, and the looks of the whole company hung with awful astonishment on my lips. Having concluded my tale, the Duke exclaimed, with enthusiasm, "Carlos, I wish I could have an opportunity of seeing your Genius." No sooner had he uttered these words, than our company was increased by one person. A white domino pushed through the chairs towards our sociable circle, and opening its cloak, turned to the Duke, and said, "Here he is!" It was really *Amanuel*. All eyes were fixed on me, to have his declaration ascertained; and my pale astonishment confirmed it. Don Bernhard started up instantly to seize the mask: however, he was, in the twinkling of an eye, in the next apartment, and disappeared among the crowd. We searched every apartment, but were unable to find him.

"My political affairs now began to assume an alarming aspect. I continued to work with an indefatigable zeal, but nevertheless received one reproof after another from the minister. Although I proceeded with the utmost care and circumspection, yet always something was omitted. I could not account for it; and, at length, was informed by a letter from a friend at Madrid, that the court was highly displeased with my conduct, though he could not divine the reason of it. I received, soon after, such plain hints to desire my dismission, that I was obliged to petition for it; and thus I was again removed from a career where I had found myself so happy, and 'till then had worked with the greatest satisfaction. I resolved, in a fit of the bitterest indignation, to bid an eternal farewell to my ungrateful country, and, after having travelled over a great part of Europe, to hide myself in some remote corner of the globe, where I could rest from my misfortunes, and in peace await their final termination. I resolved, therefore, to set out as soon as possible. A servant, and two horses, encumbered with very little baggage, were the only equipage I intended to take with me. I took an unexpected leave of my friends, and rode away with an easy heart.

CHAPTER XIII.

"The rapid rate at which I travelled, after I left Paris, soon brought me near the frontiers of Swisserland; for nothing detained me on the road, nothing was able to arrest my attention. I was dissatisfied with every tract of country which I passed, going in search——I knew not what. At length I found it.

"One evening I came to a small cluster of houses, which were situated at a small distance from the high road, where I proposed to stay over night. The small footpath led through several bushes, and at length lost itself in a spacious spot, covered with turf, in the back part of which I perceived a little cottage, illuminated by the pale light of the moon. It distinguished itself in a most pleasing manner from the verdure of an adjacent corn-field, and its neatness and natural elegance charmed me in the highest degree. Midnight was setting in, and my servant and horses seemed to be tired. A half-lighted window invited us cheerfully to request a night's lodging of its owner. I attempted to knock at the door, but no answer was returned. I knocked a second time with the same success, although we heard some person stirring within. Necessity has no law; and I opened the door gently.

"A female sat in the back ground, with a lamp before her, and occupied with some work. Her dress was more than common, and seemed to agree little with the humble habitation; although the furniture of the small apartment bespoke neatness, elegance, and even some luxury. She lifted her eyes up at intervals, to look at a picture which was suspended opposite to her; and tears started from her eyes upon her bosom, which was agitated with heavy sighs. She was so much absorpt in her silent grief, or occupied with her work, that I was close by her side before she observed me. I was in a cheerful humour, and anticipated already the little terror and perplexity in which she would be thrown by the unexpected sight of a stranger. At length, when I saw that the noise I made did not rouse her from her profound reverie, I began to cough. She started up, seized with a sudden terror, just when I stood opposite her. A piercing scream was her only answer. Merciful God! it was Elmira, my adored wife. She expanded her hands towards me in a supplicating posture. I dropt down at her feet, and she into my arms. This was the great, heart-elevating moment of meeting again.

"Elmira, for God's sake!" I exclaimed, "how do I see you here? Do I really behold my dear, my adored wife? Are you really the darling of my heart, resuscitated from the grave?—"

"Yes, Carlos, I am your faithful wife!"

"But is it possible that I should really press you again to my fond bosom? Am I not deceived by a deluding phantom of my imagination? are you really a corporeal being? Look at this handkerchief, stained with thy blood; it is the witness of that dreadful night when you was murdered in my carriage by my side. I always have carried it with me as a holy relic." Elmira looked with astonishment alternately at the handkerchief and at me.

"What did you say, dear Carlos? My blood! Murdered by your side, in the carriage! I don't know what you mean."

"How! is it possible you should have so completely forgot that dreadful night, in which we happily escaped the fury of the Spirit? Have you forgot how I carried you in my arms to the carriage, to leave with you the castle for ever? how a pistol-shot wounded you mortally? Can you not recal the least recollection of that horrid incident?" She looked at me with a smile of pity.

"Poor Carlos!" she replied, "recollect yourself. The sudden joy has transported you beyond yourself! Do you really believe what you have said just now?"

"How! Should it be possible! Meseems a veil is taken from my eyes at once.—Should it really be possible! Should I have been imposed upon a second time? Tell me candidly, dearest Elmira, can you recollect nothing, nothing at all of what I have told you?"

"Nothing at all, dearest Carlos."

"Then, by Heaven, this is the blood of an impostor!" So saying, I flung the handkerchief upon the floor.

"Most certainly, if your senses are not bewildered."

"Heavens! what scenes of purest joy did now ensue. We had so much to say to one another, and therefore said nothing at all. Never did human language appear to me so poor. Even our eyes were only imperfect and obscure interpreters of our sensations. Morning began to dawn before we perceived that midnight was past.

"So, am I then arrived at the goal* of my fondest wishes! And my sufferings are at length terminated!" I exclaimed, when I recovered the power of utterance. "How differently does Providence direct the stream of futurity, how differently from what we ominate and

---

* The first edition reads "gaol." This error occurs several times throughout the text and has been silently corrected elsewhere.

think! It has embroidered its banks for me with the gayest flowers. I press my wife with unutterable sensations of bliss to my panting bosom, and feel with unspeakable transport that Heaven has exhausted all its stores of joy to render your Carlos happy beyond conception."

"Exhausted! Carlos," Elmira replied, with a cherub's heavenly smile: "When will you cease to talk thus wildly? Does nothing remind you of the two blissful hours of my bridal state at St. Jago?"

"Elmira, what ideas do you recal to my mind!"

"Could it be possible you should not guess at one happiness more Heaven has in store for you!—But, dearest Carlos, tell me sincerely, are you *completely* restored to your faithful wife? has not another——"

"Is it possible Elmira could suspect her Carlos?"

"She pressed me with an angelic smile to her heart, exclaiming, with a heavy sigh, "Alas! Carlos, Carlos! I fear we celebrate to day the festival of a twofold reunion."

"How! should you know—"

"Yes, I know your history, dear Carlos; I know that you have been most treacherously seduced. Those infernal fiends had very obvious motives to inform me of every afflicting particular of those incidents. However, I was more fortunate than you: I escaped from their cruel fangs just in the most dangerous moment, and when they thought it least possible. I saved myself with great difficulty, and fled to this country, with no other treasure than your picture and some rings and jewels, which enabled me to purchase this cottage, and to provide for the most necessary wants. The whole wealth of your wife consisted, to the present moment, in nothing farther than two cows, a little garden, and these hands, whose whiteness and softness you will certainly admire no more."

"These hands were formerly witnesses of your beauty; but now they are far dearer to me, as witnesses of your virtue. Believe me, Elmira, I have not kissed them with more rapture at the altar than I do now. Sweet, sweet hand, thou hast commenced my happiness; wilt thou also assist me in completing it?"

"Alfonso, my good, faithful servant, now entered the apartment. He had not disturbed us all the night long, but now dropt on his knees before his mistress. She offered him her still beautiful, charming hand, which I had infolded in mine, and he bedewed it with warm, sincere tears, speechless, and stammering only broken accents. Elmira was rejoiced to see him again, promising herself, from his activity, much assistance in the occupations of our domestic life; and from his fidelity and watchfulness, a security for the duration of our love and re-union. The rays of the morning sun illuminated already the little apartment with radiant brightness, and Elmira desired to shew us her little houshold. I never beheld more neatness. Every object bespoke simplicity, which, however, bore evident marks of elegance. She had gradually purchased a little collection of books, and an excellent lute, which was neither covered with dust, nor out of tune. Her kitchen, the theatre of her little labours, exhibited all the graces of unadorned neatness; and the appearance of her buttery created appetite by its inviting cleanliness. She shewed us at last her embroideries and needle-work, informing us that she had spun the greater part of her garments herself; and yet I could perceive every where that she never had completely forgot her noble descent; and the Countess of S****** and Marchioness of G****** appeared to have retired only for a short time from her palace to a cottage, to divert herself with acting awhile the part of a charming country girl. She had derived all her assistance from a single female only, a girl, who, through the example and the conversation of her mistress, had attained such a high degree of culture, as to be able to cheer sometimes Elmira's gloominess, and to enliven the tedious hours by her sensible discourses. Her garden displayed not less natural charms; and although every little corner was carefully husbanded, yet one could clearly see that she had not forgot to provide for her pleasure. A large bower of woodbine and amaranth, enclosing a cooling dusk beneath its leafy arch, occupied a corner of that little beautiful spot, to afford my beloved Elmira a friendly asylum in the scorching heat of the day, and a fragrant shelter against the chilling blasts of the murky night-air. All her favourite flowers were planted in variegated groups around that hallowed temple of tranquil meditation. She recalled to my mind, by her sweet discourses, the recollection of former times of bliss; related the history of every flower and of every tree, generously communicating to my transported soul the joy she felt at being the creator of her fragrant and grateful nurslings, while her large blue eyes rested with delight on my chearful looks, bespeaking the sympathetic feelings of my heart, and told me, in a lively manner, that no situation is so dreadful as not to be cheered up by something or other; and that it affords sometimes moments which, even without the smiles of hope, and without a comforting prospect into a clearer futurity, can render it more supportable.

"All that you see around you," she exclaimed at length, in a kind of transport, "all that you see here, Carlos, is now your property, as well as mine, except that rosary, which I cannot share with you."

"And why not, my dearest wife?"

"Because it is not my property."

"And who is that happy being whom you indulge with a hallowed spot in your property?"

"I will make you acquainted with him, if you will promise me first to love him only with half the tenderness my heart feels for him."

"What a fire do I see sparkling in your eyes! how your beautiful cheeks are covered with a crimson hue! Elmira, my dearest wife, is your heart devoted to one more happy being besides myself?"

"To none for whom Carlos will not deprive his Elmira of a share of his affection. Will you promise me to love him as tenderly as your faithful wife does?"

"I repose an unlimited confidence in you. Here is my hand. You cannot bestow your love on any one whom I shall not be ready to cherish as much as you do."

"She now led me back to the house, trembling with joy and impatience. We ascended the stairs with winged steps. She disengaged herself from my arm, and ran before me, opening a closet, which I not observed at first; went in on tip-toe; and when I was going to join her, whispered, in a low accent, "Softly, Carlos; don't make a noise; he sleeps."

"Who sleeps?" I enquired, seized with astonishment.

"She took me by the hand, leading me towards a bed, and drew the curtains. Eternal Providence! what a scene did my eyes behold! the beautifullest boy lay half naked upon it, and seemed to be amused by a pleasing dream. His rosy cheeks wore the smiling livery of health; and the peace that throned on his lovely countenance bespoke the sweet unruffled temper of the little cherub. My wife flung her beautiful arm around my neck, and hiding her crimsoning face in my bosom, whispered, "Carlos, it is your son: shall he share your heart with me?"

"I knew him to be my son. His young features bore the marks of the raptures of that luxurious night; the innocent charms of health graced blushing his milk-white limbs; the serenity of his countenance, his heavenly smiles, and the clear forehead, bespoke him only to be the offspring of celestial bliss, but not the nursling of grief.

"While I gazed with a father's tenderness at him, he opened Elmira's black eyes. He was at first startled by the sight of a stranger; but seeing his mother kneeling by his side, expanded his little arms smiling towards her, encircled her neck, and pressed his glowing face to her bosom. She strained him with one hand to her heart, and clung the other round my waist. "Dear mother," he stammered, while I covered him with kisses, "is that father? Did you not tell me that he would love us so dearly when he should come once?"—

"Dearest Count, you have seen and experienced much: Fortune has not been a niggard to you. You have been loved by more than one woman, and adored by many. Your sister died of grief for you. However, in that one point you must leave me the preference. You do not know the enthusiastic rapture with which a father enfolds the child of his love, and re-peruses on its countenance those delicious moments in which it was engendered, while he is united to the wife of his heart by additional bonds. You never have experienced the enchanting charms of the caresses a father receives, and the gratification of those he distributes, to the darlings of his heart; nor with how much anxiety he watches over every look of his child, how he observes its attention, and contemplates all its little motions. One is never more sensible of the poverty of human speech, than in such delicious moments; yet one finds a language which affords complete satisfaction. The harmony of souls expresses itself by broken sounds, and their soft vibrations mix with the sensations we decypher on the countenance of the darlings of our heart.——

"We spent the day with making economical arrangements. I vowed to myself, and to Elmira, never to quit that charming spot. How beneficial were, at that time, the instructions and the example of the hermit to me! I took his happy life, his change of rest and labour, for a pattern. He had taught me to derive some pleasure from every labour, and to find cheering intervals of rest even in the most uninterrupted labour. I had learnt of him that one can be happy in every situation. The party-wall of rank and birth, that separated me from the inferior classes, disappeared. I did not despise that prerogative; it was only grown indifferent to me.

"With what an exhilarating freshness did evening set in! amid what enchanting plans and heavenly prospects did it steal upon me! I had improved the ideal picture of the hermit; a sweet wife was dearer to me than a friend; and I educated one for me, while I inspired my little Carlos with a susceptibility of my pleasures and sufferings. Elmira's sweet sensibility, which animated him, soon taught him to love his father. He was, in a short time, inseparable from me; and his young soul began to speak by tender caresses, when his language was too poor to express his sentiments sufficiently.

"The powerful sensations which prevailed in my soul in the morning, had not suffered me to take a minute survey of my new residence. The tranquillity I enjoyed in the evening, afforded me more liberty of contemplation, and more leisure to collect my ideas, to rest with attention on individual objects. Elmira was occupied with her domestic affairs, and her girl assisted her. Alfonso, who accommodated himself with pleasure to his new situation, watered our horses and cows; and I had finished some arrangements of our apartment, and some little jobs in the garden. I took, therefore, my sweet boy upon my arm, and ascended a little hill, which bordered on the garden, and seemed to command an extensive view. The grass was high, and intermixed with sweet scenting flowers. I sat my little Carlos down, and bade him to gather a nosegay for his mother. He told me, by a sweet smile, that he understood me, and began his task with a zeal which moved me to tears.

"The sun was setting on the western horizon with uncommon splendor, little curling clouds preceded him, as if going to form a soft bed; a long silver streak trembled over the horizon, and the evening star stood single and cheerful where it terminated. Cooling breezes gamboled already betwixt the trembling leaves, and the distant river lost itself in deeper obscurity. The creation took leave of its warming friend, and wrapped itself in its misty mantle. The feathered songsters greeted each other once more with harmonious carols, and gradually disappeared to perch on the tops of sheltering trees.

"Did I feel myself happy in that moment?—No; I did not; but was happy without knowing it. The past moment, which could have awakened the consciousness of the present, was elapsed, and not the least vestige of it left. I had changed my ideas, my prospects, and wishes, with my dress and my occupations. My manner of feeling was indeed every where the same; but being divested of its moral wants, it had been simplified to the purest nature. I was as if dropt from Heaven, or from another world, upon this globe: I had forgot, on that journey, all the incidents of my life past, and brought nothing with me but an imagination more purified by its events, and a more sensible susceptibility.

"I never had enjoyed an evening like that. All my wishes were satisfied, all my desires silenced. The stillness which prevailed in my heart, was greater than that which reigned around me; I scarcely felt the beating of its pulses. As the blushes of the evening grew paler and more extensive, my sentiments became softer, while they could extend themselves over so many objects of joy.

"I soon perceived that I was not the sole observer of the beauties that presented themselves to my delighted looks. My little boy, who, all the time, had not uttered a word, had dropt his flowers; and folding his hands, gazed at the blushing charms of the western horizon. On seeing that I looked at him, he picked up his flowers, dividing them in two halves, offering one part to me; with the seraphic smile of innocence, he crept to the spot where I was sitting, reclining his head tenderly upon my lap. I strained him to my heart, and the darling of my bosom lay with his unspeakable charms in my arm. Elmira looked out of the dark-blue softness of his clear eyes, and spoke though the eloquent features of his countenance.

"We were interrupted in our mutual caresses by an angelic being that thronged between us. Elmira encircled us with her arms, and took her little idol from my lap, to have him for a few moments to herself; yet he left some friendly looks behind, sharing his caresses with me. He decorated his mother's hair with the remaining half of his nosegay, and played with her long tresses. Now he looked with delight at her eyes, sparkling with maternal affection; and now hid his face gamboling in her bosom. Elmira's looks rested upon our little darling with a smile, with an expression which angels would have beheld with pleasure.

"When the night grew cooler and darker, we returned slowly to our peaceful habitation, leaning upon one another, and carrying the little Carlos between us. We rivalled, as it were, who was proudest of our dear burden, carrying him in a kind of triumph to our humble mansion. He appeared to us the only treasure we had happily saved out the wreck of our fortune, and viewed him as a pledge of a more cheerful futurity. Our last and best wishes rested on him; and we vowed secretly to risk and to submit to every thing his preservation should require.

"On entering our apartment, I perceived that Elmira intended to give me a specimen of her skill in keeping house. She had exhausted all her culinary knowledge, and prepared a little supper, which would have done honour to a table in a town. The plates and dishes were, indeed, only earthern and wooden; one of china made also now and then its appearance; yet I never have better relished a meal that was served up on silver. All distinction of rank was banished from our society. Our table had five covers. The Marquis and the marchioness of G****** had their little darling in the middle, and Alfonso on one and the maid servant on the other side. The latter were really no despicable companions. Alfonso had, on the wanderings in which he attended me, divested himself of all the prejudices of his situation: my misfortunes, most of which he had shared with me, had taught him modesty; and the love with which he had attended me from my earliest childhood, and with which he was attached to my fate, had given him a certain refinement of thinking that imparted itself to all his expressions. Clara, the servant of my Elmira, was still more tenderly attached to her. She had nursed her with all possible care during her lying-in, and the illness which succeeded it; and my wife had rewarded her fidelity by polishing her natural good understanding.

"Yet it is impossible to conceive a just idea of our happiness, without having tasted it in its artless simplicity; nor our occupations, without having experienced the pleasure they afforded us; nor of the whole complexion of our evening amusements, without having been prepared for them in the same manner we were. It would be in vain to attempt giving you an adequate description of the happiness which reigned in our little circle; for imagination, without experience, is never sufficient to deduce one idea *completely*, *naturally* from the other, and to represent it in a palpable manner, modified by all the preceding notions.

"Elmira directed our daily occupations, distributing to every one his task. Having spent but very little of the money I had designed for my travels, I was enabled to improve the order and the commodiousness of our house, yet without the smallest detriment to its simplicity. I took particular care to encrease the number, and to improve the quality, of our cattle, in which Alfonso assisted me, as well as in the cultivation of our garden. The profits accruing from either were placed in Elmira's hands: she stocked our pantry with a large quantity of pickled and dried vegetables and fruits, and made excellent butter and cheeses. Our meals were simple and frugal, but seasoned in a threefold manner; our hunger gave them an excellent relish; they were the produce of our diligence, and prepared by Elmira.

"The rising sun generally found us at work; and we performed our respective tasks with cheerfulness, anticipating the pleasures our sociable circle at night afforded us. We gave wings to the hours by our indefatigable diligence, and they fled with rapidity while we were absorpt in the performance of our occupations. As soon as the setting sun touched the limits of the western horizon, we left off working: Elmira rambled with me through the garden, leading our sweet boy by the hand; and we bade a cheerful farewell to the setting sun, satisfied with ourselves. The variegated colours of the clouds, the carols of the airy songsters, the first plaintive notes of the nightingale, the fragrant odour of the flowers and blossoms, and the soft whispers of the evening breezes in the air, and betwixt the leaves, filled our soul with unspeakable pleasure. We gathered flowers, making chaplets of them, and adorned one another while we joined in cheerful songs.

"When the evening was fine, we placed a bench before the cottage door, beneath a spreading walnut-tree, which was a signal for our neighbours to assemble around us with their families, and to keep us company. We then formed a sociable circle; every one contributed his share to a public supper; we ate out of one pot; and the children gamboled in the grass, while we cheerfully feasted on the simple gifts of nature. When the table was cleared, some fetched their fiddles, and we began to dance. All ages joined in that amusement; and we were merry till the chilling night air, the rising mists, and the increasing darkness, bade us to retire to our humble cottage. We talked then sometimes half an hour longer of our labours on the following day; or Elmira sang to the harmonious strains of her lute; and then I went to rest in the arms of the best of wives, and a peaceful sleep closed my weary eyes.

"When the weather did not allow us to leave our cottage, our small library was sufficient to fill up the few unoccupied hours. Elmira was far from being of a romantic turn, but a real philosophical woman. She had studied nature, and been obliged to acquire some knowledge of man. Poetry and Music gave to the seriousness of our amusements an elegant, harmonious turn, and, I may justly add, enlivened and gave them more energy.

CHAPTER XIV.

"You will, perhaps, ask me, dear Count, how we educated our Carlos. If I will be sincere, I must tell you, that we did very little with regard to his improvement. Being more afraid to infect him with some of our prejudices than to leave him ignorant, we left that sweet offspring of nature to circumstances and to his own reflections; we guarded him against all noxious impressions, extended gradually the compass of his experience, and he gained thereby the essential advantage that the ideas he abstracted himself were purer, more self-subsistent, and firmer than all those we could have imparted to him.

"I frequently took him with me when I drove my little flock into the field. Resting by my side on the turfy hill, he commenced, as it were, the course of his philosophical observations. Without my telling him: Behold the picturesque beauty of yon river, that serpentines through the trees: observe the simple and grand effect of the smoke, which rises from the ivied chimney of yon solitary cottage: don't overlook the fertility of our corn-field, the luxuriant grass of our meadow, the prolifity of our flock, and reflect upon

him who has created and given us all these blessings: Without the
assistance of these remarks, did his heavenly soul devour with silent
rapture all these scenes of nature; and I beheld joy and heartfelt satisfaction sparkle in his eyes when he contemplated the extensive
creation. Believe me, my friend, these are hours which one enjoys
with perfect gratification. While one sees one's second self gradually improve its mind, one re-peruses once more, with greater pleasure than at first, the primary rudiments of mental culture.

"But, alas! I was soon reminded of the lamentable truth, that
all human happiness is imperfect and transitory. Elmira's sickly
state of health, which generated in her lying-in, and, in spite of the
best medical assistance, rather increased than decreased, cost me
many a tear, and created many a painful hour. She was not ignorant of it; but all her exertions to hide the growing decline of her
strength from my tender looks served only to render it more visible. She struggled frequently to display more strength than she
really did possess; but the weak state of her impaired constitution
rendered every attempt of that nature fruitless. The choice of her
books grew from day to day more serious and melancholy, and her
lute had exchanged the cheerful strains of heartfelt joy with doleful dirges. This was the chief reason that prompted me to avoid all
questions and hints that could have reminded her of her adventures
during her separation from me. She began, indeed, frequently to
speak, of her own accord, of those incidents; however, her heart
was always so full, and her bosom so much strained, that I instantly
turned the discourse on some other subject. At last she said once,
in the course of our conversation, "Dear Carlos, I have employed
the first hours which I could spare in this solitude to write down my
history, and you will find those papers in yon drawer." From that
time I was anxious to avoid every word that pointed at that subject,
or could remind her or myself of the opportunity of getting possession of those secrets.

"I only shall mention here the history which I promised you in
the beginning of my memoirs, that remarkable instance of the
secret influence of those invisible confederates, which I learnt by
accident. I never knew that Elmira had a brother living, till Carlos,
one day, brought me a ring which he had found. It was a common
one of gold, on which the name *Emanuel* was engraven. Elmira

surprised me in the contemplation of that trinket, and snatching it violently from my hand, kissed and pressed it to her heart, lifting her eyes up to heaven, and exclaiming, "Alas! my poor, unfortunate brother!"

"Your brother! my dearest wife?" I replied with astonishment. "Yes, my brother, my unfortunate brother, who fell a sacrifice to that society whom we have with so much difficulty escaped by a fortunate accident. Alas! my whole family has been devoted to misery by those cruel barbarians."

"In that moment I imagined it would not be indelicate to beg her to inform me of that history, and I give it you has she related it to me.

"I had two brothers till I was twelve years of age. The youngest was of a violent fiery temper, went into military service, distinguished himself by an uncommon bravery, and soon died on the field of battle. The eldest, Emanuel, who was designed to propagate our name, staid, after my father's decease, with my mother and myself, at our estate, to repair, through his care and economy, the disordered state of our family affairs. He was a good-natured, excellent young man; open, candid, brave; a friend of his friends, a kind protector of his relations, a benefactor and father of all his tenants. He was generally respected, and sometimes almost adored. He was capable of sacrificing every thing for those he loved; and this feature of his character degenerated at last into a still more amiable weakness, which, however, some of his acquaintances abused in a most shameful manner.

"Being a friend to little amusements, and in general of a very sociable disposition, he frequently collected a large circle of friends around him, who not only spent the fine season with us, but also sometimes staid in a great part of the winter at our castle. One of them was a certain *Don Pedro G******.*"

"Don Pedro G******!" I interrupted Elmira, seized with astonishment. "Yet, go on, dearest love; the man whom I know is perhaps a different person, and only a namesake of him you mentioned."

"Don Pedro was one of the most intimate friends of my brother: he was a crooked and cunning villain, much too cunning and impenetrable for the artless Emanuel, who beheld in every one, as in a mirror, only his own image. He made him, by numberless artful wiles, dissatisfied with his family, with his limited situation, and with the nature of his pleasures; and my poor brother lost entirely that tranquil equanimity which had made him value solitude and his studies as the greatest treasure, and was involved in an uninterrupted round of pleasures and diversions. He paternal house, and the peaceful circle of his family, grew too narrow for him; and he abandoned them for the society of strangers. Even the whole neighbourhood was scarcely large enough for him; he played, hunted, and danced, uninterruptedly, and we frequently did not see him for whole weeks.

"It was very fortunate for us that my father had declared my mother his sole heir, and settled only an annuity on him, the amount of which depended entirely on her pleasure. She confined him therefore a little in his extravagancies, by a smaller allowance, but at the same time exasperated him thereby in the highest degree; and as no one attempted to reconcile him, and some hints were dropt by his bottle companion, which only served to inflame him more violently against his parent, I soon witnessed the most shocking scenes in our house. I behaved, in that state of affairs, with as much passiveness as I possibly could; consoled my afflicted mother, and endeavoured to reconcile my brother to her: but all attempts of that nature were abortive; his heart was every day more and more estranged from us, and he imagined to have a just ground for considering me as a kind of accomplice against him.

"We soon discovered the true reason of that criminal conduct, it being impossible it could remain concealed for a long time. The chief cause of his undutiful behaviour was a girl, who was intimately connected with Don Pedro; and the most artful, malicious, and voluptuous being under the sun. It cannot be denied that she was extremely handsome, and that her physiognomy and eyes were as lively and attracting as possible: however, these very charms, which she knew how to unfold, or to conceal, most artfully, as it best suited her purposes, completed the misfortune of my brother, who possessed a large share of vanity. He was an entire stranger to her great understanding, which was far superior to his. She even pretended to learn from him; and he exerted all his abilities to convince her of ideas which she first artfully had conveyed to his mind, without his being aware of it. He had such a predilection for her company, that he soon loathed all other society. He grew melancholy and morose when he had not seen her for some hours; and his furious passion for her displayed itself frequently by such shocking symptoms, that they made my mother and myself tremble for our safety.

"We could plainly see that something important rankled in his mind, on which he brooded without being able to come to some resolution. But we learnt too late what it was. The restraint which my mother put on his dissipations was extremely galling to him; and he had no other means left for continuing his enormous expences and unbridled diversions than her fortune. His heart was gradually led from thoughtlessness to criminality: he had received hints, and even was offered assistance, to attain the possession of a fortune, which he was misled to believe was unjustly withheld from him: his creditors were incited to press him uninterruptedly for payment: he saw no means of extricating himself: his pretended friends were, or dissembled to be, poor; and he began to conceive designs of a most atrocious nature.

"The waiting woman, who slept in the same apartment with my mother, was, one night, roused from her sleep by a sudden noise, and saw my brother enter the bed-chamber with hasty strides, carrying a candle in one hand and a poniard in the other; his countenance being pale, disordered, and almost entirely changed. He stept to the bed of my mother, and lifted up his arm, as if going to strike at her heart; but having hesitated a few seconds, ejaculated loud sobs, flung the poniard indignantly on the floor, placed the candle upon a table, and throwing himself upon one knee, kissed her depending hand, upon which he started up; a window flew open, and my unfortunate brother threw himself headlong into the court-yard. The petrified waiting-woman recovered the power of utterance at that shocking sight, and breaking out in loud screams, we hastened to the apartment; but, alas! came too late: he had dashed his head to pieces, and a part of his brains smoked on the pavement.

"It would be a vain attempt to give a faithful description of our grief. Suffice it to say, that my mother died of a broken heart; and I myself was at the brink of the grave. She made me promise, on her death-bed, never to mention that circumstance; and I have been as good as my word till now. Reflecting upon what I have experienced myself, and heard in the circle of my friends, of those secret confederates, I cannot but believe that they have been concerned in that lamentable event."

"Here Elmira concluded her mournful tale. "This then was thy friend Don Pedro," I said to myself, "who influenced thy feelings in so artful a manner. His settling in the neighbourhood, which guided me without my knowledge, and his theatrical gestures, which imposed on me with so much art, served to carry on a secret purpose?" I recollected his cunning conversations, and plainly saw that he designed to act the same part with me the mistress of Elmira's brother had acted with that unfortunate young man. I now plainly perceived that he had inspired me with those ideas which I afterwards imagined to have instilled into *his* mind: he then attended me to the cottage in the forest, to deliver his victim safely into the hands of his associates; and stole away to avoid every accidental discovery which the smallest oversight would certainly have produced. The mysteriousness of his behaviour, as well as the real nature of his connection with Francisca, I resolved to leave to time and to favourable circumstances. As for the rest, I was not ill satisfied with this new experience of the little reliance one can repose in the outside of mankind.

"But, alas! what sufferings awaited me! the grief of seeing Elmira's health decline gradually; to see the sweetest and best of women fade away by degrees, and the horrors of approaching death overcloud her serene countenance and her extinguishing eyes. The genius of immortality hovered already around her; she met him with a resigning smile, and extended her hand to be led by him to the mansions of everlasting peace.

"Alas! I was once more doomed to witness the dying scene of the most valuable treasure I possessed. The hermit left me when he scarcely had begun to bless my days. I was too happy in the society of these two dear persons, and it could not but end thus. Human life changes from one extreme to the other, from one dream to the other, and nothing renders it more distressing than the intervals in which one awakes from one's slumber without recovering one's consciousness entirely.

"Elmira grew soon so weak that she scarcely could quit her bed any more. I was now inseparable from her, and applied every thing in vain care and nursing could contribute to ease and to cheer her up. The art of the best physicians I could procure exerted itself in vain. A vomiting of blood deprived her at length of the last remaining spark of life; and she had scarcely sufficient time left to recommend our little Carlos to my care, to embrace me, and to kiss, with her last breath, the tears from my eyes, when she died in my arms.

"Carlos too began rapidly to ripen for eternity. He had imbibed the distemper of his mother, on whose bed he had been day and night, caressing her, and cheering her gloomy hours by his infantine prattle. When he saw that she could reply no more to his sweet talk, that her eyes were closed, and her tender looks told him no more how unspeakably she loved him; when he exerted himself in vain to awaken her from that profound sleep; when he saw me almost petrified, and Alfonso, Clara, and all our neighbours, bathed in tears, he began awfully to ominate that his dearest mother had left him for ever. He did not weep, but searched now all the day long for something, and then came to hide his glowing face in my lap, asking me, "if it would be long ere his good mother would awake? if she were angry with him; and why she did not answer me too?" My convulsive silence told him plainly enough what he had to expect, and he comprehended it gradually. When he heard that she soon would be carried from him, he gathered a nosegay of his favourite flowers, and fastened it to her bosom.

"I frequently surprised him, afterwards, walking in profound reverie in the garden, gathering flowers, and afterwards tearing them. When he happened to meet me, he divided his nosegay, as usual, in two parts, and gave me one half; but afterwards hung his head; and one flower after the other of the remaining half dropt out of his hand. He then sobbed aloud, picking them up again, and lifting his nosegay up to heaven, because Elmira had told him that she was going thither. Thus my beautiful, lovely boy gradually faded away; and before two months were elapsed, the darling of my heart had joined his mother in the grave.

"The friends whom I had gained amongst my neighbours did every thing in their power to divert my mind; and I cannot but confess that their innocent and natural sympathy contributed a great deal to alleviate my grief; their sincere concern convincing me that I still had friends that loved me, and that I was not entirely forsaken.

The little diversions they invented to amuse me, the innocent feasts that were given on my account, extended the convulsively contracted compass of my ideas; they became more easy, and less distracting, as soon as they began to expand themselves.

"However, I found the greatest comfort in Elmira's papers, from which I first learnt the whole extent of my loss. They contained emanations of a greatness of soul that could not but convey tranquillity to my heart. Her resignation to her fate, the patient submission with which she viewed all the events of her life, and the consolations which had raised her above her misfortunes, easily imparted themselves to my soul, so congenial with hers. They constituted a soothing philosophy of life, that never misses its aim under the pressure of sufferings.

"I had secured these papers as soon as I imagined to be intitled to do so, and thus saved them or me; for, I no sooner had taken possession of them, than attempts were made to rob me of that treasure. My locks were, however, too strong; and the unknown agents, that were lurking about me, did, perhaps, not think it worth their while to use greater exertions to get them in their possession. I read them in the night after Elmira's burial, and committed them to the flames the next morning, their contents being safely reposed in my memory. This precaution also preserved the secrets they contained; and I triumphed in my heart over the confederates, flattering myself to have outwitted them at least once.

"I shall now communicate to you, dearest Count, from Elmira's records, some parts of her history, that are not yet known to you. I even shall attempt to demand from my memory a great part of her own words, with which she expressed and painted the train of these events. It is pity that the papers could not be preserved; for I never have seen such striking proofs of female perfection as they contained.

END OF THE SECOND VOLUME.

THE

HORRID MYSTERIES.

CHAPTER I.

Extract from Elmira's Papers.

I awoke, at length, from that long swoon, and found myself
stretched out in a coffin. Some more of the receptacles of the
wrecks of mortality stood near me, and the odour of corruption
was the first thing that affected my senses. The spacious and lofty
vault was sparingly lighted by the faint glimmer of a single lamp,
that was suspended to the ceiling. Its dying flame plainly told me
where I was. What mortal can conceive a just idea of the sensations produced by the first breaking from sleep under such circumstances; and who could be able to recal only a single sentiment of
those that crowded on my mind, if he ever was so unfortunate to
have experienced what I did? I did not know what I should do in that
dreadful situation; whether I should call for assistance, or patiently
await the event. The lamp was a certain proof that I was in a place
not entirely deserted by human beings; and I felt no other painful
sensation, but a great weakness, and relaxation of my bodily and
mental faculties. Yet I was not suffered to remain long in a state of
consultation with myself; the sound of different voices vibrating in
my ears from a passage whose entrance the dying glimmer of the
lamp enabled me to descry. I even could distinguish the expressions
and the subject of their discourse. Some declaimed against Carlos's
inhuman barbarity, and some censured me for my imprudence; but
one person defended me, finding it very natural that a weak, love-
sick, and inexperienced girl should have been taken in by an artful
and experienced villain. The talkers, having carefully stopt a while
at the entrance, came, at length, nearer, and appeared in the vault,

exhibiting a large procession of compassionate faces of either sex. Some carried torches, some phials and glasses, and some garments and linen. The light, that now illuminated my horrid residence, enabling me to look around, I beheld myself enfolded in a cloud, and different vessels standing by my side.

"Loud rejoicings re-echoed through the vault when my visitors saw me sitting in the coffin; and they ran towards me to complete my resuscitation, carrying me out of the damp cavern to a lofty apartment, where I was put into a well aired bed. Decency bade my deliverers to retire, and only two females staid with me, to assist me in changing my dress, while I gradually was re-animated with a pleasing warmth, and recovered the full power of recollection.

"When they saw that I had entirely recovered my faculties, they congratulated me on my preservation, praising God for having made them instrumental in my restoration to life.

"Thank God, Countess," one of them began, "that you have been rescued from the cruel hands of that barbarian, and are now in the company of more humane beings!"

"From what cruel hands?" I replied, with astonishment.

"From those of your pretended lover, the Marquis Carlos of G******."

"Be silent, vile reptile," I exclaimed, "and dare not to asperse the name of a man whom I adore!"

"Don't put yourself into a passion, my Lady," she replied coolly: "You will be of our opinion before many days are elapsed. We are members of a society whose sole business it is to make the sufferer forget his sorrows, and to restore the unhappy to happiness. Indeed, Countess, we flattered ourselves to deserve, at least, your gratitude."

"What could I have replied to the declaration of that woman in my situation? I was silent; and having taken a firm resolution to conceal all my ideas, I dissembled to rely implicitly on the candour of my pretended deliverers. It was but too evident in whose power I was; and what I had heard of that society on my wedding day forced itself with additional strength on my recollection. Though I could not unfold the real purport of that incident, yet it was sufficient to ascertain to me the truth of my suspicions. If, therefore, it was possible to extricate myself from their snares, no other expedient was left than to pay them in their own coin, and to attempt to outwit them by a dissimulation superior to theirs. I began, therefore, to pretend being more susceptible of the ideas which they endeavoured to instil into my mind, and returned gradually from my gloomy reveries. I was, indeed, partial to solitude; however, it appeared to them to be favourable to their secret designs upon me; and the more the result of my contemplations seemed to make me uneasy, the less mistrust against their secret endeavours to encrease those distressing doubts did I display. I submitted, with an unaffected reluctance, more and more, to their exertions to restore me to happiness, as they pretended, and to return me to my family with an easier heart. A cheerful gaiety, which I kept in proper bounds, and strove to render as natural as possible, by an imposing varnish of truth, confirmed them in their belief of having gained upon my credulity; and I began to hope that I should find a favourable moment to give them the slip. I was not anxious to know the external circumstances of the confederates, thinking myself sufficiently happy if I could but escape their baneful breath.

"Mean time a number of fine ladies and gentlemen gathered around me. I was invited to accompany them on a nocturnal excursion to a neighbouring castle, where I learnt, the next morning, that it was to be my future residence. The situation was, indeed, beautiful; the garden extensive and elegant; walking was, therefore, my chief occupation and amusement. Although I was never without company, or at least without such attendants as observed me from a distance, and the happy period of my elopement was probably not very near, yet I cheered myself up by numberless plans of accelerating it secretly.

"My keepers studied to amuse me by numberless little diversions. Rural feasts, the charm of selected parties; beautiful, winning, females, and young, amiable men, were to accomplish, with the smiling assistance of the graces, during a constant round of pleasures, what had been devised and begun under circumstances of the most serious and awful complexion. Every one breathed a general and delicate desire of pleasing me, and of anticipating my wishes before they had time to ripen to maturity; and I cannot but confess, that they several times accomplished their designs as perfectly as they could wish. I returned involuntarily their kindness, as if enchanted. They succeeded to make me more unreserved; and if not the few hours, in which I was not in their company, had weakened the impressions of the rest, I should scarcely have been able to avoid an intoxication which would have ruined me for ever.

"Amongst the young men by whom I was surrounded, one distinguished himself particularly. He was of a most beautiful form, animated with a very dangerous fire, of polished manners, and an insinuating disposition, which rendered him pliable to all my wishes. He seemed to claim my favour in a more particular manner than the rest, depended entirely upon my looks, and was happy or unhappy as my humour changed. Never have the wiles of the most cunning seduction been applied in a more artful manner; all circumstances were in his favour: whatever the rest of the company said, supported and advanced his superiority; and being, in the sequel, convinced of the purity of his passions, by his indefatigable exertions to please me, I could not have avoided being caught in the snare at last, if not a trifling accident had rectified my opinion of him, and restored me to myself and to my plans.

"He had a little French dog; and I grew so foolishly fond of the animal, that I frequently hinted to him, it would give me the greatest pleasure if he would make me a present of it; yet he seemed not to be inclined to part with his little favourite. At length he promised me, one afternoon, to let me have it in the evening. I was walking sometime before the assembly hour in the boscage, saw him in it, seated on a bench, and occupied with his favourite, and concealed myself behind a thick hazel-bush. He tied a ribband round the neck of his little darling, and having finished the task, he could not refrain from kissing him, and uttering the words, "Poor Thonon! we must part: however, thou wilt always be dearer to me than what thou art to purchase for me."

"These words wounded my heart like a dagger; and my whole situation lay, at once, undisguised before my eyes. I was ready to faint; and could scarcely refrain from rushing forth, and letting him see an Elmira entirely different from that he had known till then. Yet rage and pain fortunately stifled my tears and sighs, and I arrived at my apartment without being seen by him.

"As soon as I had recovered my recollection, I saw plainly how necessary it was not to give up the part I had begun to act. I pre-

vailed upon myself, after a hard struggle, to assume again the semblance of cheerfulness, and an air of tranquil resignation. The dog
was presented to me, and received with an imposing pleasure: the
donor expected, and demanded, at length, a reward for the sacrifice he had made to me; but being cautioned by what I had overheard, I found it pretty easy to evade his violent caresses and tender
menaces.

"Thus some weeks more elapsed, and I could still not find out
proper means of effecting my escape. The danger of a longer stay
grew every day more pressing. I knew, however, neither the district
in which the castle was situated, nor the neighbourhood, and was
carefully guarded. At length I attempted, with a very small probability of success, what I, perhaps, under more favourable circumstances, never had dared to risk. At a feast, which was given on
my account, and on which all eyes were directed at me, I got suddenly from my throne, on which I was to receive an approaching
procession, upon a walnut-tree, and fortunately concealed myself
between the thick branches till night promised to favour my flight!

"I descended from my asylum as soon as it was dark. A foot-path
led me to an neighbouring village; and the darkness of night protected me on my retreat. Being animated with a more than common
courage, I ventured to enter a cottage, exchanged my garments for
a rural dress, dyed my face, and begged my way through the prov-
inces of Spain and France to this peaceful spot. I lost, indeed, on my
journey, a part of the jewels with which they had decorated me; yet
I saved a sufficient quantity to purchase this little solitude, and to
commence a little farm, which promised to afford me a frugal support for the remainder of my life?"

CHAPTER II.

"The above chapter, dearest Count, is a faithful, but brief, extract
from that part of Elmira's history of which I was ignorant till then.
You see how singular the turn of her and of my fate was directed
by a higher Power. If ever I had been capable of doubt that Providence guides the fate of man, the reflections which her account
produced, would certainly have convinced me of the eternal truth,

that a benevolent Being watches over our life and happiness, and produces light out of darkness.

"Give me now leave to inform you of the remainder of my adventures, which I shall be able to conclude in a few words. Clara was in love with the son of a neighbouring farmer; but being poor, and the father of her lover a rich man, the latter would not consent to a union between his son and her. Being averse to sell or to abalienate any thing my sainted Elmira had possessed, I gave her the considerable produce of my little estate as a dowry, saw the young couple married, and went through Swisserland and Germany to G******, where I had the happiness to make your acquaintance.

"You know my history from that day: suffice it, therefore, to tell you briefly, that while you was fighting the battles of your country against Great Britain, I went to B******, to commence a private, but, nevertheless, not inactive life, and to enjoy those pleasures I was accustomed to. I shall not tire your patience with an account of the little adventures, and the unimportant events, of that period in which I was constantly surrounded by members of secret societies, and enthusiasts of all sorts, got possession of their secrets, and observed that they were far inferior to what I already knew, or that they were partly connected with the confederacy in Spain."

I shall here, at last, take up again the thread of those events I have mentioned in the middle of my adventures, which I have wrote down for the Count. The reader will recollect that a man (James) settled in our neighbourhood, who, as I apprehended, was nearly connected with me. His appearance threatened me with new misfortunes; and he seemed to intend opening a new way of influence on me through the heart of the Count. However, that ominous apparition passed quickly over. He had, indeed, purchased a country seat in the neighbourhood; but disappeared after a few days. I was told that he was going to B****** on matrimonial affairs, and my apprehensions vanished. That incident left, however, some impression on my mind; and many plans, particularly that of returning to my native country, were thereby obliterated from my soul. I comprehended many a mysterious phenomenon more clearly, and could, in some degree, account for Amanuel's apparitions, the frequent repetition of which now appeared to me to be a great imprudence of the unknown confederates. They probably intended to frighten me, by letting me see that I was surrounded every where by their secret agents: however, the mystic appearance of Amanuel's presence, which had affected my senses so powerfully, lost its awfulness entirely through that oversight. I was no stranger to the artifices wrought through natural magic; and also not ignorant what a powerful influence a heated, overflowing, and transported imagination produces on our senses. The whole now appeared to me a mere scarecrow for children. The mystic farce was continued too long, and afterwards betrayed the whole confederacy. The mysterious veil was removed from that memorable moment, and my imagination being rectified by cool reflection, the miserable artifices of the confederates rather filled me with contempt than with awe. James's apparition in my neighbourhood opened my eyes; and my mind, being now liberated from the thraldom of a deluded imagination, firmly begins a new, decided career.

The Count was very much grieved at the sudden departure of the dear stranger, as he used to call him. I was already, in the beginning, strongly tempted to predict it; but cannot conceive what prevented me from doing so; and my friend was, soon after that incident, a second time obliged, by his affairs, to leave me, before I could conclude my history, and elucidate many mysterious events to him; for the various occupations in which I was engaged did not allow me, as I already have informed the reader, more leisure hours for the continuation of my memoirs than I could spare from the time of nocturnal rest.

My friend remained a long time absent, being detained by the unaccountable intricacy of his affairs. It really seemed as if they intended to exhaust his patience by juridical chicanes and petty artifices, to make him waste his precious time in the most useless manner. I very seldom received letters from him, and he always concluded them by informing me that he should not return so soon. Being convinced that I was completely acquainted with his ideas, he did not trouble himself about the management of his estates, which was an additional motive for me to be the more careful. There never was a period of my whole life, in which I knew so well to fill up every moment with such exactness; every one of them, from morning till night, being counted and designed for some employment. These tedious occupations did not at first please me much on account of their tiresome sameness; however, after a few weeks reluctant exertion, they grew so easy, and at last so amusing to me, that I could not disuse myself therefrom. I now exercised more authority over the Count's people than he ever did himself, because he had not acquired that knowledge of the inferior classes which I possessed: I conversed with every one, listened to every proposal of theirs, and frequently improved my own plans by comparing and uniting their ideas with mine. I was all the day long on horseback, or running from one part of the estate to the other, to give directions to the workmen. I never indulged myself with reading before all the labourers had finished their daily task, and my accounts were settled; and after supper, which received an additional relish from the fatigues of the day, I continued my memoirs till it was time to go to rest, when I went to bed highly satisfied with myself. The writing down of my memoirs was, from that time, continued with so much assiduity, that the manuscript was finished in less than a month after the Count's departure. I afterwards corrected it in many places, and gave it him on his return.

I was always very fond of gardening; and although my friend had an excellent taste in arranging the whole, yet he had too little patience to dedicate much time to a proper survey and regulation of the particulars. I began, therefore, to revise his excellent plans, and to polish them more carefully than he had taken the trouble to do, and altered some parts of his garden accordingly. Some old buildings and pleasure houses were sacrificed to my impatient industry. A pavilion, which was situated in a corner of the park, and visited by no one who valued his life, was one of the chief objects that had excited my dislike. It was entirely concealed by bushes and trees, and seemed to have been designed by nature for solitude, which determined me to have it pulled down, and to build in its place a little hermitage, with a few small apartments; flattering myself with the sweet hope of being able to inhabit them the subsequent summer. I formed that idea and the plan for the new building in one night; went early in the morning into the garden, took some workmen with me, who were cleaning a bason, ordering them to provide themselves with the necessary implements, and conducted them to the pavilion, with the instruction to pull the old nest instantly down. My orders were put into execution with the greatest alacrity. A part of one of the side-walls fell down of itself; and a large stone, which seemed to support the rest, being removed, we beheld the entrance of a narrow subterraneous passage. We stared at each other, seized with astonishment; and I asked one of the workmen whether he could strike fire? He affirmed it; and some of his fellow labourers tore some dry branches from a fir-tree, which, being lighted, the whole train followed me laughing into the cavern, expecting to find a great treasure, and to have some share of it. We descended, therefore, cheerfully; and I cannot deny that I also hoped to find something of value, though of a different nature from what they imagined. The scene which once took place between myself and the Count in that very garden, the small distance of the famous turf-seat from the pavilion, the communication of these two places through an almost impenetrable boscage, and the favourable concealment of the spot, seemed to promise me some important discovery, which was the reason of my being more apprehensive than the rest of my fellow adventurers. However, the consideration of my being attended by seven stout Germans, armed with their working tools, and of a brave appearance, soon inspired me with courage. I entered the avenue laughing, though with a beating heart, and called to the rest to keep close to my heels. I left one at the avenue, to guard us against all external attacks; and to alarm the servants at the castle, if we should not return within the course of an hour. Having descended some part of our way almost perpendicularly, the passage grew so small, that we found it very difficult to proceed. I constantly held the torch before me, examining the ground carefully, lest we should be caught in a dangerous snare. Yet, the passage soon grew wider, the way more even; and we had not proceeded a minute, when we came into a vaulted cave, which apparently formerly was a cellar. We discovered, in the back part, a second receptacle, furnished with a table and chairs, that were pretty new. On examining the table, I found that a piece had recently been cut out of it; and it appeared to me that some person had attempted to obliterate a character which seemed to have been cut into the wood. After a more minute inspection, I discovered some traces of an E.

I could not guess, at first, what that letter could mean, but recollected, at last, that the Count had the singular custom to delineate frequently such an E in the sand, or to cut it into the bark of trees; and I ere now suspected that letter to be the first character of the name of a former mistress. I discovered nothing else besides this; neither a new avenue, nor a continuation of the vault. I had ordered all my attendants to search every corner: however, we found no farther trace of a human inhabitation; yet, when I left the vault, to ascend the passage again, one of them exclaimed that he had found some papers. I ordered him to give them to me, and unfolded them. All of them were blank, except the fourth, on which something was written, and I was struck with astonishment when I read, *"Countess Elmira is cautioned against the young Marquis Carlos of G****** who means to impose upon her."* I did not know whether I could trust my eyes; yet it was undoubtedly the same paper. Seeing, however, that my attendants were astonished to see me start back, I added coolly, after a few moments consideration, "The D—l may make that out without the other half."

So saying, I threw the whole parcel into the same corner in which it had been found. Thus terminated that singular expedition. I left the passage with an easy heart; but my conductors hung their heads, because they had not found the expected treasures. In order to console them for their disappointment, I gave every one a dollar, under the condition to mention nothing of our adventure to the Count's servants. I could easily foresee that this would be the surest means of having it circulated in the castle, and determined to watch whether I could gather nothing from the behaviour of the servants, all of whom I suspected very much. However, the whole affair became a subject of general merriment: every one was impatient to see the subterraneous vault; and the visits of the curious to the cellar became soon so numerous, that I ordered the passage to be shut up, because it was now the general rendezvous of the servants. Thus terminated that adventure. The new pavilion was finished in a short time, and furnished, and I had the pleasure of breakfasting there before the Count returned. He arrived at length, fatigued by the incidents and the labours which had retarded his return so long. His affairs were, indeed, settled, and his law-suit was gained: however, the expences amounted to more than he had saved; and he had, besides, reason to regret the time he had wasted in that disagreeable affair. Yet he thought himself rewarded for his troubles, in some degree, by several discoveries he had accidentally made, and which he communicated to me without reserve as soon as he had read my memoirs.

"Let us act just, dear Carlos," he said, "notwithstanding those villainous artifices. We are not bound to keep promises which have been forced from us by cruelties: it would, however, be to no purpose to inform you of the history of those days when I suddenly left you. You have discovered the mysteries of the cavern: it seems to be forsaken already for some time, and I have made a solemn promise to be silent. What is, at present, of more importance to me, is to find out the persons that still are very active in our neighbourhood, that have confounded my law-suit, and, as I have reason to apprehend, will ruin us sooner or later. Marquis, are you my friend?" Here he stretched out his hand. I shook it warmly, and replied, "Yes, I am your sincere, your faithful friend."

"Will you ever preserve me your affection?" "By Heaven! for ever!" "Then come to my heart, my brother, and receive from me the same vow. I swear to be inviolably your friend; and may I be left without comfort in my dying hour, if ever I forget this promise only for a single moment. May Heaven preserve me your friendship; this is all that I wish."

"Lewis, I follow you whithersorever you go, in spite of all disasters that may befall you."

"Well, then, let us boldly meet those daring villains that intrude upon our fate; let us save the last half of life; let us sacrifice a few years more, and without mercy attack them in the centre of their mystic abode."

"Here is my hand. I follow you."

"Let us go to Paris, assemble our friends around us, and then penetrate into Spain. How willingly would I sacrifice the greater part of my fortune in that attempt, if I could purchase peace and tranquillity."

CHAPTER III.

We now exerted ourselves jointly to settle the Count's affairs as well as it was possible. Before six months were elapsed, we accomplished our purpose, and soon after arrived at the capital of France.

We were obliged to mix with the great world, in order to make discoveries, and to obtain all kinds of assistance in the execution of our plans. The Count spared nothing to do credit to his rank and title, and to introduce himself with *eclat*. His equipage was one of the most splendid at Paris; his servants' liveries were in the highest taste; his dress was selected with elegance; and before many weeks were elapsed, we were introduced in the best circles of the town, and in some received with cordiality.

The amusements of that capital are too well known to require a minute description. The play, dancing, parties of pleasure, and particularly the charm of the fine arts, never miss their aim. The Count was not much attracted by them. My character, on the contrary, impels me forcibly to seek that sort of amusement. We mixed, therefore, with the gay circles, and enjoyed the pleasures of Paris, but without being much diverted. We made new connexions, and continued the old ones, without sacrificing much to them; and spared every day at least a few hours for more important conversations in our closet.

It was very favourable to our purpose, that many of my former acquaintances and friends gradually gathered around us. Don Bernhard and Count S******i were the first, and more strongly captivated with our plans than I had left them. They were surprised to the highest degree at Count S******'s adventures, and impatient to have those mysterious incidents elucidated. The sufferings and experiences of some years had ripened our characters, and rendered them more harmonious; and we found, in the mutual exchange of our ideas, comforts, pleasures, and prospects which none of us had expected.

Our method of proceeding was also altered very much through the existing circumstances. Having divested ourselves of our former timidity, we made no secret of our plans, but spoke of them wherever we met; and while we thus gained many friends and sharers in our enterprize, we also obtained gradually more resources, and perhaps, defeated thereby many secret machinations of the confederates.

Yet all these favourable circumstances did not, at bottom, bring us much nearer to the mark; for all our power consisted, as yet, in nothing else than in firmness, and in a calculated opposition against probable future events. We had not fixed upon a plan of attack, but left the regulation of our proceedings to the direction of circumstances; yet nothing happened that could have guided us. The Count was inclined to return to Spain; and I would have faithfully followed him, if it had not been for Don Bernhard, and our associated friends, without whose assistance we could not expect to succeed in our undertaking, which, to confess the truth, promised very little, as the centre of the confederacy could easily be shifted; and we had already been convinced that it could exist any where. Thus our preparations were rendered ineffective by the confederates, while they took care to give us no opportunity of applying vigorous measures. We began, by degrees, to grow negligent, because no occasion occurred that could have given energy to our designs. Trifling amusements enervated our desire for great and important deeds; and the female world left us little time to meditate on serious occupations. A constant round of diversions unbraced our minds; and we soon looked upon our plans, which formerly had engaged our whole attention, as an object of exercising our wit. At last an incident happened which seemed to make us forget them entirely. A fatal love affair occasioned a difference between myself and the Count; deprived me, for a long time, of his affection and confidence, before I could prevail upon myself to make some sacrifice to him; and, surprising us unawares, almost terminated our investigations by an ill-fated jealousy. Chance only re-united us, and removed the veil of mysteriousness from our eyes.

Caroline de B****** was of an ancient and noble family in Picardy. She was not rich; however, her fortune was sufficient to afford her a good education, and to render her no despicable party. She was not handsome; but her complexion was fresh, her shape elegant, and her deportment natural and winning. She possessed an unaffected gaiety, which graced all her movements, and gave them diversity and novity. She neither possessed striking wit, nor an uncommon understanding: however, her sallies were always pleasing; and her modesty, good-nature, and evenness of temper, spoke highly in her favour. As for her character, I might well say, she had none; it was, at least, impossible to discern it; for she accommodated herself with so much ease and simplicity to the individual

disposition of those with whom she conversed, and adapted herself
in so natural a manner to the humours of those with whom she was
connected, that every one imagined to see in her his own picture.
As for her heart, I may truly say that it was pure and noble.

It was, indeed, very unfortunate for us that we did not get sooner
acquainted with that amiable being. If we had seen her on our
introduction into our social circle, the impression she would have
made upon us, would, perhaps, not have been so strong, or soon
have been obliterated by other charming objects. But now we were
tired by too much art; and our hearts being over-fatigued by the
intricate mazes of the most consummate female coquetry, were in
want of a place of rest in the lap of simple nature.

Caroline charmed us at first sight. We got acquainted with her
at an evening assembly which we frequented almost every day to
play at cards. Caroline had already, sometime before our arrival,
accompanied some friends into the country; and being a constant
member of the cheerful circle where we met her, her return occasioned some confusion in the arrangement of the gaming-party.
As soon as she perceived this, she declared that she would not play
with us, but was determined to be received again into the party to
which she belonged before she went into the country. This whim
threw the whole company into a new confusion. Those with whom
she desired to associate again, were already used to their new companions, and did not shew the least inclination to quit them; and
their ladies were not less disinclined to be abandoned by their partners on Caroline's account. The general commotion to which this
gave rise terminated at last in a loud laughter, which covered the
face of the poor girl with a high crimson colour, and she declared
that she would not play at all. Tranquillity and order were soon
restored, and I seated myself by her side on the sofa; not ill pleased
with the termination of that ridiculous affair. However, the Count's
mind was far from being easy. It is almost impossible to brook such
an incident with indifference with an irritability like his, which was
unimpaired by misfortunes. Anger boiled in his heart, and he only
wanted an opportunity of giving vent to it. A fire, whose nature
I was no stranger to, flushed in his eye, and seemed to search an
object. I ridiculed his agitation, and begged him to be easy: however, he replied; "Fye upon you, Carlos; how can you be so torpid?"

He then fixed his eyes upon a German officer, who played at some distance from us, and continued to smile at our disaster. "Don't you comprehend," he resumed, "that all this is pre-concerted?"

He was perhaps, not much mistaken, if he suspected the German officer, who called himself Baron de H******, to have acted in this affair with some malicious heat, and with design. Yet he was not a man that could submit to be scoffed at without chastising the offender. He knew the Baron already at Gibraltar, where he had fought with him against the Britons, and, by a strange accident, was his rival in the love of a Spanish lady. This had already incensed him against the Baron; and an affair of a later date, which I am going to relate, made him his implacable enemy.

The Count kept an actress of the royal opera, a charming girl, of uncommon wit, and a great knowledge of man; an excellent companion, but not very famous for her fidelity. Although he was not over fond of her, keeping her rather for fashion's sake than from inclination, yet he looked upon her favours as goods which he had bought, and which no one could intrude upon without violating his property. His vanity contributed to render his ambition still more tender with regard to that point; and there was a period when his mind was entirely occupied with plans of securing the fidelity of his Amasia against all temptations which might be thrown into her way. But how was it possible he could have interrupted all the connections of a vain, voluptuous, and covetous girl, who had made it the study of her life to insnare men, and to jilt them, in her fetters? In short, he had sufficient reason for being jealous, and particularly of his sworn rival, Baron de H******.

An odd incident served to blow up that dormant fire into a blazing flame. He went one evening over the Pont Neuf to pay her a visit; and intending to surprise her unexpectedly, to be certain of her infidelity, he had put on a blue coat, and taken only one servant with him. On coming to the middle of the bridge, he was at once surrounded by a troop of intoxicated citizens, who had drowned their sorrows in large bumpers, and, by their inebrity, were led to commit a number of ridiculous frolicks. One of them having engaged to discover the profession of every passenger by his external appearance, they had placed themselves upon that spot to observe every one that went over the bridge, and the Count was unfortunately the first that happened to come into their way.

He that was to guess at the profession of the passengers, was extremely puzzled by the Count's appearance; a wager of some louis d'ors having been laid. He easily conceived, notwithstanding the disguise of my friend, by his gait and shape, that he was of a superior rank. He hesitated, therefore, some moments to pronounce his opinions; crossing his arms, and gaping at the Count. The latter being struck by the oddity of that scene, could not help smiling, which inspired the drunken inquisitor with additional courage. He turned, therefore, to his comrades, who were diverted by his perplexity, exclaiming, "I will be d——d, if I don't guess that gentleman's profession: I lay you one louis d'or more than he is a cuckold." The whole company broke out into a roaring laughter; and the decision of the wager, depending on the confession of the other party, they pressed the poor Count, in their merry humour, to confess the fact. My friend being armed with no other weapon of defence, but a cane, was in danger of being torn to pieces. He defended himself as well as he could; but, without the assistance of some soldiers, who came to his relief, he would probably have been forced to make the ridiculous confession.

Thus he was seasonably extricated from the danger which had threatened him; but, far from taking the whole affair for what it really was, an accidental frolick, he imagined it to have been preconcerted, to give him a hint of the infidelity of his mistress; he fancied, at least, the whole town was already informed of his cuckoldom. His blood began violently to ferment, he quickened his steps to the house of his mistress, and entered her apartment in the height of his passion, abusing the poor, trembling girl with the bitterest reproaches. However, she soon collected herself; and having attempted in vain to soothe his rage, by tears and tender remonstrances, asked him, at length, coolly, "whether she should ring for her people, or whether he preferred to quit her house without their assistance?" He chose the latter; and she appeared the next day in public as the declared mistress of Baron de H******. This affair recurred, on the present occasion, to the recollection of my friend, and he imagined the Baron's malicious smiles alluded to it. He went, therefore, to him, whispering in his ear, "Baron, you will give me leave to ask you, how far *you* are concerned in this affair?"

The Baron made a low bow, replying, smiling, in German, "My Lord, I shall give you every explanation on that head you can wish for."

The place where we were being not proper for pushing the matter any farther, the Count pretended to be satisfied with this answer, and retired; yet I could plainly see what was going on in his mind. Caroline did every thing in her power to make us forget the consequences of her little caprice, displaying her mental charms with a most bewitching humour, nature, and elegance. She endeavoured to dispel the gloom which frowned on the Count's brow, telling him, that she would try her fortune with him the next day: however, nothing was capable of restoring the harmony of his soul; and while I felt myself as happy as a god by Caroline's side, and reviewed all my ideas to select for her the most natural and intelligible sentiments, he was absorpt in a gloomy reverie, from which he scarcely awoke now and then.

Supper was, at length, served up, and we sat down to table in tolerable good humour and harmony. The conversation turning on the siege of Gibraltar, the company were desirous to know the particulars of it. The Count was requested to favour us with a circumstantial relation of that remarkable siege; but declined it with a great deal of politeness and modesty, directing the company to beg that favour of Baron de H******, who had given many proofs of his courage and superior talents on that occasion. The Baron, having not the least suspicion that his conduct on that occasion was notorious, accepted the challenge, with a presumptuous smile, as a just tribute of his merits, and began his narrative. I was astonished to hear with how much barefacedness that fellow interlarded his relation with a number of various adventures in which he pretended to have been engaged. There was no recounter in which he had not acted a principal part: he made the whole company shudder at the dangers which he pretended to have experienced during the war; and it was merely owing to his modesty and delicacy that he forbore to speak also of those to which he was exposed by the fair sex. I am firmly convinced, that he flattered himself to have sold his rodomantades for sterling truth, as he did not take the least notice of the suspicious smiles of the company, and would certainly have carried his impudence still further, if the Count had not interrupted him at the conclusion of a most romantic adventure with the words, "And then you awoke?" An audible whisper, which ran through the company when the Count uttered these sarcastic words, roused him completely from his infatuation, and he stopped half a minute, glowing with shame and rage.

He then was going to vent his fury upon the Count, when the latter interrupted him with the greatest politeness, turning to the company, and begging leave to relate also an incident which happened at the same time. The whole company signified their approbation; but few only guessed what was to come. The Count began his story, directing some significant looks at the Baron, who wanted to continue his tale, and only could be silenced by the general clamour of the company.

"When we raised the siege of Gibraltar," the Count resumed, "most of those who had expected to gain honor and preferment on that expedition as volunteers, abandoned every idea of making a new attempt; three of my comrades, and myself, resigned on the spot, and went farther into the country, to recover from the fatigues of the campaign, and to visit an intimate friend of mine, who had married a charming and rich Spanish lady. Our journey was more pleasant than is usual in Spain. Two of my companions, who resembled me in their temper and good humour, as well as myself, found every where sufficient opportunities for diversion; and when nothing occurred that could afford us amusement, the comical lies, and rodomontades, of our fourth fellow-traveller, made us forget the badness of the roads and poverty of the inns.

"Don Antonio (thus we will call him) was one of the strangest human beings nature has produced. He had a pretty good share of understanding, and not little experience, but was of a most singular disposition. Although he knew that we had been eye witnesses of, and concerned in, almost all engagements, in which he displayed very little of the hero, yet he invented a number of adventures, in which he pretended to have acted a principal part, and endeavoured to persuade us of his veracity by a semblance of the greatest candour, as well as by numberless oaths.

"Well invented!" we frequently used to exclaim, "though it is not true!" However, he pledged his honour, and, what was still more important, his tried courage, for the truth of his tale. We resolved, therefore, unanimously, to try, on the next opportunity, how far we could rely upon the latter.

"Our common friend received us as well as we could expect, and did every thing in his power to prolong our stay with him, and to give us pleasure. His country seat united all the charms of the Spanish clime, and our rural diversions were seasoned by the pleasant flows of humorous sallies. We played most charming little tricks; and our sociable harmony prevented us from being offended when, now and then, our frolicks degenerated into something more than jest. Our hostess and host soon knew Antonio's weak side as well as we did; and we resolved to repay him with a vengeance, on the first opportunity, all the liberties he had taken with us, and soon were enabled to carry our purpose into execution.

"A sudden noise arose in the castle, one night, while we were at supper in a garden-house. Some of the servants came running, pale and with ghastly looks, to inform our host secretly, that a ghost had been seen in one of the apartments. The Marquis acquainted us instantly with that intelligence. The ladies grew deadly pale, and started up from their chairs. Some gentlemen, who happily had succeeded to suppress the first emotions of fear, began to raise a loud laughter, and to ridicule the cowardice of the servants. The Marquis, however, declared the affair ought to be treated more seriously; ordered the servants to light some torches; and begging the ladies to keep themselves quiet and easy till his return, took up his sword, and begged us to follow him.

"Now a very tender scene took place. The married ladies, as well as those of the unmarried, who had a lover amongst us, began solemnly to protest against that resolution, and conjured us not to leave them unprotected. The Marquis, however, entreated them to give him leave not to suffer himself to be robbed thus quietly; and, after a number of remonstrances, admonitions, and obsecrations, had been exchanged, it was agreed to examine the affair in the company of the ladies. The latter took fearfully hold of the arms of their neighbours, the servants led the way with a blaze of torches, and we covered the procession with drawn swords.

"I did not rightly know what to think of the matter, which appeared to me to be rather strange, and quite unpre-concerted. It was impossible to draw any conclusion from the looks of our host.

He really seemed to be rather agitated, and I knew that he was but a poor dissembler. I also could not imagine that he wantonly would alarm a whole company, merely to punish an individual. I concluded, therefore, that really something must have happened; and giving, at that time, very little credit to the apparition of ghosts, suspected some roguery, and resolved to behave with as much courage as my unhappy education would allow in that point.

"I grew, at length, so tranquil and cool, that I was capable of making observations on the company. At first, a general, profound, and anxious silence prevailed amongst us, and was only now and then interrupted by a solitary sigh, which escaped some of our companions. Don Antonio uttered, at length, the greatest oath he could find in the visible agony of his mind. His fair neighbour (for he had carefully avoided to offer his arm to one of the ladies, in order to be at full liberty to take to his heels in case of necessity) conjured him to be quiet. However, he probably mistook this for a challenge to regale the company with some more of his fine exclamations, and repeated every oath he knew, to protest that he was impatient to have the pleasure of engaging a ghost. Yet, notwithstanding these strong protestations, he could not help looking fearfully around now and then, and keeping carefully between the two servants who closed the train. He even made, at intervals, a certain noise with his teeth, which is not accounted to be a token of heroism, when the wind rustled a little stronger betwixt the leaves, and became more and more silent the nearer we approached the castle. The rest of the company were also not entirely free of fearful apprehensions; and there was not one who did not exhibit stronger or weaker symptoms of anxious apprehensions.

"A sudden gust of wind, which extinguished some of the torches, served to encrease the fear which prevailed in our heroic society: and some of the ladies protested they would not advance a step farther, if they were not lighted again immediately. We were, therefore, obliged to halt, which happening frequently, our march was very much retarded; and those that were more fearful than the rest, gained time to communicate their apprehensions to their neighbours, and to infect even the servants who, at first, had displayed pretty much courage.

"We arrived, at length, at the castle-gate. The haunted apartment was on the first floor; but the anxiety of the company displayed itself already at the staircase which led to the great hall. Numberless fears and apprehensions exhibited themselves on the countenances of my fellow-adventurers, which were rendered more visible by their painful exertions to conceal them from the rest. We now counted the company, to see whether none had stayed behind; and were struck with astonishment, on finding that the Chevalier Antonio was missing. We were already going to ridicule his cowardice severely, and felt ourselves strongly inclined to laugh at the desertion of his vaunted courage, when he convinced us that we had wronged him; for he came running out of breath, and wiping the sweat from his face. He even asked, with great clamour, why we did not proceed; and the whole company being re-animated with new courage by his noisy exhortations, advanced towards the great staircase.

"But now a new difficulty arose; none of us being willing or able to ascend the steps first. The Marquis was retained by his lady, and the rest were stopt by his example. At length, she suffered him to proceed, after he had asked her angrily, whether she took him for a child; and Antonio, who was in the rear, had exclaimed, Why we did not go on? He now ascended the stairs; and myself, with a friend of mine, who had taken me by the arm, pushed through the rest, and following him closely, while the greater part of the company were loitering partly at the bottom, and partly in the middle, of the staircase, according to their respective share of courage. We did not mind their backwardness, and proceeded towards the haunted apartment with a great show of courage, but I dare say not without palpitating hearts.

"The servants, who carried the torches, being in the rear, I went back to provide myself with one. The whole troop, who followed us slowly, watching every step of ours, were put in motion by my hasty return; and some, who were already at the landing-place, put themselves in motion to turn back on the first signal. I could not help smiling at the fear of men who had fought like lions before Gibraltar, faced all the dangers and hardships of that fatal siege with coolness and bravery, and now were overcome so much by the prejudices of their religion and education, as to give way to a most extraordinary and childish fear. Instead of being infected by their example, I derived additional courage from their unmanly conduct, returned laughing to my friend, and opening the door for the Marquis, went before him with a torch.

"However, we started a few steps back, seized with terror, as soon as we had entered the apartment; and the rest of the company, who were awaiting the event, hurried instantly down stairs. Before two seconds were elapsed, we were forsaken by the whole train, except a servant of the Marquis, who was uncommonly attached to his master, and would not leave him in the danger which seemed to threaten us. The sight which we beheld was, indeed, terrible enough. An enormous figure, with large, fiery eyes, advanced towards us; and I do not know whether an antecedent transitory fright does not sharpen the senses and the judgment; for I made, almost immediately, an observation which considerably diminished my fear.

"First of all, the figure was too grotesque. What a moderate deception would have effected, is generally frustrated by an extravagant one. I could not help remarking that the figure resembled the giant who challenged Don Quixote, that celebrated knight of the woeful countenance. This laughable idea, which forced itself upon my mind, made me suspect the whole; for as soon as I advanced further with my torch, I perceived a second figure, sneaking into an adjoining apartment, which communicated with those of the Marchioness that bordered on the garden. The room in which we were was a state-chamber of the Marquis. This train of ideas came almost in a moment in my mind; and looking around, I missed a silver clock which used to stand on a table. Having seen it in its place before we went to supper, I could easily account for the apparition.

"I took, therefore, our dubious host by the arm, exclaiming, "They are thieves, as true as I am alive! Don't you see that your clock is gone?" He was struck by that remark, and we instantly attacked the phantom with drawn swords. However, the human spectre had a long staff in its hand, with which it parried our thrusts excellently. The servant entering with a candle, along with my friend, I observed that the torch which I still held in my left hand was in my way, and threw it into my antagonist's face. His head-dress caught fire; and I threw my sword down, taking hold of his stick. The Marquis did the same: we began to embrace him in a most violent manner, and before half a minute was elapsed, came with him down upon the floor. The fellow being seized with despair, displayed a more than human strength, and could have killed every one of us if he had been armed. Being, however, engaged by four men at once, he was soon exhausted; and begged us, in a hollow accent, to spare him. The Marquis promised to pardon him; and he confessed that he belonged to a band of five robbers, who had intended to avail themselves of the bustle our festival produced in the castle, to plunder it: in short, he confirmed my suspicion.

"His hands were tied, and he was committed to the guard of the servants. The Marquis and my friend examined every apartment, in order to apprehend the rest of the gang; and I went down stairs to send some servants to their assistance. A death-like silence reigned every where, and not one human being was to be seen. They even had left some candles upon the stairs, to effect their escape with more ease. At the bottom of the staircase I found a lady who had been left there in a swoon; and a little farther I discovered Don Antonio in a condition that was not much better. As soon as he heard a noise on the stairs, he covered his face with his handkerchief, and expected a happy deliverance, seized with a most painful agony."

"Prepare thyself for eternity, Don Antonio!" I exclaimed, on coming nearer; "for thou must die!"

"Spare me, O! spare me only this time!" he stammered in a hollow and broken accent, which scarcely was intelligible.

"No mercy this time!" I replied laughing, in my natural accent. He knew me instantly, took the handkerchief from his face, and gazing at me with astonishment, said, highly rejoiced, "Dear Count, is it you? are you still alive? You have played me a fine trick."

"I now gave him a brief account of the whole affair, and recommended the fainting lady to his care. This animated him at once with new life, and he hastened to her with the alacrity of a buck to lend his assistance.

"I found the servants dispersed in different parts of the garden, and called to them to assist their master. The rest of the company were returned to the garden-house, and there awaited the event in great anxiety. When I entered the door, the ladies sat up a loud scream, because they did not at first know me, and mistook me for the ghost. I never beheld a more singular scene than that. Every distinction of rank and sex was suspended for a while. The general panic having driven the whole company into a corner of the saloon, the coyest ladies sat upon the lap of their lovers; the most obstinate shrew clung round the neck of her patient husband, and the bitterest enemies and rivals held one another enfolded in their arms in the most amicable manner.

"At length, they perceived their mistake, joyfully exclaiming, with one voice, "It is the Count! it is the Count!"

"It is impossible to describe the astonishment and the rapture with which I was received; not so much on my account, than because they saw themselves relieved from their apprehensions. I gave them a brief account of the affair; and when I had finished my report, the Chevalier joined us with the lady whom I had recommended to his care.

"Was the Chevalier also present?" one of the company exclaimed.

"Most certainly; he acted a principal part," I replied.

"This made Don Antonio suppose that I had not yet related the incident; he therefore took my assertion for a compliment paid to his courage, bowed, and began, with the greatest impudence, to relate the affair, with some additions and embellishments of his own invention. We listened patiently to his tale: however, the Marquis had mean time entered the saloon, and hearing his rodomontades, was struck with his barefaced impudence. He took his resolution on the spot, and winking me to follow him into the garden, communicated a plan to me, which was to make Don Antonio spend the night in a different manner than he seemed to expect.

"Our measures were soon taken; and we had only to give a hint to the Marchioness, in which I fortunately succeeded on my return into the saloon. She comprehended me so quickly, and so completely, that I concluded we only anticipated her design; thus much had Antonio exasperated the company by his barefaced fictions.

"Our return restored cheerfulness and merriment to our sociable circle. We sat gaily down to the desert, ridiculing one another for our fear, and the heroes of the drama earned the deserved applause. Nothing makes people more daring than a danger which has been happily overcome. There was not one amongst us who could not have defied all the infernal spirits; and but very few who did not loudly declaim against the existence of apparitions, as we had been fortunate enough to have discovered the human nature of one. It may easily be conceived who was the most clamorous amongst us. Don Antonio swore that he had laughed immoderately at our childish fear, that he had wanted to make game at me when I came down, and had been alarmed by nothing in the world than the situation of the lady.

"Our hostess now interrupted him, declaring, that her education, as well as a certain circumstance, did not allow her to coincide with the opinion most of the company seemed to have adopted. Every one being curious to know that circumstance, she was pressed to relate it; upon which she protested that it was no secret, that, every night, at twelve o'clock, such a terrible noise was heard in the chapel of the castle, that one expected it would be turned upside down. The Marquis raised a loud laugh, in which he was joined by the whole company, but particularly by Don Antonio, who, probably recollecting that midnight was already past, proposed to the company to go with him into the chapel. However, the Marchioness dissembled to pay no attention to what he said, and feigned to be offended by the ridicule which her information had been received with; declaring, that she would lay any wager, that none of the gentlemen who were pleased to laugh at her, would fetch a fan she had left in her pew in the afternoon.

"A general silence of some seconds was the consequence of this declaration. The Marquis, at length, thought proper to interrupt it, declaring, that he would cheerfully accept the wager, and that he was firmly persuaded any one of the gentlemen present would render her that service instantly with the greatest pleasure. We all confirmed his declaration, and begged the Marchioness to choose her hero. She now surveyed the whole circle, and Don Antonio always turned pale when she seemed to be going to fix upon him. Her looks were, to his greatest joy, several times fixed upon me; yet poor Antonio had, at length, the misfortune to be singled out by her. The Chevalier being bound by his word of honour, could not but accept the charge, and thank her for her good opinion of him. Having once more stolen a clandestine look at his watch, and convinced himself that it was near two o'clock, he took his sword, and left us with a very martial air. Yet his courage failed him already

at the door. Having inadvertently unfastened the red cockade of
his hat, it fell into his face. He was violently frightened; but when
we began to laugh, and declared that it was a bad omen, he collected himself again, and looking at us with an indescribable contempt, on account of our supposed timidity, flung the cockade into
a corner. We took it up, resolving to make a good use of it. He had
no sooner quitted the saloon, than the Marquis communicated his
plan and measures to the company, asking the gentlemen which
of them would act a part in the farce he was going to play? Don
Joachim F******, a man like a giant, and Don Romero L******, who
was rather of a dwarfish stature, offered instantly to act the principal parts. Our plan now was briefly concerted, and the company
rose to follow the Chevalier at a distance, and, if possible, to get the
start of him.

"Never has a plan better succeeded. The sky was indeed over-
clouded; however, it was not so dark that we could not have discerned the objects at some distance; and we could clearly perceive
that Don Antonio anxiously listened at every bush before he
approached it, and that his steps grew slower, the nearer he came
to the wall of the church-yard. He brandished his sword to frighten
away the spirits, and at length arrived at the gate of the church-
yard. He opened it with a great noise, and shut it again in the same
violent manner. He, at the same time, began to sing and to whistle
with all his might, struck against all the crosses that came in his way;
but soon lost his way, and stumbled over one tomb-stone after the
other, which enabled us to steal into the chapel from the opposite
side about ten minutes before his arrival. Having missed the large
gate, it was almost impossible for him to come to the pew of the
Marchioness, because he would have been obliged to climb over all
the other seats.

"There was only one lady in our company, who, however, had
almost spoiled the whole sport. For when she saw the poor Chevalier climbing over the pews, and heard him groan in a most rueful
accent, she broke out into an immoderate laughter, and endeavouring to stifle it, rendered it only more hideous. I had placed myself
near the organ; and being at a loss how to remedy the fault she had
committed, accompanied her with a still more disharmonious passage on the instrument. This produced an effect which surpassed

my most sanguine expectation, as but little wind was in the bellows, and I never was an adept in music.

"The poor Chevalier was almost petrified. He sat down in a pew, and awaited, in a kind of stupefaction, the things that were to come. I am sure he would have cared neither for the fan nor for his reputation, if he had had the least hope of getting safe out of the chapel. In this distress he looked anxiously about for an asylum, and seeing something of a white colour, which were the pillars of the pulpit, shine through the dusk, that prevailed around him, he climbed over the remaining pews to get at that supposed place of safety.

"We thought it our duty to light him on that expedition. A great electric machine, which the Marquis had ordered to be placed near the pulpit, served our purpose excellently, emitting from the conductor, at first, large sparks, and then a whole electric stream. We also lighted some candles of the large chandelier, which was suspended in the centre of the chapel, by means of a quantity of hemp, which was overspread with sulphur and pitch. However, we soon extinguished the candles again. Two servants, who were stationed at the church-yard, broke some panes of glass, which came with a great noise into the chapel: the doors were opened and shut again; the howling of cats was imitated; some of the company blew a strong current of air into his face by means of large bellows; the shrill sound of whistles re-echoed from every corner; and as the effect of the electrical machine grew stronger, whole streams of fire illuminated the chapel at intervals. We also had contrived to tie cords round his arms and legs, which made the poor fellow believe that he was spell-bound. In short, the effect of our contrivance was so great, that the actors themselves could not help shuddering now and then.

"Mean time, a thick smoke arose near the altar, and Don Joachim F****** and Don Romero L****** stopped forth from its grisly womb, dressed like devils. The latter being of a very diminutive size, made the former appear a great deal more gigantic than he really was. The garments of either were streaked with phosphorus; and Don Joachim F****** carried a large lanthorn on his head, on which was written, *"Sinner, prepare thyself, for thou must die!"* Don Romero had the cockade which Don Antonio had flung on the ground, and now was stained with phosphorus, fixed to his head. Both of them extended two long fiery arms, the extremities of which were armed with claws, and howled some hollow accents. Antonio shut his eyes when he saw these two frightful figures, and did not open them for some minutes.

"However, the scene was soon changed to our mutual terror. The pulpit-door opened; a man, clad in a white robe, armed with a large cross, and carrying a lanthorn, stept forth. He was soon followed by one more, clad in black.

"It was the pastor of the place, and the sexton, who had heard the uproar in the chapel. The Marquis having neglected to inform them of our nocturnal undertaking, they were come to see what was the matter. We soon knew them; however, the two disguised devils, who never had seen them before, imagined that they were apparitions from another world, their late fear seized them again, and they ran with all possible speed towards the door. They had, however, the misfortune to lose their way between the pews; Don Joachim's lanthorn dropt from his head, and fell in Don Romero's face; the one was frightened at the other; yet the latter had the presence of mind to take it up, to fasten it to one of his long artificial arms, which he took upon his shoulder, and thus happily gained the door. His giant-like assistant was close at his heels.

"But now a new misfortune happened; for when the priest began his exorcisms, both of them were tempted to look once more back; the little one, who led the way, turning suddenly round, knocked the lanthorn so violently into the face of his tall companion, that the latter, imagining to have received a blow from a spirit, dropped half dead upon the ground. Don Romero was terribly frightened at that incident, but retained sufficient recollection to disencumber himself of every thing that could retard him on his flight, and to leap with the greatest agility over the graves. Yet the terror which pervaded his agitated mind did not leave him sufficient power to proceed far, and he seated himself, at length, half fainting, upon a tombstone, patiently awaiting the event.

"The Marquis now resolved to put an end to the whole scene; and making a signal to the servants, the machinery was concealed as well as possible; every one of the actors stole silently out of the chapel, and the whole company met at the great gate. The first thing we did was to restore Don Joachim to the use of his senses;

Don Romero soon joined us; and having lighted our torches, we repaired again to the chapel.

"The priest was still preaching. He had taken the candle out of the lanthorn, and fixed it upon the pulpit, devoutly reading the exorcisms from his book. The Marquis now stepped before the pulpit, asking the priest what his strange behaviour meant, if he was in his senses, or had lost his understanding? Yet he remained some time longer in his error; and recollecting, at length, the voice of his master, was seized with amazement, and gave us a brief account of his transactions. The Marquis then begged him to go home, and we hastened to assist the poor Chevalier.

"We were struck with terror on perceiving not the least sign of life in him. His pulse ceased to beat, and the Marquis repented already the whole affair, thinking to have carried the jest rather too far, when the poor fellow, at once, opened his eyes to our greatest joy. Yet he still fancied to be in the power of spirits, and cried aloud for assistance. We scarcely could convince him that we were human beings, and come in quest of him. He now was carried to the castle, and put to bed; having entirely lost the use of his speech. When we visited him the next morning, we found him quite restored, and he informed us that he had fallen asleep at the chapel, and had a terrible dream."

Here the Count concluded his tale, which we had listened to with the greatest pleasure, though most of us had heard it already, and knew very well who the person was whom he had introduced under the name of Antonio. The Baron was covered with shame, and had lost the power of utterance, yet was prudent enough to suppress his wrath.

What rendered the whole tale most entertaining, was the presence of Don Romero L******, a man of known courage, honesty, and of an excellent temper, who made no secret of his defects; and, at the close of the history, exclaimed, "By holy Peter! I was terribly frightened."

"Then you also was present on that occasion?" one of the company asked, laughing.

"Yes, yes!" he resumed; "and the Baron yonder, too, was not far off."

The laughter encreased. However, the Baron thought it proper to bridle his passions, and not to reply a syllable, but to wait for a more favourable opportunity to revenge himself upon the Count, which he very nearly had found that very night.

We now conversed a little longer on different subjects, and then parted, as it seemed, entirely reconciled to one another. The Count saw Caroline to her carriage, and soon after went home with me, to all appearance completely happy.

He was used to sit every night half an hour with me on my sofa, and to converse on the occurrences of the day; but that time his mind was so much occupied with the past events, that he forgot it, and went directly to his apartment, which occasioned one of the drollest scenes of my life.

To make myself perfectly understood, I must premise a brief description of the arrangement of our house. The ground floor was occupied by our landlady, a mantua-maker; the first floor was inhabited by the Count and myself; and my servants lodged in the second floor. Our landlady was a young, gay woman, who understood her profession excellently, and made the utmost of every little advantage. She not only let the remaining apartments of the ground floor to compassionate ladies, but her charitable disposition was so great, that she also admitted some young gentlemen by day and night to her own room. The Count and myself being very much displeased with her conduct, we had taken a resolution to quit her house the subsequent week.

The Baron had visited us sometimes, and taken a liking to our little gay landlady. He was not used to slip an opportunity of ingratiating himself with the ladies; yet our hostess did not think proper to be kind to the Baron; and some weeks elapsed before he could make any considerable advances in her favour, notwithstanding the great pains he took to make her favourably disposed to him. But learning, at length, that two floors in her house soon would be evacuated, he paid for that which the Count inhabited beforehand, and, in return, put himself in possession of the happiness he had been hunting after for some time. He paid, that very night, a visit to his future landlady; and was safely housed in her bed when the adventure occurred which I now am going to relate.

CHAPTER IV.

The reader will recollect that the Count, on our return from the card-party, went immediately into his own apartment, instead of sitting half an hour with me as he was used to do. Having undressed himself, he observed that it was too early to go to bed: he, therefore, flung himself upon his sofa, to reflect on the occurrences of the day, and his affair with the Baron. His blood being in a violent fermentation, he tormented himself for some time with ruminating on the bad consequences the latter might produce. Yet the association of ideas at length brought him back again to Caroline; he wandered from one smiling reverie to the other, and at last fell asleep.

His situation being, however, not very easy, he awoke after he had slept about half an hour. In his drowsiness he imagined to have rested on my sofa as usual, took up his candle, and wished me a good night, supporting that I was gone to bed. He went softly down stairs, and thus came to the apartment where the mantua-maker was fallen fast asleep in the arms of her new paramour, and, notwithstanding his perceiving some change in the furniture, yet he still imagined to be in his own apartment, and was astonished at his heavy drowsiness, which, as he thought, represented every object in a different manner to his eyes. He now began to undress himself, opened the curtains, and placed the table with the candle near the bed, to extinguish it when he should have gone to bed. But unfortunately one of the Baron's boots laying on the floor, he put one foot of the table upon it, the candle dropped down, and fell burning into the face of the former. The Baron awoke with a terrible scream; and it may easily be conceived how much the Count was astonished to see his bed occupied by his mortal enemy. Being of a very irascible temper, his astonishment was turned into the most violent rage at that supposed impertinence. He uttered a dreadful oath, and ran to the corner in which he had placed his sword; but being not able to find it, he rung with such a vehemence for his servants, that the string of the bell broke; for being at a loss to account for that incident, he was determined to chastise the Baron in an exemplary manner.

The latter had, mean time, hastened out of the bed, and found his sword. Thinking that the Count was his rival, he congratulated himself upon the favourable opportunity, he imagined to have, to get rid of him at once; and while his fair companion screamed with all her might, went in his shirt to attack the poor Count, who held his breeches in one hand, and with the other, which was armed with the Baron's cane, parried his antagonist's thrusts with the greatest difficulty. Yet being an excellent fencer, he soon attacked his adversary in an offensive manner, without recollecting that his weapon was only a wooden one, beat the Baron's sword out of his hand, and gave him such a violent blow on his stomach, that he began to roar in a most rueful accent.

The lady, who had not ceased screaming all the time the combat lasted, imagined that her Adonis could not but have received some material hurt by the Count's furious blows, accompanied the vociferation of her charmer with additional force, which roused every inhabitant of the house that had not been awakened by the Count's violent ringing of the bell. A number of people appeared, by degrees, in the apartment, in their shirts, and seemed to be very much inclined to assist the landlady. Some spits and pokers began already to approach the Count, when my coachman entered the room with his horse-whip. Being of a giant-like stature, which was not inferior to his bodily strength, he could look over the heads of the rest, and soon perceived the Count's distressful situation. He, therefore, began to lay about him with his whip, and handled the naked figures so unmercifully, that the contest was terminated in a moment. The assailants dropt their arms, and saved themselves as well as they could.

The Count seeing himself delivered from his aggressors, began to reflect a little, and perceived that he was not in his own apartment. The screaming lady in the bed now attracted his attention, and he went to take her out. No sooner did he behold her face, and see who she was, than he guessed at the real state of the whole affair. Want of gallantry being not on the list of his defects, he thought it was his duty to excuse his fatal mistake, and to soothe the wrath of the offended fair one. He, therefore, told her a number of sweet

things, excusing himself as well as he could; and seeing many inviting charms, disencumbered of every envious covering, before him,
embraced her at last.

In that very moment I entered the apartment, armed with a
sword, carrying a candle, and accompanied by all the servants, who
were armed in the same manner, the Count's valet having waked
me as soon as he had missed his master. A more ridiculous scene
never has been witnessed. On stepping out of my apartment, I had
met some shopmen, who were half naked, and took to their heels
as soon as they saw me. When I came to the lady's apartment, I
saw the coachman standing on the threshold, gazing into the room,
and holding his sides with laughing. The Baron stood in the centre
of the apartment in the same posture, which, however, seemed to
be owing to a different cause; and the Count sat by the bed, caressing and, at last, tenderly embracing, a lady that was almost entirely
naked. The latter glowed with a high crimson hue, but the fire that
burned in her face was not the effect of anger. Her longing eyes
surveyed the beautiful form of the Count; she suffered his kisses,
and appeared to be displeased with nothing but the number of witnesses. Seeing me, at length, at the head of the servants, she ejaculated a loud scream, and disengaging herself from the Count's
embraces, hid herself in the bed.

The first thing I did, was to fly to the assistance of the poor
Baron. The Count, who laughed immoderately, assisted me faithfully; but our crest fallen hero was in such agonizing pains, that he
scarcely could speak. He complained of violent pains, and a great
quantity of congealed blood had gathered on the place where he
was wounded. I sent instantly for a surgeon, and assisted my friend
in putting on his cloaths. The lady in the bed declaring that it was
impossible he could remain in her apartment, we carried him into
a coach, and saw him to his lodgings, where we committed him to
the care of his servants.

We took the greatest pains to keep the whole transaction private; however, this was impossible; for it was circulated though
the whole town the next morning. We received every where con-
gratulations, and were obliged to relate all the particulars of that
strange incident. The Baron was no sooner able to go abroad, than
the Count received a challenge, in which the choice of arms was

entirely left to his option; and he was generous enough to fix upon pistols. Time and place were agreed upon. The Count seemed to presage a fatal catastrophe; having made his will, and committed it to my care, he bade a tender adieu to all his friends, under the pretext of a little journey. Caroline too was not forgotten. He imagined no one knew any thing of the real nature of his pretended journey; yet I could plainly perceive that his friends looked upon this journey as his last, at all events. Caroline almost fainted, on rising from the sofa, to offer him her beautiful hand for a farewell kiss. My rising jealousy perceived this plainly, and it did also not escape her that the Count observed it too with great emotion.

We left town early in the morning on horseback, and found the Baron and his second already on the appointed spot. Neither of the two antagonists being a great marksman, each of them had brought two braces of pistols with him, which were charged by the seconds, and then exchanged. The steps were measured, and they took their proper distance. Five shots were already fired without any effect. The Baron aimed so miserably, that he almost had wounded me, though I was more than six paces distant from the Count. I therefore called to him, when he was going to fire again, "not to tremble so much." He was, however, but too successful; for the Count dropt on the ground, exclaiming that he was wounded in the side. I hastened to assist him, and saw the blood gush violently from his wound. The Baron too offered to assist my friend; but the Count waved his hand, desiring him to flee as fast as possible. The Baron seemed really to be very much affected; and having embraced the Count and myself, mounted his horse, and rode away with his second. If the Count had been killed on the spot, I should probably have made a better use of the remaining brace of pistols than my friend. But seeing a chance of saving his life, I was too much occupied with a desire of giving him relief, as to entertain any idea of vengeance.

I flattered myself with the hope that the wound was not mortal, the ball not having penetrated deep enough as to injure his intestines materially. I only apprehended the violent effusion of blood might prove fatal to him. Having dressed his wound as well as possible with the assistance of my servant, we carried him to a neighbouring village. The surgeon was of my opinion, and the event confirmed my hope; for a few weeks confinement and rest cured him completely.

I could not prevent the duel, and the danger of the Count, from being known amongst our friends at Paris; and that incident gave us an opportunity of perceiving that we had a great many who really wished us well. All of them displayed the most anxious desire of seeing him, and of contributing something towards his recovery. The ladies, in particular, scarcely left our house; and when he began to mend perceptibly, we began again to recommence our jocund assemblies with our usual gaiety. Caroline also visited at our house under the protection of an old uncle, and seemed to be particularly rejoiced at the Count's amendment.

One evening we were sitting at table, partaking of a cheerful supper. The Count had declared that day that he intended to leave his apartment on the subsequent one, and we were talking of a little feast which was to be given on that occasion. No one was more happy at it than Caroline. She sat opposite to me, and I could plainly perceive the expressions of her secret joy on her glowing countenance. I was absorpt in the contemplation of her charms, and felt my heart beat in unison with hers. I was thrilled with a secret pleasure, which, however, was mixed with something very bitter. How nice is the perception of a lover's senses!

At once she grew pale; her large blue eyes, which were sparkling with rapture, gazed joyfully amazed at the door which was behind me; her fork dropt under the floor; she held her napkin before her face, and leaned a little back against the chair. I was just going to her assistance, when every face was turned towards the door. The chairs were suddenly overturned; every one left the table; a confused clamour filled the apartment; and turning my head, seized with astonishment, I beheld the Count enfolded in the arms of friendship.

What a feast for us to see him thus unexpectedly amongst us! We all received him as a lost and suddenly recovered treasure; the tenderest caresses were lavished upon him, but the most expressive endearments were only weak emblems of our ecstatic joy. He returned them faintly; but the languour which his words and motions expressed only served to animate them with additional ardor. We placed him in the middle; but no cushion was deemed soft enough, no chair commodious enough, to seat the dear, recovered fugitive upon. A general satisfaction prevailed in our joyous circle; he was the monarch to whom our hearts paid a willing, cheerful homage. Caroline seated herself, at length, with a charming simplicity, by his side, to nurse the dear idol of our hearts. He was deeply affected by her angelic goodness, but could not find words to express his feelings.

Wit and humour now returned to our circle in an overflowing measure, and with additional gaiety. The graces mingled with our society, and the god of cheerful hilarity presided at our table. Our conversation overflowed with witty sallies; a general desire of giving pleasure to our darling pervaded every bosom. The Count's cheerfulness was of a more gentle complexion; he smiled only when we laughed. Caroline animated him with half concealed and half visible caresses, and the warmth of friendship soon blazed perceptibly up in the flame of love. Every member of our happy society was charmed with the dear object of our love, and applauded his enchanting ideas; I alone sat mute, and, at the sight of his happiness, felt myself consumed by a secret fire, for which I neither could nor would account.

Here begins a period of my life, on which I cannot reflect without despising myself; in which I was misled by a glowing passion to forget every thing that was dear to me, and that I ever should have held sacred. And, gracious Heaven! what a passion? Not that of a first love, in which the heated blood urges us to sacrifice all prejudices, and every idea that opposes our desires; it was not that love which boldly breaks all the fetters of human nature, and even tears all other softer ties; no, it was a passion kindled by jealousy after the *first* bloom of life was past, and numberless painful experiences ought to have put me on my guard, after love even had lavished all her blessings on me; a hopeless, unhappy passion, inflamed by impossibility, and combating the most sacred duties. What a misfortune is it to *have been* for some time the favourite of fortune! Nothing had been able to resist me as yet, but here was the boundary of my power; and while I attempted to overleap it, I was in danger to lose a friend, a real treasure, in the pursuit of an imaginary one.

I was the only person in our cheerful circle that did not sincerely share the general flow of pleasure which pervaded the heart of every one present. The smile of cheerfulness sat on my lips, but baneful poison rankled in my heart. My eyes, which scarcely were able to retain the tear of painful disappointment, were over-clouded with a mist. Every innocent glance of Caroline's looks, meeting those of the enraptured Count, stung me to the heart; every tender gesture of hers threatened to choke me. I laughed immoderately, to conceal the real cause of the big tears that started from my heavy eyes, and to disguise the visible agitation of my bosom.

Yet my strange alteration did not escape the Count's keen sightedness. He now took a too small share in the general flow of pleasure as not to be a good observer, and repeatedly extended his hand to me over the table to reconcile me to him. I accepted, but could not have squeezed it for the world. My cheerfulness was so unnatural, so extravagant, that I am astonished it did not strike the whole company.

"Dear Marquis," said he, as soon as we were left to ourselves, "dear Marquis, what ails you?"

I had squeezed myself into a corner of the sofa, absorpt in a profound reverie, averting my weeping eyes from the Count, and turning them towards the window, through which the pale light of the moon trembled. A melancholy train of gloomy scenes of former times, as it were, passed visibly the review before my overclouded eyes, and I compared the overflowing measure of my sufferings with the scanty portion of my joys. Only the present moment sways in our mind in such a disposition, and reflects its hue on sufferings and pleasures past, on our wishes and fears, on our hopes and expectations. Feathers sink to the bottom when the torrent is too violent, and rocks are unrooted. In that moment the whole course of my life appeared to me to have been destitute of every joy, and futurity stared me grisly in the face. Without being rightly conscious of the original source of that agonizing state of mind, every expectation was thereby infected, and every cheering hope destroyed at once. No situation of mind is so dreadful as the moment in which a violent, hopeless passion, which we have struggled with in vain, convulses every faculty of the soul in its first inconscious rise. I scarcely heard the Count's question, yet the dubious shake of his head did not escape my notice.

"You don't hear me, dear Carlos!" he resumed. "I fear you are not well?"

"Indeed, I believe you are right," I replied mechanically; "for I feel something here," pointing to the left side.

The Count laughed at the gesture, assumed a cheerful air, and said, "So much the worse, Carlos; for hurts on that side are generally incurable." He expected I should fall in with his merry humour; yet I was entirely mute, and he resumed again:

"Tell me, for Heaven's sake, Marquis, what is the matter with you. You are entirely changed; or do you think that I have not seen the tears which you attempted to disguise by laughing, nor that I have perceived that you did not squeeze my hand when I offered it to you so cordially?"

"Don't speak of it, dearest Count. I am, indeed, not well."

"Indeed not? And that malady attacks you in the very moment in which I feel myself well again the first time?"

"Dearest, best Count; for God's sake, don't be bitter. I cannot, I cannot bear it to day."

"Bitter!" he exclaimed, with a mien which was ten times more so. "It is, indeed, the first time to day that any person taxes me with it. I was not bitter while I was unfortunate; it must therefore originate in my happiness. But," added he, in a soothing accent, "do you really think that I am such a bad and inattentive observer, that I should not have seen at whom your tenderest and most burning looks were directed?"

"Pray, tell me, at whom were they directed?"

"The former at my fair neighbour, and the latter at myself. The tears, that started from your eyes, could not extinguish their jealous fire."

"Jealous, did you say? By heaven I do not comprehend you."

"Alas! how much is my Carlos altered! Can that be *my* Carlos, whom I doat upon, who was the tender partner of my joys and sorrows, my guardian genius, the sharer of all my secrets and my inmost thoughts, whom I looked upon as my better half? I scarcely can persuade myself that he is the same person. By his kind assistance I have recovered from a dangerous illness, and he does not rejoice at his own work."

"Lewis, your reproaches are unjust. By the eternal God! I never have loved you with a greater ardour than in that fatal moment. But you are not mistaken; I am ill, very ill. I scarcely know myself again."

Here a torrent of tears relieved me at once. My pulse began to beat with uncommon violence, my whole frame was convulsed; a feverish tremor shook all my limbs. I never have experienced similar symptoms. All the agonizing feelings of my straitened heart convulsively communicated themselves, as it were, to every part of my agitated frame. The Count was almost petrified at the sight of these emotions, which thrilled me by fits, and which I struggled in vain to overcome. I wanted to speak; however, my teeth chattered so violently, that I could utter none but inarticulate accents. I wanted to shake hands with him, but trembled so excessively, that I missed his. I wanted to recline my head against his bosom, and relapsed half-fainting upon the sofa.

"What a mysterious incident!" he exclaimed ever and anon. "I cannot persuade myself that you are really ill: or shall I send for a physician?"

I begged him, in the greatest agony, for a little water and wine; my mouth being so much parched that I scarcely could open my lips. He gave it me, and I felt myself refreshed. He now seated himself upon the sofa, to wipe the cold sweat from my face with his handkerchief, entreating me, again and again, to compose myself. "All will be well," he added. "You know how little I value my life, if I can be useful to you: should I, therefore, not willingly share my happiness with my dear Carlos?"

"Dearest Lewis!" I groaned, "rather a thousand reproaches, than that heavenly goodness. Alas! I do not deserve it." So saying, I struggled to disengage myself in a fit of wild despair from his embraces; however, he would not let me go.

"If *you* don't deserve that love, that tender kindness; who else can merit it?"

"Tell me, O! tell me, my injured friend, do you really not hate a rival?"

"A rival! Is this the fatal secret? Yes, Carlos, I confess Caroline could make me happy, and obliterate the recollection of what I have suffered. My passion began as early as yours. It sways in my breast equally powerful as in your poor heart. We have the same right;

but I must tell you, that I believe my hopes are better founded than yours." I shuddered violently. "However," he continued with a deep groan, "you have nothing to fear; I cease, from this moment, to be your rival. I rather will renounce happiness for ever, than purchase it at the expense of your tranquillity and peace of mind. Here is my hand; Caroline is yours. I renounce all my claims to her heart, and leave you at full liberty to gain it for yourself." So saying, he squeezed my hand, and strained me tenderly to his bosom. How was it possible I could have expressed the grateful feelings of my heart? However, he was satisfied with himself and with my tears. Every noble, generous deed produces its own reward. Broken accents speak stronger, and with greater energy, than words; and amongst all languages that of gratitude is the most monosyllabled.

He now left me to myself with his usual gentleness. His eyes were, indeed, rather overcast with a melancholy gloom, and his brow was not cloudless; yet he restrained his grief at the sacrifice he had made, and spared my feelings. But, alas! what a dreadful night succeeded that fatal evening! my fever encreased after the Count's noble declaration, and the dawn of morning found me absorpt in gloomy reveries.

"This is then the fruit of thy sufferings, thy travels, observations, and resolution?" I said to myself: "thy most solemn vows, and thy vaunted friendship are wrecked upon a miserable passion? How deeply must he despise me! And has he not the greatest reason for it? Is he not greater than I? Did he not tell me that Caroline would render him happy for life, and restore his long lost hilarity to him? He never has enjoyed the bliss of life in its fullest extent, and I deprived him of it at his commencement of a new life: I, who am a voluptuary, a spoiled fondling of love, and have but lately wept at the early tomb of an adored wife! Carlos, thou art the meanest wretch, and not deserving of thy existence, if thou canst hesitate to return that sacrifice."

It is incredible how much pain it cost me to come to that resolution; a resolution that was too natural and just than that it ought to have appeared to me a sacrifice. I began to meditate more seriously upon it, and was astonished at the unnatural state of my mind. The first love heats a blood that rolls through a youthful, healthy frame; and the kindling fire of sensations that have just unfolded them-

selves, urges us beyond the limits of humanity; and yet my senses
never have been in such a tumultuous agitation; even not when I first
met Elmira, animated with a full sense of my pride, and conscious
of success; nor when she dropt into my trembling arms, encircling
my neck as my happy and blessing wife, and my senses were, for
the first time, inebriated, on her bosom, with every rapture love is
capable to afford; nor was my blood heated to a similar degree in
Rosalia's arms, who had taught me to empty the cup of intoxicating
sensuality to the last drop. Maturer age also had contributed to cool
the heat of passions; and Elmira's modest meekness, the dear cares
of a tranquil domesticated life, unruffled by sorrow, and flowing in
a soft and gentle stream, had blunted the edge of my desires. What
could, therefore, have deprived me of my senses in that moment;
what could have rendered me so callous against the admonitions
of a just and friendly heart; what could have been the reason of the
vehement tempest that agitated my whole nature?

While I was occupied with these and similar reflections, which
succeeded each other with an incomprehensible impetuosity, the
idea of my singular fatalities in Spain forced itself upon my soul.
Don Bernhard, who constantly frequented our house, though his
character did not suffer him to assist in all our banquets, happened
that night to be of our party. Count S******i also was present; and
both being in an uncommonly merry humour, they entertained the
company with a relation of our little Bacchanals at Toledo. The recollection of those merry scenes reminded me, by a natural association of ideas, of the separation of our society, and of the fate of its
individual members. I recollected that one was seduced by an Italian
singer to abandon our cheerful circle; that a second was called away
by family affairs; that a third was intoxicated by something mixed
with his wine. The latter idea made me start up with a loud scream.
"Heavenly powers!" thought I, "should, perhaps, the unnatural
state of my mind and body be the effect of a similar cause?" I hurried out of my bed. The dining room was separated from my bed-
chamber only by two apartments. I put a night-gown on, and went
with the greatest precaution thither, to ascertain my supposition,
if possible. The glasses were still upon the table; the servants being
used to remove every thing in the morning when the company
stayed too long. The dawn of morning peeped already through the

windows, and enabled me to discern every object without difficulty. I began to examine the glasses, but with very little hope of success, as it also was possible that something might have been mixed in my plate; nay, it even appeared to me to have been too hazardous to attempt mixing an inebriating drug with my wine or water; though I was so much absorpt in thought, that I perhaps should not have taken the least notice of whole clouds of impurity in my glass. My apprehension soon was confirmed beyond contradiction; for I discovered in one of the glasses, standing near the place where I had sat, a whitish matter on the bottom, which undoubtedly was the remainder of what I inadvertently had swallowed.

The conclusions I deduced from that discovery were of a most alarming nature. It was evident that the agent of the authors of that atrocious deed must be one of our servants, and at the same time have few accomplices, or none at all. My servants had, however, been employed very little at table; those of the Count having waited upon us from the moment he had joined our company. I had, besides, suspected two of his people for some time; for these fellows were of such an enormous and unnatural stupidity, that I could not conceive how the Count could keep them in his service. Being, however, unwilling to throw an odium upon an innocent person, I resolved to conceal that incident and my suppositions from my friend, and only to watch them with the greatest vigilance. My blood being still in a violent fermentation, I mixed some lemon juice with wine and water, which refreshed me more than I had expected. I could, indeed, not sleep; but found myself a great deal better on the subsequent morning.

CHAPTER V.

The Count, who came very early to see how I did, found me pale and languid. I entreated him to forget the whole scene of last night, because I had made the observation that I really was very ill. He sent immediately for a physician, who shook his head, declaring my illness to be a fever of a most dangerous nature, and found it necessary to bleed me. Yet I rose at ten o'clock, in health and pretty good spirits, feeling no other inconvenience than an ebullition in the blood, and an unspeakable languour. I was several times strongly tempted, in the course of the day, to inform the Count of my suspicions with regard to the affair of last night and had the best opportunity of doing it at table, where I examined the wine, and every dish, with an unusual care, which occasioned him to ask me whether I was afraid to be poisoned by him? Yet that very question sealed my lips. His extraordinary agitation, and the struggle with his heart, which was not yet entirely decided, imparted to every thing he said a certain bitterness which he could not conceal, notwithstanding his endeavours to appear open and kind to me. Thus frail is the human heart. I saw, with secret sorrow, the distress which the sacrifice he had made me inflicted upon his agonized mind. I might have soothed his agony, if I had explained to him that my singular behavior on the preceding night had been owing rather to a disordered body than to a weakness of heart; however, his silent reserve, and my being doubtful how he would receive it, prevented me from coming to an explanation.

The only thing I did was to make observations on myself; and the deeper I penetrated into the secrets of my feelings, the more coldness to Caroline did I discover in my heart. I was highly rejoiced at it, and yet apprehended that it was impossible I loved her nevertheless. I heated myself more violently in attempting to grow cooler, and secretly asked myself, "Is it *possible* you could love Caroline? It scarcely can be; and yet I apprehend it really is so. She has, indeed, not gentleness and judgment enough, and also appears to have too much self will, as to be capable to sacrifice much for her lover; however, she has a certain spirit of conversation which charms me, and a natural insinuation that flatters self-love, and must render its object happy. But is all this worth sacrificing a tried friend, whose peace of mind appears to depend on her love? No, Carlos! be ashamed, and conquer a fatal passion, that owes its existence merely to an unnatural state of thy body, lest thou becomest the sport of others that have kindled it in thy heart, and strive to gain the applause of thy own understanding, of the Count, thy friends." This soliloquy terminated in a solemn resolution to shun Caroline as much as decency would permit, and I was determined to carry it that very day into execution. We were invited to an assembly, where we were sure to meet Caroline; my indisposition affording me a natural pretext for staying at home, I resolved not to go. Not knowing how to amuse myself all the evening, I went to my closet, and searched for some books. I carried at least half a dozen to my sofa, without being able to determine which I would read. I also had got some music for my flute, and put a chair to the Piano forte. At length, I put a nightgown on, and stretched myself upon the sofa, reading aloud, to silence the voice of my heart. Thus I was in an excellent way of spending the evening in private, and to divert my mind, when suddenly a carriage stopped at our house. I was violently frightened. "Good God!" said I to myself, "I hope I shall not be disturbed by visitors!" shut my eyes, and pretended to be fast asleep.

Not two minutes were elapsed, when my closet-door was opening, and a person entered. He approached the sofa softly, while I consulted with myself whether I should not open my eyes a little to see who was so kind to disturb my sweet repose? It was the Count, and in full dress. "My God! in full dress?" I exclaimed, starting suddenly up, and surveying him with gazing looks.

"You play fine tricks, Marquis," he said coolly. "I really thought you was fast asleep, and you start up at once as if you were going to fly in my face!" So saying, he put his sword on, which he carried in his hand, went to the looking glass, and examined his head-dress.

Seeing that I still continued to look at him without making the least attempt to stir, he put his hat on, turned round, and crossing his arms negligently, said, "But tell me, Marquis, what means that comedy you are acting there in your great night-cap?"

"A comedy!" I replied, with looks of astonishment.

"I think you have had sufficient time to take your nap; though you have dined to-day with an extraordinary appetite."

"You are mistaken, Count," I began peevishly: "I have had no appetite at all."

I would have given any thing if I could have provoked him to enter into a contest with me on that point; for I was determined to prove clearly that I never had dined with less appetite. He went, however, to the window, without returning a word, began to hum an air, looking into the street, and dissembled to be occupied with some ridiculous object. At length he resumed, still looking out of the window, "How long will you let your carriage wait at the door?"

"My carriage at the door! I don't comprehend you. Have *you* ordered it?"

"Yes, I have; and it is your state-carriage. Have you entirely forgot, that I am the king of the feast which we are to have, and that the Minister of H****** and the ****sh Ambassador will be of the party?"

"Pray tell me, dear Count," I replied, "whether I am dreaming? for I assure you, I know not a syllable of it." (I really had almost entirely forgot it.)

"Have I ever seen the like?" he replied, turning round. "All the world has been solemnly invited last night. I come to fetch you, and you are not dressed. These are fine doings, indeed! I am sure the card-tables will be occupied before you are ready, and you may easily conclude that I shall play to-night?"

All my fine plans vanished in that moment: I saw nothing but the gay company, dancing, playing and laughing.

"Well, then, I must make haste to dress," I replied mechanically, taking my cap off, and ringing for my valet. He came, and used such expedition, that I was in my carriage a quarter of an hour after.

We came, indeed, too late; all the card-tables were already occupied; and Caroline having despaired to see the Count that night, had left the company to pay several visits before supper. The Count was determined to play, and succeeded at length to collect a party. Being not disposed to play at cards, I stole upon a balcony, which looked into a large yard covered with lofty trees, where I abandoned myself to pleasing reveries. The delusive dusk, the humming in the air, and the ominous rustling of the cooling breezes betwixt the trembling leaves, created sweet sensations in my mind; and my imagination was agreeably occupied with forming pleasing fancies, when the door behind me was opened at once. On turning round I beheld Caroline, who, mean time, was returned, and had left the apartment for reasons similar to mine. She seemed not to have observed me at first, being rather startled when she saw me. Yet she soon collected herself, saluting me with her usual good nature and simplicity, and inquiring how I did. I began to tremble, and replied with visible confusion, and in broken accents.

She began to laugh, resuming gaily, "I really think you have been sleeping, Marquis, for your phrases are uncommonly odd." I confessed that I had been dreaming, at least, and being asked of whom, I replied, "of you, charming Caroline."

Thus I opened a conversation on the very subject I had so firmly determined to avoid. She declined every thing I said with the gayest humour, which imperceptibly led me to add a great deal more of the same nature. In short, our conversation grew very warm. She was violently agitated, notwithstanding her cheerful humour; and at length began repeatedly to speak of the Count, pitying him with a most charming kindness for his paleness and melancholy, and even asked me whether his heart was not the prey of some silent grief? She could have chosen neither a subject nor words that could have made my blood ferment with greater violence.

When the air grew more chilling, she told me she would go and fetch her shawl, and soon join me again. I offered to do it for her; however, she insisted upon going herself. I counted every minute, but she did not return. Having waited in vain above a quarter of an hour, I returned to the company. She sat by the Count, looking in his cards, or rather contemplating his beautiful countenance, which exhibited striking marks of melancholy, and received additional charms by the languid paleness his illness had left upon it. He never had appeared handsomer to me than that night. The speaking language of his mien was indeed now and then interrupted by an indescribable perplexity; however, the goodness of his heart continued to prevail in every feature of his benevolent countenance. His dark eyes, flashing with a faint fire, spoke powerfully to the heart; and the pale enamel of his lips resembled a rose that first begins to blush.

Caroline was entirely absorpt in the contemplation of his affecting features; her face was the mirror of his, and repeated every mien of her melancholy neighbour by its movements. As soon as the Count perceived me by his side, he endeavoured to involve me in a conversation with Caroline, who just was starting up, exclaiming, "Good Heaven! I have forgot the Marquis, who waits for me on the balcony!" She was rejoiced to see that I had joined the company, and drew her chair closer to the Count.

The latter began, from that moment, to be entirely absent, replying little, or nothing at all, to her observations and questions. This offended Caroline at last, and she rose suddenly from the card-table, declaring that play did make people unaccountably insupportable. She then wished the Count, laughing, a good night; repairing to the opposite side of the apartment, where a forte piano stood, and began to play.

Yet she could relish nothing. I followed her like her shade, taking up a violin to accompany her; selected some of her favourite airs; but every thing was intolerable to her. She grew, at length, uncommonly sad and gloomy, reclining herself against the back of her chair, fetched a deep sigh, and shut her eyes.

I did every thing in my power to amuse her; but nothing would do: she returned very short answers, and grew cooler every moment. She continued to keep up that humour till the gaming parties rose; and being placed, at supper, between the Count and myself, her cheerfulness soon returned with additional lustre.

This charming change seemed, however, not to have the least effect on the Count. He continued to be sad and gloomy, however attentive and obliging she was to him. She was indefatigable in her exertions to rouse him from his melancholy stupor, displaying her wit and good humour in the most advantageous light; but nothing would succeed. The company was enchanted with her lively sallies and acute remarks; the Count only was dejected and absorpt in gloomy reveries. He had formed his plan, and nothing could tempt him to give up his resolution. His pertinacity was so firm, that neither Heaven nor Hell would have been able to draw him only a hair's breadth from his course.

At length she grew tired of that frigidity, and addressed herself to me, to punish him for his sullen reserve, thinking, perhaps, that jealousy would effect what love was not equal to perform. But she was mistaken; for the Count grew more communicative, and I was as laconic as he had been. I was but too sensible of the real motive of the honour she did me; my pride did not suffer me to avail myself of her favourable disposition, and my cheerfulness was far from encreasing. Thus the evening, for the pleasures of which so many preparations had been made, was spent in a very irksome and tedious manner.

From that time I saw Caroline almost every day; it was at least not *my* fault if I did not. The Count's melancholy encreased every day more visibly; he frequently shut himself up in his closet, retired early from all companies, or stayed entirely at home. His friends ascribed that love of solitude to the effects of his illness; and I confirmed their supposition. Every spark of generosity seemed to be dead in my heart during that fatal period; I saw him struggle against his passion with an indifference that covers me with pungent shame whenever I think of it; he was a living picture of sorrow, and I had not even so much feeling left to comfort him. In short, I was so completely, so thoroughly altered, that it is impossible my friends should not have noticed it.

The female heart is never entirely void of vanity; and none that is not pre-occupied, will be able to resist a firm and indefatigable exertion to gain upon it. I now was frequently in private with Caroline, and none of my other rivals was very formidable. I really imagined to have made some impression upon her heart, and that she had completely forgot the obstinate Count. I enjoyed that little, dubious happiness with a rapturous pleasure, when an accident suddenly overturned the airy edifice of my vanity at once.

We met at the country seat of a friend to celebrate a rural feast. The fine season was already on the verge; autumn had, however, sufficient charms left to make us forget the amusements of the town for a short time. The vintage was getting in, and that is the time when merriment and pleasure display themselves in the most natural and charming manner.

The necessary preparations were made, at the country seat of my friend, solemnly to celebrate every day of that general rejoicing. The two most virtuous girls of the village were publicly presented in the church with a garland of white roses, and received a very liberal dowry. Their beauty was, indeed, not equal to their virtue; yet they received that reward with such a grace, and so much modest innocence, that every one was convinced, beyond contradiction, that they deserved having been selected from the rest of their sisters. This enchanting harmony between gracefulness and virtue is generally no where to be met with in that high degree as among the French peasantry.

No one could deny that all his softer feelings were completely gratified among that troop of amiable country girls who, during the short time of our stay with them, never lost sight of us. These remarks had a powerful influence on my subsequent resolutions.

All of us gentlemen were greater or lesser sinners, and it afforded us the highest pleasure to exchange the coquetry and art of our ladies with the sensible and open simplicity of those innocent children of nature. Joy and cheerful mirth animated, therefore, every one of us; and we found many little innocent means of gratifying our glowing humour, and the demands of a heated blood, without injuring the virtue of those innocent rustics. Dancing and songs, little feasts and processions, fire-works and comedies, followed each other in a pleasing succession, were always different in their nature, and, nevertheless, only parts of a well arranged whole.

Even the Count began to cheer up a little, yet without being able to take his usual share in these amusements. Caroline was still a little angry with him, or at least pretended to be so; and being used to have always a declared lover, gave me the preference. I was obliged to sit always by her side, to carry her gloves and her fan, and to follow her every where as her esquire. Even when somebody talked to me at a small distance from her, she inquired, with the greatest simplicity, "where may the Marquis be?" This induced me to flatter myself to be secretly beloved by her, though she never suffered me to speak of my passion. She neither acted the prude, nor was reserved, but behaved like an offended wife that is going to lose her husband, and importuned already with proposals of a second marriage. The Count soon observed that she seemed to be very partial to me, and frequently squeezed my hand by stealth with averted looks. Yet my proud heart soon conceived a presumption upon her favour, which unexpectedly made me sensible of my mistake.

One afternoon she roved with me thro' the garden, playing numberless little pranks. She was more immoderately merry than I ever had seen her before, and her amorous gambols fired me to a degree of which I never thought myself susceptible. She was, besides, dressed with uncommon elegance and taste. Her fine shape, the activity of her limbs, the pliancy of every part of her graceful form, the luxuriant growth of her curling hair, which wantonly overshaded her forehead and bosom, and her easy, cheerful gait, made her resemble the Goddess of Mirth. I was intoxicated by the sight of her unpresuming charms, and enchanted by the jovial roguery of her sparkling eyes.

Being, at length, exhausted by her playsome gambols, we seated ourselves upon the swelling turf, where it was overshaded by a tuft of myrtles. She broke off some of the depending twigs, and began to throw them at me. I had just picked up two, and was going to fling them at her in return, when she suddenly averted her face from me towards a walk covered with lofty trees. I turned round, and beheld the Count coming slowly towards the place where we were sitting. He was alone, and so profoundly absorpt in thought, that he did not see us. His arms were crossed, his head depended upon his bosom, his eyes were half shut, and he seemed to be entirely unconscious of the objects around him. He made now and then motions, as if he conversed with some person, dropt one of his hands, covering with the other a part of his face.

Caroline suddenly grew serious; I wanted to continue our frol-icsome sport, but she paid no attention to me, replying to all my questions nothing but, "The poor Count! how melancholy he is!" "The poor Count!" I repeated with great emotion; and one of her sweet looks thanked me for my concern.

When he came nearer, without seeing us, I called to him. He awoke from his gloomy reverie a little frightened; yet he had too much power over his countenance as not to exhilarate it immedi-ately; and he always grew extravagantly merry, whenever he changed from a melancholy mood to a cheerfulness; which now also was the case. Yet Caroline could not be deceived by his unnatural jocundity; her countenance assumed an uncommon serious aspect, which impelled him to use still greater efforts to cheer her up. I seconded him faithfully; and when nothing would succeed, we grew, at last, so excessively merry, that she offered to rise, and to leave us.

"I perceive, beautiful Caroline," he now began, "that one of us is disagreeable to you, and I fear I am that *one.*"

Although he said this in a laughing accent, yet Caroline returned neither a word, nor ever a look; remaining quietly on her seat, and playing with her fan.

"No, no!" said I, "You are mistaken, dear Count; I am that person." I directed a scrutinizing look at her while I uttered these words; but she still continued to be taciturn.

"You probably think so," the Count resumed, "because she is so serious ever since an unfortunate accident has made me interrupt your conversation?"

"I don't like to enter into a contest with you; but let us make an experiment. That proud goddess may decide herself. Kneel down, and take this myrtle sprig." He kneeled, laughing, down, and took the myrtle in his hand.

"Now, fair Caroline," I began in a solemn accent, turning to her, "it is your turn to choose. Here you see two lovers kneeling before you, who adore you with equal tenderness, who would sacrifice their life with pleasure to save yours, but rather will devote it to your happiness. Either offers you a myrtle sprig, accept that of him whom you prefer to the other."

I could not help thinking that it was cruel to treat the poor Count thus: however, the present opportunity seemed to offer me that little triumph in such a natural manner, that I could not resist the temptation of enjoying it. My poor neighbour trembled, and was in a violent agitation, while I anticipated my victory with a smiling countenance. Caroline, however, instead of treating the matter as a frolic, as I had expected, rose with dignity, and in a very solemn manner, which excited our astonishment; but no sooner had she surveyed us with a dubious look, than she lost all presence of mind. Her face was alternately overspread with a deep crimson hue and a deadly paleness; her bosom heaved with greater violence, and she breathed louder, covering her countenance repeatedly with her hand, and displaying an uncommon emotion. After a few seconds, she recovered the dominion over herself, darting an unspeakable tender look at the Count, who stared at her like a statue, and another less significant one at myself, snatched with vehemence the myrtle sprig from my friend's hand, averting her face, and said, in a trembling accent, "I thank you, dear Count."

It is a kind of miracle that I did not lose the use of my senses on the spot. It rather seemed as if I had received a thousand eyes more, to see more plainly what now ensued. The Count was almost frantic with rapture, forgetting every thing, the world and myself, and straining the trembling girl to his bosom. At first, she only suffered his caresses and kisses, but soon returned them with equal fervour. Tender looks, and voluptuous sighs, were mutually exchanged, and the glowing fire of love burned on their crimsoned lips. They were infolded in tender embraces, while I continued to kneel before them in a kind of senseless stupor.

The Count observed, at length, my forlorn situation, and raised me with a grateful look. "My Caroline," said he to the sweet girl, "let my dearest friend have a share in your affection." So saying, he pressed me to Caroline's bosom. Heaven was in his looks; he believed to have regained every thing while he could strain the dear object of his love and the friend of his heart to his heaving bosom.

"Yes, Marquis," Caroline began, "I should have preferred you to all the world, if I had not known the Count. Be my friend, as you have been that of my Lewis, and you always will find my heart open, kind, and affectionately disposed to you."

I was seized with stunning stupor, and incapable of returning an answer; I even could not evince my gratitude by a mute sign. I bent my weeping eyes upon the hand which she extended to me, and felt it burn more violently than my face. This was the only sensation of which I was conscious. My heart ceased almost to beat, and a chilling tremour thrilled my frame, but was soon succeeded by a convulsive heat. My breast heaved violently, and yet I had it not in my power to unburthen it by a single sigh.

The Count embraced me, squeezing my hand. "You know, my dear Carlos," he added, "that my rapture is not unalloyed with pungent grief."

Caroline now raised me up, putting my hand between her arm, while the Count took hold of me on the other side. They spoke little; however, their tender looks conveyed comfort to my poor heart. I was scarcely conscious of being led by them.

"This then is the consequence of thy adventurous undertaking," said I to myself in the evening, when I was alone in my apartment: "fate has punished thee as thou didst deserve. Yet it is fortunate enough that that decision, that the certainty of thy fate, has cooled thy foolish presumption, and that thou hast a greater share of pride than of any other passion."

I cannot but confess that my pride only saved me, my passion being not strong enough to resist it. I never had, till then, loved without hope; and even Caroline had opened a favourable prospect to me by her innocent sportiveness. The first blow my humbled vanity received was dreadful enough, yet it soon recovered from that unexpected shock, and rendered me easy. I should have been blind, if I could have overlooked the Count's superior merits, his enchanting form, his gay and even temper, and his sensible heart, which was ever ready to make the greatest sacrifices to the objects of its love. Yet no one will expect that I should have been able to witness the felicity of the two lovers with tranquillity. I resolved, therefore, patiently to keep them company, while they should remain in the country, and then to repair to some other part of the world; a resolution, the first part of which I performed more faithfully than I had reason to expect. I took such a tranquil, but less cheerful, share in all their amusements, deceived myself so much by my equanimity, and forced myself to such an imposing unconcern, that the serenity of the Count, who firmly believed that I soon would be cured entirely, visibly encreased, and grew every day more natural.

But how great was his astonishment when I entered his apartment, a few days after our return to Paris, and informed him that I was going to leave him for a short time. He scarcely could believe that I was serious: I told him, however, that he was mistaken if he imagined my heart was as cheerful as my countenance. I alledged such strong and reasonable motives for a tour through France, and a visit to a little estate I possessed in Provence, that he approved my plan at last, though it was very visible that it gave him pain to part with me even for a short time. We found, however, some comfort in the hope of a speedy cure of my mental disease, and of my subsequent return. I had, besides, found out the most amiable travelling companion I could wish for: this was Count S******i, who was in a situation similar to mine, and sincerely rejoiced at my proposal. The Count and myself being now completely reconciled, we embraced each other with an affectionate heart and weeping eyes. He offered to spend the night with me, and to accompany me the subsequent morning a few leagues. Wishing, however, that my journey should be looked upon merely as a pleasure excursion, I desired that the farewell-scene should be as short as possible. Having, therefore, settled the manner in which our correspondence was to be carried on, I disengaged myself from his embraces, and spent the night in private in my apartment, giving audience to my thoughts, and preparing for my departure.

S******i and myself had agreed not to render our journey tiresome, by taking too much care of our convenience on the road. We provided ourselves with good horses, and very little baggage;

and were attended only by two servants. Being thus accoutred, we began our excursion, independent on the rudeness of the post-masters, who are of one cast all over the world. As for my companion, I had not the least apprehension of falling out with him, for he was good-nature itself. I called at his apartments with the first dawn of the morning; we mounted our horses, and the Count wished us a pleasant journey from the balcony.

CHAPTER VI.

S******i and I left Paris with light hearts, and cheerfully anticipated the pleasures which awaited us. Our hilarity encreased with every mile that carried us farther from the residence of every terrestrial happiness. We did not regret it in the least; and were entirely occupied with the serenity of the sky, with our plans, and the good-natured cheerfulness of the country people. Berry lay before us, and promised to afford us ample scope for observations and amuse-ment. Autumn was on the verge, and the wind whistled more chilly and bleak through the fading leaves: this is, however, the very season that agrees best with a certain weariness of soul. My companion was, besides, a man that would have been capable of soothing the acutest sorrows; for a most insinuating gentleness animated every word of his, and he took the warmest interest in the least trifle that concerned the heart. The objects that presented themselves to his eyes, made him completely forget all his cares; his exuberant imagi-nation was sufficiently purified by the trial of early disappointments and sufferings; and his similarity of mind reflected a cheerful light on every object that presented itself to his eyes. His heart was the amicable abode of tender sensibility; and he was too good-natured to confine his friendship to an individual fellow-creature, cherishing the whole human race with undivided affection.

We travelled for some time without meeting with any remark-able incident, accelerating our course whenever we thought proper, and stopping at every place which promised to afford us pleasure. Count S******i being disposed by nature, and I by my fate, by phi-losophy and stern necessity, to find every where scope for amuse-ment, we met at all places where we stopped a kind reception, and people with whom we could converse. Nothing is more ridiculous than to travel for the sake of amusement and improvement, and at the same time to pay a nice attention to one's rank. I have known very few ramblers who travelled with that intention, that did not display more or less of that foolish pomp. A traveller never ought to expect real pleasure and benefit from his rambles, if he is not initiated in the great art of being a peasant amongst country people, an artist amongst artists, and a merchant amongst merchants.

I have never known a man who possessed the different qualities and perfections which compose that art in a more extensive compass than S******i, his temper, which breathed nothing but cheerfulness and affability, appropinquating him to every open physiognomy. He spoke the language of all ranks, knew all their prejudices, their favourite ideas, and peculiar expressions. He could assume almost any shape; and no one could resist his manner, which spoke a language that is generally understood, the language of the heart. My rambling life, and the frequent changes of my situation, had taught me also a little knowledge of man; but whenever I was near him, I was but too sensible that I was obliged to exert all my attention, if I would spoil nothing. He stole almost irresistibly upon every heart; and scarcely a quarter of an hour elapsed before he was the idol of people who saw him the first time. There was no rest in the house before our horses were watered and baited, and our dinner or supper got ready. All was in a bustle: six feet were in motion as soon as one signified a wish; they assembled cheerfully around us; spoke freely, and without disguise, of every thing. The prettiest girls were selected to dance with us, or offered themselves voluntarily with the most amiable simplicity and innocence. Wherever we shewed ourselves, we beheld joy and good will depicted on every countenance; and were happy even amid the smoke of several dozen of tobacco pipes. If we stayed more than one day at a village, some little feast was generally given on our account; the best bottle of wine was fetched out of the cellar; the young girls of the place were assembled; and these poor people, who only wanted a pretext for being merry, were rendered happy for several hours by the share we took in their amusements. S******i, in return, slighted neither their dishes, nor their offers, nor their society; he ate and drank with every one what was offered to him; danced as well with the ugly as with the handsome villagers without discrimination; spoke and laughed with every one at whatever they chose; and frequently played a ballad on the guitar, or related his travels. Such silence did then prevail around us, that one could have heard the falling of a feather. The company sat gaping on the benches, and hardly dared to fetch breath before the tale was concluded; the consequence of which was, that these poor people parted with us with weeping eyes, or ran a quarter of a mile after us, on our departure.

At Blois we happened to meet the Duke of B******, and gave occasion to that proud Briton, who thought to carry every thing by the weight of his purse, to make a very mortifying experience. Having arrived early in the morning, we determined to take a ride after dinner, and to survey the environs of the town. The Duke arrived, not long before our return, with two coaches, two valets, seven or eight giant-like servants, and two led-horses. The landlady, who was preparing our supper, hesitated a while whether she should admit the proud Peer with his numerous retinue, notwithstanding the display of his guineas, as she could foresee that he would give her so much trouble that she should not be able to enjoy our society. At length she gave the keys of the apartments to the waiter, and ordered him to shew the Duke up. The purse-proud Nobleman being used to be received with the greatest respect at the inns, was astonished to see himself ushered in by the waiter, the landlady being just occupied to prepare a rice cream, which Count S******i had ordered; and the landlord gone in quest of a bottle of *Vin de la Cote*, which my friend had wished to have.

The Duke took, however, possession of his apartments, and suddenly a dreadful noise arose in the yard. Our two servants had been watering their horses, while the Duke's people had quartered theirs in our stable, which appeared to them to be more commodious, and better than the rest. Our trusty esquires were astonished to find, on their return, the receptacle of their beasts occupied by new inhabitants; and having not the least inclination to be dislodged, Antonio dismounted silently, with all possible Spanish grandezza, led the intruders into the yard, and put his horses in possession of their former station, in presence of all the servants, who were struck with astonishment on seeing the beasts of an English Peer treated thus disrespectfully, and dislodged by two miserable hacks, as they were pleased to call them.

Their indignation soon broke out into dreadful curses; and they asked Alfonso, with kindling rage, how he dared to remove the horses of an English Lord. A loud laugh was the only answer my servant returned. He locked the stable, and having put the key coolly into his pocket, was going to step into the house. The Duke's servants seeing themselves treated with so much disrespect, grew furious; and the contest soon became so clamorous and warm, that the Peer, hearing the voices of his people, opened the window of his bed-chamber, and desired to know the cause of their quarrel. Being informed of Alfonso's temerity, he ordered him, in a domineering accent, to deliver up the key, and to put his horses into another stable. The servants exulted already at their supposed victory; but Alfonso pleaded, with the greatest civility, his prior claims to the stable, and declared that he rather would lose his life than give up the key. The Peer being highly exasperated at his obstinacy, ordered his servants to take it from him by force; and his people having only waited for the signal of attack, fell furiously upon poor Alfonso. The honest fellow being assailed by seven strong and lusty men, saw no other expedient of saving the key, than to throw it into an open window, which went into the kitchen where the landlady was busily occupied with the Count's rice cream.

She had been amused already for some time by the scene which was acting under her window, and secretly applauded Alfonso's spirited conduct. He possessed, like my friend S******i, a secret charm to ingratiate himself with all the landladies we met with on our journey; and our hostess no sooner saw him fling the key into the kitchen, than she took it for a signal to come to his assistance, and instantly armed herself with her largest skimmer to terminate the contest. She was firmly resolved to hit a sound blow at the lusty fellow who had seized her dear Alfonso by the collar, when the landlord appeared on the field of battle, carrying the bottle with the costly wine, which he had got at last, after numberless fruitless inquiries, triumphantly under his arm. He was instantly informed of the cause of the contest in a most clamorous manner, and hastened with his yoke-mate to poor Alfonso's relief.

The Duke's servants being more desirous to get the key into

their possession than to vent their vengeance against my man, had already unhanded him, when they came up with them, without having done him any other harm than beating a hole into his head as large as a shilling. It may easily be conceived what a terrible clamour our landlady raised when she beheld the broken head of her favourite. "Good god! what will the dear gentlemen say on their return!" she exclaimed ever and anon. "Holy Peter! how they will be enraged!" Mean time, one of the Duke's servants attempted to get into the house to fetch the key, which she no sooner perceived, than she hit him such a dreadful blow with her culinary weapon in the face, that the poor fellow staggered back with a roaring yell.

The Duke now ordered his people to desist from all further contention; for although he was an Englishman, yet he did not possess a large share of that undaunted courage for which his countrymen are renowned; and having learnt, by the exclamation of the landlady, that Alfonso had a master, which till then had not come into his Lordship's mind, he thought it prudent to proceed with less violence. The hostess did, however, no sooner espy him at the window, than she let loose the reins of her tongue, thinking him to be the chief cause of that incident. She read such a lecture to the Englishman on the impudence of his people, as he probably never had heard before. Her husband too, who was not in the habit of agreeing with his loving spouse, was of the same opinion with her, declaring that the stable could be parted with for *no price*.

The Duke thinking the honour of his nation was at stake, looked upon this Philippic as a challenge to throw some guineas out of the window: however, that indelicate expedient only served to exasperate the host more violently; yet he contented himself with kicking them indignantly aside, and proceeded to the Duke's apartment, to remonstrate with him on his conduct. The latter was, by our host's obstinacy, inflamed with such an eagerness of getting possession of the stable, that he offered a considerable sum of money, and at last threatened to quit the house immediately. But neither the one nor the other made the least impression upon the headstrong landlord; and the Peer was, at length, obliged to drop the contest, because he knew that he could not get post-horses before the next day, and apprehended that he should find no accommodation in another inn.

The host was just going to quit the apartment, when the Duke perceived the bottle he carried under his arm. He inquired after the name of the wine, and it happened unfortunately to be his Lord-ship's favourite liquor. He began, therefore, to make new offers; but the host was equally inexorable: nay, he was even so malicious as to extoll the deliciousness of the wine to the skies; adding, that he had found it extremely difficult to get a bottle of it, and that he would take no price for it. The Duke inquiring after the reason of such strange behaviour, the host, who was impatient to display his attachment to the Count, enumerated our merits in a most hyper-bolical manner, and laid a particular stress on the description he was pleased to give of our noble spirit and bravery. "These two gentle-men do, indeed, travel in a simple and unexpensive manner," he concluded: "however, I will be hanged if they are not two foreign princes who travel incognito." These words had the desired effect on the Duke: he now began seriously to think that his heat had misled him to commit a very foolish action, and asked the landlord, with visible perplexity, how he thought Alfonso could be indemni-fied best. The landlord shook his head, declaring, that he was afraid it could not be done by money; and an attempt which the Duke made to that purpose confirmed his supposition. We returned from our excursion in the moment the landlord had finished his parley. The Duke was at the window, and seemed to be astonished at the majestic appearance of the Count, whose uncommonly beautiful horse was prancing in the yard. The noble animal was of a high mettle, and gave his rider an opportunity of displaying his skill in horsemanship. Mean-while the landlady came running out of the house to seize the reins of the horse, thinking the Count was in danger; and Alfonso, whose head was bound up, was close at her heels. We dismounted; and seeing a number of strange servants in the house, could partly guess at the affair.

Having patiently listened to the minute account of our kind landlady, we found that it was of a complexion which made it neces-sary we should wait upon his Lordship immediately. He received us with an incredible perplexity, which he strove to conceal as much as possible. My address was very short; and, without mentioning our names, or inquiring for his, I asked him what sort of satisfac-tion he meant to give to my servant for the ill treatment of which he had been the principal cause? He started some difficulties; but at length grew more reasonable, begging my pardon; and we parted with mutual civility.

We frequently met with similar instances; for the vanity of men is greater than their desire for gain. We had entirely divested ourselves of our rank and dignity; and without abandoning, only for a moment, that elegance of deportment which always distinguishes a man of noble birth and a good education, flattered the passions and prejudices of every one. *Little* friends ought not to be slighted, as well as petty enemies; and we frequently received the greatest services from people of whom we had not expected the smallest kindness. The innkeepers and their people rivalled every where to treat us as well as possible: the less we required, and the more satisfied we seemed to be with what they could give us, the more did they exert themselves to render us every kind of service, and to anticipate our wishes; the consequence of which was, that we never had any reason to complain of the insolence and the imposition of the landlords; and we were convinced, by repeated experience, that travellers generally have to accuse no person but themselves if they are not well treated by the innkeepers.

One evening we had already left Chartres far behind us, and approached a village whose solitary, but romantic, situation promised us, if not a convenient, at least an agreeable, accommodation for the night. We had made it a rule to decline as much as possible from the high road, bending our course generally towards a village on the top of a rising eminence, or secluded from the rest of the world in a deep valley. There nature was purer, happiness more artless; the inhabitants were handsomer and more cordial; and the reception was kinder than in the neighbourhood of more cultivated manners.

And why did we travel? Was a statistic speculation, or the examination of the different degrees of morality, or of churches and steeples, or of bridges and edifices; were the fine arts, or any thing of that kind, the objects of our peregrination? Certainly not. If one is desirous to travel for that purpose, one most not stop long at Paris, where speculation finds such an ample scope, and where the finest products of art, and the objects of the most luxuriant physical and moral refinement are so numerous, that a residence of a twelvemonth at that gay capital blunts the senses and the mind almost entirely; takes away every relish for such objects, at least for a considerable time; and excites an irresistible desire to fly from that fatiguing bustle, and to rest the weary mind, and the satiated senses, on the bosom of pure and artless nature. This was our aim, and constituted our sole pleasure.

The hamlet, which now hailed our eyes, seemed to consist only of a few houses; and reclined so artfully against the steep declivity of a rock, that it was almost perpendicularly suspended over a precipice. The eminence terminated, on both sides, in a plain, which was covered with a number of fertile hillocks, and exhibited a variegated mixture of garden ground, meadows, and wood. Art seemed to have joined with nature to mix the colours in the most pleasing manner.

The sensations of the traveller chiefly depend upon trifles. Nothing, therefore, produces a more picturesque effect than the rising smoke of a solitary chimney concealed between a cluster of trees. Hunger, fatigue, and curiosity, lead us to form an idea conformable to the disposition of our imagination, or to the wants of the moment of the scene which is before us: we anticipate the enjoyment of every thing we expect to find, mould the faces into the form in which we wish to meet them, and reduce the circumstances to the shape that would be the most convenient to us. Nothing is truer than that not the enjoyment makes us happy, but its approach.

CHAPTER VII.

It was Sunday when we arrived at the hamlet. All the inhabitants were assembled beneath a large wallnut-tree, and their joy was rather clamorous. One must have seen French peasants, to form an adequate idea of the scene which presented itself to our eyes. The oppressed and the poor generally abandon themselves to excesses whenever they can catch a moment of liberty, tranquillity, and superfluity; and the human heart, which much sooner is urged from one extreme to the other than cooled to moderation, destroys, without hesitation, a part of the future pleasure, while it abandons itself to the rapid torrent of present gratification.

The young people danced, and the girls were adorned with autumnal flowers. Some branches composed charming huts, where we received refreshments spread on benches. Their whole orchestra consisted of a single fiddle, a tambourine, a fife, and a clarinet: however, the female dancers moved with so much agility and natural grace, that the eyes were indemnified for what the ears missed. We passed the dancers in a hard trot, being impatient to arrive at the inn which was on the other side of the hamlet. The curiosity of seeing us ride by, put a momentary stop to the dance and the music, which began again, as soon as we were past, with the same unconstraint as if no observers were near. Our dress was soon changed: the Count put on a slight white night-gown: I followed his example; and thus accoutred, we went in our slippers to the dancing place, attended by our landlady, who gazed with visible delight at my friend's elegant form and graceful carriage. I also could not help making the same remarks I read on her countenance. He had the appearance of a king in disguise. His soft blue eye glittered with that tranquil majesty, which peacefully raises itself above the pressure of sorrows; his looks spoke the sweet language of general benevolence; and his colour, which commonly was rather pale, had been animated, by exercise and good humour, with a rosy hue, which was charmingly set off by the disorder of his brown hair. The noble grace of his gait, and of his whole carriage, easily could tempt one to believe that he was an inhabitant of Heaven's realms, who had left his celestial abode to bless the mortal race.

When we approached the dancing place, we observed some motions among the merry company. They seemed to consult how we should be received: however, we joined them with as much ease as if we had lived many years amongst them; saluted every one, and shook hands with those who were most contiguous to us. The little confusion our arrival had caused was thereby instantly dispelled; and when we told them that we wished to take a cordial share in their joy, they raised a loud shout of satisfaction. We were led to the best seat: the oldest of the happy circle offered us wine, figs, almonds, and grapes; and the music and dancing began anew.

Having refreshed ourselves sufficiently, we did not hesitate to mix with the dancers. The Count chose a partner; and I also had no difficulty to find one for myself. The vanity which our charmers felt at that preferment, soon raised them above the reserve which is natural to the female sex; and the blushing, innocent damsels joined their hands cheerfully with ours. The Count's partner was a tall, jolly brunette; and I was coupled to a little languishing girl. The former was by far too fiery for the character of her partner, and the latter too gentle for me; yet the beauty of their form, the simple, animated and well conducted dance, which unfolded their charms in the most advantageous manner, soon made us forget the reciprocal contrast of our dispositions.

Annette, the partner of my friend, had the finest shape I ever beheld; a small, pale face, full and rosy lips, and a round voluptuous chin. Her black eyes spoke, or, at least, would not speak, much that evening; for I remarked afterwards that they could be pretty eloquent. She sported with the innocent caresses of the poor Count, who seemed to be enchanted with her, though he was not wont to brook female severity. He was probably so pliant at first merely for the sake of amusement, but at last his sentiments took a more serious turn.

Lucy, my fair partner, was Annette's younger sister, and quite the reverse of her; a little, languishing, puny being, of uncommonly fine limbs, and a most pliant make. Her soft eye, overshaded with long, brown eye-lashes, seemed, indeed, not to be an entire stranger to roguish coquetry; yet it displayed more modest goodness than wantonness. It burned with a wish, with a secret desire, for a certain something, which she, perhaps, had no clear notion of, or at least, seemed never to have found as yet. Her bosom spoke the same language, as well as the blushes of her dimpled cheeks, when I pressed her little charming hand. Her feelings certainly were strong, and she only was at a loss how to express them. She had too little energy of body and of mind, and for that reason, seemed not to be susceptible of a higher culture, as she indeed was sensible of the impression of the present moment, but did not retain it long.

We spent the evening in congenial, artless pleasure, frequently changed our partners, according to the established custom, but always returned to those our good fortune had bestowed upon us at first. The Count's charming impartiality forsook him at once, and I did not hesitate to imitate his example, impelled, as it were, by an unaccountable secret enchantment. If one has, or only imagines to have, received some pleasing sensual gratification, the first impression, the first taste, always predominates strongly among those that succeed it. There were at least twenty lovely figures among these little sweet lovely figures among these little sweet country girls, that were prettier and more charming than our partners; however, we were almost entirely insensible to their beauty. The secret impulse that urged us to return to our charmers, cannot be called love, it rather was a strange sort of a nameless desire. The shape and the manners of the lovers inspired the rest with a jealousy which rather seemed to be owing to offended vanity than to a particular inclination towards us. The general good understanding was soon interrupted; the favoured fair ones indulged themselves with several little liberties; the rest did not care to disguise their indignation; and, besides, we were not the sole lovers of our partners. It was owing merely to the supposed superiority of our rank, which was confirmed by the noble carriage of the Count, that this general dissatisfaction did not break out: however, the silence which began to prevail around us rapidly increased every moment; the general inebriation of pleasure gradually vanished as one little troop separated itself by degrees from the rest; and those who were inspired with similar sentiments, retired at some distance in small groups, taking no farther share in our diversion. Our ladies, too, were sensible of our misconduct and grew gradually more reserved; and we now were the only persons that did not observe it.

I was at length reminded of it by Alfonso, who, all the evening, had been a silent observer of our behaviour, without taking the least share in our diversions. I imparted his remarks secretly to the Count, and our eyes were opened at once. We now beheld ourselves and our partners entirely deserted by the company, and the rest dispersed in several groups. However, we neglected to make a proper use of that discovery, being diverted by the jealousy of the company; and, instead of behaving with more circumspection, increased our caresses and our attention to our partners, which vexed their lovers in such a degree, that they drew nearer with glowing faces, and with looks which plainly told us that it was high time to discontinue our ungentleman-like sport.

Night was, fortunately, setting in. The families broke up, and went to their respective homes, probably very little edified by the conclusion of their rural ball and our conduct. Annette and Lucy also were impatient to go home: we offered them our arms, and attended them to their house, amid the pretty audible hisses of those that had staid behind.

There are situations in human life in which we really seem to be controuled by some magic charm, of which the events of that evening were a speaking instance. All these humiliating consequences of our conduct, the cold civility of the old people, the scornful looks of the girls, the wry faces of the young men, and even the reserve and growing coldness of our charmers, were not sufficient to make us sensible of our foolish imprudence. The landlord and his dame, who, some hours before, had received us with so much kindness, and attended us, had also changed their looks very much on our return: even our servants convinced us, by their gestures, that they did not much admire our prudence. Every thing was, besides, in a confusion to which we were not accustomed, and which we had not yet experienced on our excursion. The horses had bad stabling, and not yet got their fodder: no supper was to be seen; and having, at length, put the people of the house in motion, our meal turned out so meagre and miserable, that we went to bed with empty stomachs. We now began, almost at one time, to rail at the people of the house, instead of looking for the cause of our disappointment in our conduct; and were so much infatuated as to curse and to threaten our host, to quarrel with our servants, to beat cats and dogs, and several times were very near falling out with each other before we went to our apartment.

On coming to our bed-chamber, an additional cause of dissatisfaction threw itself in our way; only one spare bed being, unfortunately, in the house. This inconvenience would, indeed, not have given us the least uneasiness at any other time, either of us taking it rather as a favour to be suffered to sleep on a chair if the bed happened to be too small to contain both. But now, neither would resign the bed to the other; and, after a long warm contention, we squeezed ourselves at length into the narrow compass of our comfortable couch. Yet we were incapable of getting a wink of sleep, tossing ourselves from one side to the other, and murmuring alternately at our miserable situation. We had the additional misfortune to be almost suffocated by an intense heat, which, at length, drove

me out of the bed. I began to walk up and down in the room, and
the Count soon followed my example, stepping to the window, and
inhaling the fresh night air.

"What the D—l does that mean?" he exclaimed at once, starting suddenly back. "Look, Carlos, what a numerous crowd gathers
under our window." I hastened to him, and actually beheld about
twenty young people before our door, but could discern nothing else, the night being very dark. We now began to guess and
to conjecture what could be the meaning of that assemblage, and
naturally concluded that it must have some connection with the
incidents at the dancing place. I was violently enraged at the insolence of our nocturnal visitors; but Count S******i, whose good
humour returned at once, began to laugh. This inflamed me still
more vehemently; and, instead of being pacified by his unconcern,
I apprehended some danger. I fetched, therefore, our pistols; and
having made every preparation for a vigorous defence, was going to
awake our servants. Count S******i, was, however, more prudent
than myself, and stopping me at the door, with a loud laugh said,
"Don't put yourself into a passion; I will lay any thing that their
whole drift is nothing but a miserable frolic. Don't spoil the pleasure of these poor fellows, but rather let us divert ourselves at their
expense."

The event proved that he was not mistaken; for we were, after a
few minutes, regaled with an excellent serenade, whose harmony
soon informed us of its meaning. The effect this charming concert
had on my risibility was so powerful, that I could not have resisted
an immoderate fit of laughter if it had cost me my life. The music
could certainly not be called a symphony; however, so much is
certain, that the most horrid notes were borrowed from all instruments to produce a kind of chorus. As much as I could distinguish,
some horns were the principal instruments; and it may easily be
conceived how charmingly they were blown: a fiddle, with only one
string, two or three rattles, a damaged trumpet, some little drums,
and three or four kettles, accompanied the performers who played
those agreeable instruments; and some small French whistles,
which are used to call the flocks together, in the neighbourhood of
which one is in danger to lose one's hearing for ever, completed, by
their shrill notes, the harmony of the whole. Several other instru-

ments I did not know; however, the whole concert was of such a nature, that it would have been able to resuscitate the dead, and to reduce nervous people to the brink of the grave.

We were amused for some time: however, the Count took, at length, a pocket pistol out, and having extracted the ball, fired it over their heads. It caused a louder report than I had expected, and the music was silenced in an instant. The young gentlemen, who had not conceived the most distant idea of the serious consequences which might attend their frolic, did not think proper to finish their serenade, and left us suddenly to our reflections.

The Count continued to laugh immoderately, and I was infected by his merry humour. "It would be excellent sport," he exclaimed, "if we could dispossess these fellows of their pretty little girls. I would give any thing." I was entirely of his opinion, protesting that nothing could be more pleasant. Our vexation at our disastrous circumstances had divided us, and the resentment these very circumstances created united us again. We now consulted about the means of effecting our purpose, and soon hit upon measures which promised us success.

The execution of our plan was more successful at first than we had expected, as the final issue of it was more unfortunate and mortifying than we ever could have imagined. The young people had again a dance the next evening; and we prepared the whole hamlet, during the day, for our behaviour on that occasion. We were as gentle as doves, and seemed to be good-nature and condescension itself; wandered through the hamlet, paying very little attention to the girls; joked with the young men, and were serious in the company of the old ones; flattered the mothers, and treated the daughters with cold civility. When we entered a house, we were received with frigid reserve and sour looks, but pleasure and good-will beamed in the eye of every inmate when we left it: our salutes were returned with cordiality; every one was charmed with our conduct; and every thing changed in our favour. Yet we were too much exasperated as to drop our design, and impatient to be revenged for the treatment we experienced last night.

Our behaviour in the evening was also entirely changed. We betrayed not the least desire to mix with the dancers, but associated with the old peasants, discoursed of the vintage, made our observations on the wind and the clouds, presaged the weather, and pretended to know the meaning of the croaking of the frogs. The gaping peasants were astonished at the striking change of our behaviour, and listened so eagerly to our discourses, that here and there a pipe dropt on the ground. Every recollection of the events of the preceding night seemed to be obliterated, and the listening circle, that stood around us, encreased with every minute. The Count sang and played on the guittar; and I relieved him at intervals by the relation of wonderful incidents, and of ludicrous anecdotes. The dance ceased, and the girls too assembled around us; however, we took little notice of them.

Annette and *Lucy* were struck with astonishment at our behaviour with regard to themselves. They were dressed in their best apparel, and their disappointment was legibly written on their countenance. Annette affected to be entirely indifferent to the Count's inattention to her person, and strove to be extravagantly merry: Lucy, on the contrary, scarcely could retain her tears; and the more her sister exerted herself to make the company burst with laughter, the more frequently did she take her pocket handkerchief out to wipe her eyes.

Not the least of these circumstances escaped our observations, and our looks frequently met those of our offended fair ones; yet nothing was able to make the smallest impression on our obdurate hearts: they were obliged to go home unattended; and we returned to the inn, accompanied by almost all the inhabitants of the hamlet, who seemed to adore us.

No sooner were we left to ourselves, than we broke out in a fit of laughter, congratulating ourselves mutually on our excellent talents for hypocrisy, deceit, and courtly disguise, as well as on the impression we flattered ourselves to have made on the hearts of our charmers. We really had appeared more to our advantage to day than the evening before in our night gowns and slippers. The Count was dressed in his uniform, which, indeed, did not become him half so well as his white night gown: the buttons of his military dress were, however, so bright, and the rich embroidery of his coat was so refulgent, that every look was attracted by the splendor of his external appearance, which received additional charms by the bloom of health blushing on his cheeks, and the sparkling lustre of his eyes. Love, unblended with any kind of ambition, is, besides, rather unnatural; and the latter is frequently the father of the former.

The next morning we conversed, in the presence of our land-lord, on the happiness a constant residence at such a charming spot, and with such good-natured people, must afford. Our host now assumed a very sly look, assuring us that he was not so ignorant of the state of our hearts as we perhaps imagined, and declaring that he would do as much as lay in his power to put us in possession of the two girls whom we had found so charming the first evening, provided we were willing to marry them. He added, they were the richest in the village, each of them possessing a large farm of her own; and we might be sure of success, if we would avail ourselves of his interposition, as he was their uncle and godfather, and had a great influence on the family.

I feigned to be astonished at his sagacity, replying, in my and in the Count's name, that he had completely guessed the real state of our hearts, and that we should avail ourselves of his kind offer as soon as we perceived that the girls were favourably inclined to us; mean-while we wished to hire a small farm for some time.

We were fortunate enough to have the choice of two, and hired that which required the least labour; because neither the Count nor myself was over fond of too much exertion, but knew how to set a proper value on ease and convenience. It was, however, requisite we should act the part of farmers in the highest perfection possi-ble; and while we exerted ourselves to the utmost of our power to do honour to our new station, we actually incurred the danger of being rusticated. I do not know what opinion S******i entertained of me with regard to that point; however, his behaviour gave me just reason for thinking thus of him. He could easily accommo-date himself to almost any situation; and its character, which he appropriated to himself, soon became completely natural to him. He pressed, as it were, the essence out of all scenes and circum-stances of human life, and always found something agreeable in the enjoyment thereof. Ere long, his borrowed character grew habitual with him; and he never left his assumed manners before they relin-quished him, or a new situation required it.

I, on the contrary, did not so easily and so perfectly catch the spirit of a character. My disposition of mind, which always leads me back to the time past, and renders the gratification the present moment affords agreeable to me only as far as it harmonizes with the images of my fancy, embellished by the distance of time, renders every situation very soon irksome to me. Being averse to yield to the alluring charms of novelty, it gains some gratification only by a long continued study of an object, and therefore approaches it only slowly. But not one moment of human life is alike to the other; the events we experience, and our notions, are eternally fluctuating and changing; and the moment in which I begin to grow sufficiently intimate with the existing circumstances, is generally the period in which I commence a new existence.

I acted, therefore, my part a good deal worse than the Count, who found it very convenient to attend personally the pasture of his flock; to adorn his hat and bosom with ribbons and flowers; to dine beneath a spreading lime-tree, to blow a melting air on the flute, or to compose the most heart-breaking pastorals. It was, however, very unfortunate, that the fine season was already past; a flower was a rarity; not one human being heard his plaintive strains; and his verses, which savoured already of the winter, were generally obliged to be thawed before the kitchen fire along with their author, before they were palatable; and were lost to the world, and to immortality, because no person heard them but myself.

I took care of the internal economy of our house; and, with the two servants, fed and milked the cows, and prepared our meals. We three seemed to prefer having a good joint of meat in the pot, and prospect of a substantial dinner, to hunting for rhimes all the day long. When the Count returned, and had properly arranged his ideas, he began to speak with enthusiasm of the graces of poetry, and of the celestial, immortal fire of love. His character had received some fatal lunatic spots from the reading of some German novels, and his fancies more frequently breathed an odour of the grave than of sound sense. Heaven knows how it came that I never was more materially disposed than at that period. I rather endured than coincided with his fine sentiments. If the morning was serene and pure, my feelings were neither more nor less elevated than those of the brute creation: when the moon shone bright, I could, indeed, rejoice for half an hour at her silvery orb; and a sweet melancholy, now and then, stole upon me; but, instead of shedding sentimental tears, I took my gun or a net, to shoot a good bird or to catch fish, assisted by her deceiving flight.

Being occupied and diverted by labour, allured by no temptation, and safe from the corruptive poison of idleness, my heart seemed, at that time, to be as healthy as my body. I can, indeed, not deny that a certain lady of the capital of France attended me sometimes in my little occupations. She was, however, rather gay and cheerful than gloomy and sad; and, what was still more agreeable, came always in the company of a third person. I thought very little of *Lucy* and her whole tribe, but nevertheless lent always, after our meals, a patient ear to the Count's amorous complaints, laughing inwardly at my friend, that he was such a fool to fall thus violently in love.

As for our sociable life, it was regulated in the following manner: In the week every one was hard at work; for our hamlet was poor, and the inhabitants lived upon the scanty produce of their agriculture, pasturage, vintage, and the making of wooden spoons. The time lying very heavy upon my hands for want of society, I employed my idle hours in the fabrication of the latter article, and improved so rapidly, that I soon was famed in the whole hamlet for making the finest wooden spoons. I had learned, in Germany, to make baskets, and now exercised that art also in great perfection. When I was sitting in the yard bending osiers, then it grew frequently lighter in my soul than at any other time: I smiled cheerfully at the time past, and was highly sensible that nothing in the world smooths the path through life so much as constant occupation and labour, which leaves no scope for idle speculation.

This predominant propensity for activity, which, being intimately connected with my nature, has frequently urged me, in the course of my life, to commit the most adventurous follies, made me stiffer, and less sociable, than the Count was rendered by his poetical idleness. When he returned from his pastoral world with his cows and his sheep, he usually was in such a good humour, and his imagination was so bright and active, that every object presented itself to him in a rosy-coloured light; and his rapture knew no bounds when he had succeeded in being happily delivered of some fine poem, or had seen his shepherdess, and received a kind look from her. He almost choaked me with his enthusiastic extravagancies; and when I shewed him a fine spoon I had made, or a neat basket which I had finished, he left me suddenly, ran through the whole hamlet, knocked at every window where he saw a light, disturbed our neighbours in their sleep, tired them with his unseasonable discourses, found every where wit, sound sense, simplicity, and honesty, honoured, at last, his mistress with a ballad of the time of Henry IV. or of Lewis XI. and persuaded her he had composed it for her that very day. When I returned with my gun or net, I generally went for him to her house, or delivered him from the teeth of some mastiffs, who could not conceive what business he could have in the street at so late an hour.

He made, however, excellent progress in his courtship. Annette had already confessed to him that she loved and preferred him to the rest of her lovers; and nothing but the marriage ceremony debarred him from the completion of his happiness. This was, however, a point with respect to which the Count possessed as little of the spirit of cosmopolitism as myself; for he professed the just principle, that, as a man of the world could not be certain to be happy *with* his lady, one ought to take care to get something along with her, that at least would make some atonement for disappointments which might happen, and sweeten the bitterness which oftentimes is mixed in the cup of matrimonial bliss.

I was not so successful in my love, for which I probably had to thank nobody but myself; for while the fiery fair ones *seem* to make great pretensions, those of a gentler disposition *actually* demand a great deal. They do not easily forget little neglects, resent every fault one commits, and reflect at home on what one imagines to have been forgot in a moment. A great propensity for an easy and quiet life has always been a predominant stricture of my character, notwithstanding its restlessness; and my gallantry to the ladies was seldom carried to a very high degree, if my heart did not, of its own accord, urge me to tender those flattering assiduities that commonly are held to be the criterion of a fervent love.

Lucy profited, therefore, very little by my passion. I did, indeed, occasionally play a little air on the flute under her window at night, or danced twice with her on a Sunday, when the other damsels had that honour only once; or if I could get a nosegay without much difficulty, I presented it to her, entwined with a blue ribbon, in a basket of my own workmanship. I also told her sometimes, in the most elegant manner, if she was alone, and seemed to wish for it, that she was as beautiful as an angel, that I adored her, and that it depended entirely upon her to be beloved by me for ever. If I was in an uncommonly good humour, I even ventured to steal a kiss, and to repeat the sweet theft if she was angry at my boldness. This was, however, all I did for her. My rusticated phlegm did not suffer me to venture farther. The fervour of the first evening had been damped by the serenade; and I should have been vexed to death at our foolish frolic, if I had not been diverted by the cares attending my culinary and domestic employment.

It was, at bottom, nothing but kindness for the Count that prompted me to await patiently the conclusion of our whimsical farce; for love appeared to me, at that time, to be nothing else but an occupation fit only for idle people. The work I had on my hand quickened the circulation of my blood, enlivened my ideas, and rendered them more healthy, which enabled me to improve considerably, in that situation, in the true philosophy of life.

Unfortunately, our pleasure did not last much longer. The hamlet was too far remote from the high-road than that its inhabitants could have attained a great knowledge of the gallantry of the nation. It was, therefore, the custom with them to marry first, and then to commence to make love. The servants had, besides, not been over-careful to conceal our rank; and we had rendered ourselves very suspected the first night. The father of the two girls being heartily tired of the trouble of guarding their virgin treasure, and seeing their former lovers relinquish them, applied frankly to the Count, desiring him to declare whether we would marry his girls or not. S******i wanted to pacify him by an evasive answer and vague excuses: however, the farmer declared he perceived the drift of our courtship, and knew very well that it was impossible a serious alliance between ourselves and his daughters could ever take place; desiring him, at the same time, in the politest manner, never to enter his house again, nor to appear under the window, if he did not choose to expose himself to disagreeable accidents. My poor friend really was seized with despair; for although he had no mind to marry, yet he was violently in love with his charmer. He now told the fields his sorrows, and the echo repeated his desponding complaints. The moon and the stars were most ruefully invoked to witness his tears and his despair. His amorous fury and grief were, however, only poetical. He did, indeed, rove the fields, abscond himself in the most solitary recesses of the wood, gaze wildly at the waterfalls and conjure the chilling autumnal gales, which only the absence of all feeling could mistake for Zephyrs, to waft his sighs and amorous complaints to his cruel Phyllis.

I was not displeased at that unfavourable turn of our affairs: and if the girls only had been a little more of our party, this would have afforded the finest opportunity for adventures. My healthy blood spoke of nothing but of murder and elopement. Opposition made me enterprising; and I could have torn our faithless inamoratas from the bosom of their parents, and carried them to the most distant parts of the globe. But the misfortune was, that the girls were not at all disposed to elope; and I laughed, at last, at myself and the Count, and resolved to attempt his conversion to sound sense.

I never performed a good work with less difficulty; for he soon began to laugh at himself and me. He coincided with my humour, and we began publicly to act the furious lovers. We quarrelled every day with the father of the girls, and not a night passed without a serenade under their window. The whole hamlet was put into an intestine commotion, and divided in different parties. A deputation appeared, at length, at our farm, and requested us respectfully to depart in peace. This was just what we wanted: we yielded, therefore, generously to their humble request, settled our affairs, sold our cows and sheep, paid our rent, and departed laughing, highly elated by the ridiculous termination of our frolic.

CHAPTER VIII.

I forbear troubling my readers with an enumeration of the changes that little adventure, which, at bottom, was a mere nothing, produced in my character. They will be perceived, without my assistance, in the sequel of my history. The chief effect it produced was a growing coldness to Caroline. A fluctuation with regard to this point too, in which I had, till then, displayed a firmness that reflected honour on my character; a sudden breaking from a kind of mental sleep, a strong internal ebullition, fleeting sensations, hazarded presensions, a high degree of activity, and a subsequent state of apathy, made me dream, then urged me again to hunt eagerly after peace and happiness, and, when I imagined to have found them, to throw them away suddenly. The enthusiasm arising from a quicker circulation of the blood was past; and I now commence that period in which an unsatisfied internal sense, an ardent desire for activity, begins to stir, and at length relapses again into its former dormant state.

The gay periods of my life are now on the verge, and my career grows more serious. The wanton sports of an exuberant imagination are on the decline; and the reader soon will behold the birth of a new love, great and sacred, glowing and powerful, without any nourishment for the senses, new-moulding my whole character, dispelling its shades, raising the lustre of its brighter parts, artless and omnipotent. The vicious spirit of an abominable confederation purifies itself in its genial fire; and moments are dawning in which the veil of mortality drops before me, and my spirit soars beyond the confines of humanity.

I cannot conceive how it came that, after this incident, I found my disposition not quite so cloudless as before, every gratification being blended with a greater degree of care, and joy and gaiety less benevolently smiling upon me. I relapsed into serious contemplations; and although I was neither dissatisfied nor melancholy, yet I could, notwithstanding the circumspection with which I continually watched over myself, never recover that cheerful station from which that ludicrous adventure had expelled me. I was constantly obliged to spur myself to activity; and I am almost inclined to believe that my taste, and my notions of tranquillity and happiness, were entirely changed.

I was, as it were, gradually prepared for the impending period of my adventures: a serious, but inviting, shade spread itself over every object that came in my way; and I felt as if I returned from the serene luxury of an exuberant and gay landscape, to the melancholy, sweet night of a fragrant grove carpeted over with aromatic flowers, and animated with the plaintive notes of the solitary nightingale. Former scenes of joy, and the heart-expanding retrospect of the past events of my life, now represented themselves to my mind,

and absorpt me in sweet reveries. I enjoyed neither the essence nor
the external of those events, but only the sentiments and notions
which they produced and nurtured in my soul.

The Count either was infected by me; or a different cause had,
perhaps, produced the same effect. He spoke less, and was more
frequently absorpt in serious reflections. Formerly he had now
and then, and always with success, trusted to hazard; but now he
consulted carefully with himself before he attempted any thing,
and the consequence constantly turned out unfavourable. It was
very natural that he was not disposed to ascribe the cause of this
phenomenon to himself, for he found it without difficulty in the
capricious humour of fickle Fortune. He was sullen and gloomy
whenever he could find an excuse for being so; and my altered looks
always afforded him a palpable plea for relapsing in that cheerless
humour.

Do the events of human life really follow a pre-delineated trait,
or does chance sometimes produce oddly united circumstances?
Our minds were, indeed, now and then, cheered by lucid and pleasing intervals. Our good humour frequently made ample amends,
in an hour, for what we had neglected in the course of several days,
when we were refreshed by a sound sleep, if the morning was clear,
not too cold, and neither wind nor snow troubled us on the road,
which was less frequently the case the nearer we approached the
south of France. The most important morning of my life was also
the finest I recollect ever to have seen; my mind too partook of the
serenity of the sky.

January was already on the verge; and the winter having been as
mild as spring, summer seemed to be drawing near. The almond
trees were already high in blossom, and the shrubs began to be
invested with a leafy verdure. The olive woods, with their unfad-
ing green, embosomed already every where germinating wheat-
fields; and the lark, the harmonious herald of the morn, strained its
warbling throat to welcome the approach of the fine season. The
returning spring carries along with it a genial warmth, which dif-
fuses itself through body and mind; every gentle gale breathes an
animating spirit; the mystic humming in the air, and the almost visible growth of the budding plants, produces a symbol of a cheerful
resurrection. And when we behold again, for the first time, a flower,

and the sun-beams gleam through the young leaves, our heart is thrilled with a heavenly rapture, and our language is too poor to do justice to our feelings.

A secret pulsation in my blood, a mystic unaccountable pressure against my panting heart, a sudden stop of the gentle stream of my thoughts, frequently disturbed the peace of my mind on that heavenly morning. Every thing around me seemed to be animated with nameless beings; the mystic sound which pervaded the forest, the fluctuating of the sun-beams in the rising vapours, the sparkling dew-drops gliding from one leaf upon the other, the current streams of vernal warmth, formed in my busy imagination a smiling picture, without colour, without a distinct contour and centre. The whole was attended with a certain obscure presension, with an ominous, though unintelligible, meaning; and some mystic certainty lurked in my soul, without my daring to confide in it the reality of its existence. The beautifullest landscape hailed our enraptured looks: yet its beauty rather consisted in a secret charm which my soul, unknowingly and secretly, imparted to it, than in the sweet variegated mixture of its parts. On our right a beautiful country seat stretched extensive gardens and pleasure grounds over the contiguous chain of hills: smiling, picturesque groups of trees, and little neat cottages, descended from the declivity into the vale. A rosy-coloured morning vapour was still sweetly blended with the bluish colorit* of the back ground, and, where it was less intense, exhibited to our view some part of a village, the lower part of a rock, or trees whose tops towered above the vaporous ocean. The castle, whose scite we also could descry only partially, was not far distant; and the morning sun reflected with radiant splendor from its flaming windows. It was, with its light-green trees, fairy-like suspended in the misty back-ground.

We arrived at length at the park; and one of our servants (I do not recollect whether it was Alfonso, or that of the Count) began to repeat to us the information he had gathered from the landlord in whose house we had slept the preceding night, with regard to the Lord of the Manor. He was misanthrope, secluded from the

---

* The German word "Kolorit" means "colour" or "colouring"; "colorit" seems to be an error by the translator. [Publisher's note.]

world by misfortunes, who educated here a daughter famous for her uncommon beauty. Adelheid, Baronness of V******l, was the brightest ornament and the admiration of the whole province. She lived, however, a solitary life, having no intercourse with her neighbours; few had seen, and a still smaller number ever spoken to her.

This information agitated me in a singular manner. "V******l!" I exclaimed: "have you heard right?"

"I cannot be mistaken, My Lord," he replied.

"The name is very familiar to me: should he, perhaps, be the father of V******l?"

"Whose life you saved at G******," Antonio interrupted me.

"The very person," I resumed. "I now recollect that he frequently has conversed with me of his father and sister; and I am certain he was a native of this province."

In that moment I rejoiced at my good deed. When I resided at G******, that young man fell into the river. He could not swim, and was in danger of being drowned. I instantly plunged into the water, and was so fortunate to save his life. This was, indeed, no heroic action, as I was a good swimmer; and it had entirely slipt my memory; but now I recollected it with pleasure.

I took, from that moment, a warmer interest in every object I beheld. The wall was low, and I could survey all the walks. "Perhaps, (thought I) thou wilt meet young V******l in the bosom of his family, happy and animated with friendship for thee."

I was profoundly absorpt in the pleasing sensations this idea created in my heart, when Count S******i suddenly exclaimed, "Stop! Marquis: for Heaven's sake stop! You will instantly drop from your horse. Don't you perceive that your horse's girth has got loose?"

I stopped to alight, the servants not being within call. However, he dismounted, exclaiming, with his amiable kindness, "Keep your seat: my saddle, too, wants to be tied faster." While he was employed to bind the girth faster, I made some motions to make it easier to him, and in the same moment my looks catched a white object in the park. My heart began violently to palpitate; a cold tremour pervaded my limbs; and I scarcely was capable to keep myself in the saddle.

A female being, of an heavenly form, walked in the park, within a small distance from the wall. She carried a book in one hand, and

with the other screened her face against the dazzling rays of the
sun, reflecting, as it seemed, upon what she had read. A little green
straw-hat, fixed with a white ribbon beneath her chin, overshaded
her long auburn tresses, which depended in beautiful ringlets upon
her girdle: the morning breezes sported with her white gown,
which was tied round the waist with a green sash: her uplifted hand
was whiter than the muslin from which it stole forth, and the roseate smile of health was diffused over her countenance. Her gown
being unfortunately caught by a brier, she was obliged to remove
her hand from her eyes to disentangle it; and having extricated her
garment, her black eyes met me by accident. She started a little
when she saw us so contiguous to her; a deeper hue blushed over
her delicate face, and she cast her eyes suddenly to the ground, as
if in search for something. My horse, whom I inadvertently had
pricked with my spurs, began suddenly to bound; the Count called
to me to be on my guard. She looked once more at me, growing
as pale as ashes, and quickened her paces. I pacified my horse; and
while she turned round a corner into another walk, she directed
her beautiful eyes again at me; and in that moment the Count too
observed her, exclaiming, "Eternal God!" It is impossible to say
more to the praise of a beautiful object than these two words, the
astonishment and the features of my friend expressed; and yet it
was by far too little. My heart was thrilled with unutterable sensations, and an unknown something pervaded my whole frame.

I could not conceal the state of my heart, which expressed itself
legibly on my countenance. The Count observed me awhile seized
with speechless astonishment, and at last broke out in the words,
"Poor G******!" He perceived the growing passion; and knowing
that my temper was too irritable than that I ever could be fortunate
in love, wished to be able to destroy my passion in the bud. "But
how shall I accomplish this?" he said to himself. "It is impossible her
soul should entirely answer her external appearance. There is no
possibility to prevent my poor friend from getting acquainted with
her; I will, therefore, assist him; and if he sees himself disappointed
in his sanguine expectations, the cure of his passion will soon be
effected."

He told me, therefore, laughing, "I perceive, Marquis, I shall
have an opportunity to act here the same part you undertook from

friendship for me in our winter quarters." But apprehending his untimely joke would offend me, he added, in a soothing accent, "yet I hope, Carlos, you will repose confidence in me!" He accompanied these words with a hearty squeeze of his hand, which I returned cordially. Mean while we were arrived at the village, and dismounted at the inn. While I retired to a private apartment, to give audience to my thoughts, the Count mixed with the people of the house, and having made several inquiries concerning the Lord of the Manor, wrote the following note in my name, and sent it to the castle.

"The Marquis of G****** has had the honour to be intimately acquainted with a Mr. de V******l. Having great reason to believe that Baron de V******l is the happy parent of that excellent young man, he begs leave to pay his respects to the father of his friend."

His ambassador returned in the course of a few minutes with one of the Baron's servants, and a formal invitation for myself and the Count. Our horses were instantly taken out of the stable, and our servants desired to bring them with our portmanteaus to the castle. "You must be very intimate with the Baron, or strongly recommended to him," the landlord said to the Count, shaking his head.

The latter now came to my apartment, and finding me on the bed, absorpt in a profound reverie, said, "Will you not get up, Marquis? The Baron," he added coolly, "has just sent us an invitation to come to the castle."

"How! the Baron, did you say?" I exclaimed.

"Yes, yes, the Baron," he replied, smiling, and related his artifice to me. I pressed him to my bosom, transported with rapturous joy, and we went to the castle, but Heaven knows with what an anxiety on my part. My knees trembled, and my heart palpitated violently. I was obliged to take hold of my friend's arm, lest our conductor should perceive my emotion by my gait. Whenever I looked at the windows of the castle, I saw the curtains move, I was violently agitated, my tongue trembled, and I could scarcely speak intelligibly. The attention of some servants, who stood at the gate, opening the folding doors on our approach, made the blood rush into my face; and I now began first to make the observation that our dress was very indifferent; for, to confess the truth, I had nothing on but a simple green hunting coat, and my hair was in the greatest disorder. I could not help communicating these remarks, in a whisper, to the Count. However, he smiled, replying, in German, "What a vanity! I assure you, you never have looked better!" We entered the castle, at length. A man, who appeared to be the butler, welcomed us with respectful politeness, informing us that he had orders to shew us to the drawing room, till his master was dressed. We were conducted to a spacious apartment, decorated with a number of portraits and other pictures. The servant having withdrawn, we began to examine the pictures. They were, probably, family pieces. I did, indeed, gaze at every one of them, but without the least attention, my mind being differently occupied. I admired, at length, even the frames of some, declaring the carving to be excellent, when the Count quickly replied, "Dear Marquis, if you are such an admirer of frames, then come, and look at this: I am sure you never saw a finer one." I went to the other side of the apartment where he was, and he exclaimed, again and again, "Is it possible any thing could be more elegant than this frame?" "You are mistaken, dear Count; for the garland of yon picture is much more beautiful and elegant." "I am of a contrary opinion," he replied, laughing: "this is of a much better workmanship. Upon my honour the picture does not deserve such a beautiful frame." These words naturally made me look at the painting. I started back, seized with astonishment, when I beheld myself as if in a mirror. I instantly recollected to have been persuaded by young V******l, after his incident, to let him have that picture. Astonishment fettered my tongue; and I scarcely heard the Count say, "Faith, Marquis, you are grown much handsomer, or the painter has not done justice to your face."

No sooner had the Count pronounced these words, than a side door opened, and an old man, of a striking beauty, and an elegant carriage, entered the apartment. I bowed respectfully, and was going to thank him for his kind invitation, when he ran towards me, pressing me tenderly to his bosom.

"I know you, Don Carlos," he added; "and the discovery you have made just now saves me a farther elucidation. You have preserved my son's life; receive the grateful effusions of a father's heart; but, at the same time, lament with me his untimely death." With these words a torrent of tears gushed down his cheeks.

"Gracious Heaven!" I exclaimed, kissing the tears from his cheeks, "is it possible?" A violent emotion, which had been preparing all the morning, and only had waited for a pretext of growing loud, interrupted me here. A copious stream of tears relieved my heart; I pressed him to my bosom, and reclined my face on his shoulder.

"Yes, you are quite that sensible, excellent man," he resumed, "whose picture my son has so frequently drawn to us with enthusiastic warmth. Alas! his fate envied him the happiness of seeing you once more. He went into the army some years since; a few months ago he was thrown off his horse, and died of the fall." Here he paused a few moments, and then continued, "Yet you have lost nothing by his death; the son's friendship for you has devolved to the father. I do not love mankind; yet I wish you would accept of his place in my heart, and bestow, at least, a part of your affection for my unhappy boy upon his father." It was very natural that I replied I had loved him long since, and that I would endeavour to deserve his kind opinion. He now left me reluctantly, turning to the Count. I told him his name; and it fortunately happened that he was an intimate friend of the Baron in his younger years. Our reverend host was rejoiced to renew an old acquaintance, and we began soon to converse so cordially as if we had known one another for years, and were members of the same family.

Having spent about half an hour in the most agreeable manner, the Baron said to me, "I now will conduct you to my daughter, who has seen you already this morning, and instantly recollected your features. You see," he added, smiling, "how strongly your image is imprinted on our hearts."

"Our affairs are in an excellent train!" the Count whispered to me, while our kind host opened the door.

"Here, Adelheid, I bring you the friend of our Adolf!" the Baron said, on our entering his daughter's apartment. "He has promised me to be my son and your brother."

The sweet girl sat upon the sofa, holding a book in her hand. She laid it down on our entrance, and rose to meet us. She had exchanged her green hat with a ribbon of the same colour, and her bosom was adorned with a white rose. The rest of her dress was nearly the same as in the morning; her hair was in the same charming disorder, and a miniature picture depended from her swelling bosom. It was a manly face; but fortunately I thought that it was the picture of her brother.

An amiable confusion blushed on her beautiful countenance. My secret agitation did, indeed, render me very unfit for close observation: yet I perceived in her timid looks, and on the faint blushes of her dimpled cheeks, certain symptoms which gave nourishment to my hopes.

An innocent girl is chiefly swayed by instinct, when she meets the man whom her artless heart has chosen without being conscious of it. The most consummate art could not have invented a more charming reception than simple nature effected here. The visible tremour which glided through her frame was a silent confession that something more than the request of her father prompted her to do what she did afterwards. Her heart spoke through her looks, though it was afraid of being understood. The image, and, if I do not flatter myself too much, the beautified image, of her secret dreams was led into her arms by her own father, to cherish it as a brother. But who can force the human heart not to overstep the limits prescribed by parental authority?

The father did not understand his daughter completely. He imagined that she did not answer his wishes, and his tenderness for me, as much as he had expected. "How!" said he, "does Adelheid thus coldly receive the friends of her father, and her second brother?" Her looks could, however, have made him sensible of his mistake; they intreated for indulgence, and at the same time made the sweetest confession. He smiled benevolently at her confusion; and encircling his daughter with his arm, pressed her to my bosom, requesting me to embrace my sister. Her cheeks burned, and my lips quivered. This was all that I was able to observe.

I now led her to her sofa, presenting the Count to her; and she returned his courtly civility in a manner which betrayed the most accomplished education. I now was more at leisure to make observations, and my eager soul was absorpt in the contemplation of her exquisite charms. I had travelled much, and seen a great many beautiful women; I even had possessed a wife adorned with heavenly charms; and my imagination added to her image, which was deeply engraven in my soul, perfections which the original, per-

haps, never had; but here my boldest dreams were more than realized; I frequently doubted that I was awake.

Her soul which soon recovered its wonted flight, to unfold all its
perfections, enchanted me irresistibly by its romantic turn. I never
should have thought it possible that such pure and just notions of
human life could be treasured up in that beautiful mind, which evidently had received rather a singular turn. Even the prejudices of
education, the national notions of her country, and the frailties of
the human heart, had, either by accident, or by an innate talent,
given birth to adorable virtues. What an angelic heart was here to
gain!

A walk in the garden being proposed, she took hold of my arm
with the innocent familiarity of a sister; stopped at her favourite
spots, and informed me, with an inchanting simplicity, where she
sometimes had thought of me. "Don't be angry, dear Marquis,"
she added, "if I now and then, perhaps, have intruded upon your
dreams by an obscure omen; for I really believe that this is possible;
and Adolf repeated your name constantly towards the end of his
life."

How swiftly did the hours elapse in the company of that angel!
The Count, who was elated with joy at my happiness, completely
accommodated himself to the nature of her ideas, and in a short
time spoke in the same enthusiastic strain that was so peculiar to
her. Adelheid found him very amiable, and told it him without
reserve. I was several times in danger of giving way to jealousy; yet
she always reconciled me again by the tenderness she evinced for
me, and by numberless little endearments. The father took an artless and cordial share in the innocent flow of our spirits. The first
rapture of joy was, however, of no long duration.

CHAPTER IX.

The Baron had made us promise, the first evening after our arrival,
to stay some weeks with him; and these weeks were gradually
extended to months. Adelheid's natural seriousness returned by
degrees. The Baron was fond of hunting, notwithstanding his age
and infirmity; it being likewise the favourite diversion of the Count,

they were almost the whole day in the forest; and I was fond of nothing. A small, well selected library did, indeed, agreeably fill up many of my hours; yet still many dreadful chasms were left, and I was obliged to have recourse to walking to shake off the heaviness of time.

Adelheid being fond of exercise, we frequently met in the garden, where we were least disturbed. She seemed to have dedicated the morning so religiously to serious occupations, that I would have intruded upon her on no account. I was, besides, in a very anxious situation. I was sensible of her attachment to me; but could I venture to presume that this was any thing else than a sister's love?

As for myself, I loved her with an unspeakable ardour, with an uncommon patience, and an unexampled resignation. I was formerly too proud to receive laws from the female sex, but now saw myself at once reduced to the most obedient submission. A young girl directed the course of my thoughts at pleasure, and guided the current of my ideas. I had completely lost the dominion over myself, was unexpectedly deprived of what formerly constituted my greatest pride, and there were hours when I shed tears at that loss.

The name of a sister entitled her to many innocent familiarities which transported me beyond myself. The language of friendship flowed from her lips, and I was sure her heart did not give them the lie; yet she never displayed one of those finer symptoms of a strong, over-powering passion; appeared to apprehend and to divine nothing; was always of the same temper, without either reserve or caprice. I did not know that there are female hearts of a nature different from that of the generality. What Adelheid had in common with the rest of her sex, with respect to love, I mistook for a peculiarity of all passions, and tormented myself with my own feelings at a time when I could have been completely happy.

We generally took a walk when the day began to decline. She took familiarly hold of my arm when we were alone; we rambled through different parts of the garden, and a large seat of turf, in the most distant corner, was commonly the spot to which we resorted at last. Adelheid always grew more serious, and at length even melancholy, when we approached it, and I was taken with the same mood. The compass of this world was too narrow for her soul; she gathered matter for new images in other regions: night stole upon us, and threw a deeper gloom over our dreams. A sweet melancholy frequently made us weep, without our being able to account for it. I was generally so much agitated, that the power of utterance failed me. She then reclined upon my shoulder, and looked at me with eyes full of benign tenderness. One evening, when we were in the same melancholy disposition, she took hold of my hand, and pressing it with affection, said, "Dear Carlos, the disposition of your sister renders her very unhappy: it would be very well if she were not to sojourn much longer in this world. But would you then continue to remember me; and do you think you will know me again in another world?"

This and similar scenes overwhelmed me with a speechless melancholy, which gradually began to prey on my vitals. She perceived it, and caught the contagion. The Baron, too, was grieved at my alarming situation. The Count asked me, with tender sympathy, what ailed me? But what could I reply? He imagined that I was happy.

We met one evening in the garden, equally immersed in that gloomy melancholy. I had been in a violent agony of mind all the day long, and almost distracted. Being impatient to get rid of that desponding mood, I took up my gun, and went into the park, where I wandered about till evening was already far advanced. No one knew where I was; and when I was returning to the castle, I met some servants, who had been sent in search of me. Having sent them back, I climbed over the wall of the park, to come to the castle by a shorter way, and, to confess the truth, to meet Adelheid, who generally took a walk at that time.

I really met her, after a short ramble though the garden, absorpt in profound reverie, and walking with trembling steps. She did not observe me, although I was only a few paces distant from her, being occupied with a rose, which she alternately took from her bosom and replaced again. She was pale and dejected, carrying my cane in her hand, upon which she reclined, and frequently fixed her looks. I saw her start several times, looking around with a ghastly aspect, and moving her hand as if speaking with some person. At length she saw me standing close by her side, began to stagger, and I had scarcely time enough to receive her in my arms.

"Good God! Marquis, where have you been?" she said, collecting herself immediately; but that very moment a new misfortune happened. My gun being suspended round my shoulder by a strap, I pushed it back to be better able to support Adelheid; but it was unhappily cocked; the trigger came against the branch of a small tree, the fusil went off, and the ball wounded one of my fingers. It bled copiously; and my hand being lifted up, the blood streamed into the face and on the bosom of the Baroness.

This accident restored her entirely to the full use of her senses, instead of depriving her of it. "Eternal God! what have you done?" she exclaimed, terrified, and instantly pulled me towards an adjacent arbour, to examine my wound, poured the contents of her smelling bottle upon her handkerchief, and tied it carefully up. Having dressed my wound with anxious alacrity, she asked me tenderly, "Do you suffer great pains, dear Marquis?" "Very little on my hand," I replied. "Good God! are you wounded in another place besides?" "Alas! here, here I have violent pains!" pointing at my heart. "What pains you there? Will you not tell it your sister?" she resumed, taking hold of my hand. "Dearest Adelheid, how can I deserve that angelic goodness, how can I made amends for your uncommon tenderness?" "Is this all that pains you? Have you not deserved my love long since? The best amends you can make for my tenderness is to return my love."

"O, then, I have deserved it, and made ample amends; and you, Adelheid, are in *my* debt. After this poor heart of mine has wasted almost all its vital powers in a nameless grief, you ask why it bleeds? Oh! it is dreadful to love without hope; and a *tranquil* return of a *violent* passion is more galling to a spoiled, insatiable heart, than the most rancorous hatred."

A torrent of tears gushed from her eyes, and she began, after a short pause, "You are very unhappy, Carlos, if my tenderness does not suffice you. I have frequently asked myself, in the hours of silent melancholy, whether I am capable of a more ardent love than that which my heart feels for you? I do not think I am. Tell me, dear Carlos, what do you desire me to do?" "What I desire? Can words describe that? I wish that Adelheid would live only for her Carlos, who knows no other happiness but that of thinking of his sweet sister, and would shed his last drop of blood to purchase her felicity."

"Is that all my Carlos wishes? Is not your image the sweetest and the only object of my dreams and of my happiest hours? Does not every blessing of my life depend upon your affection? Does not my heart beat stronger, and my countenance assume a deeper hue, when I see you? Does not your image follow me every where like my shadow? Are you not the only object of my pride, and the sole arbiter of my happiness? Shall I quit, for your sake, father, family, and friends; or live with you in a dreary solitude upon roots? Speak only, Carlos, and your Adelheid will cheerfully obey. The world, nay eternity itself, would be a lonely desert to me without you!"

"Then you consent to become my wife; my faithful, ever adored wife?"

"Wife, or sister. Is there any difference? Or do you think I have a stronger claim to your love as wife? Here is my hand, I will be any thing you wish me to be."

On our return to the castle, we met the Baron, and the Count, who also had gone in quest of me, and with rapture embraced the recovered son and friend. I was happier than words can describe, but found it impossible to join in the lively sallies of their sportive humour. Adelheid was in the same predicament. The Baron perceived our mutual transport, and his cheerfulness encreased.

I went, on the subsequent morning, to the Baron, as soon as he got up, and discovered the whole to him. He conducted me silently to his daughter, who, as well as myself, encircled his knees, and, lifting us up with tears of affection in his eyes, said kindly, "God bless you, my children: you have prevented me." S******i almost was frantic with joy. Before a month elapsed Adelheid was my wife.

We resolved to spend the summer in the country, and to go to Paris the ensuing winter. We were unanimous in all our resolutions. The Count was looked upon as a member of our family, and had rendered himself as necessary to the Baron and Adelheid as he was to myself. How unspeakably charming was the summer to me! I never had enjoyed the fine season with so much hilarity and unclouded contentment. We became every day more susceptible of the blessings of a domesticated life; and our sociable happiness assumed a livelier complexion, and encreased with every hour. I generally spent the morning in private with my wife; the dinner bell summoned us to more common pleasures. Every one of us regaled our sociable circle, after dinner, with the new ideas and observations he had gathered in the course of his activity in the house and abroad.

Adelheid was of a very serious character, and my joviality was gradually mellowed by her turn of thinking. She soon desired me to relate my history, and loved to hear me speak of Elmira. She was pleased with her melancholy disposition, and lamented her misfortunes; but conceived more predilection for the spirit of the confederation, in which they originated, than I wished: she found its principles good, and censured me now and then for having acted with too much impetuosity of passion. We discoursed on this subject every evening which found us alone. While she attempted to penetrate deeper into the character of the different circumstances, she did, indeed, not reconcile me to a society that had caused me so many sufferings, but, nevertheless, subdued my aversion from its principles.

The choice of our sociable pleasures depended on our humour and on circumstances. Adelheid hunted, fished, or walked, with us in the park. She sang uncommonly well, and played the piano-forte to perfection. I played the flute tolerably well: the Count was an adept on several instruments, and the old Baron was delighted with our little concerts. Reading, and the mutual relation of our adventures, filled up the hours which were not dedicated to these and to more serious occupations. None of us had ever enjoyed so much unclouded happiness for so long a period, and none of our sociable circle had ever been so completely sensible of his felicity.

Thus autumn stole upon us unawares. We postponed our departure from time to time, till we could delay it no longer, if we wished to go to the capital. Having informed Count S****** of my marriage, he wrote almost every post day, urging me to come as soon as possible to Paris. We departed, at last; and at the latter end of November arrived at the capital. The political situation in France was, at that time, not yet arrived at that critical state, as to cause a great alteration in the sociable circles. I found my old friends again, united by the bonds of intimacy, and was welcomed with cordial joy. The Count appeared to be cheerful; and, although not completely happy, yet satisfied with his Caroline.

It may be easily conceived what a noise the appearance of my

wife made at Paris, where every new face charms and attracts the
general notice of the fashionable circles. She easily found out the
proper sociable tone which suited every circle to which she was
introduced; became soon the favourite of all assemblies, and the
idol of her acquaintances. She grew in a short time very intimate
with Caroline, notwithstanding the disparity of their characters.
The Baron was animated with new vigour, joined in all our diversions, and forgot the imbecillities of his advanced age. S******i was
his constant attendant and companion; and Don Bernhard was
an agreeable addition to our domestic circle. We all were happy,
or at least, appeared to be so, when a new accident seemed to be
going to disturb our pleasure. Count S****** became, soon after
our arrival at Paris, a riddle to myself and all his acquaintances. He
grew sad, dissatisfied, absent, and irascible. His whims were soon
very troublesome to us, and he frequently treated his lady in a very
harsh manner. I perceived that he preferred Adelheid's company
to all other society; but without concluding therefrom upon the
real cause of his extraordinary change, looked upon it as the effect
of the similarity of their characters, and as an encouragement of
his melancholy. I cemented, therefore, that friendship as much as
possible, instead of throwing the least impediment into his way.
Adelheid, confiding in me and my knowledge of the Count's character, made no difficulty to admit his visits without restraint, and
to receive from him an attention which she considered as a matter
of course in a friend of her husband. I do not know what particular
information S******i had received of the secret cause of his behaviour: in short, he, as well as Don Bernhard, grew every day colder
to him, and jointly endeavoured to interrupt his intimacy with
my wife, by throwing many little impediments into his way. This
served, however, only to add fuel to the flame: he intruded himself
every where upon her; and at length provoked the voice of slander to such a degree, by the violence of his passion, that S******i
and Don Bernhard thought it their duty to inform me of it in plain
terms. I did, indeed, ridicule them for their suspicion, but resolved
to keep a watchful eye over him, and to take the first opportunity to
speak to Adelheid about it.

This opportunity offered itself sooner than I imagined; for she
came one evening, after my return from company, to my apart-

ment, holding a paper in her hand, and shedding a torrent of tears.

"Dearest Adelheid!" I exclaimed, "what is the matter?" Having sent my valet away, she sat down by my side, and began, with a trembling voice, "Carlos, I cannot conceal the insult I have received any longer from you. It would be criminal in me to spare your friend on the present occasion. You certainly have observed how Count S****** has behaved to me for some time. Read this note, which I have found this moment on my dressing table." She gave me the note and I read:

"Don't fear, beautiful Marchioness, that I shall betray the secret your eyes have confessed to me. Will you receive to-morrow night, at eight o'clock, beneath the large lime-tree, a vow which my looks have made to you some time since?——Lewis, Count of S******."

It was the Count's hand writing; I could not be mistaken. My indignation was, at first, so vehement, that I flung it rather violently upon the table, and knocked a glass down. The servant, whom I had sent out of the room, returned, asking if I had rung for him? Having ordered him to retire, I embraced my wife, and promised to remove that little interruption of her tranquillity, without having recourse to violent measures. I only begged her not to change her deport-ment to the Count, and to leave every thing to me.

She seemed, indeed, to leave me with great tranquillity, but was actually far from being easy, and could not help informing her father of it. The Baron could conceal nothing from S******i, and the latter communicated it to Don Bernhard. They all agreed that I ought to meet the Count in the room of my wife, and the latter promised to be present on that occasion.

I was of the same opinion, and resolved to adopt their advice. The Count was, during the day, rather easier than usual. I repaired to the great lime-tree before it had struck eight o'clock, and was astonished to find S****** already there. He read a paper, and kissed it repeatedly; but no sooner did he see me, than he exclaimed, with the greatest fury, "Hell and damnation! I am betrayed: but you, monster in human shape, shall not escape me a second time." With these words he rushed upon me sword in hand.

I was not unarmed, and defended myself against his furious attack; taking all possible care that he should not run against the point of my sword. I exclaimed uninterruptedly, "For God's sake,

Lewis, desist, and hearken to me!" But all my entreaties were fruitless. He uttered dreadful curses, foaming and grinding his teeth.
I disarmed him, at length, and flung his sword into the adjacent
thicket. He looked up to heaven, and ejaculated the most shocking
execrations.

Loud cries behind me now attracted my attention. I looked
round, and discerned Bernhard's red coat though the gloom of
night. He was wresting with a white figure, and on the point of sinking to the ground. Now he actually dropt down. I hastened, half
frantic, to assist him: a dagger glittered over his head in one hand of
his antagonist, while the other endeavoured to stop his mouth with
a handkerchief. I pierced his opponent in the first violence of my
passion, and in that moment perceived that he was *Amanuel*. Tearing the bandage from his head, I beheld *Alfonso*, my faithful servant,
at my feet.

END OF THE THIRD VOLUME.

THE

HORRID MYSTERIES.

CHAPTER I.

My astonishment could not be greater than that of my friends; and it is impossible we could have stared at each other with more terror, if a thunder cloud had unexpectedly burst over our heads, without depriving us of the use of our senses. We were almost petrified; and *Amanuel* could safely have escaped us a second time, if his situation had permitted it.

The shades of night surprised us with an involuntary awe, and the illumination of the sky perfectly suited such a discovery. A black cloud, which seemed to terminate the northern horizon, emitted luminous streams of light, which caused a trembling in the air, as if the upper part of the heavens was, as it were, in convulsions: a universal silence rendered the pulsations of the heart audible; the leaves vibrated with a faint rustling: we were surrounded with phantoms; and even our existence seemed to be a phantom.

Don Bernhard, the boldest and coolest of the company, was the first that raised Antonio up; and the Count gazed at that awful scene, seized with amazement, and scarcely daring to breathe. The working of various passions expressed itself strongly on his countenance, overspread with a deadly paleness. Obscure bodings struggled with expiring hopes. His fury had been excited in a violent degree on seeing himself betrayed; it now had changed its object; but when he was going to give vent to his rage, his noble heart suddenly impelled him to beg my pardon: he embraced me, and wept on my bosom.

Alfonso was mortally wounded. We all were anxious to prolong his life at least a few hours, as his confession promised to clear up the mystery which hung upon the events of my life, and to remove the veil which lay on the incidents of that eventful evening.

When he opened his eyes after a long swoon, his first look was directed at me. I was sufficiently contiguous to him to be sensible of the sentiments it bespoke. It was the look of an expiring man, who reluctantly parts with the idol of his heart; of a guardian angel, who takes an eternal farewell of the object of his tenderest cares, and quits the world with the sweetest of all thoughts, to have executed his great commission. The emotions of his mind imparted themselves powerfully to my soul, recalling the scenes of former times. The ideas which crowded forcibly upon my memory almost overpowered me.

He was, at length, carried to the castle; and the surgeon declared his wound was lethal, his intestines being mortally hurt. He desired to know his real state, and received the candid answer, that nothing was to be hoped from the assistance of art. His great and noble soul seemed to brighten up at that declaration: he smiled with more than human tranquillity at those that stood mournfully around his couch, and then turning to me, seized my hand, and kissing it, said, in a trembling accent, "I have finished my career: I thank you, Don Carlos!"

I cannot recollect what my thoughts were in that awful moment; but they were undoubtedly obscure and confused. Alfonso had made me sensible, on numberless occasions, that I was dear to him: Amanuel frequently had been my guardian angel; he never had rendered me actually unhappy; I had escaped many dangers by his assistance; and if he did accompany me by order of that dreadful confederation, I did not know it sufficiently as to tax him with criminal views. Many of my ideas had been purified during that time; and Adelheid rather had inclined my heart to that mysterious society than rendered it averse therefrom. My whole existence still resembled a dream. I had derived, from my connection with the confederates, the brightest notions; he had, if not occasioned, at least connived at, my sweetest connections; and Alfonso's fidelity and attachment to me claimed my sincerest gratitude.

There are certain periods in human life, in which the thoughts rapidly cross the mind in such a firm union that one surveys them with one look. All the scenes of former times now clearly concentrated themselves in one harmonious picture; I never have seen them again in such a striking and perceptible unison. Elmira, my faithful, sweet, and loving consort, presented herself to my imagination. Alfonso, perhaps, had guided my steps to her, and to the felicity I enjoyed on her bosom; he had, at least, (nothing was more certain,) with the tenderest sympathy of soul, participated in that unspeakable bliss. Alfonso had been the dear partner of my juvenile pleasures, my companion in the sweetest hours of a serene and domestic philosophy: he had shared the sufferings of my deluded and self-deluding hopes, and all the struggles, storms and dangers of an active life. He had given me many proofs of the most cordial and disinterested friendship; and a heart so passionate and sensible as mine does not cast off its old feelings in the first moment.

Adelheid's violent emotions struck me with additional astonishment. She had watched us at a distance, from the beginning of that fatal scene, and drawn nearer on the first noise. Hearing our exclamations, and seeing us standing around the wounded in speechless amazement, she comprehended the whole instantly. She obsecrated the surgeon to exert all his skill to prolong the life of the dying at least for a short time; and being firmly determined to improve even the shortest respite for the satisfaction of her mind, thirsting after the developement of the mysterious veil that hung on the events of my life, was more zealous in assisting my dying servant than the rest. No one divined her motives so well as myself: she had derived presensions from my history, which panted after light and confirmation; they had become the subjects of her sweetest dreams, and she was determined Alfonso should speak, if possible. He surveyed us with marks of the deepest emotion and affection: my wife anxiously watched his looks, presaging, from every expression of his features, important elucidations; and the thought that now the fairest creations of her imagination either would be completed, or entirely destroyed, violently agitated her bosom, and animated all her motions with an uncommon alacrity.

We were standing around Alfonso's couch in silent, awful expectation. Our looks were anxiously cast down, and every ear watched eagerly the lowest whisper; we scarcely ventured to fetch breath. Don Bernhard stood with folded arms at Alfonso's head, closely guarding every change of his features; the Count reclined his head upon my shoulder; and my looks were fixed at my wife, who leaned over the bed, agitated with boding expectation.

We had, in the first hurry, forgot to order the servants to withdraw. They surrounded us, exchanging timid looks, without being able to comprehend or to divine any thing; and their speaking anxiousness rendered the groupe complete. However, as soon as Alfonso seemed to be inclined to speak, Don Bernhard gave them a signal to retire. They were glad to be spared the sight of that mournful scene, and left us instantly.

Alfonso now erected himself a little, as if awaking from a profound sleep, surveyed us with an eloquent look, and putting his hand to his wound, which seemed to give him great pain, lifted his eyes up to Heaven—an awful moment! His features were entirely changed; I scarcely knew him again.

"I thank you, my lady," he said, dropping my hand, and taking hold of that of my wife; "I thank you for the marks of your love, even for having occasioned my death. My friend was misguided: I have overheard your most secret conversations; and it is you to whom he owes his present susceptibility for future happiness."

My wife remained silent; not knowing, perhaps, what answer she should give; for she did not yet comprehend him perfectly. "My moments are counted," he resumed, after a short pause of reflection, "and I feel that I am on the brink of eternity. My papers contain the history of my whole life. They will inform you, my dear Carlos, more plainly of my love for you; of my designs, my fidelity, and more than human tenderness. I received you from the hands of your mother to watch over your happiness. Have you never heard of Count M******?" "Eternal God!" was my sole reply, while I dropt down by his bed-side: "Yes! I recollect you now: you are my uncle." "Yes, I am your uncle, dear Carlos. The favourite of fortune left the luxuries of life to watch in this humble disguise over his favourite's fate. I vowed to my adored sister to deserve your friendship, and I die with the proud consciousness to have religiously kept my promise. I lived for you, Carlos, and now I die for you!"

It is impossible to give an adequate description of that grand and awful scene. It was the most solemn and affecting of my whole life. The greatness of my dear uncle's affection for me, the perseverance in his noble passion, the sacrifices he had made to me during the course of so many years, notwithstanding his claims to splendour, the greatness and the magnanimity of his mind, cannot be described, and surpasses the conceptive powers of the most sensible mortal. I read this clearly in the looks of those that surrounded his couch, deeply conscious of my want of merit. Adelheid shed copious streams of tears; Don Bernhard stared silently at my expiring guardian angel, afflicted with agonizing sorrows; and the rest were without motion, perhaps, bereft of every feeling.

Alfonso resumed, at length, "You have misconceived the confederation; for I was at its head, and procured your admission. I could not design to make you great, without rendering you happy through that greatness. I could direct the circumstances, but could not command over unforeseen accidents. You must not put the latter to my account. I had violent disputes with my brethren on your account. I have saved Elmira's life; and the impostor whom they wanted to intrude upon you in her room, against my will, died by my orders. I kept you out of Spain as soon as I saw myself overvoted by the rest. Rosalia had vowed your destruction; Francisca was the first victim of her vengeance: Count S****** was present when she fell a sacrifice to the hatred of her rival. Don Pedro had betrayed us, and I could not prevent it. I watched over your life and happiness, and renewed your connection with the confederation, because the members now are united again. Carlos! I have some deserts of you."

"My dearest uncle!" I interrupted him, in an agony of grief, and yet without shedding a tear.

"Carlos, these worthy gentlemen, that now are assembled around us, are your friends. Acquaint them with the extent and the merits of the confederation, and challenge them to obliterate me from your soul. I have, indeed, not attained the mark; yet it gives me the greatest satisfaction that I chose my laborious and toilsome career for your sake. You was the sole object of my existence and activity; and now I leave you without a guide. Your genius leaves this world for better regions. You have friends; but let me give you a confidant, whose noble mind divined the aim of our confederation." So saying, he took Don Bernhard's hand, and layed it in mine. That firm and unshaken man broke out into tears and sighs, and embracing my uncle, said, "I comprehend you, my brother; receive my vow."

"Heaven be praised! few only comprehend us. The mystic veil of nature conceals her greatest and finest creations. It is so great and so sweet to be *nothing*, and to *perform every thing*. Yet it is still sweeter to die at the mark. My strength fails me before I have attained it."

"You have given a confidant and guide to my Carlos," Adelheid said, "and me you have overlooked."

"I counted you amongst his dearest and warmest friends: have you not the first place in his heart? Did I not choose you to be his wife, the partner in his future happiness; and a woman like you ought to be satisfied by the merit of having awakened the great and noble ideas which lay dormant in the mind of my Carlos."

"You make me proud, Alfonso!"

"Conclude the bond of eternal friendship in my presence, before I die!" We embraced reciprocally, and he extended his trembling hands to give us his benediction.

"May heaven bless your union! I conjure you to remain faithful to my Carlos, and never to quit the path of virtue and true greatness. No bond unites congenial hearts more firmly than that of a common great aim: strive to attain it; unite your exertions, your happiness, and life; do never forget that the happiness of your fellow creatures is the scope of your existence; endeavour to be deserving of the great confederation. The angel of peace will be your guardian! my spirit never will forsake you. The softest undulation of the air, the sweet-scenting odours, and a mystic rustling, will announce my presence, and recal to your minds the vows you now have reposed into my hand. Farewell! My eyes grow dim: the messenger of eternity draws near: the curtain is drawing between you and me. Carlos, give me your hand once more: my spirit will be with you: I die."

He had strained me to his clay-cold lips, and I caught his last expiring sigh from his lips. We embraced each other over his clay-cold corpse, and renewed the vow of eternal fidelity.

None of us was more powerfully affected by this scene than Adelheid. She reflected upon Alfonso's serene departure with an intenseness and perseverance which could not but produce the noblest resolutions. Her soul, which had a natural propensity to every thing uncommon in nature, was fertile in thoughts, and endowed with an extraordinary activity, found in her new-begotten dreams a spacious field for the secret employment of all her faculties. She was conscious that she still was in a sleeping state; yet she consoled herself with her activity in such a charming dream.

"Dearest Carlos!" she said to me, one day, "how unaccountably blind you have been!"

"Could I be otherwise?" I replied. "I not only was suffered to grope in the dark, but my ideas were also designedly confused. I never could disguise my feelings, and my whole soul lay open to Alfonso. I sometimes had formed some new idea, and taken a resolution, when unexpectedly new incidents surprised me, begetting notions of a contrary nature, and entirely obliterated the preceding ideas."

"Any other person, dear Carlos, would have learnt, from that diversity of impressions, mistrust in himself, and circumspection; but you was only plunged thereby into greater incertitude. A great confederation tenderly extended their arms to receive you; you knew that a far-stretching power proceeded from their centre, and yet you was imprudent enough to suspect those great men of a scope which would have disgraced even the meanest and most abject criminal."

"You allude to the crime of regicide, of which I suspected them, and whereby I was deterred from a more intimate union with them. But recal to your mind their words on my admission, the particulars of which I have so frequently repeated to you; consider that I always was used to take faithfully every expression in its natural and peculiar sense, that I constantly looked upon an abalienation from the existing laws as licentiousness, and then tell me, how could I otherwise understand their words?"

"I confess, Carlos, I cease being a woman, if I reflect upon the particulars of your history. It comprises something so super-human, that it transports me to a new world of ideas and wishes."

"You have made me extremely desirous to examine Alfonso's papers; but have only patience a little longer; Paris is not a place fit for studying them. We will return into the country next spring, and then read them together."

"We shall be sufficiently at leisure now; nothing is more certain; for it is highly probable that Alfonso's death has interrupted every immediate connection between yourself and the confederates."

"This is merely *probable*, dear Adelheid. The events and con-tradictions of my life have rendered me rather apprehensive with regard to that point. Alfonso's last words have struck me very much; he called Don Bernhard his brother, recommending me to his guid-ance and confidence."

"You are right: I quite forgot that circumstance. Don Bernhard is, perhaps, more intimately connected with the confederates than we imagine; for his noble mind entirely fits the great designs of that society. His eye was bedewed with tears when Alfonso bade us an eternal adieu: I am inclined to think that they have made that valu-able acquisition but a short time since."

"Any why do you think so, my dearest wife?"

"I know that lofty spirit, who stood alone in the world, proud to be able to pursue the course of his virtues without assistance; proud to be the sole father of his greatness, and to prosecute his career, free like a god, secured by his experience against all common allure-ments. He has, perhaps, received some hints; but Alfonso's dying scene renders it certain that he knew nothing of *Amanuel*."

"I comprehend you; yet the love of Count S****** is still a mystery to me."

"I think I can pretty well account for it. The relation of your his-tory has made me conclude that the confederates dislike his inti-macy with you. How frequently have they attempted to disunite you! and your plans always miscarried when you wanted to execute them in concert with him. Even his life was already once in danger; and, what is more dreadful, it was, perhaps, their intention to let him die by your hands. Could, therefore, not the affair have been a contrivance of theirs?"

"Perhaps you are right, dear Adelheid. All the circumstances attending that affair confirm and render your suspicion probable. It is not unlikely that his passion for you was excited and nourished by secret hints, without his being aware of it; and his note, which you have communicated to me, relates to another from your hand."

This supposition of my wife threw a wonderful light upon many events of my life; yet a great deal, which, by the subsequent train of incidents, was completely cleared up, was, at that period, not quite plain to me. Being now pre-occupied rather for than against the con-federation, I agreed with my wife to make sure of Don Bernhard, as we had great reason to think that he acted a principal part in it; and we beheld in his friendship, insured to us by Alfonso, certain means of attaining a mark which now was the chief object of our life.

CHAPTER II.

Winter glided away slower than usual, because we awaited the setting in of spring with the greatest impatience. My wife's suppositions soon received the strongest confirmation. Don Bernhard was no more than a novice in the confederation, whose members had been prompted, by their knowledge of his character, to slip some papers into his hands, which thawed his frozen heart, clearing up many events upon which he had reflected for some time. He naturally hated and scorned men, merely to be able to relieve them more effectually; and being obdurated against tears and sufferings, proceeded over ruins and bleeding corpses towards his great mark of perfection. This being the very principle upon which the confederates acted, it was natural that he beheld in them his brethren.

Alfonso's death evidently contributed to give the necessary impulse to the phlegmatic course of his blood. He fell with eagerness upon Alfonso's papers, reading them through with impatient haste. He then studied them with an indefatigable application, extracting the spirit of the confederation, and transplanting every thing that suited him into his own mind. He never had been so cool and so reserved as he was during that period: when I begged him to return the papers to me, he always replied, "I am now occupied to digest them; give me only time to regulate my system properly." He then seemed again to cheer up a little, visited us more frequently, and when he found Adelheid alone with me, always turned the conversation in a natural manner upon our discoveries. One could easily discern, by his expressions, that they flowed from ideas which were going to attain an unshaken stability. Being no strangers to his inquisitive and penetrating turn of mind, we were certain that he now had learnt every thing he was desirous to know.

Count S****** being firmly convinced that Alfonso had misguided him, and divining, perhaps, more of the truth than we at first could imagine, began to avoid the company of my wife ever after the fatal catastrophe in the garden. Yet his susceptible heart still carried on a very dubious contest with his understanding. On begging Adelheid's pardon, after Alfonso's death, he had vowed to her, on his knees, an eternal friendship, which could not but be very suspicious to me; and even my wife had taught me to behold him in a different point of view. I still continued to be his warmest and most cordial friend, yet I suspected the impetuosity of his passions, the deplorable disposition of a disappointed lover, his undeserved dissatisfaction with me, and finally, futurity, which constantly threatened me with unexpected momentous incidents, and the contradictions of chance. S******i and my father-in-law seemed, however, to have entirely forgot all the gloomy impressions of the time past. I may truly say, that never two men, of such different characters, were so intimate; and that never an obdurated misanthrope so suddenly was turned into a jovial rake as the old Baron. They were constantly upon their legs; and one may justly say that no person ever had more extensive connections at Paris than them. They were every where welcome, and famous for being the cheerfulest companions of the whole capital.

They involved us also, against our inclination, into their revels, dragging us to numberless assemblies, feasts, and card parties; and seeing at last no possibility of resisting them, we submitted with a good grace to their importunate and pressing invitations. Adelheid had an excellent talent for every thing; she shone in every company; and, without designing it, was every where the first person. I watched Don Bernhard strictly, and perceiving that his stern mien began to gain more mildness, found no farther difficulty to abandon myself to all the extravagancies of a gay life.

Our chief rendezvous was at the palace of the Duchess of B******u, who, at that time, was the toast of all companies. We met every night at her house to sup with her; every one had something to relate; and her table, which was frequented by an incredible conflux of people of all nations, afforded an inexhaustible source of the most entertaining observations.

We met, for instance, almost every night, two most extraordinary country squires, Lord T******d of Derbyshire, and Mr. de R****** of the Mark. Both of them were caricatures of a curious sort; unpolite, learned, and without a grain of plain sense. The latter of the two sparks became particularly remarkable to us through an adventure which made all Paris laugh.

He had taken it into his head to pay his court to my lady. Adelheid, being not inclined to disturb our common pleasure, took care not to intimidate him, but treated her admirer with the finest coquetry, which always afforded us new matter for amusement. He made verses upon her, and even honoured me with wonderful poems in my praise. But we paid him in the same coin; I did not read his verses, and Adelheid laughed at them.

He grew at length so pressing, that his love began to be troublesome to the whole company. Count S****** maintaining still some little claims to Adelheid's affection, took the trouble to grow jealous of him, and, in order to get rid of him, devised a plan, which promised to make him an object of general ridicule, and thus to drive him out of Paris.

One day Mr. de R****** scarcely had stept into a bookseller's shop, where he frequently used to spend whole days, to learn all the titles of the books by heart, to hunt after and to invent anecdotes, when an old lady, of a very unsuspicious appearance, entered, saluting him with a familiar air, and telling him that she wanted to speak a few words in private to him. Having retired with her to a contiguous apartment, she informed him, with the most honest and simple air, that a young lady had sent her to let him know she wished to have a private conversation with him.

Poor Mr. de R******, who was an amorous fool by profession, and a poetaster into the bargain, fancied to be transported to the gates of Paradise on receiving that message. His imagination got the better of his scanty portion of reason, and he began to fancy that *young lady* was dying of love for him. Yet, if he had not learnt that she was a lady of quality, he would have scorned her invitation; for Mr. de R****** talked constantly of his noble and ancient pedigree, though his real father was not known. He, therefore, accepted the invitation with the greatest cheerfulness, begging the antiquated messenger to lead on, and to be assured that he would follow her step by step. He was conducted through a number of streets and alleys, till his local knowledge of the town was entirely puzzled; and he, at last, arrived in one of the most notorious lanes of Paris.

Though his courage, which naturally was not very great, had

visibly dwindled away with every step he proceeded farther into that labyrinth, and was covered with a cold sweat, yet he replied, with an intrepid accent, to the repeated exhortations of his conductress, to fear nothing, "I am not afraid! indeed I am not, my good woman!" He possessed a natural talent of finding every thing very natural, that, perhaps, would have struck every other honest man. For all people he met with in the streets contiguous to that where he finally stopt, had gazed at him with visible astonishment; and, on his arrival in that famous lane, all the windows were opened, and a number of young ladies gazed at him with significant smiles, bowing to him as he passed them. Mr. de R****** was, however, very far from suspecting any foul play; and conceived no other idea, than that he, perhaps, was handsomer than his looking glass had told him, marching onward with the greatest satisfaction at the admiration which his fine person created.

Being elated with the flattering idea of his all-conquering charms, he was transported with the sweetest hopes, and his apprehensions were silenced at once. He stept, at last, in high spirits, into a small house, of a good and decent appearance, which was opened by his rusty conductress. Having ascended a few steps, a lady, who had been waiting for our Adonis, flung her hands round his neck, strained him to her heaving bosom, and covering his face with burning kisses, and a few tears, exclaimed in German, "Oh! my brother, my dearest brother!"

R******, who, notwithstanding the roughness of his manners, was proud of being a German, was enraptured with the melodious accent of these words; and although he could not recollect ever to have heard of a sister, yet thought proper to give the fullest credit to that artless effusion of innocent nature. He returned, therefore, her endearments with an equally ardent tenderness, and went with her to her apartment, rejoicing at having met, at last, with the first female being that had so much self-denial to receive him with tenderness, or only to endure *his* caresses.

He was shewn to an apartment, whose furniture bespoke taste, and no small degree of wealth. He beheld every where an abundance of plate, exhibited in an artless manner, rich carpets, excellent prints and pictures, and finally splendid dresses, which were negligently scattered about, most of which Count S****** had sent thither the preceding day. They were, afterwards, served by the Count's people; and the girl, who had strayed from Saxony to Paris, had been so minutely instructed of Mr. de R******'s family circumstances, that, with a good stock of natural cunning, she could not fail acting her part in a most imposing manner.

Having led him to her sofa, she began her embraces anew. Tears of joy glided from her beautiful eyes upon her rosy cheeks; her swelling lips were immoveably fixed to those of her new brother; and she imitated the tremulous accents of the most ardent and heart-felt feelings so successfully, that the poor fellow began to sob as loud as herself.

The first scene of that dumb act being successfully finished, Mr. de R****** ventured to ask the young lady how he came to the honour of being received by her as a brother?

She replied, with an oath, that no person could have a greater right to call him brother than herself. Instead of suspecting this mark of her low extraction, he mistook it for the indignation of a noble mind that felt itself injured. She availed herself, with great dexterity, of his emotion, making a seasonable use of the information she had received of her employer; and, at last, nothing was clearer than that Mr. de R******'s father had seduced Julia's (thus the girl called herself) mother at B******, where he had resided for a short time to settle some family affairs, and afterwards treacherously left her and her child to shift for themselves.

Though such incidents are not uncommon in the great world, yet Julia seemed to be half distracted at it, mistaking the son for the perfidious father, and loading him with the bitterest reproaches. She blended tears and sighs so dexterously with the most pungent invectives, that poor R******, who, in his heart, called all the saints to his assistance, begged her pardon, again and again, in his unhappy father's name, and protested, in the most solemn manner, that he would do every thing in his power to make amends for his father's cruelty.

Yet she was not satisfied with his protestations, but swore a dreadful oath, that she had come to Paris for no other purpose than to avenge herself and her mother in his person, taking, at the same time, a large knife from under the cushion of the sofa, and declaring that she would cut his cursed throat.

The sight only of an edged instrument made our hero faint. He scarcely ever had ventured to take a pistol without a lock in his hand, from fear that it would go off if a misfortune should happen. One may, therefore, easily conceive how dreadfully he was agitated at such a sight. His teeth began to chatter violently, his knees to beat together, and his hair to bristle up. He obsecrated the furious fair one in a trembling accent, and, with quivering lips, to spare his life, calling Heaven to witness, that he was as innocent as the child unborn; and, at length, called for assistance.

He wore, indeed, a large sword, but seemed to be more in fear of it than of Julia's knife. The latter being, however, not ignorant that even fear sometimes will urge a certain class of people to perform astonishing deeds, suffered herself, at length, to be moved by his supplications, tears, and solemn promises, and concluded a peace with her dear, recovered brother.

The merriest humour gradually obliterated every vestige of that threatening tempest. R****** was easily charmed, and the happiest being, if one only began to make game at him, taking the bluntest mockeries for sincere compliments; and found, in every conversation, something flattering for his family pride. Julia was, besides, very handsome; and R****** could not help wishing that she was not so nearly related to him.

The visible signs of this wish, which was legibly written on his countenance, animated Julia with the highest satisfaction, and enabled her to acquit herself of her task in a most successful manner. The liveliest sallies of wit followed each other in rapid succession; and an overflowing vein of good humour, originated, perhaps, in the Count's presents and promises, charmed the happy R****** in such a degree, that he swore never to have spent such an agreeable evening. Julia related to her new brother a number of family anecdotes, which convinced him, in the strongest manner, that she was really his natural sister, whom he ought to cherish and to respect. An excellent supper, served up on the Count's plate, completed their good humour. The most exquisite viands, and the neatest wines, completed the idea R****** had formed of the quality and fortune of his sister. She not only did not demand money of him, which would have thrown him into the greatest confusion, but even offered him her purse, if he should want it; and he secretly resolved to avail himself, on the first occasion, of that acceptable offer.

The time glided imperceptibly away amid the laughter of merriment, and it now struck twelve o'clock. The night was, indeed, extremely fine, the moon shining with an uncommon brightness: the streets, too, were still crowded with people; but Julia persuaded her brother so firmly that it would be highly dangerous to go, at that hour, through the intricate mazes of ill-famed lanes and narrow streets, that he comprehended, at last, it would be better for him to stay at her house. Being offered the use of an apartment, which was far enough remote from her's, even the nicest delicacy could not have objected against her proposal. R****** began, therefore, to be animated with additional cheerfulness, and enjoyed the good things which were set before him with an encreasing appetite. The wine did not fail to produce the desired effect; and at two o'clock, when midnight silence swayed in all the streets, he found himself inclined to go to bed. His drowsiness was so powerful, that one eye always shut itself reluctantly when he had just succeeded to open its neighbour with the greatest difficulty: in short, he found himself necessitated to desire Julia to shew him to his apartment.

She conducted him herself to a distant chamber, whose windows opened into a narrow lane; and having acquainted him with the commodities of the apartment, embraced him once more, and wished her dear brother a good night.

She had no sooner retired, than R****** began to undress himself slowly. This occupation dispelled his drowsiness a little; and having disencumbered himself of his garments, he went to the window, without either stockings or small cloaths, to enjoy the refreshing breezes of the air, the night being extremely hot. All around him was as silent as a church-yard, and he had now the best opportunity to reflect on the strange occurrences of the day. He could not deny that the whole adventure was rather unaccountable, and was incapable of comprehending how his sister could have found him out in such a large town. Yet he soon made himself easy by some conclusions suitable to the shallowness of his diminutive understanding, and, having shut the window, went to lay down.

On his way to the bed, he recollected that he had first some business to settle before he could go to rest, and opened the door of the closet, which Julia had pointed out to him, for that purpose: but, alas! while he was making the necessary preparations, the boards beneath his feet gave way, and he fell with a terrible noise into the street.

Count S****** having not had the intention of doing him the least hurt, all the mud which could be collected had previously been gathered beneath the closet, which rendered his fall extremely soft. Being, however, so unfortunate to turn himself in the air, and to arrive in his bed with his head foremost, he found it rather difficult to extricate himself from his unpleasant situation. Yet he succeeded, at last; and lifting up his head, found himself surrounded with odours, which plainly told him the whole extent of his misfortune.

He began, at first, to curse his mishap; but being as yet ignorant of the original cause of this accident, he rose patiently, with his usual phlegm, apprehending no greater misfortune than to catch a little cold before the door should be opened for him. He, therefore, hastened to knock at the house, but received no answer. He repeated his blows, and still not the most distant sound of footsteps was heard within. It is impossible to describe the despair to which this additional misfortune reduced the poor fellow. The night air sported cruelly with his shirt, and nothing was more certain than that he should catch a cold, which would confine him at least eight days to his bed.

Having knocked repeatedly, without hearing any thing stir, he grew more urgent and noisy, when a window opened, and an unknown female voice exclaimed, "What does that terrible noise mean? what do you want? what business have you here at such an unseasonable hour?"

"Open the door!" he replied; "I shall, certainly, get the toothache: for God's sake, be quick, good woman!"

"Who are you; and what do you want?"

"I am Mr. de R******, a nobleman from the Mark, and want to go to Julia, my natural sister."

"The fellow is drunk," said a second voice, which he knew to be that of his conductress: "have you ever heard of such a name? Pour the chamber-pot upon his head, Charlotte!"

Nothing could have terrified the poor fellow more dreadfully than that exhortation: he retired into the middle of the lane, to get out of the reach of that threatened inundation; and incessantly exclaimed, "For God's sake! children, don't you know me? Upon my honour, I am Mr. de R******."

"I never have heard such a name! Go about your business, good friend, and don't disturb honest people in their sleep."

His violent and repeated knocking against the door, meantime, had roused the whole charitable sisterhood from their sleep, and in a short time all the windows in the lane were crowded with female faces.

The tranquillity and honour of one of their sisterhood being at stake, all of them joined against him, loaded the poor naked fellow with the coarsest invectives, and threw stones and rotten eggs at him, threatening to come down and to tear his eyes out, if he should dare to disturb their rest once more.

Poor R****** now was in the most distressing situation; for not every one likes to be exposed to the chilling night air, without either stockings or small cloaths, and to be mocked into the bargain. He was almost distracted; and being urged to the height of his distress, ventured to knock once more against the door with all his might; but at the same moment a window was opened, a man of a most terrible aspect, which was rendered the more frightful by a pair of enormous whiskers, looked out of it, and roared, in an accent that would have terrified a lion, "Who are you? Whence do you come, and what do you want?"

R****** was almost petrified with terror, and gazed speechless, but with speaking looks, at the terrible man.

"What do you want, you dog?" the man repeated. "I am coming down directly."

With these words he shut the window, and was going to make good his words; yet I cannot say whether he really came down, for Mr. de R****** trusted to his cold, but alert, heels, and was far enough from the house before the man could reach the street door.

Mr. de R****** being happily arrived in the next street, fell, most unfortunately, into the hands of the patrol, who conducted him to the lieutenant of police, to whom he related his lamentable tale at large, and, in the course of a few days, it was repeated with many additions in all the fashionable circles of Paris.

CHAPTER III.

The winter passed away; and Adelheid was, at length, tired of all the pleasures of the capital, longing for the country, and, perhaps, also for her native fields. The Baron, S******i, myself, and my wife, returned to the country-seat of the former, which my matrimonial happiness had rendered dear to me.

We did, however, not mean to be rusticated there for ever, but had formed the most charming plan for our common pleasure and amusement. Don Bernhard, Adelheid's intimate friend, who was in a close correspondence with her about her new ideas, which yet were in an infantine state, had given us a promise to pay us a visit in the middle of the summer: we agreed, therefore, to postpone our more serious philosophical investigations to that period; and, mean time, to enjoy the innocent pleasures of the country, and of a congenial and uninterrupted harmony of souls suitable to it; to think little of, and never to mention, futurity; and to cultivate, with our neighbours, a cheerful and unrestrained intercourse. A young man, whose name was G******, and who had retired with an amiable wife into the country, was our nearest neighbour. He had travelled a great deal, and experienced still more. He now consoled himself in the circle of his family for all his disappointed hopes; was happy in his retirement from the world; rich, without possessing a large fortune; and content, though debarred from the common pleasures of the wealthy. His character was stamped with a certain cheerful philosophy, with a certain unconcern for every thing that did not immediately relate to him, which rendered his conversation very attracting and desirable to us. His lady was of a high rank, and had eloped with him from her native country. He banished himself from the friends of his youth; but his heart, which was not corrupted, but only had been afflicted by undeserved sufferings, procured him every where new ones. He consoled himself for the stain his honour had received, by the consciousness of having injured no person but himself, by the happiness of his wife, and his own contentment and tranquillity. Possessing a small independent fortune, he amused himself with writing. We read the products of his pen jointly; and I observed, with pleasure, the cheering influence the fancies from another and a better world had on his situation, and the disposition of his heart. His lady had disencumbered herself, in the arms of an attentive and tender consort, of all the prejudices of her rank, and was grateful to him for the sacrifice of his fame and friends he had been obliged to make to her. She was a woman fit for every situation, and lived amongst us as if she always had been a member of our sociable circle.

Through G******'s assistance I obtained a greater knowledge of literature. The prejudices and transformations of it, too, afforded many opportunities of attaining knowledge of the human heart; for a man of learning blends with his sentiments and foibles all the little follies which adhere to mankind in general. We all instantly know ourselves in the different pictures which are set before us; and it is rather owing to accident, than to a peculiar exertion of an author, if some individuals are more painted to the life than the rest.

"You are almost entirely secluded from the world, dear G******," I said to him one time: "fame, of course, can have no influence on you; why, therefore, do you write, and why so much?"

"I am not so much secluded from the world as you think," he replied. "I still possess friends, who remember me with tenderness; who excuse me for endeavouring to justify myself at least in their opinion; who take a silent and tender interest in my domestic happiness; who rejoice, for my sake, to see me gain the regard of other people; and, perhaps, too, to deserve it more and more. I do, indeed, not hear what my readers think of me, yet this does not lessen my joy at those compositions in which I succeed."

"But give me leave, dear G******, to repeat my first question: Why do you write so much? Would you not accomplish your purpose better, if you were to polish more, and to dedicate more time to the elaboration of your compositions?"

"This would be the case if I did occupy my pen with serious investigations. However, the subjects of which my works are composed, the airy and gay children of a warm and active fancy, to which the language naturally accommodates itself, always appear to greater advantage at the first stroke, than if produced by a slow and anxious elaboration. I observe every thing that is going on around me as much as possible; however, I observe my own imagination with more attention; and the principal fault of which I find myself guilty, rather consists in an irregular exuberance than in a sterile dryness."

"I find (said I) that an author is exposed to so many mortifications, that I do not think I should be able to prevail upon myself to publish any thing. For instance, criticisms."

"Not to so many as you, perhaps, think, (he replied,) in a situation like mine. I hear not much either of praise or censure, and derive all possible advantage from the little that comes to my knowledge. I frequently imagine that the critics speak of some other person when they censure me; and being used to apply the errors and defects of every one to my own improvement, I coolly select those remarks which I think can be applicable to myself too. Thus, dear Marquis, we advance in perfection, and vex our enemies, and those that envy us, by the consciousness of having, against their will, contributed to our perfection."

"I admire the equanimity which you oppose to public fame, though you know that it is not much in your favour; particularly, as your domestic situation urges you strongly not to let a discovery be made that would justify your character at once."

"Do you know what consoles me for that trifling misfortune? My happiness, the felicity of my wife, my independence, and the firm persuasion, that the truth will unfold itself sooner or later without injuring us, if prudence only has prompted us to conceal it for some time."

We lived extremely happy together; and what else could we have wished? The Baron, S******i, G******, myself and our two amiable consorts, composed a more than tolerable society. We had no other care but that of enjoying life; and sweetened the unavoidable, but transient, difficulties of it as much as possible.

V******l is a charming spot, and possesses every thing that can render a rural life agreeable. Adelheid and G******'s lady were very fond of fishing; V******l and S******i partial to the pleasures of the chase; I loved agriculture; and G******, mean time, composed some pretty tale, whose moral and application represented some scene of our life and nature in an amusing and useful manner. Our time being unemployed by serious occupations, we were at leisure to criticise him: little amicable disputes arose; he altered, or persisted, in his opinion; but always confessed to have derived some benefit from our criticisms, particularly from those of the ladies; for a female ear is the best judge of the purity and the graces of diction.

Don Bernhard arrived, at length; and the presence of such a man produced some change in our diversions, to which the gaieties of awaking nature, our liberty, and the temperature of our blood, had habituated us. I reluctantly sacrificed the simple and unrestrained exchange of our ideas to the more serious and important train of thoughts which a new companion produced within me, and I could not but perceive that the rest were in the same predicament with myself. Even Adelheid, who naturally was inclined to melancholy, had, till then, been as thoughtless as the rest of our sociable circle, and taken a more than passive share in our sports and diversions; and if, sometimes, our little feasts and amusements really were blended with some romantic charms, they were certainly the produce of her enthusiastic turn of mind. Yet it was high time a change should take place in our manner of living, lest we should have awoke of our own accord, sooner or later, from our sweet dreams, which, without doubt, would have been attended with more painful sensations: it was highly beneficial to us that Don Bernhard roused us softly to restore energy to our minds.

His soul, mean time, had conceived great designs: he felt an internal irresistible impulse to realise his resolution: and being sensible that his remorseless severity had, indeed, proved advantageous to himself, but that he could expect to derive no benefit therefrom as an active member of a far-stretching confederation, he condescended with more mildness to men. He took a friendly share in our notions, so widely different from his; and while he seemed to embrace them with ardour, found an opportunity of removing them imperceptibly from the theatre of our souls.

One may easily conceive how frequently the confederation became the theme of our conversations. G****** knew very little of, or seemed to have scarcely any feeling for it; and not being destitute of a sufficient share of perceptivity to form a proper idea of its greatness, his silent indifference vexed the proud Don Bernhard more than the most decisive enmity would have done. Long and never decided disputes arose. We could, at least, not decide, at first, on which side victory had inclined; yet Don Bernhard carried, at last, the palm; for his cause was just; he was cooler, and not so discordant, as G******, whose chief argument always was deduced from his own happiness and patient tranquillity.

"Of what use would it be," said he, "to sacrifice the gratifications which are within our reach, to a happiness that is placed at such a distance, and perhaps not even attainable for us?"

"So *you* think, Mr. G******," Don Bernhard replied: "and I confess it is easily believed in a narrow domestic circle, to which one has been habituated by degrees."

"I think I see your whole system in these words. You imagine that I have been obliged to habituate myself first to that domestic circle, which premises a different disposition: I protest, however, that nothing in the world ever has been less difficult to me than that; that I looked upon all the disasters of my life only as so many rocks, through which one must steer to a peaceful port; and that I have left nothing of that elevation of soul which *you* may have experienced. Thence, I conclude, that, if you will allow me to possess some ability and feeling, men may have similar talents, and yet a different calling and compass of activity."

"Then you suppose *you* are called to adorn a single apartment in the great edifice of the world, and I to make some alterations in the structure of the whole?"

"Very right. Yet I do not think that I am bound to confine myself absolutely to my apartment when I have put it properly in order."

"By that you see what a difference exists between you and myself. You possess talents for particulars, and I believe to possess some for generals; yet I think it is evident which of the two dispositions is more important to the world, and which of these internal impulses excites activity most powerfully."

"With regard to the latter, the spirit for generals is undoubtedly the most forcible incentive to activity; and as for the former, it is equally evident that talents which confine themselves to particulars are more important to mankind. Nothing is plainer than that a man who is born for great purposes, who is hurried on by an irresistible internal impulse, and feels himself endowed with extraordinary faculties, boldly overleaps the limits which are set to the rest of his brethren; yet I also am firmly convinced, that a complete and convenient edifice would be raised, if every individual would exert himself to the utmost of his abilities in the station allotted to him by the great Disposer of the world."

"This is perfectly true; and you have, against your own will, proved my system more strongly than I, perhaps, should have been able to do. The world would be perfect, if every one did *occupy* his proper station; but it is a difficult matter for many to *know* which place is most proper for them; and let me tell you, we believe it to be our calling to remove that obstacle."

"And with what right?"

"With more right than the profoundest moralist defines the duties of mankind, and enforces the observation of the same: for, do we aspire to any reward; do we claim any compensation for our trouble? Is it not a fundamental principle of our society, that titles, rank, and splendour, are nothing but fools jackets; and that it is the first step leading to perfection, and real activity, to wander through the world unknown, and subject to few wants? And do we not apply that voluntary independence to study men whom we design to lead towards the goal of happiness, even against their own will? A long and uninterrupted active experience; a compass of activity, which one can change without difficulty in every moment of life; a far-stretching and noble family, upon which one reclines; a certain futurity, which the firmness of our dispositions at least renders pretty independent on fate; all this must rouse even the most phlegmatic spirit to an indefatigable activity. And, finally, my dear G******, you will confess that, to have built a house upon a high mountain, and above the clouds, is materially different from having erected one in a valley, where every loose rock exposes us to the danger of being buried under its weight."

CHAPTER IV.

Towards the autumn Don Bernhard proposed to return to Spain. S******i had taken an amicable interest in our union, while he was spared the trouble of taking an active part in it; but now he pleaded numberless excuses for staying with the old Baron at V******l. Count S******, too, who was invited to accompany us on our jour-

ney to Spain, started many objections; and Don Bernhard, myself,
and Adelheid, departed without them.

We arrived at Alcantara, at the house of my mother, the best and
tenderest of parents. I had informed her previously of the death of
her brother, and we now mingled our tears. Her bosom was animated with sentiments, the force of which I scarcely deserved. It
is so sweet to love a mother, and to be beloved by her! Adelheid
soon became her favourite. Her mild seriousness, her melancholy
sensibility, open to the sufferings of her fellow creatures, and ever
active to alleviate the misery of the distressed, and her attachment
to every thing that belonged to me, rendered her dearer to my heart
every day. I certainly should have relinquished the confederation
with all its great prospects, if Adelheid had not been capable of
taking an equal share in it with myself: but Don Bernhard pacified
us on that head, and seemed to have sufficient authority for doing
it. He was very active for the confederation, but carefully concealed
his proceedings from us.

With how much pleasure did I now introduce my dear wife to
the theatre of all my former sufferings and amusements! The voracious tooth of time had, however, made great havock at my castle
during my short absence. Every thing was suffered to decay after
the death of Don Antonio, the friend of my juvenile days. The
castle was in a ruinous state; and its dilapidated walls now let me
perceive secret communications, of which Alfonso could avail
himself with safety in executing his plans. The whole fabric of my
mysterious adventures now was exhibited to my view in a palpable
sketch. Don Pedro's castle had met the same fate after his disappearance; and I found no where a monument of my happiness, not
a vestige of my tears was left; all the favourite spots, where I used
to give audience to anxious and serene meditations, had lost their
attractive charms, and even the rivulet was dried up. This scene of
general destruction seemed to have been designed to prepare me
for the succeeding events. I relapsed into my former melancholy.
Adelheid having a natural propensity the same way, sympathised
with my ideas and feelings; yet our reveries opened our mind to the
most elevated hopes, notwithstanding the melancholy gloom that
hung upon them.

Don Bernhard returned, at length, from a secret expedition, and our discourses soon turned upon a single object; and it dawned gradually in our souls. After Don Bernhard had left us repeatedly on secret business, he returned, one morning, from one of those excursions, more cheerful and serene than he was used to be. "To-morrow night, Don Carlos!" he said smiling: "To-morrow night, Adelheid!" We had left every thing to him, and instantly comprehended the meaning of his words. My dear wife was violently affected by this intelligence; I felt all her limbs quiver in my embraces: soft blushes overspread her charming face; her sparkling eyes were animated with the smiling dawn of new hopes. We mounted our horses the subsequent day with the setting in of night; and the wild, mystic forest, with its awful terrors, received us. I conducted Adelheid to James's cottage; and all the former scenes crowded again upon my imagination, yet without creating the least sensation of fear.

Don Bernhard made us proceed by an easier path than that which the old man had led me. The setting sun concealed his blushing orb behind the lofty trees, but left a soft twilight behind, which, being blended with the nodding shades between the mossy rocks, the ancient oaks, the colonades of tapering fir trees, and the ruins of decayed buildings, reflected an unspeakable grandeur upon all the surrounding objects, and elated our souls, which expanded themselves more and more with the gradual encrease of the awful shades of night.

Adelheid was of a manly turn of mind, but had not yet divested herself of all womanhood in such a degree as to be able to meet with tranquillity a moment, the presension of which always had thrilled her frame with a chilling tremour. We endeavoured, indeed, to inspire her with courage: however, her perturbated heart made her change colour more than ten times in a minute; she scarcely could keep the saddle, and the reins visibly trembled in her hand.

Night having thrown, at length, her mystic veil over the face of the earth, we alighted from our horses, and tied them to a tree; I took Adelheid's hand under my arm, and we followed Don Bernhard, who turned into a narrow foot-path. Profound silence reigned all around; scarcely a breath of air was stirring, and the palpitations of our hearts were distinctly heard. A low humming noise vibrated in our ears from a distance like confused whispers, and lights skipped through the bushes. The sensations I had formerly experienced on this awful spot crowded on my memory. The scene changed, and my ideas imperceptibly turned into the recollection of Count S******'s history. I beheld again the bushes he had described to me in such a picturesque manner. My imagination led me through the various mystic scenes he had experienced, and, at length, into the bower where Francisca's arms received him.

Adelheid felt my heart beat violently under her hand, whispering, in a tender accent, "What is the matter with you, dear Carlos?" I pacified her anxiety: however, Francisca's fate rushed irresistibly on my imagination; and, alas! I felt that the burning kiss she had pressed on the Count's glowing cheeks was intended for me.

A sudden glare of blazing flames now illuminated the forest. We directed our looks to the alley which was before us, and beheld a numerous procession moving towards us in an awful pomp. A low, majestic song, interrupted, by intervals, the solemn silence in which they advanced. A train of priests and priestesses unfolded themselves gradually from the confused throng. They were clad in long white robes; their hair, which was decorated with flowers, floated down their shoulders in artless ringlets. I beheld again most of those apostolic faces at which I had gazed with trembling awe on my first reception. They saluted me with serene heavenly smiles on passing by with their torches. I beheld my brethren celebrating my return with rapture.

Amongst the priestesses, who carried covered baskets, I instantly descried my dear Rosalia. She glanced at me with soft blushes, and the tears started from her beautiful eyes. Her looks then turned with the smile of heavenly resignation on Adelheid, who squeezed my hand tenderly, whispering in my ear, "Is this Rosalia?"

Don Bernhard joined the train at last. We followed his example, and soon approached the avenues of the castle. We descended the long vaulted passage, and, while I exhorted my trembling wife, entered the blazing hall.

The members seated themselves on the exalted chairs; the reverend old man embraced me, and all my brethren advanced to give me the fraternal kiss. The vow was now taken from Don Bernhard and Adelheid, and blood streamed mingled with tears. Awful, immortal words were uttered; and, on raising our looks from the ground, a curtain was drawn. Unspeakable, mystic rites commenced; celestial sounds struck our ears with rapture; heavenly visions astonished our gazing eyes; all presensions were accomplished, and the boldest hopes silenced by reality.———

CHAPTER V.

I must once more take up the pen, which I imagined to have laid down for ever on the close of the last section of my memoirs. All my misfortunes seemed to have happily terminated at that period, being blessed with the possession of a faithful and dear wife, an attentive confidant, who was animated by the same spirit with myself, encircled by a large number of tender friends, arrived at the pure source of the most exalted ideas, and at the goal of my fondest wishes. My fate seemed to be settled for ever, and unadulterated felicity appeared to have firmly rooted in my mind for the first time. But, alas! while I was preparing myself to enjoy the blessings of life in peaceful serenity, treacherous time secretly engendered new events. The life of some people is never blessed with a long point of rest; and the few hours of enjoyment and serenity which now and then come to the relief of their worn-out spirit, seem to be designed merely to revigorate them as much as is required, if they shall not sink entirely under the load of their adverse fate. An invisible hand administers a strengthening cordial to them to revive their desponding spirit against the eruption of new tempests.

My adventures are of that complexion. The power of the storms, which hunted me through the variegated but gloomy scenes of my eventful life, seemed frequently to be exhausted: however, the roaring thunder always burst again over my head, when I scarcely had proceeded a few steps on a flowery ground, exhilarated by the smiles of a serene sky. I frequently imagined my strength was completely exhausted; but an unexpected event always enabled me to discover new resources hitherto unknown to me. I was oftentimes in the situation of a weary, exhausted wanderer, who, surrounded by midnight darkness, enfeebled by hunger and fatigue, and drenched by pouring tempests, flings himself down on the slippery ground in an agony of despair, and suddenly discovers, by the light glare of a vivid flash of cracking lightening, a hospitable cottage close by his side. Thus they teach us to know ourselves, and that every thing changes, as well as that this mutability is of great benefit to ourselves. One says very little if one compares human life with a *romance*; it is much more than a *fairy tale*, or a *summer-midnight's dream*.

CHAPTER VI.

We spent the whole night in the performance of rites, whose simplicity and harmony rendered them very fit to impress upon the affected heart those things whose symbols they were. We considered ourselves as one family, and the whole world as our habitation. Being initiated in the plans, and the most secret connections, of the society, surveying all its collateral branches, and the whole extent of its influence, knowing how to direct and to preserve the latter, and being informed of its internal strength, it was but natural we should be transported by the consciousness of our importance, and that all former ideas of joy and happiness were obliterated by the impressions our minds received from the ecstasies of that night.

I do not know how it came that I took a cooler and more inconsiderate share in the general festivity than the rest. The first powerful impression I received from the mystic pomp died soon away, my senses grew more sober, and I plainly perceived that several rites were inadequate to the purpose for which they were intended. My feelings being not quite the same with those of the rest, I was, as it were, already excluded from their circle, reflected seriously upon the relaxation of my imagination; and, while I watched the other members with attention, to find whether none of my brethren was of my opinion, my coldness encreased gradually. Having never been able to disguise my real sentiments for a long time, my inattention and absence of mind was noticed, and this naturally encreased it.

A faint sensation of jealousy stole, for the first time, upon my heart: I observed that Adelheid's senses were intoxicated with ecstatic rapture; and saw her mingle with the rest, elated with the highest enthusiasm. Her ardent and eager fervour distinguished her in a most striking manner from the other females; and she even appeared to me to take more notice of her new brethren than of my self, and to seek Don Bernhard's hand and looks in an uncommon and striking manner. The recollection of former intimacies and familiarities I had observed, but not much regarded, forced itself, at the same time, again upon my mind. I frequently had heard her launch out into the warmest praises and admiration of his under-standing, which never appeared weaker and more diminutive to me than in that moment. If, therefore, I would not believe that a secret sympathy existed between them, I could not but suspect Don Bern-hard's mysterious sneaking officiousness towards her.

The whole throng of these ideas, unfolding themselves with so much the more violence and rapidity, the longer they had, perhaps, fermented in my soul unknown to me, blunted all my senses, enfee-bled my attention, and gave to the awfullest solemnity the appear-ance of a miserable farce. These ideas received an additional force by Rosalia's patient, modest, and affecting deportment. Her char-acter seemed to have been totally divested of that incredible firm-ness and energy with which she seasoned her tenderness for me on that blissful morning, and which afterwards occasioned Francisca's horrid catastrophe. The progress of time seemed to have weaned her from love, and instructed her mind in the patient humility of a saint. Her speaking looks were directed at me with expressions of a silent grief, yet I could not discern whether I or herself was its object.

Alas! I recollected but too well that blissful time, that day which Rosalia made fleet away like a single hour, all her heavenly charms, and the ecstatic rapture of my senses. My soul was involuntarily absorpt in that charming recollection. Sensations which admit of no description pervaded my whole frame: I felt that my face was cold, and all my blood rushing towards the heart; a tear of sensibil-ity started from my eye; and turning round, I beheld the astonished looks of the assembly directed at me. Rosalia's beautiful face was covered with blushes; I lost the use of my senses, and was ready to drop from my seat.

Some drops of water, which were sprinkled in my face, restored me to recollection, and I beheld all my brethren anxiously occu-pied with my person. Rosalia leaned mechanically over my head. I searched for Adelheid, and beheld her leaning upon Don Bernhard, and absorpt in deep conversation. She even had not perceived that I was not well; and observing it, at length, she gave me a look which almost petrified me. Such a want of tenderness and attention was certainly unpardonable: my pride awoke; I resolved to be revenged for her negligence. A few moments of reflection restored me to the full use of my faculties, and I beheld the whole extent of my misery. "This is the fruit of the influence of such societies," thought I: "this is that very Adelheid who doated upon me before she had seen me. Who would have thought that she could have changed thus?" The mystic rites were, at length, finished with less devotion and awe than they had excited at first. I had interrupted their course; and as, perhaps, no one, but Rosalia, guessed the real ground of the violent emotions which agitated me, the whole assembly were alarmed at the consequences which might follow. My uneasiness was raised to the highest degree by Adelheid's visible unconcern. She dissembled, perhaps, designedly, not to have perceived any thing, whispering, more than usual, to Don Bernhard; attempting to cure me, thereby, of every sensation of jealousy, and preparing a severe curtain lecture against our return to my castle.

The poor woman was, however, much mistaken; for she sooner could have tamed a furious lion than appeased my boiling anger. Don Bernhard, who had studied my character better than her, seemed to have a secret presension of it. I am certain they consulted what was to be done: he appeared to dissuade her from her resolution; however, she would not listen to his advice. We took leave, mounted our horses, and returned home in profound silence; neither of us uttering a single word. My heart was agitated with certain melancholy sensations, for which I know no name; and Count S****** occupied my mind more than ever. The tenderest friendship had united us for many years. It was very well known to the confederates that, while I should continue to love him, no other sentiment would be able to get the sway over my mind. Was it honourable to separate us in such a manner? "Alas!" thought I, "love is nothing in comparison with the intimacy of two congenial friends. The years of our union glided away like minutes. Not one gloomy hour disturbed our life, before the fatal influence of that society began to exercise its baneful sway over me. Our friendship was so cordial, so disinterested, and afforded us so many hours of heavenly bliss! May the blessing of God attend my dear Count, and reward his unspeakable love for an ungrateful wretch!"

These sentiments almost overpowered me, and loud sobs interrupted the profound silence which prevailed in our society. I clearly saw Don Bernhard give a hint to Adelheid, who stopped her horse, and then turned him towards me; yet she could not directly find words, and relapsed into her former reverie.

"What does that change mean, Carlos?" she began, at length.

"I know of none, Madam," I replied, in a cold and cutting accent, which came naturally from my heart. That woman was then an entire stranger to me, and methought I never had known her. My resolution was taken, and I did not care for the rest.

The tone in which I spoke to her had the desired effect. It was the first time she ever had heard such a disagreeable sound from my lips. She was confounded, and seemed to look for advice in Don Bernhard's gestures. But, probably, the good man had none for her; and she attempted to disguise her perplexity by boldness, like people that have no good conscience.

"I am astonished, Don Carlos, to hear you answer in that unkind accent; I never have heard you speak to me in such a strain. What ails you? what is the matter?"

"Nothing, Madam! as I already have had the honour to tell you."

She relented when she perceived the agitation of my mind, and resumed, in a milder accent, "What ails my dear Carlos? Does he know his Adelheid no more?"

However, she uttered these words in such an artificial, trembling accent, that they only served to increase my contempt of her. The heart cannot be deceived when the enchantment that has fettered the senses is removed. I beheld that comedy with the eyes of an indifferent spectator, shook the hand she offered me with cold civility, and then dropt it again, though she endeavoured to hold me by one finger.

This polite and firm coldness, which was not blended with the least bitterness, offended her in the highest degree. She set spurs to her horse in the first ebullition of her anger; but instantly stopped him again. The animal raised himself upon his hind legs, while the body reared up in the air; she staggered, and I scarcely had time to alight, and to receive her in my arms.

The horse, in the mean time, ran away in full speed, and Don Bernhard went after it, while I was occupied with my lady, who was ready to faint. Having restored her to the use of her senses by the application of a smelling bottle, I mounted her upon my horse, and led it by the bridle.

"You will excuse me, Madam, for taking the bridle in my hand, for a short time; but I think you don't ride so well to day as you are used to do."

She returned no answer to this remark, which stung her to the heart; yet I could plainly see that her bosom almost burst with boiling anger. We exchanged not a word more on our way to the castle: I walked slowly by the side of the horse, without letting the bridle loose; and although I perceived, unobserved by her, that she surveyed me sideways with scrutinizing looks, yet I did not once lift my eyes up to her. We arrived, at length, at the castle; and having assisted her to dismount, handed her up stairs. When we came to her apartment, I opened the door, and making a low bow, said, "I dare say you will lay down a little, though this morning is already far advanced;" and left her without staying for the answer she was going to return.

She shut the door of the anti-chamber softly, but that of her own apartment with uncommon violence. I went into the garden to let my passion cool, and soon after heard Don Bernhard return with the strayed horse. He enquired, with evident concern, after the Marchioness: however, she sent word she could not see him, upon which he left the castle without inquiring after me.

CHAPTER VII.

I was at a loss how I should treat Adelheid properly. It is of the greatest importance to behave, in such a case, with the utmost delicacy and circumspection, as an unjust and foolish world is but too apt to make the honour of a husband dependent on the conduct of his wife. My suspicion being not yet sufficiently confirmed, I resolved to inform the Marchioness, by way of letter, of my will, to postpone more rigorous measures till I should be able to collect more convincing facts, and to continue to live with her on a polite footing, but to refrain from every familiarity, which only would serve to render her more secure. I determined, at the same time, to treat Don Bernhard as usual; to watch, however, his conduct, and to keep my jealousy in proper bounds. This plan was, indeed, prudent enough, but not adapted to Adelheid's violent temper, which could not brook a state of dubious suspense, and urged her to insist upon an explanation. It was, however, certain that I was in danger to be thrown off my guard on such an occasion. She really demanded such an explanation with a zeal that could not have been more ardent if the happiness of her whole life had depended upon it. I am certain the poor woman had, at that time, not yet anatomized her own sentiments; and being strongly persuaded not to have done wrong, boasted upon her innocence, and taxed me with injustice. I apprehended, at first, Rosalia's unguarded looks had excited her resentment, and prompted her to shew more attention to Don Bernhard than usual; however, her refusing to see him was a certain proof that she misunderstood, and wanted to persuade me that he was nothing to her.

I went, at the usual hour, into the dining room. The Marchioness made me wait a long time for her; and having sent the servant twice to inform her that the dinner was on the table, I sat down in pretty good spirits, and with an excellent appetite. I was so much altered, that I scarcely knew myself again. A twelvemonth before I should have been distracted under such circumstances, and incapable to have eat a morsel: but on that day I had a better appetite than ever. I did not think a syllable of Adelheid; the events of the preceding night appeared to me like a dream; and my whole soul was with Count S******, whose image presented itself so lively to my imagination, that no other thought could obtrude upon my mind.

The first course being finished, Adelheid's valet came to inform me that she could not come to dinner, and begged to be excused. I ordered him to tell the cook to lay the cloth in her apartment, when she unexpectedly entered into the dining room, having either repented the message she had sent me, or followed the servant to hear my answer. I returned her silent salutation, without suffering myself to be interrupted in my occupation. She unfolded her napkin, and seemed to expect for some time, that I should help her: I was, however, too much occupied with myself, than that I could have had the least idea of answering her expectation, scarcely taking the trouble to glance now and then negligently at her. Her looks were cast down, and her countenance was pale and disordered; her hair, which was curled in natural ringlets, depended upon her heaving bosom. I remarked by myself that she looked much better than when dressed for a ball. Yet my ideas returned soon again to my dear Count, to our cordial intimacy, our common adventures, the duration of our union, and the worthless wretches who interrupted it.

She began, at length, after a long pause, during which she scarcely had breathed: "I see you have a very good appetite, Don Carlos!"

"Nothing, my dear, is more natural." Having given a hint to the servant to retire, I continued, "you know I have not slept a moment last night, and this morning I have run about in the garden and the park to dispel my drowsiness a little; and exercise, you know, sharpens the appetite. But shall I help you to this or to that dish? You seem to have not much appetite, and your face is extremely pale. I hope last night has not hurt you?"

"Very much, as it seems, Don Carlos."

"Is it possible? yet this is the course of this world. No pleasure is unmixed with some bitterness. (The Marchioness did not reply a syllable, struck with astonishment at my merry humour and the volubility of my tongue.) In short, the most amazing and unexpected changes happen in this life. Last night no person could be happier, more attentive, cheerful, and communicative, than that very Marchioness who now is sitting before me, mute, musing, pale, and without the least appetite. Who would think, my Lady, that you are a native of France?"

She held her napkin before her face, probably, to conceal the tear that started from her eye. Her countenance was overspread with a glowing redness, and her eyes sparkled with anger when she removed her hand. I pretended to be struck with astonishment, exclaiming, "Gracious Heaven! you are in a high fever, Madam! Shall I give you a glass of water?" So saying, I pushed my chair back, and started up.

"Don't trouble yourself, my Lord," she replied mildly. However, she could not disguise her rage, gnashing with her teeth, and adding, in a trembling accent, "And, believe me, you would be the last person of whom I could accept a service."

"Then I shall ring for a servant." I rung the bell. "James, you will find a glass with a red powder upon my writing desk; make haste, and fetch it; your Lady is not well."

"I don't want it, Marquis!" The servant having withdrawn, she added, with a killing look, "It is, perhaps, poison, my Lord?"

I was going to give vent to my rage, but fortunately recollected the part I was acting. "No, it is the red powder you bought for me at Paris. Who could have thought that you would want it first? Poison!" I added, after some reflection, "A man of understanding could draw a number of fine conclusions from that question. For instance, that you have adopted very strange principles, and are totally infected by the spirit of a certain society."

"Is this the only cause of your displeasure?" she said, with visible satisfaction, deceived by the unexpected turn of my discourse. "Is that all? And who made me first acquainted with that spirit?"

"Did I do it? Look at these glass panes, on which the name of *Elmira*, a sacred name, is inscribed. This is a fragile glass, and has stood storms and tempests; and my heart is a marble, from which time can obliterate nothing."

She comprehended me entirely, and shuddered; I do not know why. She either envied Elmira, or apprehended to meet with a fate similar to her's. The first passion that steals upon the heart is always the most powerful, and it might, perhaps, have hurt her that I recollected it.

"You are right," she replied: "it is very difficult to obliterate old and powerful impressions."

It appeared to me that she wanted to lead me, by this observation, imperceptibly from the chief point; I, therefore, interrupted her: "I did not make that remark with regard to you, but to that society, with which you seem to be entirely captivated. You tax me with having pre-occupied you in favour of it, and nothing is more untrue. I was entirely tired of it before our marriage. It tore me out of the arms of my best friends, because they did not suit the plans of the confederates: those infernal fiends connected me with people whom I did not love, perhaps with no other view than to carry some of their secret purposes."

"Do you speak of me, Marquis?"

"I speak of no particular person; my remark is entirely general;

however, I was born free, Madam; and it is insupportable to be governed by a master whom we have not chosen ourselves."

"Who has forced that master upon you?"

"Can you seriously ask that question? First of all my unfortunate fate, from which I, at last, succeeded to disengage myself, after it had robbed me of every thing dear to me; and then you, Madam."

"I! Marquis?" she replied, more joyfully than she, perhaps, ought to have done. I saw but too well how much it was her interest to mislead me from the point in question. I was, however, less ductile than she had expected.

"Undoubtedly, you!" I resumed with some heat. "Recollect only your new discoveries; your secret conversations with *your friend* Don Bernhard, who, sometimes, was locked up with you for hours; and your warm disputes with me, which were the result of the ideas he instilled into your mind. This will always be the consequence, if a married woman presumes to reform the world. She cannot avoid getting into numberless dangerous connexions; and our worthy friend G****** justly observes, that real domestic happiness entirely depends upon the tender and undivided love of a wife that is attentive to her duties, and sets no value on other goods, that can contribute nothing to the improvement of the former."

Adelheid shed a torrent of tears during that lecture, to which she wantonly had provoked me. Her sobs and tears made, however, very little impression upon me; my heart was obdurated, and I had begun to persuade myself firmly, that much art was concealed under her pretended innocence and candour. "Yet," I replied, with some acrimony, "these are only general remarks, which have no relation to you."

"Is this the consequence of my tender love for you, Don Carlos?" she replied, wiping the tears from her face. "One ought to expect such abuses, if one is so inconsiderate as to lay one's heart too much open to you proud lords of the creation."

This awkward shift of eluding me vexed me uncommonly; and I exclaimed with rising indignation, "What name do you give to those little hints which I have taken the liberty to suggest as a friend? Abuses, Madam? I think the Marchioness of G****** needs to fear none, particularly from her husband. Your expressions are very severe. You will excuse the liberty I presume to take. No one will be better able to judge of the motives of your behaviour than yourself. I always have reposed an implicit confidence in your understanding, and I hope you will never forget that your own honour depends entirely upon the preservation of mine."

"May I make bold to ask you, my Lord, what part of my conduct is so offensive to you, that you cannot see the motives of it? I hope you are not jealous of Don Bernhard?" This question was attended with a laugh, which rendered her completely despicable in my eyes; and I replied very seriously, "Madam, you have just now given me an instance of the principles of your nation; but I must tell you that in this point, I am a true Briton. If you were only my mistress, I should demand nothing else of you than not to endanger my health; but having honoured you with the rank of a wedded consort, I insist that you betray the weakness of your heart to no person but myself."

In lieu of an answer she gave me a look, which, at any other time, would have made some impression on me; but the times were past in which beauty could divert me from the execution of a plan. She now abandoned herself to a profound reverie; being, perhaps, astonished at the discovery of a new side of my character. I did not stay for the dessert, but made a low bow and retired.

I imagined that I could let the whole affair rest here. "It is impossible (thought I by myself) that Adelheid should have been so entirely debased in such a short time. A prudent woman is not likely to risk much if she knows that her steps are closely watched. The most violent passion only can urge her, under such circumstances, to go great lengths; and it is not probable that it should have rooted so firmly in Adelheid's heart. Too much love on my part has, perhaps, rendered me indifferent to her; and Don Bernhard may have seduced her from her duty by too much art and flattery. The hint I have suggested to her will assist her to see the impropriety of her conduct, and I shall be able to restore harmony between us without exposing her to the world."

Thus I endeavoured to dispel every apprehension from my boding mind; but I was mistaken; and, in the course of a few minutes, had an opportunity of perceiving my error. I was scarcely arrived at the door of my apartment, when I heard the Marchioness call to the servant in a most vehement accent, that she should not be at home whenever Don Bernhard should inquire after her.

This order, which bespoke but too plainly the real state of her heart, afflicted me more than words can express; and I was on the point of running down stairs, and recalling it; but considering that this would only serve to encrease the painful consequences of her imprudence, and expose us to the servants, I desisted from my intention.

The more I reflected upon this circumstance, the more dreadful did its secret import appear to me. Adelheid's temper was extremely violent; I had offended her; nothing was more certain than that some secret understanding existed between her and Don Bernhard; I frequently had observed clandestine hints, and almost imperceptible assignations; though I had reason to conclude, from their imprudence, that my honour had not yet been injured. I could, therefore, not suppose that Adelheid would sacrifice her friend to a mere suspicion on my part, and that she must know some expedient to make him amends for that public denial of admission. The horror which that clandestine correspondence caused me can be better felt than described, for I was but too sensible that this would totally ruin my domestic peace, and encourage Adelheid's secret aversion from me, which was but too evident. Not having deserved the latter, I could not but ascribe it to Don Bernhard's artifices and cunning; and it would have distracted me, if I had not possessed so much pride, and suffered a considerable abatement in my love for the Marchioness, since the last fatal night. This, however, enabled me to think with more coolness of the properest measures for obviating the injury my honour was threatened with.

I determined to sift Adelheid more closely, in order to fix on the best plan of recalling her to her duty, and made repeated attempts to see her: however, she always pretended to be busy, and begged to be excused, which made me conclude that she was writing. Don Bernhard came to the castle against evening. I observed that he was received by one of Adelheid's waiting women, who, for some time, had been very suspicious to me. She went with him into her own apartment, whence I justly concluded that she either informed him of my difference with my wife, or wanted to give him a letter. Having staid some time with her, he mounted his horse, and rode away, absorpt in profound thought. This incident fixed my resolution either to carry Adelheid back to France, or to confine her in a cloister.

Thinking, however, that it would be proper to consult my mother previously, I ordered my valet to get my horses ready the following day against noon, informing him that I intended to make a short excursion to Alcantara to see my mother.

My chief motive for doing this was to let the Marchioness know it in time, and thus enable her to prevent the execution of my design if she should suspect my intention. However necessary such a step appeared to me, yet I did it reluctantly, on account of several circumstances, and I sincerely wished to avoid it.

At night I ordered the cloth to be laid in my bed-chamber. Adelheid generally used to come to me; but that time she sent me an invitation to sup with her in her own apartment, which I declined. Alas! how weak is the human heart! This little incident rendered me unable to get only a wink of sleep all the night long, in spite of my weariness. I was repeatedly tempted to get up, and to pay her a visit; only the uncertainty how she would receive me kept me back. I dressed myself; but laid down again, groaning, complaining of her want of love for me, and cursing my fate, Don Bernhard, and myself. The night elapsed amidst numberless follies; and I do not know what would have been the consequence, if the rising light of the sun had not restored me to a proper use of my understanding. But, fortunately, the inebriation of my reason was dispelled by the encreasing splendour of the morning. I settled my little affairs with the greatest tranquillity, in order to lose no time after my mother should have given her opinion, and gave all necessary instructions to my confidential servant to keep a watchful eye over the Marchioness during my absence, and at last sent up a good morning to Adelheid, letting her know that I was going to Alcantara for a short time. Having settled every thing, I flung a small gun over my shoulders, which I always used to do on my excursions, mounted my horse, and rode away.

While I was going through the castle gate, I turned once more round. The Marchioness stood upon the balcony, and looked after me: her countenance was overspread with the rosy hue of health, and her eyes sparkled with pleasure. She was dressed in a loose gown, and wore a hat exactly of the same shape and colour with

that in which I saw her the first time in her father's park. This observation afflicted me severely. I waved my handkerchief, which I carried in my hand; she returned my farewel salutation, but went into
her apartment before I had passed the gate.

This new mark of indifference and disrespect tempted me
strongly to return instantly, and, instead of going to Alcantara, to
order the carriages to be got ready, and to set off with her for France
that very day. Finding, however, on maturer consideration, that
it was my duty to see my mother first, at all events, I dropt that
design; and no sooner was in the open fields, than I forgot all the
injury I had received.

CHAPTER VIII.

When I drew nearer towards the famous forest which was the theatre of my most remarkable adventures, the image of Rosalia stole
suddenly upon my heart. Her soft looks had made a deep impression upon my mind; I now reflected upon them, and on her ardent
love for me, which made me think that it would be very unkind to
quit her, perhaps for ever, without taking leave. My hand directed
the horse mechanically towards the castle in the forest; I was on the
road which led thither without intending it, and arrived at James's
cottage before I was aware of it. I had sent my servant before me,
and ordered him to await my arrival in a public house on the road
to Alcantara: I, therefore, tied my horse to a post in the cottage, and
went in search of Rosalia.

I was soon profoundly absorpt in the reflection on the memorable incidents in which I was engaged in these environs; and every
object I met, every tree, and all the vestiges of former cultivation
my eyes beheld, reminded me of past events. The tears started
from my eyes when I arrived in the avenue leading to the castle,
which had been repaired, and received a more decent and modern
front. I was told that Rosalia was in the garden; and a cold tremour
pervaded my frame on that intelligence; my heated imagination
recalled all the images of former times, and filled me with anxious
bodings. The setting sun seemed to imitate, with his faint rays, the
serene morning which led Rosalia into my arms. The aromatic

exhalations of the orange trees, the hollow murmurs of the purling rills, and the rustling between the young leaves, recalled former
scenes of happiness to my mind; and every soft, melodious vibration of the warm vernal air seemed to convey to my listening ears
one of those sweet accents with which that enchantress ravished
my organs on that happy day when I saw her the first time arrayed
in fairy charms.

My impatient looks descried her, at length, on the very spot
which had witnessed our first interview, and I hastened with eager
steps to meet her. Her form was the same as on that momentous day, except that the budding roses of her virgin charms had
unfolded themselves in full splendor. I gazed with enraptured looks
at the harmonious symmetry of her elegant shape, which was set
off in a most advantageous manner by the simplicity of her dress,
and could not help groaning, "Alas! that master-piece of plastic
nature once was in thy possession!"

She saw me when I came nearer, but suddenly turned into a bye-
path. I imagined she wanted to shun me, though I perceived nothing in her steps that indicated flight. A secret voice in my bosom
urged me to follow her; and no sooner had I stept into the bye-path,
than the charming enchantress enfolded me in her arms, imprint-
ing burning kisses on my eager lips.

"Dear, dear Carlos!" she whispered, "how much am I obliged
to you for this kind visit! I knew that your generous heart would
remind you now and then of your Rosalia; I knew that the man upon
whom she doats could not forget her entirely." I pressed the sweet
girl to my heaving bosom. Her glowing face, which she reclined on
mine, had a freshness which I then felt for the first time; the tender
sentiments of her heart spoke plainly through her sparkling looks,
the soft enamel of love blushed on her dimpled cheeks, and the
quickening pulsation that heaved her swelling bosom thrilled me
with sensations of unspeakable bliss.

"Beautiful angel of love!" I exclaimed, with admiration, "have
you really fostered these sentiments so long in your breast, to bless
thereby once more your unfaithful Carlos without either hatred or
jealousy?"

"Unfaithful, indeed!" she replied: "you have called it by the right
name. But don't speak ill of that sweet traitor: I have forgiven his

treachery, and am changed from a mistress into a warm and tender friend."

"This renders you dearer to my heart than ever. The flame of passion lasts for months; whereas the tranquil, modest and unassuming warmth of friendship unites two congenial souls for ever. Entertain these sentiments always for me, sweet girl; count upon me as a brother in every emergency. Where could you hope to meet with the same sentiments in a higher degree than in the heart of a man whom you have loved once?"

"I am rather vexed, Carlos, that that time is past; yet it is better to have something than nothing at all. I receive you with unspeakable joy as a brother, and always shall take a fond sister's share in your happiness."

She then gave me one of *her* kisses, which were the children of purest nature. Her inmost sentiments ascended upon her rosy lips, imparting their original warmth to them. Her soul resided visibly, and, as it were, embodied in her looks, or mixed itself with a soft sentimental tear gliding down her dimpled cheeks.

Perceiving that the day was on the decline, I disengaged myself from her embraces. "Dear Rosalia," I said, "you see, by my gun, that the chase and accident have brought me hither. I thank my stars that I have met you; but now I must be gone. Give me one kiss more, and then farewel!"

"You say that with smiling looks, Carlos," she replied; "but I have no great confidence in them. Your visit has some mysterious meaning; and it is a stale invention of yours to ascribe it to the chase and accident."

"If it has any, it is no other than the desire of seeing you once more."

"Once more, Carlos!"

"I mean in private, and without being interrupted. Are we not watched by more than an hundred eyes, and who knows what may happen?"

She shed a copious stream of tears, whispering, "I comprehend you, Carlos: but I fear nothing; I am your sister, and thank you for this melancholy proof of your love. You could, undoubtedly, be more explicit with your sister; yet do as you think proper." "But swear," she resumed, after a short pause, "that you will return once more.

No! no! do not swear. You have already sworn a dreadful oath in yon bower, and dared to break it." (She shuddered, and grew deadly pale.) "I have kept it sacredly, Carlos." So saying, she enfolded me again in her tender arms, and, reclining her wan face against my shoulder, continued, "I always have been faithful to you; and what woman would not have done the same?" I sighed. Fortunately she mistook the real motive of my visible agitation, which her last words had wound up to the highest pitch. "Farewel. May Heaven's best blessing attend you, Carlos!" she added, sobbing. "I know your heart. Our cursed fate has forced you to be forsworn; else you would certainly have been more faithful to your Rosalia. She would not have been obliged to be satisfied with the mere name of a sister; and, alas! you would, perhaps, have been as happy with her as with another." "I certainly should, dear Rosalia; and perhaps happier! You justly call our fate cursed: Heaven only knows how it will terminate."

"Take courage, Carlos. I will watch over your safety; and endeavour to warn you of every danger with may threaten your happiness and life."

With these words she strained me again to her panting bosom, and then disengaging herself reluctantly from my arms, fled into an adjacent grove.

I returned to the cottage, and was so profoundly absorpt in various thoughts that I almost missed it. The difference between Rosalia and Adelheid was, indeed, extremely striking; and yet the latter had not the least reason to complain of me. I loved her most ardently, and never missed an opportunity of convincing her of my fondness. "Thus women are! thought I. They are flattered by a conquest only as long as it is not entirely accomplished, or threatened by some danger." The refreshing shades of evening were already descending when I arrived at the cottage; and I consulted with myself, whether I should join my servant, and spend the night in a sorry public-house, or sleep in my own bed, and make up for the delay in the morning.

After a short consideration, I preferred the latter, and rode so slowly back, that I did not arrive at the castle before it was completely dark. I also had missed the road, diverted by various thoughts which crossed my mind, and was at the back-gate of the park when I imagined to be arrived at the drawbridge.

I dismounted, and fastened the horse to a tree, intending to send a servant for it, opened the gate with a master-key, and went through the little myrtle boscage towards the castle. I could see no light in the bed-chamber of my lady, which looked into the garden, and a general silence prevailed in the environs of the castle. I imagined the Marchioness was already gone to bed; and although the evening was not far advanced, yet I reflected no farther upon it, opened the castle gate softly, and went with all possible precaution up stairs. I met not a single person; but heard some people converse in the kitchen, and in the apartments of the servants.

I do not know why I feared being discovered; whether I was prompted to tread so softly by a desire to see how the servants behaved while I was supposed to be absent, or whether the human mind really has a presension of future events. I trembled like an aspen leaf, and feared every moment to meet some person, without being able to account for it. However, I collected myself, and was going to proceed to my apartment, when I saw the door of Adelheid's anti-chamber wide open, and beheld a faint light in her sitting room.

"I will bid her a good evening, I thought; lest she might form no favourable opinion of my stealing thus like a thief into my own house. I, therefore, went boldly onward, but found her apartment empty. Two candles were burning upon her working table, which had very large snuffs. "Where can she be?" said I to myself. "I hope she is not running about in the damp night-air; she will certainly catch cold."

I sat down to await her return; but feeling something under me, I got up, and saw a man's hat lying on the chair. I imagined, at first, that it was my own; but, on closer examination, found that it belonged to Don Bernhard. I flung it vehemently upon the floor, in the first heat of my passion, stamping it with my feet; snatched a candle from the table, and ran into Adelheid's bed-chamber. The bed was, however, empty, and in perfect order. I recovered a little from my violent agitation, returned slowly and softly to the sitting room, and having laid the hat on its former place, waited a little longer; but hearing some person approach, concealed myself behind a screen, where the Marchioness used to have some cloaths hung up, and made an opening with the bayonet of my fowling-piece, large enough to enable me to see what was doing in the apartment.

The Marchioness appeared almost instantly, led by Don Bernhard, who made room for her on the couch; and having pushed the table a little farther back, seated himself by her side. I certainly should have imagined the whole scene to be the produce of fairy art, if I had had the least belief in enchantments and transformations, either being wonderfully changed. Adelheid's face was all in a glow; her beautiful countenance never had expressed so much life and internal emotion. My blood began to ferment; and yet I could not help gazing with admiration at the heavenly form. Her handkerchief was disordered, and, gracious Heaven! it also was doubled in numberless folds.

She trembled, and breathed with difficulty. Her looks breathed wanton desire; her mien, and every motion of her limbs, spoke the language of the most unbridled voluptuousness. There was not a vestige left of that innocence and modest reluctance with which she used to bridle the bold caresses of her husband, nor of that virgin pudency which granted nothing, but yielded every thing to compulsion. I imagined to see a lascivious woman before me who loves the first time, her looks and gestures being bold, nay encouraging beyond expression. Nothing was more certain than that Don Bernhard had mixed something with her wine. The latter appeared to have studiously prepared himself for such an adventure, having changed the simple frock which he generally used to wear for the full dress of a Parisian beau. The roughness and gravity of his language and expressions was changed into the soft whisper of fine flatteries. He always had appeared to me a handsome man, in his natural character, but on that occasion I thought him so absurd and grotesque, that I should have laughed at him at any other place.

His eyes flashed with a wild and criminal fire; his bosom was violently agitated, and his frantic passion almost bereft him of the power of utterance. There was, indeed, no occasion for the assistance of words, as his convulsively trembling hands bespoke but too plainly the wild desires of his heart. The accursed, attrocious villain now prophaned the pure throne of love; and, alas! Adelheid did not prevent the vile attempt.

Having imprinted thousands of ardent kisses upon her agitated bosom, he prepared to consummate the most infernal crime. Adelheid was exhausted, and seemed to be willing to yield to his brutal lust without reluctance. I scarcely could keep myself upon my legs, and was ready to drop on the floor: however, the nearness of the impending danger restored me to the use of my faculties, which the fear of it had deprived me of. Despair roused me from the stupor to which fury had reduced me. I stept forth from my lurking place, cocked my fowling piece, and was going to terminate the existence of the two vile wretches with one ball.

A guardian angel watched, however, over Adelheid's life. The noise I made in cocking my gun made Don Bernhard, who had enfolded my wife in his arms, start up, and turn his head on one side: but he had not a moment's time to recollect himself; I discharged my piece, and he relapsed lifeless upon his mistress.

Adelheid lay in a deep swoon beneath the corpse of her seducer. I was, at first, vexed at her having escaped her doom, and, seizing her by the hand, roused her from her swoon. "Accursed woman!" I exclaimed, with a thundering voice, "awake, to receive the punishment of your hideous crime!" As soon as I perceived that her senses were returning, I pressed her bleeding lover into her arms, and went into the anti-chamber to appease the servants, who, as I apprehended, might have been terrified by the report of my gun. I really met some with candles in their hands, and told them not to be alarmed, as my gun only had gone off through my carelessness, without doing any harm. The waiting women, and particularly Adelheid's confidant, were hastening toward their lady's apartment; but I desired them to retire into a contiguous chamber, and locked them up. I then ordered my confidential valet to go down stairs, and not to suffer any person to stir. I gave him my gun, enjoining him strictly to shoot the first that should offer to be disobedient. He was a brave German, and I could rely upon his fidelity. On my return to the Marchioness, she had entirely recovered, and awaited, not far from the corpse, which lay on the floor, her impending doom. She was firmly persuaded that instant death would be her portion, and wished for it; for how could she ever have looked at me again, without shame and pungent remorse? She lifted her eyes up when she heard me step into the apartment. Her face was horribly distorted: the roses of love, and of libidinous desires, were faded away;

and the grisly spectre of impending death had thrown his grey veil over it. The horror which agitated her mind erected one part of her hair, while the rest, stained with the blood of her seducer, depended upon her forehead. Her eyes were dim, and stared motionless, like those of a midnight spectre, blinking convulsively when they beheld her supposed executioner. Her lips were contorted, and opened only when her straitened bosom could no longer retain her dying groans.

This shocking sight served, however, only to render my indignation more relentless, instead of affecting me with sentiments of compassion. I opened the window, seized the corpse by the throat, and flung it furiously into the garden. "Rise, madam!" I now exclaimed. She endeavoured to get up, but dropt down again. I, therefore, took her under the arm, and helped her up. She imagined, without doubt, that I would throw her after her lover; and said, in a trembling accent, "I thank you, Don Carlos: make haste to rid me of an existence that is a burden to me" Having raised her up, I resumed, "I have seen your wash-hand bason behind yon screen; fetch it, and wash up that blood."

She went to fetch it, obedient to my order, and finding no cloth, took out her pocket handkerchief, wiped her eyes, and kneeled down to clean the floor. She was, however, repeatedly obliged to stop, and to fetch breath. The tears streamed down her face, and mixed with the congealed blood. I stood by her side, lighting her with the candle, and exclaiming repeatedly, "Rub a little more, Madam; there is another spot!"

Having finished her painful task, she dropt with her face upon the floor. I raised her up again; and having lighted a torch, gave it her in her hand, and ordered her to go before me. I then took the bason with the blood, and went into the garden, where I gave the vessel to the Marchioness; and having taken the corpse upon my shoulders, ordered her to conduct me to the hermitage, as the remotest part of the garden. She did not utter a sound, not even a sigh, but trembled violently, and spilled a great deal of the blood. I called repeatedly to her, "Hold the bason faster, Madam!" but she endeavoured in vain to obey me.

We arrived, at length, at the hermitage, and I began to dig a grave in the remotest corner. The ground being very loose, I soon had finished my task; taking the torch from her hand, commanded her to give a farewell kiss to her lover. She kneeled patiently down by the corpse, like a lamb that is going to be slaughtered, and kissed his livid lips; and I was pleased to see that her looks bespoke some aversion. Having buried the body, I poured the blood over the grave, and broke the bason, adding, "Thus I devote thee to damnation and eternal remorse: thou hast robbed thy friend of his greatest treasure!"

Adelheid shed not a single tear during that awful transaction, being, perhaps, too much occupied with reflections on her impending doom. Her dark eye was only now and then directed at me with marks of horror and fear; yet I shunned her anxious looks, and ordered her to lead me back to the castle.

We were not far advanced when I heard the report of a gun. I instantly conceived the meaning of it; but Adelheid shuddered, and the torch dropped from her weary hand. Having taken it up, I took Adelheid by the arm, and led her to her apartment. On our arrival in her sitting room, I placed her on the couch, and said, "Here, Madam, is the key to the apartment in which I thought proper to lock up your attendants: you will be pleased to order your trunks to be packed instantly, that we may depart in an hour's time. On the road you will tell me whether you wish to return to your father, or prefer a cloister in France."

This unexpected lenity overpowered her; she dropt down upon her knees, and kissed my feet. The sudden transition from the fear of death to the certainty of having her life spared, was too much for her, and she was unable to rise again. I lifted her up, seated her again on her former place, sprinkling water into her face, and rubbing her temples. She perceived the emotions of my mind, which must have been strongly marked in my countenance, and was going to kneel down again; but I prevented it, exhorting her to prepare for our departure without delay. "For God's sake! Carlos!" she now exclaimed, in a trembling accent, "For God's sake! Carlos! don't distract me by your kindness: I have deserved death; here is my breast; have pity with me, and put an end to my dreadful agony." With these words she bared her bosom; but I turned my face another way not to see it. "Make yourself easy, Madam," I replied, coolly, "and thank God that I did not surprise you after the consummation of that horrid crime. My vengeance terminates here. I have forgiven you." So saying, I stretched out my hand to her. She covered it with burning kisses, exclaiming, with an unspeakable emotion, "How shall I thank you, best of men, for your forbearance, and more than human kindness, to a criminal, to an ungrateful wife, that, however, rather had erred and strayed than abandoned herself to vice. Heaven will reward your virtue! Alas! I never shall be able to do it!"

She sobbed violently, and I began to fear the consequences of her unspeakable agony. In the first stupor, which had suspended the use of her faculties, she had not had sufficient consciousness to come to a resolution; but in that dreadful state of the bitterest remorse and contrition, the effervescence of her blood rendered her capable to attempt any thing. I trembled to see her absorpt in profound meditation. The whole extent of her guilt, of her lost happiness, her ignominy, and her future misery, the dreadful thought to be torn from me for ever, to be deprived, for the rest of her life, of the care and love of a tender husband, and to pine away her days in the melancholy solitude of a cloistered confinement, to be buried, as it were, alive: all these ideas forced themselves upon her agonized soul; and I could clearly perceive that she wished for annihilation. Every convulsed motion of her ghastly looks thrilled me with the apprehension of a horrid catastrophe.

I seated myself down by her side, taking hold of her quivering hands: "Adelheid," said I, "my poor, seduced wife; do not abuse the weakness of your husband; he has forgiven you; give him no cause for repenting his lenity. Endeavour to convince him, by your future conduct, that you have been seduced only for moments, and that you deserve his compassion. You are yet in the bloom of your life; and a good and noble wife always has it in her power to make amends for past errors, if she is but inclined to do it."

She pressed my hands to her bosom, and then reclined her face upon them. Her speaking eyes, which seemed to rejoice at the preservation of her life, thanked me with an enthusiastic look. But more she did not venture. She resembled a repenting angel, that beholds new hopes at a distance.

"I now shall call your women, Adelheid," I added, "and hope you will make haste to be ready for a speedy departure. We have no time to lose: I am surrounded with lurking spies; the shot you heard fall in the garden, has, probably, terminated the existence of one of them that attempted to escape. I request it as a favour of you that you will discharge Isabel in the next town."

Isabel was her confidant, and Adelheid understood the motive of my request, and, kissing my hands, replied, in a tender accent, "Fear nothing, my Lord: I shall endeavour to obliterate every vestige of my crime." I pressed her hands affectionately, and retired, enlarging her waiting women, and ordering them to go to the Marchioness. My valet had done his duty. We buried the corpse in the garden. The carriages were got ready, and the first dawn of day found us on the road to France.

I asked the Marchioness on the road whether she had fixed upon her future place of abode? She replied that she could not bear to see the face of her worthy father with the deep impression of her guilt, and that she should prefer the cloister at D******, the Abbess of which was a near relation of her's. We now consulted what she should say to her, and the rest of her family, with regard to our separation, and arrived, after a pretty pleasant journey, at D******, where I was to leave her with two of her attendants. No language can express the sensations that agitated my mind when I took leave of her. I scarcely was equal to stand the parting scene. Adelheid had spoken very little during our journey; a deep, mute melancholy had reduced her almost to a shadow; and her woe-worn countenance moved every one who saw her to tears of compassion. A fine woman, suffering with silent resignation, and with the meekness of a repenting or guiltless heart, is irresistible. All our servants, and all those who saw her on the road, were infected by her melancholy. I myself could not resist that secret influence, notwithstanding the strong reasons I had to hate and to despise her. I did as much as lay in my power to cheer her up, and to divert her mind, but all my kindness and attention only served to encrease her affliction. She thanked me with silent tears, and with the modest warmth of a broken, contrite heart; but at the same time proved that she despaired of every thing.

When we got within sight of the cloister, she began, for the first time, to weep aloud, and to bemoan her melancholy fate. She had spent some happy years of her innocent virginity at that place, and the recollection of the rosy hours of her youth crowded on her

mind. She beheld in every object we met a witness of her mirth-
ful age and her juvenile sports; and felt the deepest compunction
that she had rendered herself incapable of enjoying the pleasure
her heart would have derived, under different circumstances, from
a visit to that scene of former happiness. I read these reflections in
her countenance, but hoped that solitude would heal her bleeding
heart sooner than she dared to flatter herself.

We were, at length, obliged to part: I recommended Adelheid
once more to the care of her relation, and then went to her apartment to take leave. She started up from her chair when she saw
me, and rushed without hesitation into my arms. My heart did not
suffer me to repel a wife that I had loved so dearly in such a solemn
moment of affliction; and pressing my lips upon her ice cold cheeks,
said, in a soothing accent, "Be easy, my dearest wife; endeavour to
be reconciled to yourself, and Carlos will not be totally lost to you.
Although that sweet ecstasy of former bliss, that unconstrained
confidence, and that artless and unsuspicious love, which brightened the horizon of our life, should not return quite unimpaired,
yet you will have no warmer and nearer friend than me. My heart
never can wean itself entirely from an object to which it has been
once so completely devoted."

"No, Carlos, take your friendship back again; I will not have it. Do
you think a single drop would satisfy me, since it was in my power
to have emptied the whole cup of love and matrimonial bliss? Do
you think I could impose my miserable delusion upon my glowing
feelings? No, man of my heart, Adelheid would never have deserved
your love, if she could live without possessing it unimpaired. My
destiny was so beautiful; and I have wantonly shortened it; what
else is now left to me, but to die nobly? I have rendered myself
undeserving of your love, but I wish to merit at least your regard.
Give me a parting kiss, Carlos! Alas! I shall see you no more!"

I did not know what to reply, thinking it imprudent to let her
hope too much; and yet I wished to speak comfort to her agitated,
desponding mind. My senses almost denied me their service; her
dying charms, the deadly paleness of her beautiful cheeks, and the
dimness of her eyes, touched the tenderest parts of my soul; and I
replied, in a tone which plainly bespoke the agitation of my mind,
"Do not despair, dear Adelheid; futurity may soften the rigour of

your fate: who knows whether it may not unite us again? Time weakens the strength of all impressions, obliterates their dark sides, and leaves only those that are of a brighter complexion."

"No, no! I will not delude myself by these hopes: and if you would generously receive me again to your bosom, and bless me with the same tender confidence, with the same fullness of unsuspicious affection, which I formerly enjoyed, yet I never would return to it; for every tear of pleasure that should glide from your eye would burn upon my cheeks like corroding poison. But will you grant me one favour more, dear Carlos?" she resumed, after a short pause. "I wear a picture of you on my bosom, which my poor brother gave me, and was my idol before I knew you: will you let me keep it?"

She trembled violently while she took it from her heart, and dropt upon her knees, when I hesitated to return an answer. My feelings were powerfully affected: I rung for her attendants; and as soon as they entered the apartment, quitted it with the greatest precipitation.

CHAPTER IX.

I now resolved to pay a visit to Count S******, being certain that I was not mistaken in my opinion of his noble heart. I did not doubt that it would depend entirely upon myself to find again in him the warmest and tenderest friend. The love which abalienated myself from all other sentiments, and from the whole world, was not able to throw even a light veil over the genial splendor of his friendship. He never hesitated to sacrifice every thing, even the greatest happiness of his life, to me; and I was convinced that nothing but the firm persuasion that Adelheid did not love me, and that I detested her, which was effected by the infernal viles of the confederates, had tempted him to pay his addresses to her.

I went first to the old Baron, where I met S******i; but there I heard that he was returned to his estates in Germany. I informed my father-in-law of the residence of Adelheid, and of the motives of her retirement, pretending, as we had agreed, that a slight indisposition and nervous weakness prevented her to follow me to Germany. The good Baron, who doated upon me, promised to visit his daughter at D******, to write frequently to her during my absence, and complained bitterly of her having preferred a cloister to the house of her father. This affected me more than I can express: and I hinted to him, that Adelheid had been subject, of late, to an unaccountable melancholy, which made her so much inclined to cloistered retirement.

Having engaged myself solemnly to see him again in a short time, I took the road to the estate of Count S******. I was, at first, inclined to inform him previously of my visit, and the plan I had formed; however, it is so unspeakably sweet to surprise a dear friend, that I have dropt that intention; and could I have seen so plainly the amiable disposition of his soul towards me, if I had given him time to prepare himself for my reception? When I came within sight of his country-seat, I dismounted, to get, by a private path, with which I was well acquainted, into the garden; and sent my carriage to the public house, ordering my servant to wait there till he should hear from me. On my entrance into the boscage, the theatre of so many sweet and dreadful events, all the feelings which formerly had pervaded me singly now rushed united upon my heart. The recollection of those events was, at the same time, associated with all the subsequent incidents of my life: I saw the turf seat where Amanuel appeared to the Count, and where his and my life was in the most imminent danger. The ruins in which he was buried alive for some time, every tree, every grassy spot, the undulation of the air, which received me as an old acquaintance, reprocreated in my soul those sensations which they formerly had occasioned or witnessed. I also recollected many children of my invention, and many creations of my sweetest hours; for most of the alterations the garden had undergone, either had been begun or pointed out by me; and I plainly recollected to have sown the seeds of many sweet-scenting shrubs and flowers, which now hailed my organs by their odoriferous exhalations. A father cannot return into the lap of his family with a purer and more heartfelt rapture than I felt when I was saluted by my mute acquaintances and favourites.

Having reached the terrace, the first object I beheld was a sweet child sitting on the turf, and playing with two large dogs. I was, at first, terrified at the danger of the little cherub; but my apprehensions vanished, when I saw him defend himself smiling; and the dogs, who seemed to be used to his childish sports, scarcely daring to touch him, awed by the charms of innocence, or fearful to hurt their little play-fellow. What a soft sweetness did his infantine features express! It appeared to me like the soft blushes of the morning sun smiling on the eastern sky, when the emerging king of day unfolds his cheering rays, growing gradually warmer and more distinct. The sweetest innocent joy, young and unimpaired, sat modestly on his brow; and the happy unconcern of his infantine soul smiled in his serene looks. The sight of that little cherub enraptured me with silent happiness; and the celestial tranquillity of the charming boy imparted itself imperceptibly to my mind; but, alas! recalled, at the same time, former times to my memory, reminding me of my unexpected meeting with Elmira. I beheld again the beautiful nursling of her love, saw him stretched out on his couch, enfolded in the arms of peaceful sleep, adorned with the budding roses of health, and by instinct expanding his little arms to encircle the neck of his long-lost father.

My reflections were interrupted by the approach of a third person. It was the Count, who anxiously hastened to drive the dogs away. He then took the sweet boy upon his arm, pressing his face tenderly against his glowing cheek. What a grand expression of delight and joy did his countenance display! Paternal love, the noblest sentiment of nature, beautifies every countenance, and it gave the Count the appearance of a celestial being. His little darling understood the tender meaning of his caresses, and returned them with a speaking smile. I was transported by that heavenly scene.

The dogs ran, mean time, towards me. They were two old acquaintances and nurslings of mine, and recollected me instantly, bounding joyfully against my breast, whining, and expressing their pleasure by numberless antic gestures. The Count, who, mean while, had seated the boy again upon the turf, was rendered attentive by the barking and whining of the dogs, and, turning round, beheld his old friend. A moment of astonishment, and he jumped down the terrace, and pressed me to his panting heart.

"Oh, Carlos!"

"Oh, Lewis!"

"What fortunate accident has brought you hither!"

"How happy am I to see you again! Best, dearest Count, I already had despaired to press you once more to my bosom." Our tender and rapturous embraces suffocated even those simple and abrupted sounds with which exhausted nature expresses the highest degree of pleasure. Our tears mingled upon our cheeks. Heaven smiled with sympathetic serenity upon us; and the feathered choiristers of the air celebrated our joyous meeting with their sweetest strains. The glowing and sensible imagination never produces more blissful fancies than on the happy re-union of two congenial souls.

He took my hand under his arm, and led me towards the castle. "Although you know but too well all these objects, dear Carlos," he said, "yet you will find a new one." That instant we came to the spot where the boy still was sitting on the turf, playing with flowers, and offering a nosegay to his father as soon as he saw him. The Count took, with paternal affection, his child upon his arm, resuming, "This is my son, Marquis; and your namesake; our little, sweet Carlos!"

"May Heaven be more propitious to him than to his namesake!" I replied.

"How, Carlos?" gazing at me with astonishment, "are you not happy? Indeed, you are paler than usual, and your looks are clouded! But come, the philosophy and sympathy of your friend will soon cheer you up. That angel of goodness that once endangered the peace of your heart, will now assist me to dispel the gloom that hangs over your tranquillity." The good Count imagined to speak in a prophetic spirit; but, alas! how far was he from divining the impending horrors of futurity!

I encircled his waist with my arm, and we proceeded. When we came opposite the balcony, I observed a lady that was leaning over it, and seemed to survey us with uncommon curiosity and attention. Her dress bespoke her to be a person of rank, but her face was entirely unknown to me. It appeared to me extremely ugly; and having reflected for some time who it could be, I asked the Count, with some surprise, "Have you got visitors at the castle?"

"Not a soul."

"Then who was that strange lady on the balcony?"

"I thought you would not recollect her; it is my lady, the mother of this boy."

"Eternal God! then Caroline is dead?"

He smiled bitterly. "No, my friend," he resumed, "I will not surprise you in an unpleasant manner. It is that very Caroline with whom you was so violently in love. The small-pox have disfigured her thus."

I wrung my hands in silent grief.

"But don't be uneasy, Carlos," he added: "I warrant you, you will be more pleased with her than ever. She is, indeed, less handsome, but much, much more amiable than she was at that time."

My understanding did in vain attempt to persuade me of the truth of that assertion, my refractory heart representing her to me as an utter stranger; and my natural aversion from new connexions inspired me with a secret dislike to her. She was once the idol of my soul; and my vile pride was pleased that I now should have nothing to fear from her charms, but even find many opportunities of humiliating her, in case of necessity. A number of vicious inclinations, which I thought to be entirely rooted out, unexpectedly reappeared in that fatal moment: my attention withdrew, however, from the object that had recalled them, and I began to despise myself.

In this state of mind I entered the apartment. Caroline rose from the sofa, where she seemed to have awaited our arrival; and a secret emotion, which blushed on her countenance, urged her to advance a few steps towards us. I took all possible care to disguise my astonishment at the uncommon alteration of her features; yet her own consciousness probably told her more than my looks could have expressed; and she cast down her sweet, unchangeable eye, while she saluted us with a silent curtesy.

The Count came to the assistance of her lovely confusion, and taking me by the hand, said, "Madam, you will be happy to see our old friend, the Marquis of G******, who returns to us after all his adventures; and being, perhaps, satiated by the gratifications of love, means to taste again the sweets of friendship." He pronounced these words slowly and smiling, to give her time to collect herself. Caroline soon recovered her equanimity, and replied modestly, and in an accent which affected my heart, "You are welcome, dear Marquis; but I should be sorry if the latter were the case."

The conversation soon grew more animated; and our former confidential familiarity was completely restored before half an hour was elapsed. I found her face not quite so disagreeable as it had appeared to me at first sight. The marks which the small-pox had left had, indeed, given a different form to her countenance; but the natural softness of her features had resisted all the efforts of the malady. Her lips were as fresh and rosy as ever; her looks were rather more captivating and sweet than formerly; the paleness of her complexion diffused a charming langour over her face; and the consciousness of her loss imparted to all her motions and gestures a soft modesty, which, however, served only to gain upon the heart of the beholder with invigorated irresistibility.

But nothing can be compared with the charms of her conversation. Her voice, which received a sweet insinuating tone from sentiment and some internal pain, the stamp which her feeling heart imprinted upon her words, the vivid flashes of a naturally rash but good-natured wit, bridled by a light tincture of melancholy, and the harmony of her words emanating from the bottom of her soul, rendered her charming beyond conception. If one had loved her formerly, one could now not help adoring her.

She took the boy from the arms of her lord; and the strongest maternal feelings, the most heart-felt tenderness, animated her looks. The boy was sensible of her affection, and seemed to exchange his heart with hers for the first time. The additional warmth which pervaded her blood, blushed sweetly on her countenance. The strength of her amiable feelings deprived her of the power of utterance, and she kissed the innocent smiles eagerly from the lips of her little darling. I now was but too sensible that the name she had given to the child had some secret meaning.

The Count put me again in possession of my old apartments. I found every thing in them in its usual place, and unaltered; and even met my former sensations again. The most tranquil, unpassionate, and happy period of my whole life returned once more into my soul; and the sweetest tears glided, on that evening, from my eyes, while I was sitting on the same sofa where I was so frequently and anxiously occupied with the ideas of the confederation; a secret tremor pervaded my frame at the sight of the memorable turf-seat, which I could discern from my chamber windows; and I spent the greater part of the night with listening to the plaintive strains of the nightingales, whom my heated imagination introduced to me as old acquaintances.

The Count did not fail to ask me, the following day, when we were in private, about my history. He was astonished when I gave him a minute account of the whole; but, after some reflection, said, "Alas! Carlos, I forboded it but too strongly. A connection with such a set of people was fit neither for myself nor for you; and that I fostered that idea in my bosom, and instilled into your mind as much of it as I could, that the confederates had proofs of those attempts, and endeavoured to dissolve our union, could have been very fatal to me; but actually contributed to establish my happiness. How much misery did I, perhaps, escape, because they thought me incapable of bearing it!"

"It is but too true, dear Lewis, that you frequently have hinted it to me; but the greatness of the idea, and the extent of their imposing plan, deluded and charmed me, as it were, to their interest."

"Alas! it is but too true that you was deluded; for your late adventures cannot but convince you, that you was ignorant of the real nature of the confederation. Does it not appear, by the visible familiarity Don Bernhard was suffered to keep up with your lady, that a complete communion of all things was a fundamental law of the order?"

"Who could suspect that the imposing appearance of the most perfect virtue could conceal crimes of such an atrocious nature?"

"They are crimes in *our* eyes; but may not those people be of a different opinion? They, perhaps, are among the number of their greatest virtues."

"But who knows whether the confederation really were privy to Don Bernhard's design upon Adelheid?" I replied.

"This is entirely indifferent; for it was a fault of the society if they did not perceive it in its beginning; nor endeavoured to obviate such crimes before they could be brought to maturity, and exposed themselves to the danger of being undone by wantonly provoking the resentment of an individual member, who was not previously initiated in such an important mystery. And what can you expect of a set of people, who tear the noblest and most natural bonds of love and friendship asunder, to obtrude upon you, against your inclinations, plans, against the usefulness of which your temperament and disposition constantly object, though they should succeed to convince you of their real importance?"

CHAPTER X.

The Count was too much enamoured with his silent domestic happiness than to have any relish for other pleasures. Our natural indolence, particularly if we have been harassed by misfortunes, and want recreation, renders us fond of that peace; it charms all our senses, and grows dearer to us, because it makes us prouder of ourselves; as we feel no want in the deprivation of all other goods, and obtain a more intimate knowledge of our own resources and treasures than in any other situation.

Our course of life, and the train of our occupations and amusements, soon were again the same they had been before the Count's marriage. I endeavoured, as much as possible, to dispel, or at least to conceal, the gloom that hung on my mind. Caroline did not only not interrupt my sweet familiarity with the Count, but also contributed very much to give it a proper relish. She was the arbiter of all our little disputes, and possessed the great art always to satisfy both parties. She accommodated her humour to our respective dispositions, laughing and joking with her lord, and roving with me through the solitary parts of the garden, harmonizing with my melancholy, complaining of the mutability of human happiness, and sometimes even mixing her tears with mine.

The good Count, being completely occupied with his domestic concerns, was glad that I had found in his lady an agreeable companion of my idle hours during the day; but insisted to have my company entirely to himself in the evening, and the beginning of night; his friendship for me prevailing so much over love, and every other sentiment, that he was jealous of every thing that deprived him of my society. He was always the first who rose from supper, and wishing a good night to the Countess, took me by the arm, and staid two or three hours in my apartment; or roved with me through the garden, when the night was warm and serene. These walks frequently were continued till the dawning morning reminded us of the fleetness of time. While we disclosed our inmost thoughts to one another, and mutually unfolded the most secret recesses of our hearts, our minds expanded themselves, and great and new hopes reconciled us to the time past, and the gloom of frowning futurity was gradually cleared up.

Yet my melancholy must have made a greater impression upon the Countess than on my friend. The more the latter saw my gloominess encrease, the more did he exert his good humour to dispel it. Caroline, on the contrary, caught the cheerless disease of my over-clouded mind; and the despondency which my looks expressed but too strongly frequently bedewed her eyes with tears of compassion.

Some heavy and insupportable secret seemed, at length, to depress her amiable heart. The Count did, fortunately, not observe it; but it did not escape me, that she neglected him more than usual, that her caresses gradually grew colder and more ambiguous, and that she even shewed less anxious attention and care to the tender nursling of her love.

She did not choose to disclose her mystery to me, and I would not intrude upon it; though her friendship for me would have sufficiently justified such a step. A secret instinct, which frequently guided my actions, without my knowing it, did perhaps make me ominate that I should find more in such a discovery that I expected. I left it, therefore, to time to unfold that secret. Yet I thought it was my duty to consult the Count about it. "I have made the same observation some time since," he replied; "but being persuaded that her melancholy cannot originate in a moral cause, I have ascribed it to a physical one, and think I ought to apply to a physician."

Being desirous not to let him see the whole extent of my anxious apprehensions, I replied, "Has she had this melancholy turn for a long time?"

"I perceived it for the first time after her lying in. I have found her frequently weeping over her son; and whenever I tenderly enquired after the cause of her tears, she always pleaded an unaccountable internal anxiousness which her last illness had left behind. You know that I spare no pains to exhilarate her; but I think travelling will do her more good than any thing else, and intend to make a journey to Italy next year."

I approved his plan, although I was unable to explain why I did not repose much confidence in the efficacy of that expedient.

Her beautiful eyes were frequently fixed at me; I always met her affectionate looks when we were in private; and what struck me most, she never enquired after my lady, or my late adventures, or the cause of my separation from Adelheid; though I knew that the Count never had betrayed my secret to her.

Autumn set in at last; the country seats were again visited by the inhabitants of the town, and our neighbourhood grew more lively. We received, of course, more frequently, company, which interrupted the train of our usual occupations to our greatest regret. The Count, being an utter stranger to dissimulation, could not disguise his displeasure at that change; and I joined him in declaiming against all those idle talkers who intruded upon our social happiness, but we endeavoured in vain to get rid of their tiresome company. They struck like burs, and there was no possibility of shaking them off. The poor Countess suffered most by their importunity; for we left them frequently to their gossiping, and escaped into the field, while she was exposed to their tedious, inane chit-chat. Not being at liberty to give vent to her grief, it rankled in her heart, and almost reduced her to a shadow.

Chance, which is as unpropitious as favourable to lovers, unfolded, at last, on a fatal day, her unfortunate secret. We had a great number of guests at the castle; and being at a loss how to amuse them after dinner, proposed a walk to a neighbouring mill. The company set out in high spirits, and myself and the Count led the way. The path grew narrower and narrower the nearer we came to the mill, and, at last, scarcely permitted us to walk abreast. Our situation was, therefore, highly disagreeable, on our meeting the miller's man, with a loaded horse, walking strait towards us with his sacks, in spite of the driver's exclamations. We separated to let the animal pass. The Count was so fortunate to escape by a dexterous turn the danger of being knocked down. I got upon the outermost extremity of a deep ditch, squeezing myself into the smallest compass that was possible; but in vain! the horse brushed against me with his sacks, and I glided with a piece of loose ground into the ditch, which was overgrown with briars and thistles.

When the company, who walked behind us, saw me sink down, they raised a loud scream. The ditch being, however, perfectly dry, and not the least danger to be apprehended, they soon began to laugh loudly at my awkward situation. The Countess almost swooned away, at first; but being restored to her recollection by the exultations of the company, her apprehension turned into a violent rage, and she began to exercise her walking cane most unmercifully upon the back of the animal and his driver, who was in the greatest confusion, and received her blows in a humble, supplicating posture.

The Count beheld the uncommon rage of his lady with astonishment, and seemed to guess its secret motive. I also was struck by the extraordinary behaviour of the Countess; and no sooner had disengaged myself from my uncomfortable situation, than I took again hold of his arm, and endeavoured to dispel his gloomy reverie by lively sallies of good humour. Yet his overcast eye remained gloomy, although I could perceive that he was not in the least angry with me. That day was very trying for the Countess; for a new adventure was awaiting for her. We arrived at the mill, where the Count had ordered an excellent collation to be prepared. We were, in general, in a pretty good humour. After our repast was finished, we began to amuse the ladies by various little sports, and, at last, attempted to walk upon the balustrade of a bridge. The experiment was rather dangerous; and those that were subject to giddiness separated themselves from the rest. Most of us having shewn their skill with success, the Count too tried his dexterity, to the satisfaction of the company; but when my turn came, I saw the Countess suddenly grow pale: "It is enough, it is enough!" she exclaimed: "these dangerous tricks make my head quite giddy." Seeing, however, that I paid no attention to her exclamations, she ran without reflection towards me, and took hold of my arm, exclaiming vehemently, and with a look which expressed the anxiety of her soul, "Marquis, you know you have a weak head; why would you expose yourself to such a neck-breaking danger?"

I made a silent bow, and withdrew. The Count was almost petrified, and the whole company struck with astonishment. I was not able to utter a word. The Count was the first that spoke. "I think, Caroline," he said, "it grows late; will you conduct the ladies back to the castle?" That heavenly goodness would have moved a stone; and the Countess was feelingly affected by the kindness of her lord. She recovered, however, soon from her emotion, and began to be naturally cheerful and merry, taking two of the ladies by the arm, and returning gaily to the castle, as if nothing had happened.

The Count said nothing, but his countenance betrayed silent grief. I exerted myself in vain to dispel the gloom of his mind; yet I was firmly persuaded that his great and noble heart could harbour neither suspicion nor bitterness against me. He was sure that I was incapable of a perfidious breach of friendship. His regard for me drew a glory round my image; and he could not suffer that the least spot should appear in it. My passion for Caroline, before his marriage, was too violent than that it could have lain dormant so long, and now suddenly awake in its pristine force. Nay, I am certain that not even one of those reflections came into his mind.

Our guests left us soon after our return to the castle; and the Count was as cheerful and obliging at supper as ever. He behaved with more than common attention and kindness to his lady, anticipating every wish of her's before she could form a complete idea of it. He dressed with more elegance than usual, was attentive to the least trifle, invented numberless little amusements for her diversion, and did every thing a man of feeling can do to recal a strayed heart to the right path.

I, on my part, carefully avoided every opportunity of thwarting his tender endeavours, shunning Caroline's company as much as decency would allow. I was, indeed, as cheerful as ever at table; but appeared rather in the character of a guest, and a polite companion, than in that of her former confidential friend, who took a tender share in all her little family concerns. I spent the greatest part of the day with attending to the Count's domestic affairs, or with forming new connections amongst our neighbours; received company, or joined some pleasure parties; paid my addresses to every fine woman; was the disposer and king of all feasts and balls: in short, I was every where more at home than at the castle.

This change of my conduct made a very bitter impression upon the Countess. A more keen-sighted connoisseur of the female heart than the Count and myself, would easily have foreseen the fatal consequences of that conduct. The Count's tender and studious attention appeared affectation to her, and rendered his company irksome and tedious; and my constant absence gave an additional charm to the few accomplishments I possessed. Jealousy contributed to make me dearer to her than ever, and her heart was infected with a baneful poison. A speechless melancholy rankled in her soul, preyed on her vitals, and rendered her a riddle to her acquaintances. The Count apprehended a public eruption of her passion, and, therefore, avoided all great companies; but this almost imperceptible constraint only served to add fuel to the flame.

I ordered, mean time, my trunks to be packed with all possible secresy; and being firmly resolved to depart without delay, only waited for a proper opportunity of acquainting the Count with my intention. I was convinced that he secretly wished for the same; and that nothing but a tender regard for his lady's honour prevented him from disclosing his real sentiments to me without reserve. But I was mistaken; for he thought, on the contrary, that such a step would only make bad worse, and that one ought to have recourse to it if all gentler means should have been applied without success.

One night I came home after twelve o'clock; and having been absent from the castle all the day, joyfully anticipated the pleasure of spending a few hours with the Count in confidential talk. The Countess at that time, being generally gone to bed an hour or two, I was astonished to see her apartment still illuminated. A heavy load fell, at that sight, upon my heart, a number of ominous apprehensions pervaded my mind, and I slackened my horse's pace not to come home so soon.

My astonishment was raised to the highest pitch when I found the Countess waiting for me at the landing-place, leaning her head against the balustrade of the staircase. She no sooner saw me, than she exclaimed, in a trembling accent, "Oh! Carlos!"

I could not conceive what that strange ejaculation meant, and quickened my paces, expecting every moment that she would faint away. When I came to the top of the stairs, she added sobbing, "Merciful God! O my God!"

"What has happened to you, Madam?" I replied. "Are you not well?"

"I am very ill, Carlos," she resumed, raising her head. I never saw a more haggard and ghastly countenance than hers. "Have pity with me, Carlos!" she added: "For God's sake, have pity with me!"

I thought her intellects were disordered, or very near being so. What could I do? Prudence forbade me to flatter her passion even for a moment only; and if I had been prompted by an ill-timed compassion with her lamentable state, I should have run the danger of being overheard by the Count, whose heart was dearer to me than life. I did not know what to reply.

"Heavens! have you no feeling at all, Carlos?" she exclaimed.

"For God's sake, my lady," I replied, in a low whisper, "what is the matter with you? Consider the place, and that the Count is not yet gone to bed."

"Well, then, come into my apartment."

"I believe the Count has seen, and waits for me."

"Come into my apartment!" she repeated, with great emotion.

"Best, dearest Caroline," I replied, frightened at her situation, "what is the matter with you? You are beyond yourself. Shall I call somebody?"

She shook her head.

"You want to communicate something to me? But consider the unseasonable hour and the place. I rather will meet you to-morrow after midnight in the garden, if you insist upon speaking to me in private."

"Will you, Carlos? Will you indeed?" she exclaimed, with the greatest emotion. "Yes, yes, I knew that you still have some love for me." She was going to press me to her panting bosom; but I turned suddenly round, pretending to hear a distant noise, and led her to her apartment. Having placed her on her sofa, I withdrew silently; but she called after me, "To-morrow night, Carlos! To-morrow night!"

CHAPTER XI.

I was in the greatest distress about the properest measure I was to take. I could not avoid the nocturnal meeting without treachery; and yet felt myself bound by every tie of honour and friendship to inform the Count of the whole affair. I pretended, therefore, to go to my apartment, but went on tip-toe to the Count. He was already undressed, and occupied with reading; but I could perceive, by his looks, that his mind was agitated. Being desirous to know whether he had had a dispute with the Countess at supper, I began, in a tender accent, "How are you, Lewis? How does the Countess?"

"I don't believe," he replied, "that she is gone to bed. She was, to night, uneasier than I ever saw her. She has wept from morning till night, and found fault with every thing. What shall I do with that whimsical woman?"

"Send her to the cloister where the Marchioness is," I replied imprudently.

He stared at me with wild and anxious looks, exclaiming, in an agony of despair, "Oh! my God! Oh! heavenly Father! for what a dreadful fate hast thou preserved me!"

"You see, Lewis, you are to have no preference before your friend. A similarity of our fate and our sorrows is to cement our union more firmly!"

"But have I deserved it, Marquis? Have I neglected one of the conjugal duties? Have I not done every thing to please her, and were not all my most anxious endeavours fruitless? My very tenderness seemed to make her more averse to me?"

"And I, Lewis?"

He fell into meditation. "You are right, friend of my heart!" he resumed after some reflection. "I repeat the words I have already alledged; let the world never say that a *woman* has interrupted the union of two souls like ours."

"This openness is a proof that you know me! Rely upon the fidelity of your Carlos."

"But what do you intend to do?"

I acquainted him with the whole of my adventure on the stair-case. Expecting that my relation would reduce him to despair, I was astonished to see him smile, while a few gentle tears glided down his cheeks, and the gloom that overshaded his brow gradually brightened up. That uncommon phenomenon was, at bottom, not difficult to be accounted for. He had, indeed, never doubted the rectitude of his friend, but was surprised to find him so totally devoid of vanity and of presumption, so candid and open. The sweet sympathy uniting our souls was more to him than the most ardent love; and was it matter of astonishment that the raptures of the former gradually obliterated the sufferings of the latter? He was too much occupied with my image, than that any thing else could have found room in his noble soul.

"Oh! my Jonathan, my second self!" he exclaimed with ecstasy, when I had concluded my narrative, "are you really a *mortal?* are you really *my friend?* Or is my happiness only the work of a delusive dream?"

"No, no, Lewis! my love for you is reality. Your Carlos is not ungrateful. Has he not reason to prefer you to all mortals? Have we not repeatedly tried each other? You have, perhaps, frequently found me weak and irresolute; but false!—Lewis!—

"Never, never! Let us frequently renew the bond of eternal friendship! Heaven and earth may dissolve, but our friendship shall last for ever!"

We agreed to try gentle means once more with the Countess. He hated all severity; though it was the only thing that could have been applied with success in the beginning. The appointed rendezvous promised to give me the best opportunity for an explanation; and the Count left it to my eloquence, and to the influence I had gained upon Caroline, to render that explanation as strong and affecting as possible. I insisted upon his being a secret witness of our discourse. He started numberless objections; but consented at length, when I vowed to keep the assignation only under that condition.

Heaven only knows in what a state of mind I spent the rest of the night, and the subsequent day. My soul was so violently agitated, that I have only an obscure idea of the sensations that pervaded my mind. I was entirely occupied with thinking of what I should say to combat her foolish passion, and even neglected to observe the Count and his lady meantime.

My friend appeared to be neither more nor less attentive to Caroline during that interval; for it was of the highest importance to make her secure, as our intimacy easily could have excited her suspicion.

The Countess ate not a morsel at supper, being scarcely able to conceal the tremor that pervaded her frame and at last entirely lost the command over her wandering, imprudent looks. The Count was as kind as ever, but struggled in vain to conceal his anxiety. I, on my part, was intolerably merry, jocose without wit, talkative without sense, and gallant without any desire of pleasing.

The Countess had not the courage to rise first from table, notwithstanding her impatience at the long duration of our meal, being fearful to excite suspicion. Yet her internal displeasure could not be disguised, speaking loudly through her gloomy looks, and, at length, venting itself through half-stifled sighs. The Count did not lose sight of his lady for a single moment, and was obliged to rise first, his agitation encreasing so violently, that he feared not to be able to conceal it any longer. He pretended to have a violent headache, wished Caroline a good night, pressed her hand tenderly, and retired. I staid a few minutes longer, and insinuated to her, that we could not trust the Count, and ought to be circumspect. We then began to converse on indifferent subjects; but I could not prevent her rising, and pressing me violently to her bosom. Having disengaged myself from her arms, I retired to my bed-chamber, after I had given the pre-concerted signal to my unfortunate friend.

The night was fine and serene, as warm as one could expect it in October. I was half an hour before the appointed time at the spot fixed for our interview. My heart beat anxiously, my senses were agitated by every distant rustling, and I struggled in vain to conquer the ominous bodings which assailed me.

The vapours of the pond, which was before me, rose in wonderful shapes, and floated over the turfy back ground of the garden. The pale orb of the moon emerged from the gloomy womb of a dark cloud, and trembled in the blue ether, her silver rays skipping on the curling waves of the water. My heated imagination transformed the nodding shades of the trees, and the floating vapours, into spirits celebrating their nocturnal revels, and produced strange, unutterable sensations in my heart. The soft stream of my fancies transported me to fairy regions, and totally avocated my ideas from reality. I had forgot Caroline, and all my fine plans, when suddenly a soft, warm hand took hold of mine. An unexpected electric stroke could not have surprised me more violently. I shuddered vehemently: it was the Countess, who said, with an angelic smile, "Have I surprised you, Carlos! But why are you frightened at your Caroline?" She gave me no time to return an answer. Before I could collect myself sufficiently, I felt myself enfolded by her soft arms, and my face covered with burning kisses. I scarcely could resist a human weakness, the desire of returning to her rosy lips the animated kisses, which thrilled my whole frame with unutterable sensations; only the idea of the Count's presence enabled me to disengage myself from the sweet enchantress. She was startled;

but I left her no time for a moment's reflection, taking her by the hand, and leading the trembling woman to a turf-seat contiguous to the pond. She perceived my carefulness, and sank again enraptured into my arms.

I do not think that it would have been in my power to resist Caroline's ardent kisses, her supplicating posture, and her tears, if she had been capable to rekindle a single spark of my former passion for her, and if we had been unobserved. This was one of the motives that urged me to insist upon the Count's presence; for I had made the unfortunate observation that Caroline had, for some days, appeared to me handsomer than ever. Her impatience had, besides, made her as charming that night as a woman can be. She saw that I endeavoured to disengage myself from her; but thinking that this was nothing but affectation, would not let me go. "Why do you struggle to disengage yourself from my arms, Carlos?" she said smiling. "No, no! you shall not escape me this time, as you did yesterday!"

"And yet, I must, Caroline. Recollect yourself, dearest friend. You know I am your friend; but I am also the intimate friend of your husband."

She shuddered violently, starting from my arms with a convulsive emotion, as if I had been a hideous monster. Her looks sparkled with burning rage; and she replied, with a contemptuous sneer, "Vile wretch! is this the reception you have prepared for me, and that your perfidious looks promised?"

"Yes, it is. Did you not want a confidant to communicate some secret sorrow to in private? Did you not choose me to be your friend, and demand any thing better and more noble from me, than the sincerest friendship?"

The accent of my words plainly bespoke the emotion of my heart. She was affected, and eased her straitened bosom by heavy sighs; and dropping on her knees, said, in a supplicating posture, "No, no, Carlos; I neither wish for friendship, nor for confidence: what I desire is love, an ardent and everlasting love. I have no secret to disclose to you, besides that of my love. Love for you is the only burden that bends me down; I lay it down at your feet; and, God knows, if you don't accept of it, I shall patiently bear it to my grave."

I sobbed and wept aloud; and am sure the Count, who witnessed the whole scene, also could not retain his tears. They flowed for his erring, unhappy wife; mine flowed for him. I endeavoured to raise the Countess up, but she was stronger than myself. "Rise, Caroline," I replied: "you desire too much of me. My heart has been deadened by severe afflictions, and beats only faintly even for its dearest friends. Could such a heart be acceptable to Caroline?"

I imagined this expedient would be the safest and gentlest to recal her to her duty; but it did not succeed. "No! no!" she exclaimed, "You cannot deceive me, Carlos; love is more keen-sighted than you think. I know and have observed you secretly for years, and am convinced that your heart is but too sensible. Alas! you are so good, so kind to every one, and only to me you would be cruel."

"No, Caroline. The wife of the friend of my bosom always will be dear to my heart. I loved you once with a violent, juvenile ardour: you repelled my passion with scorn; and in that moment I reposed all my claims to your heart into the hands of the worthiest, the best of men."

I chose this language on purpose, hoping that it would exasperate her; but she misunderstood me, imagining that it proceeded from a kindling spark of love and jealousy; and exerting herself to the utmost of her power to blow it up into a flame, "And can you really make me that reproach?" she replied. "Can you be so cruel to a poor unhappy woman, dead for the world, and for herself? Have I not sufficiently atoned for my dreadful error? Have I not lingered away the rosy time of my youth, the bloom of my life, separated from you? And can you now repel me with scorn, when I return repenting to you, offering every atonement I can make?"

She lifted her hands up to heaven, and dropt upon the ground entirely exhausted. I availed myself of that opportunity to raise her up, and to place her by my side upon the turf-seat. She shed a torrent of tears, and wrung her hands in a convulsive agony. No man ever had been in a situation like mine. I was watched, and yet entirely left to myself. I could expect no assistance in that dreadful distress but from myself. I implored all the powers of Heaven to come to my relief. "Dearest Countess," I now resumed, "you never was in a greater error than at present. I do not deserve your love, nor ever did. Were it otherwise, would you then have forgot me so soon, and so completely?"

"*So soon! so completely!* did you say? Heavenly powers! Can you persecute me with such a dreadful, unrelenting ire? And have I nothing to hope, Marquis? Nothing at all? Good God! why don't you speak? Why have you appointed this meeting, in such a damp, foggy, and dark night?"

She began to rave. The images her troubled fancy formed were incoherent and wild; her words disjointed. Her whole frame was in a convulsive tremor, her face wan, and her eye dim and over-clouded. The pale light of the moon rendered her aspect still more ghastly and horrible: The moral lecture which I was going to read to her, all the fine sentiments of wisdom and virtue I intended to urge, were silenced at once. She seemed to hear me no more, ejaculating only hollow and unintelligible accents. I was bereft of the power of reflecting, and held her hand mechanically in mine.

A low rustling excited her attention; and she raised herself slowly, directing her fearful looks at the spot whence it proceeded. But she averted them suddenly, seized with horror; her hair began to bristle, and her face to glow. She pushed me violently back; and starting up in a fit of wild frenzy, was going to plunge into the pond. I caught her in my arms.

Her looks had catched the Count, who hastened to my assistance. Shame, fury, disappointed and scorned love, deprived her of the use of her intellects: the pain which had been rankling in her heart for a long time, now broke forth with impetuosity, contracted her veins, and stopt the course of her blood. The poor Count was reduced by that shocking sight to a state not much better than her's. Caroline resembled a lifeless corpse before we arrived at the castle.

All our endeavours to restore her to life were fruitless for some time. At length she opened her eyes, and began to speak; but, alas! her understanding was disordered. She mistook me for the Count, but would suffer neither of us to come near her.

She recovered but slowly, and had frequent relapses. We went but seldom to her apartment; and she seemed to have lost all recollection of us. She spoke to no person, her little boy excepted, with whom she amused herself constantly. He sat all the day long on her bed, and they diverted themselves with infantine gambols.

Nothing was spared to exhilarate the gloom of her mind; but she seemed to be dead to every thing, having completely lost all recollection of her former friends. A deep melancholy preyed on her mind, and all the faculties of her soul were in a kind of lethargy.

The Count was at a loss what he should do, and, at length, asked me whether I did not think a journey to Italy would be of service to her? I advised him to propose it to the Countess, but she could not be persuaded to return an answer, staring at him like a person that hears some words without comprehending their meaning, and casting her eyes down again.

I now thought that it, perhaps, would be better to carry her to the cloister at D******, where Adelheid was; being firmly persuaded that their former friendship would revive again, and some happy change might be effected by the reciprocal communication of their sentiments; for nothing is more capable to rouse the torpid senses from their lethargy, than the sweet recollection of past times, spent in a happy congeniality of soul with a dear and deserving friend.

Being, however, ignorant of Adelheid's real state of mind, about which her tender letters were entirely silent, I hesitated to expose the Countess to a far greater danger, instead of curing her. I also apprehended Adelheid's returning love for me might provoke the Countess's jealousy, and then every thing would have been lost. I agreed, therefore, with the Count, to make a little excursion to D******, to inform myself of the real state of Adelheid's mind. I began my journey without delay, and wrote to the Marchioness on the road, informing her of an intended visit from the Countess of S******; painted my face and eye-brows, laid a large patch upon my right eye; and having exchanged my garments for a peasant's dress, proceeded on foot for D******, to deliver the letter myself, disguised as a messenger.

The nuns were at chapel when I arrived; and I had sufficiently time to sift the portress about Adelheid's state of mind.

"Is this the cloister of D******?" I began with an affected rusticity, and gaping at the direction of the letter.

"Where else should it be, master blockhead?" she replied, in a morose accent. "But what have you got there? For whom is that letter?"

With these words she was going to snatch the letter from my hand, but I retreated a few steps, resuming, "Does a certain Marchioness of G****** live in this cloister?"

"The poor Marchioness! Is the letter for her? I will run and inform her of the joyful news; for I dare say you come from the Marquis. She almost devours his letters, even before she has read them." She was going to shut the door in my face, and run to the Marchioness, but I exclaimed, "One word more, mistress! one word more, if you please!"

She turned round, and replied, "Well, what do you want? Don't detain me long; I have no time to lose."

"Will you not tell me who that Marchioness of G****** is?" I asked, apprehending that her fatal hurry would leave me no time to sift her sufficiently. But I had scarcely touched the floodgates of her eloquence, when they opened at once, discharging an overflowing stream of thoughts, which, perhaps, had burdened her mind for some time.

"What!" she exclaimed, "are you so impudently curious to ask me such questions? The Marchioness of G******, you must know, is such a great lady, that you don't deserve to pronounce her name."

"Well! well! my good lady," I replied, coaxing her, "I have seen the King of France, and the handsome majestic Queen, the dear Dauphin, and the charming Princess, who has such fine eyes, that I could have given her a kiss." I made, at the same time, a pantomine with my hand, which plainly and strongly expressed that desire. The nun crimsoned at that profane expression, but, nevertheless, could not help smiling at it.

"What an abominable fellow you are! But to return to the dear Marchioness, I must tell you, that I did not call her a great lady on account of her high rank, but because of her mildness, gentleness, kindness, and virtue."

"And virtue?" I repeated mechanically.

"She did nothing but weep, at first; and grief almost reduced her to a living skeleton. None of us could prevail upon her to speak. What ails you, dear Marchioness? what is the matter with you? all of us asked. There was not one sister in the cloister that was not curious to know the cause of her grief."

"I believe it!" I replied smiling. But, fortunately, I recollected that this was too witty for a simple clown adding, "I should like to know it myself."

"No person can tell it with certainty."

"But what do you think may be the reason?"

She seemed to hesitate; but, at length, resumed, "They say the Marquis is very hot; and who knows how he may have treated her?"

"Good God!" I thought, "some person must have betrayed her; but who can guess at the real ground of her melancholy, besides ourselves?"

"Has the Marquis, perhaps, been jealous?" I replied. "That would have been very natural, if she is really so handsome."

"No, it is impossible she could have given him a reason for it; for she is a pattern of goodness and virtue. Several people have been here to see and to speak to her: however, she never would receive a stranger. I rather think the hot-headed, wild Marquis is the cause of her grief."

This took a great load from my heart; and I cared little for the slander which was directed at me, if but the honour of my poor wife was spared.

"There you are right, mistress," I exclaimed: "the Marquis is really a very hot-headed man. He has already played numberless wild tricks; and Heaven only knows how many more he will play."

"Then you know him?"

"Who should not know him? But only from hearsay; you under-stand me, mistress? All the world speaks of it."

"Will you not tell me a little of it?"

"By and by, dear lady," I replied. "The service will now be over; and I am directed to give this letter into the Marchioness's own hands. Will you be so good to inform her of it?"

"I fear she will not consent to see you."

"Tell her only that I come from the Marquis, and have orders to deliver the letter to nobody but herself."

I was sure that she would admit a messenger from her consort, how great soever her aversion from strangers might be. I, therefore, prepared already answers to a thousand anxious questions; and my imprudent heart flattered itself with the hope that, perhaps, a secret boding would whisper to her who was concealed under that mask. But that was the surest way of betraying myself, if the tender tenour of the letter should leave her only a little attention for other objects.

The portress returned after a few minutes, with the intelligence that she had orders to shew me to the parlour. My knees shook, and my legs scarcely could carry me. My heart either must have palpitated audibly, or my impatience have expressed itself by some hasty gesture. In short, my conductress gazed at me with a dubious look when she opened the parlour door.

Adelheid was waiting for me when I came to the grate. Without deigning to look at me, she took the letter eagerly out of my hand, examining the direction and the seal, kissed and opened it. She read, however, with so much impatience, that she was frequently obliged to begin again, in order to understand the import of its contents. I was, mean time, at leisure to examine the countenance of my wife, and found her features exactly corresponding with those that were deeply engraven in my heart. My looks gazed with inward rapture at her sweet Madonna-face! Her pale and interesting features unfolded themselves clearer and heavenlier the more she comprehended the import of the letter. I saw her pure soul restored again to the throne of innocence, candour, and tender friendship, which she formerly had graced in such an adorable manner. "I thank you, ye benevolent heavenly powers!" I said within myself: "My wife is again deserving of my love."

A big tear sparkled in her eye when she had finished the letter, dropping upon the paper, while she kissed it once more.

"Do you come directly from S******, good friend!" she said, putting the letter into her bosom.

"Directly from S******, Madam."

"Do you know the Marquis of G******?"

"Who should not know him? He is kind to every one, and wishes to make all the world happy."

These words struck her heart. "You are right," she sighed; "but he may frequently lavish his benefactions upon ungrateful people."

"The world is full of such wretches, Madam."

Her eyes glistened again with a pearly dew; but the internal consciousness of her guilt rendered those tears suspicious; she averted her face, wiping her cheeks with her handkerchief.

"Do you see him frequently?"

"Yes, Madam!"

"You are happier than me!"

"Why, Madam? you too will see him again!"

"God bless you for that word, good man. I will remember you if I ever shall leave these cloistered walls. Take this little badge of my gratitude for your gladsome message." With these words she offered me a piece of gold through the grate. I seized her hand, and imprinted fervent kisses upon it. But while I kept it enfolded in mine, I took a diamond ring, which was well known to her, out of my pocket, slipping it on the finger on which she wore her wedding ring, and left her abruptly. "Eternal God! what is this?" she exclaimed, when I opened the door. "Should it——For God's sake, stay a little!" But I shut the door, and hurried away.

CHAPTER XII.

It may easily be conceived what reflections occupied my mind on my return to the Count's castle. I was almost frantic with joy, and felt myself regenerated to a new life. My blood circulated quicker and warmer; a benign fire glowed in my breast, animated my feelings, and gave wings to my ideas.

What a delightful plans did I now devise! They appeared to me to be founded on a firm, unshaken base. Heaven smiled upon me with additional brightness; every threatening cloud had disappeared; the tempest was blown over; a train of rosy hopes danced cheerfully before my enraptured soul.

I was certain that Adelheid was able to cure the Countess entirely from her mental disease. They were intimate friends in their infantine and juvenile days, and female sorrows can meet with no safer asylum than a female bosom affords. The meekness of my wife promised Caroline a sweet encouragement; her experience held out to her a safe guide; her sorrow a warning example; and her returning virtue, and unshaken friendship, assistance, advice, and lenient sympathy.

But, alas! how prone is the feeble heart of man to deceive itself! Being a stranger to futurity, deluded by self-created dreams, intoxicated by its own feelings, and easily to be imposed upon by lively hopes, it raises its own foolish belief to convincing certainty, scarcely has conquered the impediments debarring it from happiness, and no sooner begins to feel the blessings of sweet tranquillity, than it is suddenly overtaken again by new tempests of adversity.

How could I, unhappy man! have ominated, on drawing nearer to the castle, the new misfortune that, during my absence, had been prepared for me by my unhappy fate? The Count stood at the window, waving his handkerchief to me when he saw me at a distance, and turning aside, wiped his eyes.

"Gracious Heaven!" I thought, "what can have happened? Should, perhaps, Caroline?—But, no; it cannot be. She was visibly mending when I left the castle. His last letter was, indeed, melancholy enough; but he did not speak of himself; and rather seemed to be desirous to be capable of speaking comfort to my heart, and of reconciling me to the mutability of fate. *Me!* But what can have happened? Should, perhaps, accounts from Spain? Impossible!" My breast was straitened by anxious bodings, and I scarcely could fetch breath when the carriage stopt at the castle. The Count came down the steps to meet me. His face was extremely pale and disordered: his gloomy looks were fixed at me with some dreadful mysterious meaning; and he encircled me warmer and closer than usual when I rushed into his arms. His wandering eyes were big with tears, and his hand trembled in mine.

I gazed at him with marks of the highest astonishment. He seemed not to be able to bear my look, and cast his heavy eyes to the ground. "Are you not well, dearest friend," I began.

"I am very indifferent, dear Carlos."

"How is Caroline?" I resumed hastily.

"She is much better, and easier: very melancholy, but knows me again. She was very serene yesterday. However, you shall see her yourself."

The good Count endeavoured to divert my attention from himself, and to prevent me from asking more questions; but my heart was too full, and I resumed, trembling, "has something else happened?"

He meditated a while, and affecting an indifferent tone, replied, in a tranquil, but audibly trembling, accent, "Nothing, that I know of, Carlos!"

"And yet your looks are so ominous, so entirely altered!"

"Can you really wonder at it? Does my situation afford me any ground for cheerfulness?"

"But for despondency neither!"

I now gave him a brief account of all my hopes and prospects. He thanked and embraced me. "Believe me, Carlos!" he added, sobbing, and with an agony which he could no longer conceal, "I ever, ever shall love you."

We now approached the apartment of the Countess. He opened the door. I looked at him with astonishment; but he replied, smiling, "You see I live on a very friendly footing with her. It would certainly have grieved her, if you had not surprised her once more."

The Countess sat at her usual place, reading in a book. When we entered the room, she laid it down, looking at us without either surprise or astonishment. Her beautiful eyes were more serene than usual. She rose, extending her hand to me without any affectation, and gave me a cordial welcome, making room for me on the sofa. She then enquired after my health, and the history of my journey, with so much unconcern and natural grace, that I scarcely could conceal my surprise. Yet this only served to encrease my apprehensions. I knew but too well that wounds which close so soon generally break open again in a most dangerous manner. The Count's downcast looks plainly told me that he was of the same opinion. She endeavoured to smile, but the tempest through which the sun shone was not quite blown over, and it was uncertain whether it was drawing nearer or passing away. Her eyes still stared too much at the objects, or strangely wandered from one to the other. Her countenance had lost its amiable expression; and being inanimated, and devoid of every passion, it caused disagreeable sensations in the beholder. It is extremely disgusting to hear sentiments uttered that are not expressed by a concomitant gesture bearing their beautiful stamp.

However lamentable this was, yet it did not appear to me a sufficient ground for the Count's desponding melancholy; for all these symptoms contained nothing that was not a natural effect of her illness, or could not be expected to be cured by the lenient hand of time. I was impatient to be alone with my friend, to learn what gloomy spot in his soul my hopes could not brighten up, and to pour the healing balsam of sympathizing friendship into his wounded heart.

We supped earlier than usual, that I should go to rest in good time. I never had spoken so little at our meals. The Countess looked staring at the light, pursuing the flight of a fly, which, at last, burned itself, and dropt dead upon the table. "Don Carlos!" she said, "do you think that there can exist a beautifuller symbol of love than that fly, who plunged into the light to be consumed by the flame?"

I trembled at that new eruption of her passion, and was at a loss what answer I should return to that unexpected question. I consulted the looks of the Count: however, he played with his knife upon the plate, and seemed to be entirely absorpt in thought. I took this for a hint to do the same, and cast down my eyes as if I had heard nothing. The Countess darted a cutting look at me, but did not deign to repeat her question.

This little incident changed at once the situation of my mind. My breath was straitened, the rosy dawn of hope died away, and I trembled at the idea of her being sent to my wife, with whose conduct I was so highly satisfied. Nothing is more catching to a sensible heart than melancholy; and who could foresee whether it would not finally turn in my wife into bitterness and hatred against mankind, if frequently provoked by jealousy in Caroline's company. These reflections were so much the more painful and alarming, as I durst not communicate them to the Count. We retired, at length, to my apartment. The Count seated himself by my side upon the sofa, and affectionately took hold of my hand. I stared with astonishment at him, while he meditated upon what he was going to say. "But why am I anxiously searching for words to explain myself to you?" he, at last, began: "Is not Carlos a man? Have we not jointly borne so many evils, and has not our union rendered the load of misery easier?"

"Dearest Count," I replied resolutely, though trembling, "your anxious looks, your circumstances, your ominous preparations, are worse than death itself. Let me hear the worst at once! Why would you agonize the heart of your friend by your tormenting anxiousness? Do I appear so cowardly and pusillanimous to you, as not to be able to face boldly the most dreadful calamity? Have you ever seen me tremble at a danger?"

"Your glowing fancy raves too wildly, dear Carlos. I intended to prepare you neither for death, terror, nor danger. I am going to disclose to you a most affecting scene, that will lacerate your feeling heart, and for which you cannot be prepared. Come with me, friend of my bosom. Your Lewis will mingle his tears with yours. Your friend will once more swear the solemn oath of eternal fidelity and love at the altar of grief."

He encircled me with weeping eyes, raising me from the sofa. We went into the garden, and he conducted me to the labyrinth in gloomy silence. The night was cold and stormy; the dry leaves rustled beneath our footsteps. Black clouds swept the horizon with great velocity; a solitary star twinkled now and then through the leafless branches of the trees; a damp mist obscured the objects that surrounded us, and was raised in various shapes by the swelling wind. The general torpor of decaying nature harmonized with the numbness of my heart; the horrors of death were passed over, and methought the eternal silence of the grave surrounded me.

The Count led me towards the pavilion which I had caused to be built over the famous, mysterious grotto. As soon as we got within sight of it, my friend said, in a trembling accent, "Know, Carlos, that James has brought me the dear treasure I am going to shew you now."

"James!" I exclaimed, seized with astonishment.

"He told me that was his name, and that you did know him very well. He was going with his lady to a country in the North, and expecting to find you at my castle, called here, but staid only a few moments. We too are old acquaintances, for he was the stranger who wanted to settle in our neighbourhood, and disappeared so suddenly. He told me, on taking leave, "Inform your friend that the *confederation* has been dissolved, and that he is safe. The death of Don Bernhard and the servant excited the attention of the police: we were surprised in the centre of our residence, and only a few escaped."

"Eternal God!—and Rosalia?"

"He did not mention a word about her: I believe she did not live to witness that scene."

"*Not live?*"

"It is but too certain, dear Carlos!"

So saying, he opened the door of the pavilion. The walls were hung with black: a solitary lamp, suspended to the ceiling, spread a pale melancholy light through the awful space; and two more burnt with a dying glimmer on an altar in the back ground. An alabaster urn stood in their middle. I disengaged myself from the Count's arm, and rushing towards that melancholy sanctuary, beheld these two words, written with black letters, upon the urn: *"Rosalia's heart."*

"Be a man, Carlos!" the Count said.

"Do you see me swoon, at the foot of the altar, like a woman? Or do I weep like a child over the sacred relics in that urn?"

He saw that my agony was the more violent, because it was not attended with tears, and enfolding me with his arms, sighed, "Carlos, you have a tender friend, that shares your grief."

"I know it, and thank you for that token of your love. If ever I could have doubted it, this testimony of your love would have gained you my affection for ever. You honour the memory of my dear, departed Rosalia: this deserves my eternal gratitude."

We dropped speechless upon our knees at the foot of the altar, and mingled our tears. I do not know by what accident, the Countess happened to be in the garden at the same time. She saw us walk arm in arm, and with an unusual impetuosity, through the garden: a natural impulse of curiosity tempted her to follow us; and seeing us kneel down at the foot of the altar, dropt also on her knees behind us, without knowing the meaning of our posture. Her straitened bosom seemed to have watched for a pretext to vent its cutting agony through sighs and tears. A rustling at the door disturbed us in our devotion: the Count started up, and looking round, beheld his wife, kneeling behind him. He raised her up, and leading her towards me, said, with tender emotion, "Rosalia's heart is enclosed in that urn; mourn with our unhappy friend!" The dear woman encircled me with her arm without reserve or fear; the Count pressed her to my bosom, and she kissed the tears from my cheeks.

CHAPTER XIII.

The Count now carried Caroline to D******. Adelheid was animated with new life on seeing her old friend again. The sweet reunion with the partner in her juvenile pleasures seemed already, in the first hour, to ease the heavy load of her sorrows. The Count beheld with pleasure the happy change the society of Caroline's new companion had produced, during the short time of his stay, on his wife's mind, and returned with sanguine hopes to the castle, where I, mean time, had spent my hours with pleasing reveries. Futurity serenely smiled at me through the tears of the present moment; and prospects of better days soothed the melancholy that hung on my afflicted mind. The Count found me easier on his return than he had expected, and thinking that a change of objects would completely cure both of us, brought the journey to Italy again upon the carpet. The time of the carnival was near, and we resolved to go to Venice. Having informed our ladies of our resolution, promising to return in a twelvemonth, we departed.

We stopped some time on the road, James's account having made me secure. I ought, perhaps, not to have put such an implicit confidence in his assurance; but my poor heart eagerly grasped at every friendly support on the stormy ocean of grief. I had taken the firm resolution to be tranquil, and to grieve for nothing in the world. I strove to enjoy every pleasure with an unpassionate mind, and found in the novelty and variety of the characters and manners I met with, an ample scope for attention and diversion. The highest warmth of human nature blown up to a devouring flame by a voluptuous clime, a lubricious wit, a hot and insatiable temper; jealous men, who, at the same time, are reduced to abject slavery by the gratifications of sensuality; confined and libidinous women; all this could not but produce a mixture of forms that wanted no disguise to compose a masquerade. Although I was susceptible only of a tender and reasonable love, yet I found, as a distant spectator, numberless new charms in the most violent eruptions of a passion whose power I had experienced but too sensibly.

The Count shared my observations and feelings. We imagined to be already too old and experienced than to have any thing to fear of that omnipotent passion. But that infatuation nearly had proved fatal to us on several occasions, where no danger would have threatened us if we had been more cautious. We escaped with the greatest difficulty those little snares which the least circumspection would have discovered to us; the seducing, wanton gestures which every Italian has at her command; the flatteries which allured, and then repelled, us again; the licence that knows no restraint; the charms of the fashionable tone; and, finally the unbounded licentiousness to which the mask seduces or intitles every one at that season.

The conflux of foreigners at Venice was uncommon, and no one remembered to have seen such a splendid carnival. The place of St. Mark was crowded all the day long by numberless whimsical masks: plays, balls, and pleasure parties, afforded a spacious field for intrigues, and every day produced new sorts of amusement.

The man who is not successful with the ladies of Venice ought to give up all farther claims to love. We were met half-ways in various manners. Our names went before us; and as we had not the least reason for living incognito, we endeavoured to do honour to our rank by a becoming splendor. We were, therefore, looked upon as very good conquests. The Count was, besides, one of the finest and handsomest men I ever saw; his pleasant and more flattering than offending wit enchanted every one, while the generosity and openness of his character conquered all hearts. I possessed, indeed, more knowledge of the world, and the female sex, than my friend; but, nevertheless, acted always only a subaltern part in great circles when I was in his company. I was tempted neither by envy nor jealousy to impede him in his splendid career, arresting him only occasionally, when I thought he encroached too much upon Caroline's rights. He loved me so tenderly, that he would have entirely submitted to my guidance; however, his warm temper, and the uncommon sensibility of his heart, urging him to return every inclination, seduced him into many excesses which I could not behold with indifference.

He was, indeed, not inclined to mere sensual love, which prevails at Venice; yet it was concealed under such a charming cloak of tenderness, sentiment, and disinterestedness, that it became dangerous to him. I frequently wished that he were attended by a guardian genius, who could have watched him when he was out of the reach of my looks.

The Duchess of F****** fixed, at last, his taste. She was adorned with all those qualities which the Count admired in a woman; that expression which a nice sensibility imparts to a form rather fine than perfectly handsome; a humour that rather was good natured and cordial than bright; the art of not confessing her love, but of conceding every thing to importunate desires; of enhancing her favours, and of rendering them more valuable, by a seasonable coyness; and of sacrificing and yielding every thing to her lover, while she checked him and herself in the midst of the highest enjoyment of the pleasures of love. Such a female character could seduce the Count to any thing.

He confessed his sentiments to me without reserve. I rejoiced sincerely at it: for a serious passion could not but divert him from excesses of a more dangerous nature. He viewed his mistress merely in the light of a feeling woman, that was willing to render him happy by a tender friendship. I confirmed him in his persuasion of the disinterestedness and purity of her love, in order to make him averse from an attempt against a virtue that probably was too weak as not to yield without great resistance. The Duchess being, however, not over partial to a long continued restraint, and used to fetter her countrymen through the senses, did not choose to make an exception from her principles in a connection with a foreigner.

She was married to an old and intolerably jealous man, who confined the poor woman, that thirsted after gratification, and, perhaps, had not been guilty of an essential breach of trust before she got acquainted with the Count. The Duke had, till then, watched her so closely, that she was incapable of giving so much encouragement to any man as to animate him to undertake something extraordinary; and no one had, as yet, found out the secret of gaining the confidence of her lord, so far as to be admitted by him to the company of his lady. The Count succeeded, however, to gain the friendship and confidence of the Duke, and was introduced by him to the Duchess. He afterwards was obliged to sup or to dine almost every day at his house, and generally spent the rest of the night with his new friend, either with playing at chess, or with roving the streets, or frequenting all balls, plays, and masquerades, in his company. They used to mix in the most whimsical disguise with the general bustle, to play numberless foolish tricks on their acquaintances, were several times in danger of being soundly cudgelled, and committed a thousand merry follies.

Although I knew that the Count reluctantly suffered himself to be dragged through a constant round of irrational pleasures, and that his sole view was to ingratiate himself with the Duchess, by removing her jealous sentinel, yet I thought he went too far. The price for which he sacrificed his time and health appeared to me not to be worth the trouble he took of attaining it; and I endeavoured to restrain him as much as possible in his rakish course of life. I had, indeed, not much reason to fear that he would ruin his health and fortune, but trembled at the fatal impression a continual dissimulation would make, at last, on his amiable openness, and even on his unrestrained friendship for me.

The Duchess was highly sensible of the great obligations she owed him for that dissolute course of life, which afforded them the best opportunity of availing themselves of the first propitious moment to gratify their mutual wishes. Love, which had stolen into their heart already, before the Duke introduced the Count to his house, taught them a thousand little arts to impart their sentiments to each other unobserved by the world, and to devise the means of eluding the jealous vigilance of her lord.

I also gained, at length, free admission to the house through the Count's intercession, but displayed so little care to improve that acquaintance, that the Duke did not think it worth his while to be jealous of me. I took, besides, very seldom a part in the amusements of these two friends; but when I did, always shared their revels with so much warmth, that the Duke imagined some secret grief was rankling in my heart, and did every thing in his power to amuse me. This I became gradually his confidant, and had the pleasure to render many essential services to the lovers. Yet they were still very far from the goal of their wishes; for although the Duchess was not so closely watched as usual, yet the Duke never lost sight of the Count. This restraint inflamed, at length, the desires of the fair Italian in the highest degree, and she resolved to risk and to hazard every thing.

The lover was informed of this resolution; receiving at the same time, the severest reproaches for his want of spirit. The Duchess threatened him with a nocturnal visit as soon as she should be able to give the slip to her vigilant keeper; and the Count, who now plainly perceived that his love was rather the effect of whim than of a serious passion, trembled at the danger which the execution of that resolution would expose him to, and took every possible precaution to obviate the fatal consequences it might produce.

The night which the Duchess impatiently was wishing for

arrived at length. Her lord returned, one evening, in such a dreadful state of intoxication to his palace, that the Duchess was obliged to send for a physician; but he was seized with such a violent fever, that he began to rave, which rendered it necessary that he should be removed from his lady's apartment. No sooner was the latter delivered from her jealous sentinel, than she went through a back door out of the palace, and got into a gondola, which had been waiting for several nights.

The Count had taken every precaution at our house to admit her without noise. He never went to bed before day-break; and I was always on the watch, when he was obliged to go out, to let her in, and to send him intelligence of her arrival. The Count always came home at an early hour, because he expected her every night; and we generally beguiled the time by confidential agitation; not relying much on the prudence of his mistress, who seemed to be entirely blinded by the impetuosity of her passion. The least noise, a distant rustling, a cracking in the wood, made him start and tremble; his countenance changed at every knock, even at the house of a neighbour.

One night we heard, at length, a rap at our door: it was opened, but profound silence resumed its former sway. The Count started up, and listened; but some minutes passed without any farther noise being heard. It was improbable that some other person than the Duchess should have knocked; and yet she knew all the opportunities of our house perfectly. We could, therefore, not account for the silence which continued to prevail.

The Count grew, at length, impatient, and taking a candle in his hand, went softly to the door. Having listened a while, he opened it, and saw something white lying on the uppermost step. He ejaculated a loud scream, which prompted me to follow him precipitately. He had placed the candle on the ground, and was raising up a lady that seemed to be lifeless. Her veil was torn to pieces, and her garments were in visible disorder. I stept nearer, and, to my utter astonishment, beheld the Duchess in his arms.

Our nocturnal visitor was only with the greatest difficulty restored to the use of her senses, which, however, continued to be in great disorder. The first sound she uttered was a request to be carried back to her palace. We promised to see her safe home, entreating her to make herself easy, and anxiously enquired by what accident she had come into that situation.

"Order your house to be searched instantly," she replied, all in a tremor: "some stranger must be concealed in it." The Count having rung the bell, and ordered his servants to search every corner, she resumed, "I arrived above half an hour since at your door on the channel, but seeing two young men engaged in a deep conversation before your house, could not leave the gondola. They were dressed in a kind of uniform, and spoke very low, which prevented me to discern the subject of their discourse. Having waited a long time, and being afraid to lose too much time, I ventured, at length, to go on shore, and to knock at your house. The door was opened, but in the moment I was going to enter, one of them threw me down, tore my veil from my face, and beat me till I fainted away. You know that I durst not venture to call for assistance, which encouraged them to treat me in such a manner, that the marks probably will remain on my frame for the rest of my life." So saying, she bared her arms, and a part of her neck, which was black and blue: we even found several marks of nails. "I assure you," she continued, "there is no part of my body that has not suffered by those furious hands."

The Count grew almost distracted at that fatal accident. He fetched his sword, and swore that the ruffians should pay with their lives for their villainy. However, the Duchess retained him, declaring that she had no time to lose, and conjuring us to conduct her home without delay.

My friend seeing that the morning was dawning, was sensible of the reasonableness of her request. We, therefore, armed ourselves, and saw the Duchess to her palace. On our return, we searched every corner of the house, but were not more successful than the servants.

The Count apprehended that accident would have greatly lessened the passion of his inamorata, or at least make her very careful for the future; and he was well aware that a woman that begins to reflect coolly on her passion, is not very far from suppressing it entirely. Yet the Duchess was far from realizing his apprehensions, and grew more daring than she ever had been.

This created apprehensions of a different nature in the Count's mind. The Duchess's courage, which rather had encreased than

abated since that nocturnal adventure, made her neglect all rules
of prudence and sound reason. Her eyes glistened with impatience,
and her looks wandered about every where without reserve. The
Duke was fortunately too much occupied with his illness to take
notice of his lady's strange conduct: her lover was, however, nevertheless, constantly on the rack.

The Duke was soon able to leave his bed, and resolved to give a
little feast to his friends at his villa, in spite of winter and the badness of the weather. He was determined it should be as splendid
as possible. The first nobility were invited; the best musicians and
singers engaged; and he stayed whole days there to make the necessary preparations.

Two days previous to that feast, the Count happened to fall out
with him at a coffee-house, leaving him abruptly with a kind of
challenge, and taking the firm resolution to break off all connection with his house. He came instantly home to inform me of the
incident. On seeing him heated with a violent passion, and his face
as red as crimson, I could not help laughing aloud at his complaints.
He asked me, with kindling anger, what I meant by that strange
behaviour. "You ought to rejoice; for nothing could have happened
more fortunate, if you will take my advice."

I then explained my whole plan to the Count, who could not help
laughing at it, though he did not think it would succeed. Having
settled the proper measures, we went, without delay, in search of
the Duke, who scarcely recollected the incident, and, without difficulty, was prevailed to settle all differences in an amicable manner.
He went the next morning to his villa; and I repaired, without delay,
to the inquisitor of state, to inform him of the Duke's quarrel with
my friend. Having already received intelligence of it, my information only served to confirm the fact, and to render the general
opinion that a duel would be fought more certain. No one having
heard of their reconciliation, the danger seemed to be cogent, and
the Duke was ordered not to stir from his villa. The Count being a
stranger, was obliged to give his word of honour that he would not
leave the town within three days.

Thus our plan succeeded as well as we could have wished. The
Duke was almost frantic with rage, and for some time racked his
brains in vain to trace out the cause of that order. This state of sus-

pense grew, at length, so intolerable to him, that he disguised himself in the garb of a peasant, and arrived at Venice after midnight.
Being afraid to go directly to his house, he went to all the public
places, expecting to learn, by the general talk, something of the
true nature of that mysterious incident.

He really heard all the world talk of nothing else; but the opinions were so different, that he was not a jot wiser for it. He was
just going to leave the place of St. Mark, when he was accosted by
a stranger, in the dress of an English officer, who whispered in his
ear, "My Lord, you will do better to go home than to remain any
longer in the streets. You will find Count S****** at your house."
With these words the stranger retired, leaving the Duke in a state of
utter astonishment.

"The Count of S******?" he said to himself. "What business can
he have at my house at this late hour? And why did that stranger
inform me of it in such a mysterious tone? But, what is still worse, I
am betrayed, and it will be dangerous for me to rove the streets any
longer. The good Count had, perhaps, heard of my misfortune, and
is consulting with the Duchess about the best measures of extricating me from my disagreeable situation." Jealousy, fear, vexation at
his arrest, attachment to the Count, and mistrust of his lady, caused
a strange conflict in his shallow brains. The Count, who had previously informed his mistress of the real nature of that event, went,
against night, to her palace, to reap the fruit of our artifice. She
received him with marks of the greatest tenderness; and her conjugal fidelity would undoubtedly have fallen a sacrifice to her desires,
notwithstanding the Count's resolution to respect her virtue, if
not a sudden violent knocking at the street door had relieved my
friend unexpectedly from his perilous situation. The two lovers
were seized with terror when the Duchess's waiting woman,
who was on the watch, entered the apartment, out of breath, and
informed them that a man, in a peasant's dress, was at the door,
and that she believed it could be no other person but the Duke.
The situation of the apartment made it impossible for the Count
to escape; and even if the Duchess could have concealed him some
where, yet she could be certain that the Duke would search every
corner, if he had only the most distant suspicion, and undoubtedly
sacrifice her lover to his fury. They agreed, therefore, to face the

unexpected intruder boldly, and to have recourse to art. The chess-board was placed on the table, and they began to play a party in a most furious manner. This expedient was by far the best they could have chosen. The Duchess laughed immoderately at her situation and artifice, which the Duke could hear in the anti-chamber. The Count too was seized with a fit of laughter; and thus the whole scene received such a harmless, unsuspicious air, that it would have imposed upon a more keen-sighted man than the Duke was. They appeared to be profoundly absorpt in their play, and the Duchess to have made a decisive move. The Count, who sat opposite to her with a grave and meditating air, seemed to be in the greatest dis-tress; and the Duke advanced on tip-toe, to see whether he could not unexpectedly extricate him from his difficulty. But how great was his astonishment, when he perceived nothing but confusion on the chess-board, and was utterly unable to make any thing of the position of the men. He imagined the night air had dimmed his sight, and rubbed his eyes: however, the Duchess left him no time to examine the matter more minutely, and, starting up, when she saw him, exclaiming, "Jesus! Maria!" overturned the table. "These are fine doings, my Lord!" she said; "you know that the least thing in the world is apt to frighten me!"

"Don't be angry, my angel!" the Duke replied, with a profound bow: "I imagined it would give you pleasure to see me thus unex-pectedly."

"A fine pleasure, indeed!" she resumed scolding. "You have spoiled the finest game in the world."

"I assure you, I only wanted to come to the Count's assistance; but, upon my honour! the men were in such a confused, strange position, that I found it impossible to form the least idea of your plan."

The Count now welcomed his friend, laughing, and, without the least mark of perplexity; but the poor Duke had so much to do to pacify his frightened and scolding lady, that he was not at leisure to return his salutation. He succeeded, at length, to mollify her by his caresses; and having staid half an hour with her, went with the Count to his closet, to consult with him upon the best means of terminating his affair before the next night. The latter promised to settle every thing on the subsequent morning; but insisted upon his returning immediately to his villa, and accompanied him part of the way. The Duke informed him, on the road, of his adventure at the place of St. Mark, and of the alarm that incident had given him. The Count was, as well as myself, astonished at that mysterious incident, which pervaded our minds with numberless apprehensions, particularly when we reflected that the villain who treated the Duchess, before our house, in such a barbarous manner, also was an officer, and probably the same person that accosted the Duke at night.

The decree of arrest was repealed the following morning; and the feast at the Duke's villa was celebrated with the greatest pomp and gaiety. The general bustle afforded the lovers frequent opportunities to settle a plan for the last public masquerade. It was agreed the Duke, his lady, the Count and myself, should go together to the ball. The former consented cheerfully to be of the party, and requested me to take charge of the Duchess. But I declined that honour; protesting that his lady would find me but a dull and awkward companion. He laughed at my philosophy; and it was, at last, settled, that the Count should take that charge. We agreed that the Count and the Duchess should go in the mask of shepherds, the Duke as Pantaloon, and I in my usual domino.

When we arrived at the assembly room, we found it extremely crowded; and scarcely had proceeded a few steps, when our poor Pantaloon was completely hemmed in between the masks, and struggled in vain to disengage himself from a Harlequin who had taken hold of him. We left him to shift for himself; and, after the shepherd and his shepherdess had taken some turns through the room, they slipt into a private apartment where they were to exchange their dress, and then to repair to our house. The Count had ordered one of our servants, who resembled him much in stature and shape, and a girl, to mask themselves as shepherds, and never to lose sight of the Pantaloon, who could not well be mistaken. They acted their part with admirable dexterity; and the poor Duke could not conceive the least suspicion, particularly as we had agreed to speak only through signs. His situation grew, however, at length, so irksome and tedious, that he endeavoured to persuade his supposed lady to go home with him; but being not able to prevail upon her and her shepherd to coincide with his request, he grew highly exasperated at their obstinacy, and went to a contiguous card room.

However insignificant my mask was, yet I saw myself already, in the beginning, surrounded by a number of persons, who endeavoured to involve me in a dispute, and to separate me from my friend. Another domino even knew my person, asking me, in broken Spanish, "How do you like the ladies of Venice, Don Carlos?" Yet I disengaged myself from the importunate crowd, returning no answer to their troublesome questions, and kept a careful guard over my friend and his inamorata, till I knew they were in a place of safety. But I was no sooner returned into the midst of the crowd, than a mask, who passed me, hastily whispered in my ear, "Marquis, your friend is in danger; the Duke misses his lady. Not a moment is to be lost." I was almost petrified; and in the same moment saw our Pantaloon run through the room like a madman, making signs to and staring at all the masks, to know who they were. I took hold of his arm, asking him, in a whisper, "What is the matter? What has happened?" He answered me with the pantomime of a striking poniard, and left me abruptly.

I now thought it high time to inform my friend of his danger, and met him with the Duchess on the staircase, just as they were going to leave the house. I briefly acquainted them with that alarming incident; and we agreed, after a short consultation, that it would be best to enquire more minutely into the matter. We, therefore, returned to the ball-room, and, on seeing the Pantaloon still running up and down like a distracted person, the Duchess said, "Let us avoid him, and go into one of the card rooms."

The Count observed, mean time, a white mark on my back, which some person probably had made, on my entrance, to know me again. He erased it; and we stept into one of the card rooms, where we beheld our Pantaloon, to our greatest astonishment, sitting at a faro table, and staking with the completest tranquillity. He knew us instantly, and was inseparable from us all the rest of the night.

On coming home, we made our remarks on those mysterious and singular incidents. All our plans were rendered abortive by some unknown persons, and Heaven only knew what interest they could have in vexing us thus. "Who can those persons be? (said I to myself.) Should perhaps a new *Genius*, a new *Amanuel*, watch our steps? Yet, suppose the *confederates* should not be dispersed, what interest could they have in meddling with the love affairs of the Count, whom they always kept at a proper distance? and has not their invisible influence over me ceased since Alfonso's death?"

The two officers, whom the Duchess observed at our door, seemed, nevertheless, suspicious enough to keep our attention fixed to that point. It was certain they had some design upon us; and although their secret influence appeared rather to exert itself to keep us in certain limits, than to hurt us, yet it soon displayed itself in several more instances.

The Duke grew visibly cooler to his old confidential friend. We ascribed it, at first, to the numerous serious occupations which took up the greatest part of his time: however, his reserve continued to encrease even when he was more at leisure. He behaved in a similar manner to the Duchess, who was rendered miserable by that sudden unaccountable change. The Count too was vexed, but soon composed himself. The Duchess comforted him as much as possible, promising that she never would lose sight of their mutual interest, when a new incident happened, which, at once, entirely changed their situation.

The Count loved women rather from a predilection for an easy and agreeable conversation, than from other less honourable motives. He did, therefore, not care where he could meet with it, and Venice, where the number of the ladies of pleasure is pretty large, afforded him sufficient opportunities of indulging that propensity, by a familiar but cautious connection with some of the first rate beauties of that class. His favourite was Irene, a Greek, who united, with an uncommon beauty, all the charms of art and wit, and of an uncorrupted heart. She was very delicate in the choice of her admirers, and admitted only a few, though she could have seen half Venice at her feet. The Count was one of that number; and we spent sometimes whole evenings at her house. Our little suppers were a repetition of those I formerly had enjoyed at Toledo in the lap of the most intimate friendship. Good humour, and the gayest sallies of the most luxuriant wit, gave to our moderate suppers the highest relish, and we spent the happiest hours at Irene's house.

One evening, on which we intended to meet at the house of our charming Greek, the Count was detained by some urgent business. He desired me to go without him, and promised to follow me as soon as possible. I was engaged in a familiar conversation with Irene, when, unexpectedly, the Duchess of F****** sent up her name. I was ready to faint when that name was mentioned, and begged Irene to conceal me somewhere. She directed me to an alcove with glass doors. I just had time enough to get in, and to conceal myself behind the curtains, through which I could see every thing that was doing in the apartment. I never trembled so much for the Count as in that fatal, ominous moment, when I saw not only his life exposed to the fury of a jealous and deceived Italian, but also his tranquillity and happiness at stake. The Duchess entered the apartment with all the dignity natural to her rank, and her large eyes wandered inquisitively through the room. Irene received her with her natural grace, and asked her modestly, to what she was to ascribe the distinguishing honour of such a visit.

"Your great fame, Signora," she replied, "has made me so bold. I wanted to convince myself personally, whether your charms really are so irresistible, and your manners so polished and agreeable, as I have been told. You will excuse the injustice I have done you; for you know that our sex is not over credulous with regard to these points."

Irene never was at a loss for an answer, and easily found a way to every heart. The Duchess now declared that she was so much charmed with her amiable manners, and mental accomplishments, that she begged leave to stay supper; and, without waiting for Irene's answer, fixed herself upon a chair, firmly determined to make good her words.

Irene protested she was extremely sorry that she could not accept her condescending offer, as she expected some strangers, who probably were not prepared to meet with company at her house. The Duchess crimsoned at that reply; but, nevertheless, declared that nothing would be able to alter her mind. Irene certainly would have been able to find out means of getting rid of her fair visitor, if she had had the least suspicion of the Count's connection with the Duchess; but being entirely ignorant of it, she thought he would not be displeased to meet with one lady more at her house.

It is impossible to conceive how great my anxiety was, as it was not in my power to escape, or to receive the Count at the door, without going through the apartment where the Duchess was. Nothing was more certain than that she had heard of his connection with Irene, and that she was come to be an occular witness of his infidelity. It was equally certain, that, if she should meet the Count, it would be most adviseable to quit Venice as soon as possible, as every thing was to be apprehended from the vengeance of a Venetian lady under these circumstances. I resolved, therefore, rather to run any risk, and threw a glass, which was on the table, on the floor. Irene understood the hint; but despairing to get rid of her visitor, rung for the servant, and said, "Go into the alcove, and look whether my little dog has done no mischief:" She could not come herself, as the Duchess probably would have been close at her heels.

The servant entered my asylum with a candle in his hand, when I whispered, "Go instantly down stairs, and if Count S****** should come, tell him to go home immediately, because his life is in the greatest danger." The servant took the little dog from the bed, where he was sleeping quietly, and turning him into the apartment, said, "He has broken a glass, Signora." But, alas! Heaven had decreed it otherwise; for while the servant was going to leave the apartment, the Count entered, humming an air, and in high spirits. He went familiarly to Irene, bidding her a good evening, and then turned to pay his respects to her visitor. But a clap of thunder from the blue serene sky could not have surprised him more than the sight of the Duchess. He staggered a few steps back, and dropped senseless to the floor. Irene was seized with terror, and wanted to fly to his assistance; but the Duchess took hold of her arm, exclaiming, in a voice choked with rage, "For God's sake, Signora, let him die!"

"Barbarous woman!" replied the dear girl, disengaging herself from her furious gripe, and ringing the bell vehemently. I now also broke forth from my lurking place, and hastened to the Count's assistance. "You too, Marquis?" the Duchess said, with Cesar's words.

The Count recovered at length, staring wildly at the Duchess, who felt an infernal pleasure at our confusion, changing her colour more than ten times in a minute. I was on the point of reading a serious lecture to her, when she rose with uncommon dignity, leaving the room with slow steps and silent contempt.

The Count was in a lamentable situation; but soon grew sensible that certain disasters become less heavy the longer they are borne. On our return to our lodgings, I took occasion, from that fatal incident, to read him a severe lecture, reminding him how foolish it was to seek abroad what he could have enjoyed in the highest perfection at home; and recalling to his memory the scenes of former bliss, of the tenderest friendship, and of the most attentive love; the exhilarating joys of a small but happy circle, animated by a gay humour; and the sallies of an innocent wit, which art can neither produce nor improve. The recollection of domestic happiness awoke at once powerfully in his soul; and he longed for his peaceful fields, which bloomed beautifuller under his hands; for the serene, uninterrupted tranquillity of an artless life; and for the heart of his Caroline, of which he believed to have made himself not entirely unworthy.

These reflections could not but make him entirely indifferent to the Duchess. Every moment divested her of some of those charms which love had lent her; he considered her as the principle cause of his infatuation, and of the painful consciousness not to return so pure and innocent to Caroline's arms as he had left them. The last scene of a more than female fury, which threatened to endanger his life, finally destroyed every remnant of that fatal passion.

We could not comprehend how the Duchess could have learnt the Count's connection with Irene; nothing but the certain knowledge of which could have determined her to stay, notwithstanding the excuses of the fair Greek, and to convince herself of his infidelity. The idea that those unknown strangers, perhaps, had had a hand in that dangerous affair, was the only one that afforded us some light, and rendered the Count impatient to leave Venice as soon as possible. I was highly pleased with his resolution; and we agreed to wait only for the remittance of our money; and, mean time, to live as retired as our situation would allow.

Yet our tranquillity was of no long duration. The Duchess meditated upon nothing else but plans of bloody revenge. The Duke, who probably had been more firmly convinced of his friend's treachery, and was prevented, by family reasons, from venting his fury against his lady, was determined to punish the Count for his temerity. We received, almost every day, anonymous letters, in which our danger was represented with the liveliest colours; and our servants informed us that our house was, every evening, beset with masked persons, who seemed to have no good intention. We knew the revengeful spirit of the Venetians but too well as not to be on our guard; but at the same time were so firmly convinced of the excellence of their police, that we were not afraid of an open attack. We, therefore, provided ourselves with good cuirasses, and, without fear, went abroad every day; but always avoided narrow lanes and alleys, and returned as soon as night began to set in.

One day we staid later than usual at one of the coffee-houses, near the place of St. Mark; and the day being fine and serene, I desired the sherbet I had ordered to be brought before the house, where we seated ourselves upon a bench. We waited a considerable time for it; but, as the house was crowded with company, I ascribed the delay to the confusion and bustle which harassed the waiters. We saw, at length, one of them press through the throng; but while he was going to present the sherbet to us, a man, in a green cloak, ran against him, and threw the poor fellow upon the ground.

Although the stranger endeavoured to make that accident appear natural, yet he behaved in such an awkward manner, that we could clearly see it was premeditated. The Count being of a very irascible temper, took it as an affront, and was going to chastise the stranger for his impudence: however, I retained him by his cloak, whispering in his ear, "For God's sake! Consider that we are at Venice!"

His dog began, mean time, to lick the broken plate on which the waiter had carried the sherbet: the Count kicked him with his foot; and rose with boiling anger, reminding me that it was very late, and high time to go home. He was, however, so dry, that we were obliged to stop at another coffee-house to drink lemonade. I now observed that his dog was very uneasy, and soon after he began to howl in a most pitiful manner. The Count, who was very fond of the animal, took him on his arm, to carry him home; but we had not proceeded twenty steps, when he ceased howling, and expired. My friend could not retain his tears at that sight; and throwing his little favourite into the canal, said, "Marquis, the poison was strong."

"Very strong!" I replied, shuddering with horror.

When we came to the bridge before *Santo Giovanni e Paolo*, which was only a few steps distant from our house, we heard a shrill whis-

tling on the opposite side. Night was already setting in, and no
human being to be seen in the street and on the canals. I instantly
drew my sword; the Count did the same; and we disengaged ourselves from our cloaks, to have both arms free in case of an attack;
for I had a poniard in my left hand, with which I could parry pretty
well.

We were no sooner arrived at the opposite side of the bridge,
than we saw three masked men rush forth from an alley, and join
with a fourth, who seemed to have been on the watch. The contest
was very unequal; yet we were not disheartened. The Count was
an excellent fencer, and I had an exceeding steady hand. Our only
care was to keep our backs free; and just when they rushed upon us
with their long swords, exclaiming, "Death! death" we had gained
the wall of the church. I threw my cloak into the face of the first
who attacked me; and while he endeavoured to disengage himself
pierced his breast; but while I extracted my sword, I was wounded in
the shoulder by one of his associates. I dropt the dagger to take hold
of his sword; but he drew it with so much force through my hand,
that some of my fingers were severely wounded. The Count had,
mean time, also wounded one of them, and the combat became
more equal. The wound in my shoulder burning violently, I apprehended it was poisoned, and despair made me fight with unspeakable fury. Yet our three antagonists were no common banditti, but
excellent and cool swordsmen. I lost a great deal of blood, and the
Count too was entirely exhausted, when suddenly two strangers
attacked our adversaries from behind, and soon obliged them to
give up the contest, and to fly to a contiguous narrow lane.

One of our preservers now withdrew, without staying for the
effusions of our gratitude. His companion seemed to be danger-
ously wounded, and to follow him with great difficulty. We hastened after them, and found they were dressed in a red uniform; but
we could not get the least answer to any of our questions, nor to the
warm expressions of our gratitude.

We took the wounded between us, leading him to our house,
and were astonished to hear him sob violently. The Count asked
him repeatedly whether his arm, which bled copiously, pained him
much? But not the least answer ensued. His companion, too, seemed
to be speechless, and walked musing with a drooping head, by our

side. We arrived at our house; and the servants carried the wounded unknown, who had fainted away, to my apartment. While we sent for a surgeon, and my valet dressed my wound, which seemed to be of no consequence, the Count began to undress our kind preserver; but when he took his large hat off, he dropt the candle. I turned round, and saw my friend lying senseless at the feet of his patient, and the latter encircling him with his arm. I wanted to fly to his assistance, when the other stranger suddenly threw off his cloak, and dropt down at my feet, encircling my knees. I now looked in his face, and—heavenly powers!—it was *Adelheid*.

"Adelheid, my dear, adored wife!" This was all that I could say. I raised her up, and led her to the Count, where we jointly embraced *Caroline*. "Do you see, Carlos," my angelic wife said, "you have not lost your guardian *Genius!*"

CHAPTER XIV.

I now shall bid an eternal adieu to my friends, wishing to be remembered by them as often as the incidents of their lives may have some resemblance with mine. I do, indeed, not flatter myself that fate will suffer me to proceed in sweet tranquillity on my pilgrimage to a better world; however, as the future events of my life, probably, will be similar to my past adventures, I shall not trouble the patience of my friends by a communication of them. All that I have to add, is confined in the sincerest wish that the life of my friends may resemble mine as far as all the evils that have befallen me have contributed to put me in possession of a felicity, which, at present, is so complete, that it even does not require a witness.

THE END.